Praise for K   Silver Dragons Novels

Up in Smoke

"Filled with action ... yet there is also plenty of humor and affection."   —*Midwest Book Review*

"This zany paranormal, with its madcap plot and screwball characters, will work its magic with MacAlister's many fans and make some new ones along the way."   —*Booklist*

"An action-packed, never-a-dull-moment thrill ride."
          —Romance Novel TV

"Ms. MacAlister works her humor-filled magic to entertain readers with the action and scorching romance that keeps them glued to the pages."   —*Darque Reviews*

"An upbeat, funny paranormal. . . . You won't be disappointed!"   —Romance Reader at Heart

"Ms. MacAlister has done it again and provided me with an enjoyable and very entertaining series to read!"
          —The Romance Studio

"*Up in Smoke* ... may not be as laugh-out-loud hilarious as the Aisling Grey series but is no less fun, entertaining, or addictive."   —A Romance Review

Playing with Fire

"Fast-paced. . . . Katie MacAlister proves her skill as a magician when *Playing with Fire*, she places Aisling in a secondary role yet enchants her audience."   —*Midwest Book Review*

"Ms. MacAlister works her creative magic and adds a fabulous new layer to her world of sexy dragons. The dialog is as witty as ever. . . . *Playing with Fire* has all of the danger-filled action, steamy romance, and wonderful humor that fans know and love."   —*Darque Reviews*

"It's packed with all her signature hilarity and adventure, as well as many familiar faces. The cliff-hanger ending will leave you breathless."   —*Romantic Times*

continued ...

Praise for Katie MacAlister's
Dark Ones Novels

Zen and the Art of Vampires

"A jocular, action-packed tale . . . [a] wonderful zany series."   —*Midwest Book Review*

"Has all of the paranormal action, romance, and humor that fans of the author look for in her books. This is a fast-moving read with sizzling chemistry and a touch of suspense."   —Darque Reviews

"Pia Thomason just might be my favorite heroine ever . . . an entrancing story, and a very good escape."
                    —*The Romance Reader*

"I completely loved *Zen and the Art of Vampires*! . . . The chemistry between Pia and Kristoff sizzles all the way through the novel. . . . I don't think I can wait for the next Dark Ones installment! Please hurry, Katie!"
                    —Romance Junkies

"Steamy."   —*Booklist*

The Last of the Red-Hot Vampires

"MacAlister's fast-paced romp is a delight with all its quirky twists and turns, which even include a murder mystery."
                    —*Booklist*

"A wild, zany romantic fantasy. . . . Paranormal romance readers will enjoy this madcap tale of the logical physicist who finds love."   —The Best Reviews

"A fascinating paranormal read that will captivate you."
                    —Romance Reviews Today

"A pleasurable afternoon of reading."
                    —*The Romance Reader*

"The sexy humor, wild secondary characters, and outlandish events make her novels pure escapist pleasure!"
                    —*Romantic Times*

STEAMED

A STEAMPUNK ROMANCE

Katie MacAlister

A SIGNET BOOK

SIGNET

Published by New American Library, a division of
Penguin Group (USA) Inc., 375 Hudson Street,
New York, New York 10014, USA
Penguin Group (Canada), 90 Eglinton Avenue East, Suite 700, Toronto,
Ontario M4P 2Y3, Canada (a division of Pearson Penguin Canada Inc.)
Penguin Books Ltd., 80 Strand, London WC2R 0RL, England
Penguin Ireland, 25 St. Stephen's Green, Dublin 2,
Ireland (a division of Penguin Books Ltd.)
Penguin Group (Australia), 250 Camberwell Road, Camberwell, Victoria 3124,
Australia (a division of Pearson Australia Group Pty. Ltd.)
Penguin Books India Pvt. Ltd., 11 Community Centre, Panchsheel Park,
New Delhi - 110 017, India
Penguin Group (NZ), 67 Apollo Drive, Rosedale, North Shore 0632,
New Zealand (a division of Pearson New Zealand Ltd.)
Penguin Books (South Africa) (Pty.) Ltd., 24 Sturdee Avenue,
Rosebank, Johannesburg 2196, South Africa

Penguin Books Ltd., Registered Offices:
80 Strand, London WC2R 0RL, England

First published by Signet, an imprint of New American Library,
a division of Penguin Group (USA) Inc.

First Printing, February 2010
10 9 8 7 6 5 4 3 2 1

My heartfelt thanks and appreciation go to Aleta Pardalis, Zita Hildebrandt, and Kat Robb for all their support, no matter how wacky things get. I hope you all enjoy this taste of something new and different.

A Plague on Sisters

"Good morning, Jack. Is that a molecular detector in your pocket, or are you just happy to see me?"

The voice that called out as I passed was female, soft, and sultry as hell. I paused to toss a grin at one of the two women who were occupying the big kidney-shaped desk that graced the front lobby of the Nordic Tech building. "Morning, Karin. Would it be against human resources policy if I was to tell you how much I liked that top?"

The red-haired receptionist giggled and leaned forward, giving me a better-than-normal view of her cleavage in the skimpy tank top that she liked to wear on casual-dress Fridays. "Probably, but I'm not going to tell anyone. You know my rule, Jack."

"What happens in reception stays in reception?" I asked, winking.

She giggled again. "You're so naughty. You look really yummy yourself in khaki. Is that the new Airship Pirates shirt?"

"It is. Saw them last night at the Foundry," I answered, naming a local hot spot favored by bands that were a bit out of the mainstream. I turned around so she could admire the design on the back of the T-shirt.

"Oh, and I was hoping you would ask me to go see

them," she said, pouting just a little, and leaning over a bit farther. She traced a finger down my arm as I turned back to face her. "We had such fun the last time we went out. Well, until I got sick and had to go home, but I just know we would have fun again."

She paused, clearly waiting for me to do my duty and ask her out again, but the memory of her lying in a drunken stupor in the back of my car—not to mention the money I had to pay to have the vomit cleaned up and the car deodorized—was enough to warn me against any such thing.

That wasn't the Jack Fletcher she wanted, however. It was the fake Jack she was appealing to, the fictional Jack who had somehow garnered a reputation as a wild ladies' man. I did what was expected and slapped a quasi leer onto my face as I leaned in close. "You know I would snap you up in a minute if it wasn't for your boyfriend."

"Oh, him," she simpered, brushing my hand with her fingers. "Jerry's jealous of everyone."

"He threatened to rip my head off and spit down my throat the last time he saw me," I said, dropping my voice. "I think he meant it, too."

"I don't for one minute think you're scared of Jerry," she said, looking both pleased and coy. "Not you. Not the famous Jack Fletcher. Oh, Jack, this is Minerva. She's going to take over for me while I'm in Cancún for two weeks."

A girlish face hove into view, her eyes wide and somewhat vacant. "Hi, Dr. Fletcher. I've heard so much about you from Karin."

"Don't believe a word of it," I cautioned, giving her a wink, as well. I had a reputation to maintain, after all. "I doubt if any of it is true."

"Of course it's true," Karin said, squeezing my arm

as she heaved herself a little farther over the counter so her breast could press against my arm. "Everyone knows you're a hero! You're just too modest to admit it."

Or perhaps resigned to people's determination to ignore the truth in favor of more attractive and entertaining fiction that had started several years back.

"Karin said you tracked down a notorious ring of industrial spies in Cairo," Minerva said, breathless with excitement. She started to lean toward me over the counter, but a gimlet-eyed glance from her friend warned her off.

"He didn't just track them down—he beat the crap out of them, and got secret plans back for the government."

Minerva ooohed appreciably, her eyes filling with hero worship. Honesty prompted me to correct that particular fallacy. "I didn't actually track anyone down so much as accidentally ran into a meeting of some folks selling proprietary information. They thought I was following them, but I was really just lost and trying to find my way back to my hotel so I could rejoin my tour. In fact, I wasn't even in danger from them, since Interpol had them under surveillance, and the Cairo police were hidden around the bazaar, but it was exciting for a few minutes until everything was straightened out."

"And then there's Alaska," Karin said, ignoring the boring truth just as everyone did when I tried to explain what really happened in Cairo.

"Alaska?" Minerva asked her. "What about Alaska?"

Karin turned to her friend. "It was so amazing! It's all over the Greenpeace Web site."

I groaned to myself and prepared to explain that incident, as well.

"What happened?" Minerva repeated, a rapt expression on her face.

"I was on vacation, doing some fishing, and my rented boat had engine trouble. I got picked up by some animal-activist people, and they—"

"He hijacked a whaling ship!" Karin interrupted, a triumphant note in her voice as she beamed at me.

"Ooooh!" Minerva breathed.

"I wasn't even part of the group," I said quickly, wondering why no one was ever willing to believe that I had been the victim of odd circumstances. "My engine had died and the Greenpeacers picked me up on the way to attacking a whaling ship. It was just the purest of coincidences that I was even on the ship at the time, and that picture of me holding a gun on the captain was totally misleading. He'd dropped it and I was going to hand it back to him when a photographer took a picture of us—"

"You went to jail for that, didn't you?" Karin asked, squeezing my arm a little more insistently now, her face filled with sympathy.

"Three months," I said, resigned. "It took that long for my lawyer to convince the judge I had nothing to do with the whole whaler fiasco."

"But the really amazing thing was in Mexico," Karin told Minerva.

"I love amazing things," she said, grasping my other arm. "What happened? I'm dying to know!"

Oh, Lord, not Mexico. "It's really not worth talking about—"

"Jack was in Mexico City with Mr. Sawyer on some business matters, and Mr. Sawyer was kidnapped by radical Mexican antitechnology fanatics!" Karin said, her gaze earnest and fervent as she told the story to her friend. "Jack rescued Mr. Sawyer right as the fanatics were about to sacrifice him on a Mayan altar! He *saved* his *life*!"

"Saved Mr. Sawyer's life!" Minerva gasped.

The addition of the Mayan altar to the whole crock of bullshit was too much for me. "There was no altar, Mayan or otherwise," I said firmly.

"Mr. Sawyer totally swore his undying gratitude," Karin answered her, nodding vehemently.

"And it really wasn't so much a group of radical fanatics as it was a couple of people who had been unemployed and took Mr. Sawyer's limo for that of the labor secretary."

"He told Jack that he would have a job at his company for the rest of his life," Karin added in a confusion of pronouns.

"They drove us straight back to the hotel after they realized their mistake," I said, a hint of desperation entering my voice. Why the hell did no one ever listen to me?

"Well, I would promise that, too," Minerva told her. "Being sacrificed on a Mayan altar would scare the bejeepers out of me! That was so brave of Dr. Fletcher!"

"The whole thing got blown out of proportion when the police had a report of a kidnapping, and brought in some military troops to try to find us, which was ridiculous because by then we were back at the hotel, safe and sound, having margaritas next to the pool. It wasn't until the next day that we realized they were looking for us," I finished, but I knew my breath was wasted. People, I have frequently noticed, hear what they want to hear.

"Well, you know, Jack was in the military," Karin said, her voice dropping to a confidential level, apparently forgetting I was standing right there. "Secret military research."

"Wow," Minerva said, her eyes huge. "What sort of research?"

"I don't know, but it has to be something pretty juicy because Jack never talks about it."

I sighed, gathered up my leather satchel and the morning's paper, and headed for the stairs.

"He's just like Indiana Jones, isn't he?" I heard Minerva say as I started up the stairs to the fourth floor, where my office was located. "Right down to the hat. I wonder if he has one of those long whips he could wrap around his waist."

"He should totally get one...."

"Hey, Jack." I entered the first in a connected set of rooms that were our research labs, unloading hat, satchel, and newspaper onto my desk. A tall man with curly black hair emerged from the far room. "You're late."

"Had a late night." I slumped into the chair behind my desk and pulled out my laptop.

"Foundry?" Brian, the graduate student who was interning for a year, plopped down on the corner of his desk.

"Yep. Airship Pirates were playing last night."

"Airship..." His face screwed up in thought for a few seconds. "Oh, that goth band?"

"Part steampunk, part goth, part industrial." I frowned as the e-mail started loading into my in-box. "You should go sometime."

"Like I have time to go hang out at the Foundry? You may, but I have work to do." He nodded toward the clean room behind him. "If I don't get those dots set today, I'll be out of an internship. Speaking of that—Dr. Elton's been asking for you. He says that latest version of the quantum gate you sent him refuses to reverse, and could you fix it by noon so he has a working model to show Sawyer."

"It's on my list of things to do today," I murmured.

"Feeley called and said if you don't get that budget to him by the end of today, he'll sauté your balls in garlic and wine sauce."

I made a face. I hated dealing with the yearly budget.

"Oh, and a woman was here to see you."

"A woman?" I looked up in surprise. "Who?"

Brian shrugged and picked up one of the small canisters of liquid helium we use to cool down the computer equipment. "Didn't say. Said she'd be back, though."

"I wonder who it could be." I racked my brain for any female acquaintance who would be willing to brave the geekified air of Nordic Tech.

"Someone you met last night?" Brian offered as he headed for the clean room.

"Doubt it. I went with a couple of Friends last night."

He paused at the door, his eyebrows raised. "You went with Quakers? To see a goth band? Isn't that like a sin or something?"

"Of course it's not a sin," I said, giving him a quick frown. "It's not like they decapitated a bat."

"Yeah, but *Quakers*! At a goth concert! It's just so wrong!"

"Hardly. I've been a part of the church my whole life, and I assure you, there's nothing anywhere in the Bible that says goth concerts are on the forbidden list," I answered, quickly scanning an e-mail from the CEO, Jeff Sawyer.

"I know you're one and all, but you're kind of like Quaker Lite, aren't you? I mean, you drink, and you swear better than my old man, and he was in the merchant marines. You go out with women. And you were in the army. I thought that was, like, totally anti-Quaker."

"Many of us are conscientious objectors, but still manage to be useful in ways that don't compromise our beliefs."

"That's right. Karin at reception said you did research in the army in lieu of seeing action in the Middle East. High-tech stuff, huh? Spy technology and all that?"

I looked up and cocked an eyebrow at him. "I could tell you, but then I would have to kill you."

His jaw dropped a smidgen.

"You don't see the irony of that statement, do you?" I asked, unable to keep from smiling.

"Well, I see the irony in you threatening to kill me when I'm the only intern you've got," he answered quickly, edging closer to the door.

"Tempting as it is to explain, we both have work to do. If you expect to get those quantum dots down before the afternoon, we'll have to forgo a discussion of my personal philosophy for another time."

He glanced at the clock, uttered an expletive, and bolted into the changing area for the clean room beyond, where we did the bulk of our construction on the quantum computer we were building.

A half hour later, when I was doubled over a minute circuit board, soldering on a tiny circuit, the door opened.

"Good morning, Indiana. What adventures have you had this morning? Rescued a damsel in distress? Saved a priceless amulet from being stolen by ruffians? Smuggled innocent baby seals from a fur-processing plant?"

"Hallelujah," I said, looking up and waving a small soldering iron at her by way of greeting. A minute piece of silver solder flew toward her. "What are you doing here?"

"Avoiding internal injury, evidently," she said, side-stepping the solder. "And don't call me that. You know I hate it."

"Not nearly as much as I hate being called Indiana."

"He who weareth the hat shall be calledeth by the name," she said, grabbing a stool and hauling it over to my worktable. "At least you haven't gotten a bullwhip. *Yet.*"

"You've been talking to Karin."

"Bah," my sister said, waving away the subject. "I hope you're not serious about her, because she's totally the wrong type for you."

"I'm not serious about anyone, not that it's any of your business," I said, looking through the microscope for placement of a minuscule part.

"Ah, but it is, big brother. I am here in my official capacity to hook you up with an absolutely terrific woman."

I set down the soldering iron. "Not another blind date, Hal? You promised me you weren't going to set me up on any more of those hellish experiences."

She picked up a piece of circuit board and toyed with it as I went across the lab to grab some wire. "Trust me, you're going to like Linda. She's different. She likes all the things you like."

"Such as?" I took the piece of circuit board from her. Absently, she picked up a pair of forceps meant to position small pieces, and used them to poke at my notes.

"She has a laptop that she takes everywhere, so she's clearly a computer geek, just like you. And she likes reading, and you always have your nose in a comic book."

"Graphic novel. They're called graphic novels."

"Whatever." She forcepped a piece of muffin left over from my breakfast and popped it in her mouth. "She likes those—she was reading one that she said was a retelling of a Jules Verne book, and it sounded just like something you'd read, what with all those Victorian rocket ships to the moon, and people marching around with ray guns and goggles."

"I'm delighted that you have a friend who enjoys steampunk and computers, but I fail to see why you would want to match her up with me. I'm perfectly happy as I am."

She slid off the stool and moved around the lab, tidying papers, rearranging boxes of computer components, and generally doing what she referred to as "straightening up." "It's . . . well . . . you see . . ."

"Spit it out, Hallie," I said, squinting through the microscope as I wrapped wire around a semiconductor.

She took a deep breath, then said very quickly, "I promised you to Linda."

I looked up at that. "You did what?"

"I promised you to Linda. That is, I sold you to her." She held a small canister of helium in her hands, absently twisting the top as she watched me with anxious eyes.

"You sold me? Like a slave or something?" I asked, completely confused. "What do you mean, you sold me?"

"No, not like a slave, don't be stupid," she said, biting her lip. "It was an auction. A charity auction."

I closed my eyes for a moment before shaking my head. "Which charity?"

"Now, don't you get that tone of voice," she said, adopting a defensive attitude. She shook the canister at me as she spoke. "I know what you think about my charities, but this one is fabulous, Jack, just fabulous. It's for care and rehabilitation of released parakeets."

I was so surprised by what she said, I stopped worrying about whether the top had been loosened on the helium. "Released *what*?"

"Parakeets! Do you have any idea how many parakeets each year are shoved out of their homes and left to fend for themselves? Hundreds, Jack! Hundreds and hundreds of poor little innocent birdies just tossed out the window, and they have no idea how to forage for food, or where to sleep, or even where to live. It's a horrible, senseless tragedy, and we at the People for Humane Treatment of Parakeets are doing what we can to try to rescue parakeets, and rehome them with good people who will take care of them."

Hallie always had a cause. Ever since she was a little girl, she had been a joiner of causes. When she grew up, she had taken to throwing herself wholeheartedly into whatever cause appealed to her at the moment.

"What happened to that group you belonged to that was supposed to knit sweaters for hairless dogs who lived in animal shelters?"

"Oh, that fell apart months ago," she said, twisting the lid of the canister again. "We couldn't decide on whether mohair or acrylic yarn was best. This group is totally rock solid, Jack. And you like animals!"

"That doesn't mean I want to be sold into slavery on their behalf. What did you sell me for?"

"Five hundred dollars! Can you believe it? No one else's husband or brother went for as much. It was a shame you couldn't be there to model yourself, but I took that picture of you that was in the paper that time you and Jeff Sawyer were in Mexico, and you rescued him from being disemboweled by crazed Mayans."

I sighed to myself again. It was pretty sad when my own sister refused to listen to me.

"Anyway, everyone loved that picture, and lots of ladies bid on you, only Linda won, and that's so perfect because she's just the woman I would pick out for you. She's smart and she likes the things you like, and she paid *five hundred dollars* just to spend some time with you."

"I wasn't asking how much she spent; what services of mine has she won?" I asked suspiciously.

"Oh, well, that's up to Linda," she said, waving the canister at me.

"Stop shaking that!" When I realized what she was doing, I jumped to my feet and lunged toward her in the hopes of getting the canister before it blew up.

"Now, I know you're a bit peeved that I sold you without telling you, but really, it's for a very good cause—" Hallie skirted the lab table, keeping just out of my reach as she pleaded with me.

I cut her short, worried about her safety. "No, you idiot! The lid is off and you're shaking the canister. It's very volatile!"

"This?" She looked down at the helium. "It's just a thermos of coffee. How can coffee be volatile?"

"It's not coffee—it's liquid helium."

"Helium?" She held the canister up as if she could see through the stainless steel walls. "What on earth are you doing with helium?"

"We use it to cool the core of the chip when it's being tested. Now set it down very carefully."

"Oh, like canned air? I use that all the time at home on my stereo. I like the way the bottle frosts up when you use it for a while. You're not mad at me about the auction, are you?" she said with sublime unawareness of what she held. She reached for the lid, jamming it down on top of the canister.

"My emotions at this moment are rather indescribable," I said, moving around to take the canister from her.

"Stupid thing won't go on," she grumbled, trying to force the lid on, but the inner valve had been jostled and was out of position enough to keep the lid from screwing on properly.

"Just set it down, Hallie, and I'll deal with it."

"Maybe it's got an air bubble or something that's keeping it from closing properly." She tossed aside the top, right on top of the circuit I had been finishing. Several tiny LED lights lit up, indicating the computer's brain was receiving power.

"No!" I yelled, lunging for her. Just as my hand closed around hers, she flipped up the valve, sending liquid helium boiling out to the circuit below. Hallie snatched at the precious circuit, obviously to save it from being harmed, but it was too late. A brilliant silver light filled my mind as she grabbed the circuit board. In the dim distance, I could hear voices talking, but couldn't make out what they were saying. The light expanded until it seemed to fill the room, filling me with a soothing, calming presence.

Hallie screamed as the light erupted around and through and inside me.

Log of the HIMA *Tesla*
Monday, February 15
Forenoon Watch: Four Bells

"Cap'n Pye! Cap'n Pye!"

"The word is 'captain,' Dooley. We are not pirates, nor are we yokels who cannot expend the extra effort to pronounce words correctly, and judging by the nonstop chatter I hear from you in the mess, I am reassured you have the vocal capacities to do so. Yes, I see it now, Mr. Mowen. The valve to the left of the intake cylinder, isn't it? It's cracked, you think?"

"Aye, Captain."

I sat back on my heels after examining the valve in question. Cracked, my three-legged uncle. It was no more cracked than I was.

"Captain Pye, Mr. Piper, he says you're to come to the forward hold immediately!" Young Dooley fairly danced with agitation as he spoke, but that was nothing new. Dooley was a quicksilver sort of lad, always moving or talking, apparently unable to sit still for even the shortest amount of time. In a way, he reminded me of a hummingbird I'd seen in the emperor's aviary, for

Dooley flitted and dived around the ship just as the hummingbird had done in the high-domed aviary.

"Can you fix the valve, Mr. Mowen?" I asked the chief engineer, fully confident of an affirmative answer. "Or will we need to land at Lyon?"

"An unauthorized landing?" Mr. Mowen looked scandalized at the thought. "That would put us off schedule, lass. Er . . . Captain."

"Captain Pye—" Dooley tugged at the sleeve of my new scarlet-red Aerocorps jacket.

I quelled both the tugging and the excited dancing with a look, one I had honed on lesser crew members for a decade. "I will be with you in a moment, Dooley. Mr. Mowen has my attention now."

"But Mr. Piper said you must come quick—"

"Mr. Piper would never condone your interrupting an important discussion about the ability of the *Tesla* to fly, Dooley. You have delivered your message, and may return to your duties." I spoke in what I hoped was an authoritative, yet kindly, tone. I didn't want to be perceived as an ogre to the crew, not on this, my first assignment. Yet the seven other individuals on board must acknowledge my position of command, or it would all end badly. Firm but tempered, that was the key.

"But, Cap'n—"

Mr. Mowen watched me with interested, somewhat amused eyes. He was waiting to see how I handled the overexcited teen who was the bosun's mate, no doubt curious to see whether I would let him ruffle me. Ah, but had he known I had long since lost that ability . . .

"You have duties, Dooley, do you not?"

"Aye, miss. Cap'n. *Captain.* I'm to be cleaning the galley, then tending to the boilers as Mr. Mowen likes."

"You are excused to attend to your duties."

Dooley responded to the voice of authority, reluctantly tugging on his smart black cap as he left the cramped quarters of the aft boiler room. "Aye, aye, Captain."

"That wasn't nearly so bad as you thought, now, was it?" Mowen asked with the hint of a smile beneath his big salt-and-pepper walrus mustache.

"Not at all, and how did you guess?" I asked, a little surprised by the perspicacity in the older man's eyes. "Is it that obvious that I was expecting such a test?" One of several that were laid all ready for me, no doubt.

"I've been sailing the skies betwixt Rome and London long enough to see a full score of captains come and go," he answered, his eyes now twinkling with amusement. "The first run is always entertaining, with the crew watchful, waiting to see what sort of man the company has saddled us with."

I glanced at him, curious as to the meaning behind his words. "I can't believe that no one from the Aerocorps told you anything about me. I received a dossier on the crew; surely you had something about me?"

"It wasn't so much a dossier as it was a note telling us that you were taking command of the ship."

I waited, sure there was more to come.

There was. "Mr. Francisco has a mate in the Corps offices, and he told us a bit more about you. He said you were a woman, which we'd guessed from your name, that you had red hair and brown eyes—not that it matters, you understand, but Mr. Francisco, as you might have noticed, has a bit of passion for redheaded ladies, so he was particularly overjoyed about that bit of information—that you joined the Corps when you were sixteen, and have been in it just as many years, and that you have some friends in high places."

My brows rose just a smidgen. "The Aerocorps files say that?"

"Ah, well . . ." Mr. Mowen slid me a sidelong look. "Perhaps that was my own speculation."

"Indeed." I made my voice as neutral as possible. "On the whole, that is an accurate summation. I hope the crew will not be disappointed with me."

"Time will show," he said, nodding, idly rubbing a spot of grease on his cuff. "Good or bad, there's naught we can do but accept."

"Oh, I imagine there are all sorts of things a crew could do to make an unwanted captain feel less than welcome," I answered, deliberately keeping my tone light. "Food that is oddly inedible when compared to the crew's fare, unpleasant surprises of the insect and rodent nature to be found in the captain's bed, repeated rousing during the sleeping hours to examine strangely malfunctioning equipment that was sound only a few hours before . . . Yes, I have heard of such dealings, and imagine it would be quite easy for a dedicated crew to take care of an unpopular captain."

Mr. Mowen gave me a long look. I allowed myself a little smile, at which he relaxed. "True enough, Captain, true enough."

"I trust that this valve, which strangely appears to have been wrenched to the side and thus is no longer seated properly rather than cracked, can be returned to its proper position without delay, Mr. Mowen." A light of respect shone briefly in his eyes. I waved away his offer of help as I rose to my feet, dusting off my long navy wool skirt and the edges of my knee-length jacket. "I also expect there will be no further tests to determine if I am familiar with the workings of an airship steam engine and boilers. I assure you I am."

The engineer saluted me. "And right glad I am to hear it, ma'am. It's about time the *Tesla* had a captain who understood her."

"Even one who is female, Mr. Mowen?" I couldn't help but ask as I made my way along the narrow metal catwalk.

He replied after a few moments of silence. "I would be prevaricating if I was to say that, Mr. Francisco aside, we did not have concerns about having a lass as a captain."

We reached the gangway. I gave the engineer a considering look. I had expected a token amount of resistance when I took over as captain, but surely in these enlightened times no one could protest the fact that I was a woman. "There are several female captains in the Southampton Aerocorps, Mr. Mowen. It is not at all uncommon."

"Aye, but those captains are limited to domestic routes. You are the first we've heard of taking command of an international route."

"An oversight on the part of the Aerocorps, I'm sure. I served for several years under Captain Robert Anstruther, and he, as you might know, commanded the largest passenger airship to travel the empire. I am quite familiar with both the routes and the duties of a captain, even those that fall under the domain of a small cargo transport, such as the *Tesla*."

"Captain Anstruther will be well missed," Mowen said, his face now somber. "Those damned Black Hand revolutionaries have much to answer for, killing as fine a captain as ever sailed the skies."

"Indeed they do," I answered, squaring my shoulders at the pain that always followed the memory of Robert Anstruther's last hours.

"You knew him well, did you?" Mowen asked, watching me closely.

I made an attempt to present a serene expression. "I did. He was my guardian, and a very great man. I consider him my father."

The engineer's eyebrows rose above the steel rims of his spectacles. "Then I am sorry for your loss, Captain."

I acknowledged his sympathy, the pain that rose at the memory of Robert's sacrifice a familiar burden. "I was given into his care when I was very young, and both he and his wife treated me as if I was their own child. I miss them very much."

"The captain's lady—she died, too, in the airship explosion?"

I closed my eyes for a moment as once again the vision of the burning aerodrome rose in my mind's eye, the figure of Robert Anstruther silhouetted against the flames licking the black sky stark and hard.

"There is no other way, Octavia," he had said, and I felt again the pain in his voice. "The emperor will not be appeased this time. If it was just myself, I could bear what would follow. I am old, and my time has almost run its course. But there is Jane and you to consider. I will not let my shame destroy your lives."

"I will go with you," I had begged at the time. "Let me go with you and Jane. I can help, I know I can."

He had merely smiled sadly, and cupped the side of my face. "I bless the day the old emperor brought you to me. Do you remember it, Octavia? You were just a wee little girl, lost and confused, talking of wild, impossible things, and trying so very hard to be brave and not cry. Jane called you our little miracle, coming as you did right after our son died."

My throat ached as I fought vainly against tears.

Robert considered me for a long moment, ignoring the wetness that rolled down my face and over his hands. "You have a bright future ahead of you, my dear. If we are lost to the fire, nothing will taint that future."

"Am I to never see you again?" I asked, my voice cracked with pain.

"No. We cannot come back to England. We are too well-known. But you will always be with us, in our hearts."

I bowed my head, overcome with the grief, wanting desperately to cast aside all my burdens and flee with the two people I loved best in the world.

"Fight for what is right, little Octavia. Do what Jane and I cannot."

Those were his last words. No more had been needed—I stayed behind to do my duty while Robert Anstruther, decorated three times by the emperor himself, and a hero to the entire empire, walked toward the burning aerodrome, and into the pages of history.

"I'm sorry, Captain. I did not mean to distress you."

The voice had softly spoken, but pulled me from my dark memories back to the present. Robert and Jane had been gone for almost a year. It had all come to pass as he predicted—the inquiries that had swirled around his activities had withered to nothing, and a nation mourned its lost hero.

I squared my shoulders and gave the engineer a little nod. "Thank you, Mr. Mowen. If any other issues arise, I will be in the forward cargo hold seeing what it is that has Dooley in such a swivet."

He touched his cap in a salute as I moved down the narrow gangway, past the two rear boilers that powered the steering engines. The low thrum of the engines as they turned the propellers sounded in time to the throb of movement felt in the metal framework structure that ran the length, breadth, and height of the ship. It was a familiar sensation, one I didn't even think of now, and certainly not one I noticed until I was on land, and it was missing. Indeed, the feeling of the ship as it sailed through the air was as much a part of me as breathing was, and I could tell instantly—as could every man on board the *Tesla*—when something was awry with the engines. A slight change in tempo in the vibration, or a higher tone in the thrum, was enough to have the crew looking to me with concerned eyes.

"You're not going to have any problems, though, are you?" I asked the ship softly as I made my way down a small metal ladder to the lower gangway. "You know how important this trip is. You know how valuable the cargo is. You know what will happen should we fail."

The ship didn't answer, but I felt an odd sort of kinship with it. The engineer might find it remarkable that an international route had been given to me, but I knew better—it was a payment for services rendered, nothing more. My silence had been bought with the most insignificant, smallest cargo supply route in all of the Aerocorps. The *Tesla* was a minnow when compared with the new airships that graced the skies, an outdated model that showed visible signs of her age, from the stained fabric that made up the envelope, to the forty-year-old engines that were far from the highly efficient machinery that ran the bigger, longer, sleeker airships.

I knew all this, and yet I was proud of the *Tesla*, proud to be commanding her. If only everything would go right. If there was the slightest delay or problem that kept us from landing the ship in the small aerodrome outside Rome, all would be lost. I had argued with Etienne that such a tight timeline was tempting disaster, but he ignored my warnings and pleas, as he always did. "The man may be the leader of the Black Hand," I murmured as I strode the gangway toward the forward hold, "but he'll always be a presumptuous, stubborn idiot when it comes to listening to me."

I pushed down the worry of what might happen should things go awry, and focused instead on ensuring they didn't. "That includes unwanted problems," I grumbled to myself as I arrived at the hold, one of four compartments that filled the middle section of the gondola.

"Captain Pye." An elderly, grizzled man who shuffled with an almost-crablike walk moved forward in his peculiar gait to greet me. I knew from perusing the crew dossiers that his odd method of movement was due to injuries sustained when he'd flung himself from a burning airship. "I was hopin' ye would come soon. We have a great hairy bollock of a problem, we do."

"I'm sorry to hear that, Mr. Piper. I assume the hairy bollock must be very great indeed if Mr. Christian is unable to deal with it." I kept a mild expression on my face, despite the urge to laugh at his colorful language, well aware that it could be another test or an attempt to rattle me.

At the sound of his name the tall, very thin redheaded man who was my new chief officer jumped, his pale blue eyes wide with distress as he stammered out an excuse. Amusement faded as I considered him. There was no denying I was a bit disappointed in my right-hand man—thus far, he seemed ineffectual and totally unsuited for the job—but I reminded myself that everyone deserved a chance to prove himself, and that he might grow into the job. I certainly hoped that was so.

". . . and I only just arrived here before you, Captain. Didn't I, Piper? I just arrived here. A matter of seconds, isn't it? I couldn't know what's going on when I only just got here myself, could I?"

"Aye, that ye did, arse-backward and shittin' coal."

Aldous Christian looked almost panic-stricken, and I was quick to absolve him before he worked himself up any further. He looked on the verge of an apoplectic fit as it was. "My apologies for my false assumption. Since we are both here now, perhaps we could know the extent of the situation?"

"But I don't know!" he all but wailed, his face turning beet red.

"I was directing that comment to Mr. Piper," I said in a soothing voice, giving the chief officer's arm a reassuring squeeze. He stopped blushing, but looked as high-strung as a racehorse before the wire. "Proceed, Mr. Piper."

"It's bodies, Captain," the bosun answered with brevity.

"Bodies?"

"Oh, mercy," Mr. Christian said, looking for a moment as if he was going to swoon. He clutched at the edge of the nearest stack of crates and weaved for a moment.

"What sort of bodies?" I asked, eyeing the chief officer lest he suddenly totter toward me.

"Bloody great bodies, that's what sort," Mr. Piper answered, scratching absently at his crotch. "Gettin' in me way, they are."

"There's blood?" the chief officer wailed, his eyes filled with horror as he grabbed the bosun. "I . . . I . . . faint at blood."

"Where exactly are these bodies?" I asked, almost positive that I was being tested again.

"Over yonder, behind the barrels of salted meat." Piper nodded toward the far side of the hold, where

stacked neatly were three dozen barrels of salted veni-
son, pork, beef, and fish destined for the emperor's
troops in the south of Italy. "Neptune's salty cods, man,
let go of me arm! Ye'll have me uniform wrinkled."

"Dead or alive?" I asked.

"Alive, we think," Piper answered, plucking Mr.
Christian's hands from his arm. "That is, there ain't no
great big pools o' blood soakin' into everything."

"Urk!" Mr. Christian said, swallowing hard.

"And no severed limbs that we could find, nor any
entrails or guts spewed out everywhere."

"Entrails," Mr. Christian whispered, his voice hoarse
with horror as he groped blindly for the stack of wine
barrels. "Entrails would be the end of me."

"Aye, and they're a right shiv up the arse to clean up,
too," Mr. Piper agreed, sucking his teeth for a moment
before he continued. "Ye need sawdust to proper clean
up after entrails, ye do. An arseload of sawdust. And so-
dium carbonate, and we don't be havin' much of that on
board."

"It's good, then, that we will have no need for it," I
said, finding it difficult to keep my lips from twitching.

" 'Tis the truth ye're speakin'," he agreed, before
adding, "It's hard to tell if they be alive or dead, Captain.
Ye'll just have to be lookin' for yerself."

"An excellent suggestion. Mr. Christian, you will
come with me, please."

I took three steps, but paused when the chief officer
made an inarticulate noise of horror in his throat before
falling over in a dead faint.

It was going to be a *very* long trip.

"Son of a whore's left leg," Mr. Piper swore, looking
with interest at the chief officer's prone form. "He's light
in the ballast, that one is, Captain. Ye should have seen

him carry on when Auld John—he were the steward two seasons ago, before Mr. Ho joined us—when Auld John had three toes drop off."

I paused on my way toward the cargo in question. "His toes dropped off?"

"Aye." He sucked his teeth for the count of three. "We'd been to Marseilles, and ye know how it can be there—lads'll go out lookin' for a good time, and get mixed up with a strumpet or two, and the next thing ye know, someone's lopped off a few of their toes."

I stared at him in growing horror. "I don't believe I've ever heard of anyone losing their toes because of promiscuous activities, even in so rough a city as Marseilles. None of the crew I've sailed with have ever done so."

"Aye, well," he said shrugging, and poking at the inert form of Mr. Christian with the highly polished toes of his boot. "Could have been the pox, too. He had that right enough. He thought his rod was going to drop off one time, but it turned out to be the clap."

I opened my mouth to respond, but there was just nothing I could say to that, so instead I gestured toward the unconscious officer, and asked, "Would you see to him while I view these bodies of yours?"

"They ain't me bodies, at any rate," he said, shuffling over to the door. "As if I'd leave them lyin' about me hold. I've been on airships for the last forty years, and never once have I left a body in the hold where anyone can trip arse over ears on it. Dooley! Where are ye, ye useless sod? Mr. Christian's taken one of his fits again."

The old man bellowed as I moved off, carefully picking my way around the stacks of scientific equipment and supplies, wondering what on earth bodies were doing on my ship. If they were dead, I would have some explaining to do before the emperor's men in Rome. If they weren't . . . I gritted my teeth. Stowaways would spell disaster. Either it was someone Etienne had sent to watch me, or a spy for the emperor. The former I could deal with, but the latter? It didn't bear thinking about.

A foot came into view as I hiked up my skirts and scrambled over a long packing crate. The crate had shifted slightly during the last day, and now rested a good yard from the wall of the hold. The foot lay in plain view, with the rest of the body assumably wedged between the crate and wall.

I didn't usually carry firearms, preferring instead the blade hidden inside of the walking stick that Robert Anstruther had given me on the occasion of my thirtieth birthday, but that was unfortunately in the tiny captain's cabin, whereas the standard-issue Empyrean Disruptor that was given to all captains was strapped to my hip. I pulled out the small weapon, turning a switch that would allow the galvanic charge to be released upon firing.

"I am armed," I told the foot in what I hoped was a calm voice. "If you intend on attacking me, please be aware that I will defend myself."

The foot didn't move, nor did its owner respond. I edged closer to it, frowning at the foot. It was clad in a strange sort of half shoe, with only the front of the foot covered. The rest was bare, as was the ankle. I moved around the crate, leaning over it to peer behind, my grip firm on the Disruptor. "Are you injured?"

It was a man. He lay half-propped-up against the wall, half-flung across another person, a woman. Both appeared to be asleep—or dead—although there was no blood to be seen, and no sign of injury.

"Has Mr. Christian been roused?" I called over my shoulder, straightening up.

"Aye, but he looks as pale as watered piss."

I counted to ten, then said, "Tell him there is no blood whatsoever, and ask him to come forward."

Both the chief officer and Dooley appeared, the former looking as if he was going to be sick.

"Are they . . . dead?" he asked in a thick voice. I wondered if he was likely to keel over again.

"No. Their chests are moving, and there is no sign of injury. I believe they are merely unconscious."

His eyes widened as he glanced around wildly.

"Mr. Christian, please remember you are an officer in the Southampton Aerocorps," I said purely to brace him up. "Officers do not panic when faced with unconscious stowaways. Nor do they faint repeatedly, or vomit willy-nilly." That last bit was added in reference to the green cast to his face.

He swallowed hard, his pronounced Adam's apple bobbing a bit wildly, but in the end he squared his shoulders and gave a nod. "Aye, Captain. I'm ready."

Oh, I had my doubts as to whether he was ready for the stresses and strains of life aboard a Corps airship, but that was something I would have to deal with at a later time. Right now I had to figure out who the stowaways were, and what it would mean to me. Etienne would kill me if anything happened to mess up the Black Hand's plans. "Help me move them out from behind the crate. Perhaps they swooned due to lack of air."

It wasn't a horribly good theory, but I didn't dwell on that as we pulled out first the man, then the woman, laying them tidily on the two long crates near the door Piper indicated as suitable resting spots.

"Where's their velocipedes?" Mr. Christian asked as we stood back to gaze down on the inert man and woman.

I stared at my chief officer. "Their velocipedes?"

"Aye." He gestured toward the woman. "She's wearing bloomers, so she must have been riding a velocipede."

I glanced at the woman, wanting to point out the obvious. But I was captain now, and I had a duty to my crew. "Those are trousers, Mr. Christian, not cycling bloomers."

"But . . . she's a lady." A puzzled frown pulled his eyebrows together.

"There's more to a lady than a pair of titties," Mr. Piper offered as he eyed the woman.

"Mr. Piper," I said, goaded into admonishing him.

He gave an odd little half shrug. "I'm just sayin' that a woman ain't necessarily a lady."

"I do not have argument with your sentiment, just your method of expressing it." I moved around him to consider the man lying on the crate.

"I've heard tell that some ladies wear trousers," the earnest Dooley offered. "In America. Before the war. I don't know that they do now, but I did see pictures of ladies in trousers walking in a parade."

"You aren't old enough to remember the time before the war," Mr. Christian scoffed. "It's only been over for four years, and it was on for eighteen before that."

"I've seen pictures!" Dooley said stubbornly, and I knew the two would get into what I feared were perpetual arguments about trivial matters.

"Dooley, please ask Mr. Ho to join us. Perhaps she can ascertain if there is any injury to the stowaways."

"You think they really are stowaways?" Mr. Christian asked, looking both scandalized and thrilled. "Will we have to throw them in the brig?"

"Considering we don't have a brig on board the *Tesla*, that might be a little difficult. Let us first find out who they are and what they were doing in the hold. Perhaps they had some sort of an attack while the cargo was being loaded, and are here by mistake."

I didn't believe that for one minute, but I couldn't bear to contemplate the repercussions of the pair being spies.

Mr. Piper gave me a long look, but said nothing, just cocked his hip up on a nearby barrel and watched silently as I made a cursory examination of the two.

"Well, they don't seem to have any weapons upon them," I noted as I finished my examination of their pockets. The man was wearing an undershirt, and dark gray trousers. The woman was clad in a long blue tunic made of silk, and matching trousers. It was beautiful material, and I couldn't help but touch the hem of the tunic with longing. Reality returned quickly, however, and I surreptitiously brushed down the heavy wool of my uniform jacket and skirt before turning to the bosun. "I wonder why the man is wearing nothing but an undershirt?"

"And a black one at that," Mr. Piper said, squinting at it. "Black as the devil's cods, it is. Ain't never seen one that color."

"Could be he's a thuggee," Mr. Christian piped up.

I looked at him in surprise. "A thuggee? The Indian thuggees, do you mean?"

"Aye." He nodded, his expression earnest. "My mum used to tell me tales of the thuggees. Before the Moghul imperator took it over, the whole of India used to be ruled by these thuggees. They were dangerous men, very deadly and skilled in the ways of murder. My mum said that they all ran around in naught but their underthings, on account it made them silent and stealthy."

We all looked at the prone man. "He certainly is silent, but I don't know how stealthy he is," I commented. "He doesn't look particularly Indian, either."

"That's probably part of his clever plan," Mr. Christian said, nodding as if it all made sense. "He wouldn't want to look like a thuggee, now, would he? That would warn you to beware of him. They're cunning, those thuggees. My mum always said they were as cunning as a cat."

"What would a thuggee be doing in the hold of my ship?" I asked, making another quick search of the man for weapons. I found none.

"Well," Mr. Christian said, making himself comfortable on a wine barrel. "What if he was a master thuggee, and had a job to do in Rome to kill someone important, say one of the emperor's representatives? There's a lot of them there now, what with the wedding and all."

"That is true," I said slowly. The very reason Etienne had chosen my ship to hide his cargo in was the opportunity it presented to strike a blow against the number of imperial representatives who were in Rome. "I've heard that there is a large delegation in Rome to work out the terms of the treaty with the king of Italy."

"So the thuggee needs to get there, but with everyone watching all the passenger ships, he can't take one of those," Mr. Christian continued, clearly warming up to his theme. "So he stows away on an insignificant cargo ship, intending on catching the crew—that's all of us— by surprise one night, and killing us all in our beds. That way he can land in Rome without anyone knowing he was there. His plan is no doubt to slip away once he lands, and conduct his nefarious affairs."

"God's bollocks!" Mr. Piper said, looking askance at the still-unconscious man. "The brig's too good for him! Let's toss the murdering son of a scabby whore over the side, Captain."

"The Southampton Aerocorps frowns heavily on

tossing people out of airships," I said mildly, adding, "And even if they didn't, I would not suggest that as a course of action in this case. There are two flaws in your reasoning, Mr. Christian."

"Oh? What's that, Captain?"

"One," I said, ticking the item off on my finger, "you did not account for the woman's presence. If this thuggee was sent to kill one or more of the emperor's men, then why is the woman with him?"

The young man's face fell while he eyed the woman. "Well . . . mayhap she's his accomplice?"

"Doubtful," I said, shaking my head. "Not knowing any assassins—or thuggees—personally, I am forced to rely on the testimony given by those who have, and never have I heard of assassins roaming the countryside in packs. They are solitary folk by nature, I believe, especially those who strive to achieve an unsurpassed level of stealth."

"What's the second flaw?" Mr. Christian asked, a touch acidly, I thought.

"He's not armed. Not only would that make it impossible for a man to single-handedly kill the eight people on the *Tesla*, but it also leaves him at a distinct disadvantage when trying to assassinate an imperial official."

"The captain has a point," Mr. Piper said slowly, nodding his grizzled head. "I'm not saying the lad isn't a murderin' bastard, but it's a damned sight harder to throttle people by hand than it is to stick a shiv in their heart, or blast their brains out the back of their head with a Disruptor, or shove a red-hot poker—"

"Thank you, Mr. Piper," I said, quickly cutting off his gruesome catalog.

"Course, there's nothin' to say he couldn't be gettin' a knife from the galley, and spillin' all our guts on the floor. Nothin' is easier than a quick disembowelin', says I, though it takes ye a bit to die—"

"*Thank* you," I said louder, giving him a gimlet look.

He pursed his lips and said nothing.

"Mayhap we should toss him over the side, just to be sure," Mr. Christian said, clutching his abdomen.

"I don't think such an extreme action will be necessary. The simple fact is that we have no proof that this man and woman are thuggees."

"Then who are they?" Mr. Christian asked, and I had to admit that there he had me.

"We will have to wait for them to wake up to ask them," I said calmly.

"Could be the murderin' sod is from the Corps, sent out to watch you," Mr. Piper said, absently picking his ear. "But he's not wearin' a uniform, so I don't think that's likely."

"I know!" Mr. Christian said, raising his hand as if he were in the schoolroom. "He's from the emperor, and he's in *disguise* as a thuggee."

I ignored him, my eyes once again on the strange man. "It is a very curious thing, no matter who he is. As for his companion . . . I wonder what Mr. Mowen would make of this."

I held up a small rectangular white-and-black object. It was made of some sort of chrome, smooth and rounded at the corners, with dangling black wires.

"What is it?" Mr. Christian asked, craning his head to peer at it.

"I don't know," I answered, turning the object over. It was about the size of my hand, and cool to the touch. "There is a maker's mark here: iPod. How very odd. I have never heard of such a company."

"Do you think it's a bomb, then, miss?" Mr. Christian's eyes came close to popping right out of his head.

"It's not ticking, and doesn't appear to be active, but it does have wires, and everyone knows bombs must have wires. However, I've never seen one like this. It's quite dainty."

Mr. Piper leaned over my shoulder to examine it. "I wouldn't be thinkin' a thuggee would carry a dainty bomb. A wicked-sharp shiv, now, that I could see. But a wee little bomb like that?" He shook his head. "Don't make sense."

"I'm inclined to agree, but despite it appearing to be inactive, I believe we should get it off the ship. Since we are almost to Marseilles, we will drop it over the side into the Étang de Berre, where it will not harm anyone should it explode."

Mr. Christian's gaze swiveled to the couple still draped over the crates. "A petite bomb! That must mean . . . Captain, do you think they're"—his voice dropped to a hoarse whisper—"revolutionaries?"

Mr. Piper sat up a bit straighter, but his eyes were on me, not the strangers. I didn't mind him looking to me for direction, but the speculation in his eyes was a bit daunting.

"I doubt that," I said slowly, looking back at the man and woman, picking my words carefully. "I did not find the Black Hand insignia on them, nor do they have any weapons. It's been my experience that revolutionaries always carry weapons."

"Oh. I suppose that's so," Mr. Christian said, his face falling. "Still, would have been exciting to have caught some revolutionaries, wouldn't it? I've heard that the emperor himself rewards those who turn them in. I'd love to see him, just once."

"I've seen him," Dooley said as he reentered the hold, his chest puffing out with self-importance. "He rode by when I was on leave in London. He was in a beautiful black carriage, made of glass it was, and there was a lady next to him, a glorious princess all dressed in gold, glittering and sparkling in the sun just like my brass buttons."

"Your buttons are a disgrace to the Corps," Mr. Christian answered, his lip curling as he gestured toward Dooley's jacket. "And that wasn't a princess next to the emperor—it was the Duchess of Prussia, the one he's marrying in ten days' time."

I ignored their banter as I chewed over a possibility that had just struck me—could it be that Etienne had sent the couple to assist me? It wasn't unknown for him to send assistance when he thought it necessary, but he knew me well. A memory rose of him pulling on his clothes as I lay tangled in the sheets, exhausted and sated, his gray eyes warm with amusement as he said that he could always count on me to be proficient in all that I did.

A faint blush rose at the memory. The knowledge that I had given myself to a man who was using me for political reasons was not one of my finer moments, but I had survived it, just as I had survived everything else. No, Etienne would be confident in my ability to do my job. Besides, he would tell me if he was sending a couple of members incognito—and he hadn't said anything of the sort the last time we'd met. Although it was true we hadn't had more than a few snatched minutes, it not being at all the thing for a captain in the Aerocorps to be seen in the company of the head of the revolutionary force determined to overthrow the emperor.

I sheathed the Disruptor. "Dooley, did you find Mr. Ho?"

"Aye, Captain. She'll be along directly," he answered, hovering around the bodies.

I directed a pointed glance at him. "Then please, about your duties. Mr. Christian, would you be so kind as to ask Mr. Mowen if he could spare a moment to examine the device we found?"

"Aye, aye," he answered, giving a brisk salute as he hurried out of the hold.

I waited until the sound of their footsteps on the gangway faded into nothing before I turned to my companion. "Well, Mr. Piper?"

"Well, Captain?" the old man said, his gaze skittering away from mine with cagey awareness.

"Do you think they're revolutionaries?"

His eyes met mine again for a moment before turning to the two people. "What ye said about revolutionaries never bein' found without weapons ain't true, it ain't true at all."

"No, it isn't, but it's better if Mr. Christian thinks so."

"Aye, the lad's been dropped on his head once too often," the old man agreed, idly scratching his rear end. "Could be they *are* revolutionaries. They have the look of strangers about them. But what would such as them be doin' on the *Tesla*?"

"Doing what revolutionaries do best, I suppose," I answered, contemplating a miserable future that started with the people in front of me, and ended in disaster, possibly death. Probably my own. Or, God help me, worse. "Sowing dissent, attempting to overthrow the emperor, and destroying all things imperial. It's going to be a nightmare when we land."

He slid me another odd look. "Perhaps."

Before I could ask him just what he meant, the unconscious man moaned, and lifted his hand to his head. "What the hell hit me?"

His words were slurred slightly, but that wasn't what concerned me—it was his accent. An American accent.

"Ratsbane!" I swore, pulling out the Disruptor. "He's American!"

"I ain't never heard of an American revolutionary," Mr. Piper said meditatively. "Is there such a thing as an American thuggee?"

"Sir," I said, addressing the man with both words and the weapon. "You will regulate your movements. I am holding a firearm, and the setting is on sensitive."

"What?" The man rubbed his face, then opened his eyes, squinting at me. "What's sensitive? Ow. Other than my head. Would you mind me asking who you are, and just what you're doing in my lab?"

"Could be he's not so much a revolutionary as he is lackin' in wits," Mr. Piper murmured.

I couldn't help but wonder if that was true. A lab? What was the stranger talking about? He certainly appeared befuddled, his face expressing a combination of pain and confusion. Perhaps he was just a poor soul who had wandered onto the ship by mistake? No. That would be too much of a coincidence. He had to be there for a reason, a reason I was sure to dislike intensely.

"Jupiter, Mars, and all the little planets," the man said in a manner that indicated he was swearing. He rubbed his head, then turned to look at me. With a start, I realized his eyes didn't match—one was brown, while the other was mossy green. Oddly enough, it was attractive on him, not discordant, as I would have supposed. In fact, his face was attractive, too.

What the devil was a handsome spy doing on my ship?

"Did I ask who you were?" he asked in a voice that was still a little thick.

"Yes. I am Octavia Emmaline Pye." I bit back an oath at my words. What on earth was I doing giving him my full name with such casual disregard? Captains in the Aerocorps demanded and received respect; they did *not* engage in common chitchat with suspected criminals. I strove to put the stowaway in his proper position, saying in a stern voice, "You may refer to me as Captain Pye."

With a sudden move that had me scrambling backward, the man swung his legs over the edge of the crate and got to his feet. He wobbled for a few seconds, then straightened up to his full height. He blinked in surprise at me for a few moments; then a smile curled his lips. "Did I miss the memo about a masquerade party?"

Log of the HIMA *Tesla*
Monday, February 15
Forenoon Watch: Five Bells

"Er ..." The man rubbed his head as if it pained him. His fingers moved around from his forehead to the side, causing him to wince. "Sins of the saints—that's a hell of a goose egg."

"You're injured? We didn't see any signs of that. Allow me to look," I said, cautiously moving around to his side. I held the Disruptor firmly in case he was attempting to fool me, but he made no move other than to duck his head when I gently parted his hair.

"Careful. I don't know what happened to me, but it hurts like hell."

I sought, and found, the source of the pain—a lump on the side of his head the size and approximate shape of a quail's egg.

"What's the fancy dress about? Ow! That hurt!"

"I'm sorry." I stopped gently probing the injury, taking a step back from the man.

He grinned at me, a lopsided grin that tugged on something inside me. "'Sokay. It's just that the pain is kind of ebbing and flowing, although at least it seems to be clearing now. Kind of. Sorry, did you tell me what the occasion is? I seem to be a bit rummy, still."

"Occasion?" I tried not to openly examine the man, but he seemed quite different now that he was animated. He seemed much . . . well, much more. More handsome, more alive, more vital. And oddly endearing, which was a very odd emotion to feel about a person who could turn out to be a spy or worse.

He waved a hand toward me. "For the costume. Is there a con going on?"

"Con?" I mentally chided myself for repeating his questions in such an idiotic manner, but I didn't for the life of me understand what he meant.

"Convention." He touched the lump on his head, winced again, and rubbed his jaw, instead. "Like a cosplay one? You heard of cosplay?"

"No. Mr. Piper?" I glanced at the bosun. He looked as confused as I felt.

"Nay, Captain. Codsplay, now, that I have. There's a whore in Marseilles who can wrap her tongue all the way around a man's cods and still have enough left over to—"

"I'm afraid you have us at a disadvantage, sir," I said loudly, interrupting Mr. Piper before he could go into any further detail. I gave him a sharp look, but he was too busy staring at the stranger to notice it. "What I would like to know is who you are, and what you are doing on my ship."

"That sounds like a useful sort of woman to know," the man said to Mr. Piper with one of those male-to-male knowing looks.

"Aye, that she was," he agreed, propping himself up on the crate again. "She could milk a man dry with both her mouth and her—"

"I think I've heard just about enough of your . . . *friends* . . . in Marseilles," I interrupted again, this time managing to catch the bosun's eye.

He grinned. "Sorry, Captain. Forgot ye was a woman."

"Indeed." I transferred my gaze from him to the stranger, who was examining me with a look of admiration that would have, had I been a lesser woman, had me blushing.

"That's a hell of an outfit," he said, and, before I could say anything, moved around behind me, examining the back side. "Incredible. It's just incredible. I love the scarlet coat. Steampunk, right? You don't see much scarlet in steampunk outfits. Most folks go in for browns and blacks, but the scarlet looks really good, even though you have red hair. I was always under the impression that redheads weren't supposed to wear red, but it looks good on you. And I *really* like the corset."

I gasped a little gasp, looking down at myself, fearing for a moment that I had forgotten to don a blouse, but no, all was well.

"I wouldn't be a man if I didn't," he said, winking at Mr. Piper. "I mean, what man wouldn't love the effect of a corset on a woman's . . ." He made a gesture toward his chest.

I straightened up and glared at him.

"Although I thought you were supposed to wear the corset on the outside?" he continued, tipping his head to the side as he stared at my breasts. "Not that the lacy top isn't pretty and all. It really frames your . . . er . . . breasts nicely. But every other woman I've seen had hers on the outside."

"Her tits?" Mr. Piper asked, his eyes bugging out a bit as he, too, stared at my chest.

I hurriedly started buttoning up the long row of brass buttons on my coat.

"No, corset. You know how ladies are—they go to all the trouble of making a corset, and they want to show it off. Don't blame them at all," the stranger answered.

Mr. Piper considered me speculatively.

"I assure you that I did *not* make my corset, not that it is apropos to anything," I said in a voice that sounded aggrieved. I never realized how many buttons the uniform jacket had until that moment. Both men watched with what seemed to be disappointment as I buttoned it across my breasts. Immediately after the last button was slid into place, I began to sweat under the effect of all that heavy wool bound tightly around me.

"Nothing wrong with an off-the-rack model, either. I bought a great Victorian frock coat that way, although I haven't had a chance to wear it to any steampunk events yet. I don't have much in line of a costume, to be honest. You know, I have to say that your modded gun is awesome. I've tried my hand at converting a couple of Nerf guns to something steampunk, but they never turn out. That looks really authentic. I particularly like the brass tubing. Can I see it?"

"Sir!" I said, perhaps louder than was strictly polite, snatching back the Disruptor that he had managed to take from me, so baffled was I by his speech. I pointed the gun at his chest, and donned my most austere expression. "I am bound by the laws governing the Southampton Aerocorps to inform you that you are under arrest for unauthorized presence on a ship under contract for imperial business."

"Wow, you have the whole persona down and everything," the man said, little lines around his eyes crinkling as he laughed a rich, deep laugh that I could swear I felt reverberating in my bones. I told my bones to stop being so susceptible, and frowned at the stranger. "That's really great. And what about you?"

Mr. Piper straightened up as the man turned to him. "Piper's the name. I'm bosun here."

"Wait a minute—Aerocorps? Bosun? Captain?" He looked at me again, delight filling his mismatched eyes. "You're an airship fan, too? I know a lot of steamy folk consider them way too overdone, but I have to admit, I've always had a fondness for them, and although I don't have a persona, I always thought that if I did, he would have something to do with an airship."

"Are you daft?" The words slipped out of my mouth without my brain agreeing they were at all right and proper to say, which of course they weren't. I rubbed my forehead, a small headache starting to blossom there. "Sir, I fear we are talking at cross-purposes. Perhaps if we were to start with a few simple facts, we might proceed to those of a more strenuous nature. What is your name?"

"Jack. Jack Fletcher."

I examined his face, mentally trying out the name. It suited him. He looked like a Jack.

His smile faded into a frown as he looked around. "Hey, where's Hallie?"

"Would that be your female companion?" I asked, ignoring the prick of sweat that formed under my arms. I did not normally wear my coat buttoned except when required by protocol, and certainly not in the warm, airless confines of the hold.

"My sister. She was with me. I think. We were . . ." He touched his head as his voice trailed off, a puzzled look on his face. "We were talking about something."

"Your companion is here," I said, moving aside so he could see behind me.

With a cry of, "Hallie!" he rushed over to the prone woman. "What's wrong with her?"

"Nothing that we could see, although I must admit that we did not notice the injury to your head," I answered, moving around the woman's feet.

"Hal? Wake up!"

"Nrrng." The woman frowned, licking her lips for a second before rolling over onto her side.

"Come on, Hal, make an effort to wake up." Jack tried to roll her over, but she mumbled something incoherent as she slapped at his hands. He looked up from her to me. "What have you done to her?"

There was ire in his voice, ire and an unspoken threat. I straightened my shoulders. "We have done nothing but move you both from where we found you."

"Found us?" He looked around again, his gaze this time taking in the visible contents of the hold, his expression growing more and more dark. "What the hell? Where are we?"

"You are in the forward hold of His Imperial Majesty's *Tesla*, an airship that is under my command," I said, allowing a little sting of irritation to sound in my voice. "Perhaps, Mr. Fletcher, you would be good enough to tell me how your sister and you happened to be found behind a crate of salted beef?"

"Jack," he said, moving away to examine a crate of surveying equipment.

"Mr. Fletcher," I repeated, a bit more forcefully, following after him as he suddenly jetted down a narrow aisle between crates. "Sir, I must remind you that I am armed."

"Wow, this is really impressive. What is it, a warehouse?" he asked, pausing next to the salted meat, tracing the logo of the Aerocorps that had been painted on the wood. "I have to say, your group has gone to a tremendous amount of trouble to create an authentic setting."

I cast a glance behind me to Mr. Piper, who hobbled over to us. "If you could please answer my question, Mr. Fletcher, we might be a little forwarder."

He grinned at me, his laugh lines crinkling at me in a way that made my stomach flutter. With stern determination, I ignored the sensation.

"You even talk like something straight out of a Victorian book. Brava, Octavia."

"Captain Pye," I said sternly, taking a good firm grip on the patience that was fast slipping through my fingers.

"But Octavia is such a pretty name," he said, winking at me. "It fits you well. This isn't by any chance a film set, is it? I hadn't heard through the grapevine that there was a new steampunk movie being made, but this—" He turned around, gesturing toward the stacks of crates in the hold. "This is really amazing."

I gasped at the sign painted on the back of his undershirt, staring at it in disbelief. "You dare?"

"Satan's stones!" Mr. Piper gasped, as well, as soon as he caught sight of it. "Aw, lad, and ye seemed like such a nice fellow."

I leveled my gun at the man as he spun around. "What's wrong?" he asked. "What do I dare?"

"Your arrogance," I said through a tight jaw. "Well, at least we know what you are now."

"I'm a nanoelectrical systems engineer," he said, giving me a puzzled look. "I don't see how that's overly arrogant, although I have to admit to being labeled as a nerd once in a while. But usually the stories about Alaska and Mexico get out, and that reputation wipes out anything else. If I was to tell you that I was accidentally swept up in a group that hijacked a whaling ship, but had nothing to do with the whole thing, what would you say?"

"That you were a scoundrel, rogue, and the worst sort of adventurer," I said, indignant that my inner workings seemed to be wholly at odds with my brain. For some inexplicable reason, the confounded Mr. Fletcher seemed to hold an attraction for me. Well, I would have none of it. I had not been the wisest of women in my choices of male partners, but I was not stupid. I would learn from my mistakes.

"Oh, man," he said, rubbing his face. "You've heard those absurd stories? I swear to you, I was just a victim of circumstance, nothing more. I'm not an adventurer. I'm not dashing and romantic. I'm not Indiana Jones."

"But you *are* an airship pirate," I said, gesturing toward the entrance to the hold with the Disruptor. "You will please return to your sister."

"Airship . . . Oh, you mean my T-shirt," he said, the puzzlement in his face fading into amusement. "It's a band. I'm surprised you haven't heard of them. They're pretty good. You should listen to their latest CD—I bet you'd like it. It's got some goth overtones to it, but it's still very listenable."

"Sir, I have had quite enough of your conundrums. You will return to the entrance now, or I will be forced to use the Disruptor."

"Knock yourself out," he said easily, looking interested. "Does it have working parts?"

My patience was gone. With a silent oath, I pointed the gun toward the edge of the crate nearest him, one containing uniforms, and fired. The weapon spat out a single pulse of charged aether, blasting the corner of the wooden crate into a thousand little slivers. The smell of scorched wood drifted back to me as Jack examined the results.

"That's pretty impressive. Did you have one of those special effect squibs rigged to blow up?" he asked slowly, reaching out to touch the still-smoldering remains of wood. With a yelp, he jerked his hand back, blowing on his fingers as he looked up to me. "That's hot. How did you do that?"

"Am I to assume, Mr. Fletcher, that you deny the fact you are an airship pirate when the sign on the back of your undergarment states the opposite?"

"I got the T-shirt last night at the concert," he said, looking back at the destroyed crate corner. "It wasn't a squib you used, was it? It looks like the wood was hit by a high-temperature bullet."

"Pulse, not bullet. The Mark 15 Empyrean Disruptors use pulses of heated aether rather than bullets," I corrected him. "And now I've had enough of this farce. Please return to your sister."

"You really are taking this to quite a length, aren't you? Well, I'm afraid that I'm not going to be able to play along with the whole thing much longer. I've got a lot on my plate today, and my boss will be on my back if I don't get some things done. Hal? Wake up. We've got to get going."

"Will you see to it that Mr. Christian has the brig arranged properly, Mr. Piper?" I asked the bosun.

He eyed Jack for a moment or two. "Ye sure ye'll be all right with the blighted bastard?"

"Bastard?" Jack said, frowning at him. "Look, I don't want to pick a fight with you, but I don't appreciate being called a bastard when I haven't done anything to deserve it."

"I will be perfectly safe, Mr. Piper," I reassured him, nodding toward the Disruptor.

"Aye, Captain." Piper scurried around Jack, careful to give the younger man a wide berth.

Jack watched him go with a disgruntled look that he turned upon me as the door closed behind Mr. Piper. "OK, it's just you and me and my addled sister, so you can drop the act. What's going on here, Octavia, if that is really your name?"

"It is. I've told you repeatedly, Mr. Fletcher—you are my prisoner. It is you who seems to have trouble accepting that fact. There you are, Mr. Ho. I have been waiting some time for you."

"My apologies, Captain," the woman who was our steward's mate said hurriedly, a bit out of breath. "I was up in the starboard stabilizing plane, helping Mr. Mowen. Dooley said someone was injured?"

Beatrice Ho, a slight woman of Asian descent, gazed at Jack with frank appraisal. Although I had been with this crew for only a few days, I had marked the steward's mate out as someone I would enjoy knowing. She seemed a sensible young woman, hardworking, and knowledgeable in her job. I had no doubt she would rise in rank within the Aerocorps . . . but that didn't explain why I was taken with an idiotic urge to shove her out of the room.

"*Mr.* Ho?" Jack asked, giving her a considering look.

The hairs on the back of my neck stood on end.

"It is a custom in the Aerocorps to refer to all members of the crew in the masculine form, regardless of gender," I said, annoyed with how stiff my voice sounded. I would not be influenced by this scoundrel! "It is an archaic rule, I agree, but we are bound to follow the traditions of the Corps, and thus Miss Ho is referred to as Mr. while she serves on board this ship. Mr. Ho, this gentleman's sister is indisposed. She appears to have no injuries, but I would feel more comfortable if you were to examine her."

"Certainly."

"Mr. Fletcher, perhaps you would step out into the gangway while Mr. Ho works," I said, gesturing toward the door.

Jack gave the steward a long look, then nodded and opened the door, waiting for me to go through.

"You will precede me, please," I said, fighting the urge to brush back a lock of his hair that had fallen forward on his brow.

"For God's sake . . ." He went through the door, stopping abruptly just beyond it, moving only when I gave him a gentle shove between the shoulder blades.

"Good God in heaven . . ." His voice held an odd mixture of awe, surprise, and disbelief as his head tilted back, his gaze going upward.

"Is something the matter?" I asked, trying to hold on to a shred of patience. I had to admit that one part of me was dying to know what outrageous thing he would say next. What came out of his mouth wasn't at all what I expected.

"This is an airship," he said, spinning around to face me as he gestured toward the aluminum girders and struts that made up the framework containing the balloon envelopes. "It's really an airship."

"What did you expect?" I asked, confused by the honest astonishment visible on his face. I searched his eyes, but found nothing there but profound surprise.

"But . . ." He turned slowly in a circle, his gaze darting from the balloon envelope directly above us to the six others that spanned the length of the airship. "But this is real. It can't be, but it is. I've never seen anything like this before in my life."

"You've never been on an airship before?" I couldn't help but ask.

"No." He turned back to me, his gaze earnest as he took my free hand. "Octavia, what's happened to me? How did Hallie and I get here?"

I stared at him, not wanting to believe the evidence before me, but I couldn't deny the truth—he was genuinely confused.

"I wish I could answer that, but I cannot," I said, strangely touched by the way he clung to my hand as his gaze rose once more to the supporting structures of the airship. "But we will find out, Mr. Fletcher. You may rest assured that we will find out."

Sing Hallelujah, C'mon Get Happy

"I don't understand, Jack. I just don't understand. Explain it to me. Explain how this could happen to us!"

"I don't know exactly what happened to us, Hal." I held my sister in my arms, more to keep her from running amok and possibly hurting herself than to comfort her. She was too distraught to gain comfort from anything but a serious dose of Valium.

"I know what it is." Hallie pushed back from me, her face tight with suspicion. "You're having me on, aren't you? This is some great big elaborate joke you've concocted to pay me back for selling you at an auction. Well, it isn't going to work, Jack. You and your skinny little buddy there aren't going to make me believe we're in some sort of weirdo fantasy world. I don't know how you got me onto this blimp, or whatever it is, but I want down now. I have a lunch date with a really fabulous personal trainer, and I'm not going to miss it because you've dreamt up some grandiose practical joke!"

"It's not a joke," I said. "It's real. This ship is real. This guy is real. Er . . . what was your name again?"

The tall, skinny kid who looked like he was about twenty, with slicked-back red hair and the vaguest hint of a mustache, straightened up and cleared his throat. "I am Aldous Christian, the chief officer on His Imperial Majesty's Airship *Tesla*."

"Nice to meet you, Al. I know Octavia told you to keep an eye on us, but is there somewhere else we can go other than this cabin? I think my sister needs to see a bit more of the ship."

He frowned. "The captain didn't say anything about you leaving the cabin."

"Then she can't mind if we do," I pointed out, taking Hallie by the arm. "Come on, Hal. This is something you have to see."

"I think the captain meant for you to stay here—," Al started to say, but I had other plans. I pulled a lead-footed Hallie out into the corridor, and up a curved flight of stairs, stopping at a landing that was open to the main part of the airship. "There. See?"

She looked around, her expression bored. "It's a movie set."

"Not even close."

She shook her head. "It has to be. Where did you get the sort of money to rent a whole movie set, Jack? That has to run to thousands, especially with the actors you had to hire to go with it."

"Such a skeptic," I sighed. "Hey, Al, is there a window somewhere that Hallie can look out? There's no way she can say we're on a movie set if we're a thousand feet in the air."

"There's the observation platform, but we've landed in Marseilles to fill the boilers," he said.

"Maybe that'll convince you," I told Hallie, taking her by the hand and pulling her back down the stairs. There had to be an exit somewhere on the lower level of the ship.

"What, more sets? Not even close. And stop pulling

me around. I want to go to lunch with Luis and admire his abs."

"Sir! Mr. Fletcher! You can't do that!" Al the officer said, running after us. "The captain wouldn't like it at all. No one is allowed off the ship while we're taking on water."

"There has to be some sort of an entrance down here," I said, dragging Hallie down another flight of stairs with me to the area where we'd woken up. "If this is a cargo bay . . . ah, daylight!"

"I'll give it to you, it's quite an elaborate set," Hallie commented as she looked around curiously. "Hi. You must be one of the actors my brother hired."

A boy of about fifteen whirled around from where he was peering out of a door, staring at us in surprise. "Er . . ."

"Pardon us," I told the kid, pulling Hallie after me as I jumped down into hard-packed dirt. "There. Now tell me this is a movie set."

"What's he doing?" the kid asked Al.

"Get the captain," he answered, his narrow face worried as he jumped down after us. "Sir, I must insist that you return to the *Tesla*. The captain will be very angry indeed if you violate the ship's rules."

Hallie was silent as she looked around us. I had to admit that the sight was somewhat awe inspiring, at least to our eyes. The small wooden building in front of us was nothing out of the ordinary, nor were the two huge water towers behind it, one of which was currently pouring water into an opening in the airship, assumably loading up the steam boilers. But it was the scene that lay beyond that had Hallie's eyes opening wide.

"It's . . . a city," she said, blinking a couple of times.

"Yeah. A hell of a city," I said, shaking off the hand

that Al had placed on my arm. I walked past the wooden building, my gaze following the dirt road that snaked away from us, down a gentle slope to the town below. "Holy shit, that's amazing. Look, Hal—carriages and horses and ladies in long skirts."

"I'm not seeing this," she said, moving to stand next to me. She shook her head. "It's not possible. Tell me it's all a joke, Jack."

"Sir! Madam! You must return to the ship now," Al said, almost dancing with agitation behind us.

"You said this was Marseilles?" I asked him, not taking my eyes off the town. It was a busy seaport, the streets clogged with horses and carriages, big open wagons hauling cargo, a couple of traditional sailing ships in the harbor, and people everywhere—women in long skirts like the one Octavia wore, men in frock coats and hats, or shirtsleeves, vests, and derbies. Most of the activity was centered around the piers, where men loaded cargo onto a seemingly endless line of empty wagons.

Beyond the busy port area, the streets stretched out in a fan shape, the buildings just a few stories tall, but beautifully built with cream stone, tall arched windows, and all those fiddly, fancy bits stuck around the front that tourists oohed and aahed over.

A Klaxon sounded from above. We turned just in time to see the long metal chute that spouted from a water tower withdrawing from the airship.

"No," Hallie repeated, her face set in a shocked, disbelieving expression. "I am dreaming. I will wake up and go to lunch with Luis, and the after-lunch sex will be really fabulous, and then I will call you and tell you about this amazing dream I had. That's all. It's a dream."

"I wish it was that easy," a woman's voice said. Hallie turned toward Octavia, standing in the doorway of the ship, the kid behind her. "Mr. Fletcher, would you please escort your sister back to the ship? Our schedule is very tight, and we need to leave immediately if we are to not fall behind."

"I tried to tell them, Captain," Al said, scurrying over to her, his hands wringing and gesturing wildly as he pointed to us. "I told them you don't allow anyone to disembark during refilling stops."

"Wake up, wake up, wake up," Hallie said, scrunching her eyes tight and pinching her arms. "It's not real. Time to get up and get dressed."

"Hallie—"

"What's goin' on here?" The man named Piper with the odd hitch in his walk pushed past Octavia, the teenage kid right behind him. "What's the thuggees doin' out here, Captain?"

"Thuggees?" I asked, distracted for a moment.

"They're escaping!" the kid shouted, fumbling with something in his pocket.

"We're not doing anything," I said, turning around to help Hallie back into the airship. She sidestepped me when I tried to take her arm.

"Escapin', are they?" Piper grimly hobbled toward us. "That they'll not do."

"We're just standing here taking a look around," I protested. "And since Octavia asked us to return to the ship, that's what we're going to do, isn't it, Hal?"

"I don't care what you do," Hallie said, her eyes wild. "I'm getting the hell out of here so I can wake up and have a rendezvous with Luis."

"Take her!" Al said as he flung himself at me.

A chunk of dirt flew up at Hallie's feet as I was knocked to the ground.

She stared for a moment at the kid holding the same

sort of odd gun that Octavia had pointed at me, then turned and ran screaming down the hill.

"You idiot," I yelled, rolling over to shake the skinny first officer at the same time Octavia shouted something at the kid with the gun. "Get off of me! She's in no shape to be running around on her own."

"Ye're not goin' anywhere, ye murdering canker," Piper yelled as he, too, threw himself on me.

"I haven't murdered anyone, although I'm sure as hell thinking about it right now," I snarled, trying not to hurt the old man too much as I shoved him off me. I was a bit less careful with Al, getting a good right hook in that sent him flying backward with a dazed look on his face.

"Mr. Piper! Restrain yourself! Dooley, for the love of God, if you fire that Disruptor one more time, I will remove it from your person!" Octavia stormed down off the ship and helped Piper to his feet. "Mr. Fletcher, are you injured?"

"A visit to the chiropractor might be in order later, but right now I have to get my sister." I got to my feet and rubbed at a spot on my back where it felt like an anvil had hit me.

"I shall accompany you," she said, turning to glare at her crew. "You will remain here, all of you. Do I make myself clear?"

"Aye, Captain, but—"

"All of you!" she said firmly, then, picking up her skirts, ran past me down the hill. I didn't wait to add my two cents; I just took off, my eyes on the rapidly shrinking figure of Hallie as she entered the town proper.

"Please, Mr. Fletcher, I can't run as fast as you," Octavia said from behind me a few minutes later.

I slowed up and waited for her, scanning the outer

fringes of the town. There was no sign of Hallie at all. "Great. We've lost her."

"She shouldn't be too hard to find in that ensemble," Octavia murmured, breathing heavily.

"You should take up jogging," I told her, turning to scan the opposite direction. "Does wonders for your cardio."

"I have no idea what that is, but if you are referring to the fact that I can't breathe, I would remind you that I'm wearing a corset you found so intriguing a short while ago. There—people are staring after something. It is probably your sister garnering undue attention. Thank God the emperor doesn't have men in this region of France."

We took off at a fast walk in the direction she pointed. "Sorry. I forgot about the corset." I couldn't help but slip a little look over to her chest, where her lacy white top framed the tops of her boobs so nicely. They heaved now as she tried to catch her breath, plump little mounds that had my mouth watering.

"I would appreciate it if you could refrain from ogling my chest in public," she murmured, pointing to a side street. "There's nothing extraordinary there, and I'm sure your attention would be better spent watching for signs of Miss Norris."

"A man would have to be dead six months to not want to ogle your breasts, but I am sorry if I've embarrassed you. Over here. She went this way."

She paused as I stopped in front of a dark alley that seemed to lead into a less bustling area of town. "I highly doubt if she's gone into the refugees' quarter. She must be north of us, toward the market."

I looked again at the alley. In its entrance, a man was bent over, picking up a basket of apples that had been dumped out onto the ground, his glare over his shoulder down the darkened alley very telling.

"You don't know my sister. Causes are like magnets to her. If there are refugees to champion, she'll find them." I plunged into the darkness of the narrow alley, its coolness and stale smell hitting me at the same time. The air itself was close and dank, earthy with an overtone of too many unwashed bodies packed into too small a space. But it was the despair that seemed to hang heavy overhead and seep downward, like rain on crumbled stone ruins.

"Mr. Fletcher, I'm quite sure she's not—oh, bloody hell!" Octavia muttered a few things to herself, but followed after me. I emerged from the alley to what probably once was a courtyard, but now appeared to be a tent city.

"What the . . ." I stared at the small dwellings crammed together in the courtyard. The smell and sense of despair was even greater here than it was in the dark alley. "What is this?"

"Refugees," Octavia said, her voice emotionless.

I was startled by her callousness, but one look at her face told me she was struggling to keep her voice neutral. A deep sadness filled her eyes, her face reflecting the suffering shown by the people crouching over a small fire, a ratty cook pot hanging from a makeshift spit.

"Refugees from what?" I asked.

"War. You were quite correct—there is Miss Norris."

A flash of blue told me she was right. Octavia wove her way through the clusters of people to the far side of the courtyard, where Hallie perched on a partially crumbled stone bench that sat beneath a half-dead olive tree. The people clustered here were strangely silent; only a few snuffles and coughs were punctuated with the occasional groan of pain. Men, women, and children all alike were clothed in what amounted to rags, an ever-present miasma of hopelessness combining with dirt, lack of hygiene, and probably lack of edible food to make them indistinguishable from one another. Lank, stringy hair hung down over faces that would haunt me at night.

Some of the refugees had missing limbs, or bore dirty bandages. Others just sat in boneless heaps, leaning against rickety wooden shelters curtained with torn, colorless blankets. As we passed by them, one or two reached out dirty hands toward Octavia. She stopped at each one for a moment, speaking too softly for me to hear, but at last we arrived at Hallie.

"Hal? You OK?"

She sat hunched on the bench, her hands around her knees, rocking slightly, her eyes glazed as if she couldn't process what was happening to her. Carefully, in case the bench was going to crumble away entirely, I sat down next to her and put my arm around her. "It's OK, Hallie. Octavia and I are here."

"It's real," she said to her knees, her eyes unfocused. "Those people are real. I touched one of them, Jack." She held up her hand. Her fingers were stained with drying blood.

"We had better get her out of here," Octavia said in a low voice, casting a glance over her shoulder. A few of the refugees had risen and were watching us with numb indifference. "Can you walk, Miss Norris?"

"Is there nothing that can be done for them?" I asked, nodding toward the people as I pulled Hallie to her feet.

"Where there is war, there will always be victims," was all she said, taking Hallie's other arm.

"I was actually asking if there wasn't something that

could be done for these people, rather than a discourse on philosophy," I said somewhat acidly.

She glanced at me as we piloted a silent Hallie through the gathered people. "Why do you care?"

I frowned. Octavia didn't seem like the sort of woman who would be so unfeeling about those less fortunate. She was so intriguing, so attractive and sexy, I forgot for a moment that sometimes the inner package didn't match the outer. And what a damned shame that was. She was just about perfect in every other way. "Hallie and I were raised to help others when possible. I realize my money probably isn't going to be good here, but I have a few bucks on me if you thought it would help them. Or I could give one of them my watch—it's nothing fancy, but it's worth a couple of hundred."

Octavia stopped at the alleyway, shooting me a look full of disbelief. "You'd give them your possessions?"

I shrugged, mentally striking her off my interest list. Just looking at her might make me want to lick every inch of that lovely freckly skin, but I'd been around enough shallow, self-centered women to know there was no way we'd mesh. "If it would help them, yes. I prefer working with folks who need a helping hand rather than doling out charity, but you said you had to be on your way, so that's the best I can do."

A little blush came to her cheeks as she touched my hand, apparently forgetting about Hallie for a few seconds. "That's very kind of you, but not necessary. I left some provisions for them at the way station. They will be brought down later, at night, when the townspeople won't be able to confiscate them."

It was my turn to stare at her. "You left provisions?"

"Yes. It's against the rules of the Corps, naturally, but I, too, was raised to believe it is my duty to help those less fortunate. My father always laid by extra provisions to be distributed at the way station stops, and I have continued his tradition."

She moved to the top of my mental Women I Want list again, with a couple of bullets and big arrows pointing to her name. "Has anyone told you that you're just about perfect, Octavia?"

Her eyebrows rose slightly. "What a very odd question. I am in no way perfect, I assure you, Mr. Fletcher. Especially when I am in danger of being so delayed that my schedule is irreparably harmed."

"I think we're going to get along well." I smiled and took Hallie's unresisting arm again, gently tugging her down the alleyway. "Really, *really* well."

She looked disconcerted at that thought.

Log of the HIMA *Tesla*
Monday, February 15
Forenoon Watch: Six Bells

"Well, that brandy did the job. It shook her out of the stupor she was in, and she's taking everything better than I thought she would."

I straightened up from where I had been leaning against the wall outside my cabin. "Indeed. I—"

A woman's scream interrupted me.

We both turned to look at the door. The scream was one of fury, and died off into a loudly shouted stream of profanity that made my eyebrows rise.

Jack's lips twisted in a wry smile. "Or not." He winced at a particularly profane reference coming from the cabin. "I think she's finally accepted that this isn't all a dream. She's . . . upset," he added, as if that explanation needed to be made.

"It's understandable. I find myself having somewhat the same sort of difficulty believing your tale. You realize, of course, that you are asking us to believe something quite outrageous."

The door to the cabin was jerked open, and the passive, glassy-eyed woman whom we had brought back to the *Tesla* a short while before now stood staring out at us, her hair as wild as her eyes, her breath somewhat ragged as if she'd been under an extreme exertion.

"Quite outrageous!" she yelled, the strained note in her voice giving proof that she was perilously close to hysteria. *"Quite outrageous?"*

"Hallie, calm down, or the steward will be forced to sedate you."

"Go ahead," she said, marching out of the room, glaring at her brother. Her clothes, the lovely silk tunic and trousers, were dirty and wrinkled from the visit to the refugee quarters. "Sedate me! Knock me out! Maybe that way I'll get out of this nightmare and back in the real world!"

"I don't think you've been properly introduced. This is my sister, Hallelujah Norris, better known as Hallie," Jack said, giving me a wry smile. "She doesn't normally swear like a sailor."

"The hell I don't!"

"Hal, this is Octavia Pye. She's the captain of this . . . er . . ."

"Say it," Hallie snarled at her brother, her eyes narrowing. "Go on, say it. Drive me over the edge! Drive me over the goddamned fuc—"

"Hal!" Her brother interrupted her with a worried look my way. "I don't think Octavia appreciates swearing."

I gave the distraught woman a quelling look. "Indeed."

"Fine!" Hallie yelled, tossing her hands in the air. "I won't swear, because it will offend this pretend woman's delicate sensibilities! Have it your way! I'll just go quietly insane on my own, then, shall I? Without swearing?"

"Pretend woman?" I asked, eyeing her lest she should

try to escape again. We were once again under way, but I worried that in her distraught state she hadn't taken that fact in.

"Now she thinks this is a delusion," Jack said quietly to me as his sister paced back and forth across the narrow hallway, her hands gesturing as she mumbled to herself. "She thinks that we somehow ingested some sort of hallucinogenic, and that we're imagining all of this."

"I must admit that I find your story just as unlikely as she finds us," I said, relieved to see Hallie stop muttering as she stopped before one of the portholes that lined the corridor.

Jack gave me an odd look. "You say unlikely, but not impossible."

I raised my eyebrows. "Does that matter?"

"I don't know. I think it's telling. I would think that anyone else would tell me I was out-and-out lying, or delusional. But you just say it's unlikely."

"I did say that your story is outrageous," I pointed out. "And so it is."

"I don't know. Maybe. Let's look at the facts," he answered, holding up his hand to tick items off his fingers.

"Yes, let's look at the facts. Facts are good. Facts are solid. Facts never, ever spirit one away from one's normal world and into something of make-believe," Hallie said quickly, her knuckles white as she gripped the brass porthole frame. "I like facts. Give me facts, Jack."

"One: earlier today we were in my lab at work. The year was 2010, and I was a nanoelectrical engineer working on a quantum computer project."

I considered him carefully. His eyes were steady on mine, nothing in them but a slight look of worry. Either he was telling the truth, or he believed that what he said was the truth.

"Indeed," I said a third time.

"What year is it here?" he asked me.

"It's 2010."

"No, I mean what year is it for you? I'm no expert on Victorian fashion, but you appear to be wearing a bustle, and I thought those went out of style before the turn of the century, so I'm assuming that your present is something in the late eighteen hundreds?"

"Today is February 15, 2010, Mr. Fletcher," I answered.

"But . . ." His gaze dropped to my chest. I had unbuttoned my jacket earlier, in an attempt to keep from sweating profusely. "But you're wearing that corset you keep mentioning."

"On the contrary, you are the one who repeatedly brings it up," I corrected him.

"And long skirts. And a bustle. You can't deny you have a bustle."

"Why would I wish to?" I asked, frowning at him. "Truly, Mr. Fletcher, you seem to have an extremely bizarre preoccupation with my undergarments."

"And button boots," he said, pointing at my feet. "The kind you have to use a button-hook thing on."

"Granny boots," Hallie said suddenly, having turned to stare at my feet. "Mom had a pair of those. My God, Jack, you're right. She does have granny boots on!"

"I do not have a grandmother, so these boots could hardly have belonged to her," I corrected Hallie. "And once again I must say that I do not see what my clothing has to do with you both being here on my ship."

"How come your skirt is so short?" Hallie asked, frowning at my ankles. "I was in a production of *Hello, Dolly!* and all the dresses we wore swept the floor. It was a pain in the ass always having to hoist the skirts to walk up and down the stairs. But your skirt is at your ankles."

"The uniform of the female members of the Southampton Aerocorps includes skirts that are ankle-length for safety reasons, Miss Norris. It would be impractical to attempt to climb around in the ship's rigging with skirts that touched the floor."

"Hrmph." She went back to looking out of the porthole.

"Point two . . . damn. I forgot what point two was," Jack said, frowning.

"I'm sorry to hear that. Perhaps instead, I might have a word with you?"

"You're going to talk about me, aren't you?" Hallie asked, her hands on her hips. "I know you're going to talk about me."

"Yes," I said simply.

"I think I'm going to lie down," she said in a sudden reversal of attitude, her hand to her forehead. "Maybe if I go back to sleep, the drug will work its way out of my system and I can see normal things again. Er . . . this room looks like someone is living in it."

"That is my cabin. Since it is unsuitable for you to remain with Mr. Fletcher in his cabin, you will share mine."

"Unsuitable?" Jack asked, looking as if he wanted to laugh. "She's my sister."

"She is an unmarried woman, sir," I pointed out. "The Aerocorps has standards of conduct upon their ships, and I would be in violation of several of them were I to allow your sister and you to share a cabin."

"I'm divorced, not unmarried," Hallie said, sounding somewhat forlorn as she stood in the doorway of my cabin.

"That makes little difference to the Aerocorps. You will share my cabin. The window seat converts into a bunk; you are welcome to use that. We'll worry about finding you some clothing at a later time."

She nodded, but said nothing until she entered the cabin, pausing to look over her shoulder at us. "We didn't eat magic mushrooms, did we, Jack?"

"No, Hal, we didn't."

"Those people we saw, they were real?"

"Yes. Octavia is having some food and stuff sent to them. I added my watch and the money I had, in case they could be used, too."

Her face grew pinched. "It was the explosion in your lab?"

"I think so," he said, his voice calm, but I sensed an underlying unease. "I think when the liquid helium that you spilled hit the quantum circuits . . . well, I don't know exactly what happened except it knocked us unconscious, and out of our reality and into this one."

"Why don't you look more disturbed by all this?" she suddenly wailed, her hands wringing themselves before she gestured toward Jack Fletcher. "Why aren't you upset about her? About all of this? Why aren't you insane with anxiety over this whole thing?"

Oddly enough, I was wondering much the same thing. After his initial confusion and disbelief, he'd settled down into a sort of excited anticipation that I had a hard time explaining.

He took one of his sister's hands in his. "This is the chance of a lifetime, Hal. Don't you see it? We've done something remarkable, something miraculous. We're not in our world anymore—somehow, something changed on an atomic level. I don't know how or why, but I do know this—we're explorers in a strange new territory.

The ramifications of what happened to us are mind-boggling. Just think of the research we can do! Just think of the knowledge we can gain from our experiences. I really wish I had my laptop to take notes on."

Hallie was silent for a moment, her expression unchanged. "Can we get back?"

The excitement in Jack's face faded as he stared at her, the question hanging heavily in the air.

She nodded again, just as if his silence had answered her question, and went into the cabin, closing the door softly behind her.

I was a bit taken aback by her sudden acceptance of, or at least resignation to, her presence on the airship. "She will not do herself any harm, will she?" I asked Jack.

"Hallie? No," he said, shaking his head. "You wouldn't believe it from her little freak-out, but she's really a very levelheaded person. Feet on the ground and all that. It's just that . . . well, you have to admit, this whole thing is really bizarre."

"It is very trying for everyone. I feel in the need for a strong cup of tea," I answered. "Just as soon as you've changed your garments, we will indulge ourselves, and have a discussion about the situation."

"Why do I need to change my clothes?" he asked, looking down at himself.

I stopped outside of the storage cabin that Mr. Piper had emptied in order to convert it to what was either a brig or a passenger cabin, depending on your point of view. "Mr. Fletcher, you may not be bothered by the sign on your back proclaiming you to be an airship pirate, but I assure you that the Aerocorps takes a very hard view of such people. Mr. Piper has found some suitable clothing for you to wear. I trust they will fit well enough for you to don them."

He chuckled, outright chuckled, as if what I said was too amusing. "You know, I'd be tempted to freak out right along with Hallie, except for one thing."

"What is that?" I asked as he opened the door and stepped inside.

"You," he said, a twinkle in his mismatched eyes as he closed the door.

My heart did an odd sort of flip-flop in my chest.

"I am *not* going to be charmed by that rogue," I muttered to myself as I stalked down the hallway toward the galley. "He could be deranged. He could be lying. Or he could be up to something nefarious. And besides, three rogues in my life were quite enough! There is not room for one more!"

Log of the HIMA *Tesla*
Monday, February 15
Forenoon Watch: Six Bells and a Smidgen

Robert Anstruther once told me that it was funny how fate chose certain moments to listen in to one's thoughts. It had certainly done so to mine—a wish to escape an unhappy childhood with an alcoholic mother had led me to places I had never in my dreams imagined. And at that moment, as I walked down the passageway toward the mess, I had an uncomfortably itchy feeling that fate had once again chosen the present to poke its head into my business.

"Captain!"

"Mr. Llama?" I winced when I spoke. Addressing the second engineer always left me with the regrettable feeling I was speaking to a child's toy. I had a suspicion that the man in question wasn't born with the dubious name he had given the Aerocorps, but it was not for me to insist he adopt something less eccentric.

"There is a rumor floating around that spies have come on board," the slight, dark-haired man said as he closed the door of the mess. Mr. Llama—I sighed to myself as I even thought of his absurd name—often entered a room in such a manner, or so I had noticed during my four days on the *Tesla*. He had a long face, black eyes, and a manner of keeping himself to himself. He also had an uncanny knack of popping up behind me without me being aware, startling me to the extreme.

"We have some unexpected guests, yes, but I have no cause to believe they are spies," I said carefully, watching him closely. I had yet to actually catch Mr. Llama in the process of entering or leaving a room; he just seemed to appear or disappear as if he were made of smoke.

"If you would like a hand at . . . *interrogation* . . . I am at your assistance," he said, making a little bow. "I have some knowledge of methods of ascertaining if someone is speaking the truth or not."

"Really?" I asked, setting down the pen I had been using to write in the ship's log. "That's a rather odd skill for an engineer, isn't it?"

"I haven't *always* been an engineer," he said, sliding a glance to the side, his body stiffening as if something he saw shocked him. I looked to see what it was, but there was nothing else in the mess but Dooley, at the far end of the table, whistling to himself as he performed his chores.

"I'm sure you haven't, but—" The words stopped when I looked back to find that Mr. Llama had disappeared. "Damnation. He did it again."

"Who did what?" Dooley asked, looking up from a boot he was blacking.

"Mr. Llama. Did you see him leave the room?"

Dooley scratched his head, leaving a smear of boot blacking on his forehead. "I didn't know he was here."

"He was. How very odd."

"Aye, that he is. Mr. Francisco says he doesn't sleep at night."

"He doesn't?" I asked, confused. "Who doesn't?"

"Mr. Llama." Dooley leaned toward me with the air of one sharing a confidence. "Mr. Francisco says that Mr. Llama slips out of their cabin at night, and never sleeps in his bunk. Never! Not once has he seen him there! Isn't that strange? Mr. Francisco says that Mr. Llama learned strange Oriental skills when he was fighting the Moghuls, and that he knows thirty-seven ways to kill a man with naught but a bit of string and a pair of tweezers."

I looked at the door with speculation, wondering what the mysterious Mr. Llama did at night, and made a resolution to keep a closer eye on the crew.

When the door opened again, my heart jumped into my throat.

"Better?" Jack stopped in front of me and pirouetted, his arms held out at his sides.

"Quite suitable," I said, my fingers tightening around the pen. That's what I said—what I thought was entirely different.

He wore the standard Aerocorps uniform jacket, but there was nothing standard about the way it fit his body. He was handsome in his black undershirt, but in the knee-length scarlet jacket, he was downright devastating. The snowy white wing tips of his shirt sat over the silk cross tie, below which an embroidered double-breasted gold waistcoat hugged his torso. The fact that Mr. Piper had given Jack the waistcoat of an officer was neither here nor there—it suited him very well, the twin rows of black enameled buttons with the gold leaf Aerocorps logo glinting in the light streaming in through the viewing-platform window. Black trousers and boots completed the outfit, and left me, I was distressed to note, with an overwhelming urge to run my hands over his body.

With an effort, I pulled my mind back from unwelcome desires and gestured toward the teapot. "Would you take tea?"

"Sure."

"Cream or lemon?" I asked, pouring him a cup as he took the seat opposite me.

He glanced around the mess, empty except for Dooley. "Lemon is fine. So, where do I pick up my goggles?"

"I beg your pardon?" I asked, adding a bit of sugar to his tea before handing it to him.

"Goggles, you know?" He made circles with his fingers and held them to his eyes. "Every good steamer has goggles. Don't you?"

"Certainly not," I said, wondering if I would ever really understand him. "I have safety spectacles for when I examine the boilers, naturally, but goggles? No."

"Oh." He looked disappointed for a moment, then took a sip of his tea. "So, we're here to get down to brass tacks, right?"

I set down the pen and put the cap on the bottle of ink, lest it spill on my logbook. "Dooley, if you have finished with the boots, you may take your tea with Mr. Francisco in the galley."

"Aye, Cap'n," he said, reluctantly gathering up the boots and shuffling out of the far door, his gaze never leaving that of Jack. "Mayhap Mr. Llama will be there, and he can tell me how to kill a man with tweezers."

"Bloodthirsty little devil," Jack said, watching him leave. "Cabin boy? Wait—did he say Mr. *Llama*?"

"Dooley is the bosun's mate. He is young, but enthusiastic, and yes, one of my crew is named Mr. Llama. He is the second engineer, and is rather . . . well . . . different."

"With that name, I don't doubt it."

"Mr. Fletcher, I take it from the somewhat confusing discussion that you had with your sister both in and outside of my cabin that you and she were involved in some sort of an industrial accident. Is it your supposition that you were both knocked unconscious and placed on board my ship without being aware of that fact?"

"Not quite," he said, touching the side of his head briefly. "It took Hallie to prod the memory forward, but after your Mr. Ho brought Hal around, she reminded me that we'd been in my lab when the accident occurred. That's the only possible thing I can think of that would have made this happen."

"I see. I will tell you now that I am not scientifically trained, and thus am not prepared to say whether or not what you say is possible, but I will warn you that I do have a friend who is an amateur inventor, and he will offer me such advice as I find necessary."

"Do you always talk like that?" he asked.

"Talk how?" I asked warily.

"So formal, like you're straight from the pages of a Victorian novel."

I looked at him for a moment, not sure how to take such a comment. "I'm sorry if my method of speech distresses you, but I'm afraid it is something I would be unable to change without great difficulty."

"It doesn't distress me," he said with an engaging smile.

I refused to give in to the smile.

"I like it, as a matter of fact," he continued. "It's kind of charming. You don't talk like any of the women I know."

"And have you known many women?" The words were out of my mouth before I could consider the wisdom of speaking them. Blushing with embarrassment, I clapped a hand over my mouth for a few seconds before saying, "My apologies, Mr. Fletcher."

"Jack."

"That was rude of me. You will not, of course, answer such an impertinent question."

"You look even more charming when you blush," he said, grinning. "I don't mind telling you. I've had four official girlfriends, the last one about two years ago. If you're asking how many women I've *known*—" The emphasis he put on the word was unmistakable. My cheeks grew even hotter. "That would be seven. I wasn't much for girls until I got to college. Then I had a few wild years before settling down to study."

"I see." I busied myself with pouring a dollop more tea.

"How about you?" he asked over the rim of his cup.

I looked up, startled at the insinuation.

"How many men have you known?"

That question was almost as impertinent as what I thought he had been suggesting. "That, sir, is none of your business."

"Oh?" His eyebrows rose. "I told you how many women I've been with. Fair play would demand you do the same."

It was on the tip of my tongue to retort that I hadn't wanted to know, but honesty wouldn't allow me to lie to save my self-pride. "Three," I said finally, after a brief inner struggle. I watched him closely to see if he would display any signs of repugnance at the number, not that I cared one way or another. I was a captain, I told myself. I just wanted to make sure he didn't lose any respect for me in order to avoid undermining my authority. "Not that it's any of your business whatsoever, I have had three lovers."

I lifted my chin, throwing out that last word as almost a challenge.

"Ah. You're not hooked up with someone right now, are you?" he said without blinking so much as one eyelash.

"No," I said, startled enough to answer without thinking. I set down my teacup and gave him a firm look. "Mr. Fletcher, we have strayed from the purpose of this conversation. What I wish to know is—"

"*El capitán!*"

"Oh, dear God," I moaned softly.

The door leading to the small galley was flung open, the figure of a man silhouetted in the doorway. He stalked toward us slowly, his head tipped forward as he pinned me back with what I was coming to think of as the Francisco Smolder. "*El capitán, mi capitán,* Dooley, he says that you are here alone with a man. I will tear his heart out and cook it with his kidneys if he has laid so much as a finger on you, my sweet, delicious *capitán.*"

Francisco García Ramón de Cardona, better known to the crew as Mr. Francisco, rushed forward and flung himself onto his knees at my feet, grasping my hand and pressing wet kisses onto it.

"Mr. Francisco, I have asked you not to do that," I said sternly, trying to pull my hand back.

His grip tightened as he made cow eyes at me. "*Mi capitán,*" he said, his voice simmering with sensuality and sexual promise. "My luscious, delectable *capitán.*"

Jack snorted, turning his laughter into an awkward cough.

I ground my teeth and, with an effort, jerked my hand from that of the steward. "And I've asked you not to address me with such familiarity."

"You do not love your Francisco anymore?" he asked,

adopting a suddenly coy look as he batted his eyelashes at me. "My heart, he is yours, all yours. And the rest of me, as well," he added, standing up.

I averted my gaze from his bulging pelvis, which unfortunately was right at eye level. "In addition, I believe I have addressed you on the subject of those wholly inappropriate breeches that you insist on wearing rather than the standard Aerocorps trousers."

He waggled his hips at me. "You do not like my breeches, oh, glorious one of the flaming sunset hair?"

Jack made another bark of choked laughter that I did my best to ignore as I gave the steward a very stern look, indeed. "Given that your breeches leave little, if anything, to the imagination, I am quite confident that everyone in the crew would be happier if you were to don the regulation trousers."

Francisco pursed his lips in what I'm sure he thought was a seductive pout. "It is impossible that you could resist my breeches. You are having your time of the monthlies, no? That is why you do not crave poor Francisco's body, which is so hot and hard for you."

"Really, Mr. Francisco—," I started to say when Jack interrupted.

"It doesn't seem to me that the lady is overly interested in what you're offering," he said, his smile fading. "Maybe you should just do as she asks and put on a pair of pants that don't let everyone see the outline of every vein and ridge."

Francisco drew himself up to his full height, which was no more than mine. He was small but sturdily built, and, like many Spaniards, held his pride dearly. He puffed out his chest as his eyes narrowed into obsidian slits focused on Jack. "You dare speak to me, you son of a she-dog?"

"Yeah, I do," Jack answered, getting to his feet. "It's clear that Octavia isn't interested in you, so why don't you just take yourself off and leave us in peace."

I sighed, drooping for a moment at the explosion that I knew, even after only a short acquaintance with Francisco, would be forthcoming. "Sometimes men are so pigheaded," I said to the teapot.

"You address the flaming *capitán* by her so-precious name?" Francisco snarled, storming around the table to where Jack stood. His hands danced wildly in the air as he spoke. "She is not to you belonging that you can speak so! The *capitán*, she is mine! I claimed her the moment I saw her shining, glorious hair of the hottest flames!"

"That's for her to say, not you," Jack said, his hands fisting as Francisco snarled a word that I suspected was not suitable for polite company. "Look, I have a rule about not fighting people, but if you continue to bother the captain, I will rethink it."

"You do not frighten me, you pirate of the most scabulous ancestors!" Francisco yelled.

"Scabulous?" Jack asked.

"I think he means scurrilous," I suggested.

"*Sí*, scurrilous. You are scurrilous of the most great level!" Francisco said, still waving his hands around. "I will enjoy cutting out your liver and frying it with tomatoes and capers and *un poco* basil!"

"I think that's about enough." I gave in and stood up, as well, giving my errant steward a look that by rights should have had him cowering. "You will cease threatening Mr. Fletcher. You will also cease making absurd statements regarding me. I am not yours. I will never be yours, as I told you the very first night when you burst into my cabin and threw your naked person upon my hair. I am not interested in you in *any* capacity but that of a steward. Now, please, stop making these embarrassing scenes and return to your duties."

"Mi capitán—"

"Now!" I said, pointing to the door to the galley.

Francisco looked like he wanted to spit on Jack, but thought better of insulting the larger man, contenting himself with a stream of Spanish that left a profane tint to the air as he stomped dramatically back into the galley.

"You really do have some characters on this ship, don't you?" Jack asked as I slumped down into my chair.

I was unable to deny that. "They are good people nonetheless. And I would have been able to control Mr. Francisco if you hadn't enraged him."

"You didn't look like you appreciated him hitting on you."

"I would never tolerate any man striking me, let alone a crew member," I said primly.

"That's not what . . . never mind. It's not important. What were we talking about before the Spanish drama queen entered?"

"I don't quite remember." I rubbed my forehead. "Oh, yes, the situation with you, and—"

"—how we got on board an airship in what is evidently a steampunk world, that's right. I'd like a definitive answer to that, too, but I think the best we're going to get at this point is conjecture."

"What is this steampunk you keep mentioning?" I asked, distracted by the word.

An indescribable look came over his face as he retook his seat. "It's . . . well, it's all this," he said, waving his hands. "At least I think it is. Let me ask you—what is the source of power of this airship?"

"The boilers," I answered promptly. "They turn the propellers, and heat the air that fills the envelopes."

"Steam engines, in other words," he said, nodding. "I noticed that there are gas jets on the wall. Is there any sort of electricity on board?"

"Of course not. Electricity is highly dangerous. I wouldn't have it in my home, let alone on an airship."

"Right," he said, as if he expected that answer. "And if I said 'nuclear power' to you . . . ?"

"I would suggest you define that term."

"Got it. So in other words, it's present-day, at least so far as the year is. You're dressed in a late Victorian outfit, steam engines run your airship, and you have a gun that shoots heated aether, which is an archaic term that has no real meaning."

"I assure you that should you be struck by it, you would change your point of view," I said with complaisance.

"Ah, but that's because in your world it has a definition that doesn't apply to the real world."

"The world is only as real as you make it."

"True, true, but in this case, it's hard to define just what real is. My real is different from your real."

"Is that so?" I said politely.

"Yes. Somehow, Hal and I were popped from our real world, into yours. I'm not going to speculate how that could happen, except to say that when you deal with things on a quantum level, as I was with my research project, things aren't necessarily what you expect them to be."

"So you hold to the statement that you were not placed on board the ship by persons unknown, but that you were . . ." I struggled to find a word for the action he was suggesting.

"Zapped. We were zapped here, yes. That's what I think happened. How the hell we're going to get back is another question, but right now, I think I'll just settle for coping with the fact that we're not where we should be. You have to admit that this offers a tremendous opportunity to learn about you."

"Me?" I asked, my eyebrows once again rising. I told them to stop being so dramatic.

His gaze dropped to my chest for a moment. "Your world. Although I don't mind saying I'd enjoy knowing you better, too."

There was a slight emphasis on the word "knowing" that didn't escape me.

The question was, why did my pulse race at the thought of it?

Log of the HIMA *Tesla*
Monday, February 15
Forenoon Watch: Six Bells and a Half

"You look skeptical," Jack said, watching my face. "You don't think this is the perfect opportunity for exploring a truly remarkable opportunity?"

I pulled my mind back from thoughts that were highly improper, most of which concerned him lying naked on my bed, and said slowly, "I am more concerned with what I'm going to do with you now that you're here, regardless of how you came to be on my ship. The Aerocorps takes a narrow view of unauthorized personnel on board their ships, and frankly, I have no idea what explanation I can give the emperor's officials when we land in Rome."

"Emperor?" he asked. "There's an emperor?"

"Emperor William VI, yes. The empire consists of the United Kingdom, and the duchy of Prussia."

He was silent for the count of five, then nodded. "OK. You guys have an empire, and Prussia is part of that. Gotcha. So the emperor will have guys waiting for you in Rome? Is Italy part of the empire?"

"No. The king of Italy is a cousin to the Duchess of

Prussia, who is marrying the emperor in about a week. Relations between Italy and England have been strained for several decades due to the Moghuls reclaiming Constantinople."

"Moghuls," he said, blinking.

"Italy liberated Constantinople from the Moghuls three decades past," I explained. "But seven years ago, the imperator—he's really an emperor, but for some reason they call him imperator—Imperator Aurangzeb III retook the city. The king of Italy was distraught at this, and asked for aid from Emperor William, but he was busy fighting the war with the Americas, and could not help."

"You guys had a war with us?" he asked, his eyes narrowing. "Another one?"

"There have been several," I said, shrugging. "An empire is neither won nor held without casualty. The war with the Americas ended four years ago. However, I should warn you that there are still hard feelings about citizens of the countries who fought against the empire. If it was possible to modify your accent, I would urge you to do so, lest you encounter trouble because of it."

He straightened up, an indignant look on his face. "I'm not ashamed that I'm American, and I'll be damned if I pretend otherwise."

"I'm not suggesting you pretend anything; I'm simply warning you that your accent may cause trouble. If you do not wish to modify it, fine. But don't be surprised if you find a hostile reaction to it."

"I'm used to getting flak for a lot of things," he said with a wry smile that made me want to kiss him.

I ground my teeth against the unruly thought, and poured myself more tea.

"So, back to your problem. You say that unauthorized

people on your ship are going to get you into trouble. Is there anything that says you can't tell this emperor's dudes that Hallie and I are part of your crew?"

"Unfortunately, yes. The Aerocorps offices have a list of personnel on all ships, and they check all arrivals closely. It's not just the emperor's officials who pose a danger—Akbar has been making raids upon Italy in retaliation for the battle over Constantinople, and he has been hitting Rome particularly hard."

"Akbar is . . . ?"

"Aurangzeb's son and heir, a ruthless warlord who lets nothing stand in his path," I said, clearing my throat when I noted how singsong that came out, almost as if I was reciting it. "Of late, he has attacked several Aerocorps ships in the name of the Moghuls."

"Well, of course he has," Jack said, nodding, his smile fading. "What else would a ruthless heir do? And you think these Moghuls may attack you?"

"Attack by one's enemies is always a possibility," I said, tracing the pattern of flowers on the china teapot.

"That's a very odd answer," he said, his eyes thoughtful on me.

"Is it? I hadn't intended it to be. There is one other threat," I said quickly. "The revolutionaries who oppose William have, in the past, focused their attentions on matters in England and Prussia. For the last two years, however, they have spread their attacks to include imperial forces in other countries; most notably they have made a number of strikes against ships bearing imperial cargoes. Their raids have targeted the Rome aerodrome three times in the last few months, which is why there are bound to be imperial officials present when we land."

He looked at me askance. "You have two emperors, a bloodthirsty prince, and revolutionaries? Have you ever thought of writing all of this down? It would make a hell of a story."

"I am trying to have a serious discussion, Mr. Fletcher. Under the circumstances, flippancy is neither desired or appreciated."

"Go with the flow, Jack, go with the flow," he murmured before taking a deep breath and saying, "All right. So there are three threats to you landing safely at Rome."

"Only two—the Moghuls and the Black Hand."

"The latter being the revolutionaries?"

"Yes." I tightened my lips. I didn't want to go into details about the Hand, but I had a suspicion that a man of his curiosity wouldn't leave it alone. "They are opposed to the empire."

"That's it? They're just opposed to it?" he asked after a few seconds of silence passed.

I watched my fingers trace out the rim of my cup. "They are opposed to Prussia being under the power of William. There is a lengthy history of Prussia attempting to gain its freedom from the empire, but with no success."

"And yet the duchess is going to marry this emperor of yours?" Jack asked, his gaze shrewd.

"He's not *my* emperor," I said stiffly.

He watched me for a moment, leaving me with the uncomfortable sensation that he could see my thoughts. "That was a little too much, you know."

I sighed, allowing my shoulders to slump for a few seconds. "I know. It was stupid of me."

"So you know the emperor?"

My fingers ran around the rim of the cup again as I wondered how much to tell him. I decided to be prudent rather than garrulous. "When I was very young, I was separated from my parents. William found me wandering around the garden of one of the imperial palaces. He took me to his father, the old emperor, who made me a ward of a friend of his, a man by the name of Robert Anstruther. Because we were of an age, and because William had few playfellows, I was allowed to visit him periodically. We had some wonderful times together, William a brave knight to my fairy princess as we fought dragons and trolls and all sorts of wicked beings." I smiled at the sweet memories. "We more or less grew up together, although once the old emperor died, my visits to play with William were at an end."

The other visits, the ones made later in my life, were not so sweet, although filled with a wonder of their own.

"Sounds like you had a good childhood," he said, still watching me closely.

"My childhood is not of importance at this moment," I said, firmly closing the door to any further introspection. "I have quite enough on my plate with your arrival."

"It seems that way, doesn't it?" he said thoughtfully. "Let me make sure I have all this straight—there's an emperor of England who also rules Prussia, who was at war with the US until a few years ago."

"The Americas—the United States, Canada, and Mexico."

"All three together?" he asked, looking surprised.

"Yes."

"What exactly comprises your empire? Britain and Prussia? No Australia or Canada?"

"No, just the British Isles and Prussia."

"Got it. And this friend of yours, William the emperor, is going to marry a duchess."

"Constanza, yes."

"Right, and she's the cousin of the Italian king?"

"That is correct. King Iago."

"How Shakespearean of him," Jack said absently, rubbing the bridge of his nose. "Iago is at war with some guy whose name I can't pronounce, dad of a bloodthirsty heir."

"Aurangzeb III. His son is Akbar, but it's not Iago who is at war with Aurangzeb—he doesn't have the force to battle the Moghuls on his own. It is our empire that is at war with the Moghuls. We have fought for almost a century, checking their attempt to take over Europe. Countries such as Italy lend aid as they can, but our people bear most of the responsibility. The empire's men and women have paid the highest price for freedom from the Moghuls."

"You guys were fighting two wars at once?" Jack looked astonished.

"Yes. It was a very grim time," I said, refusing to remember the long, dark years. "You must understand that William wants nothing more than a cessation of the war with the Moghuls, but Aurangzeb is reputed to be working on a siege machine that is impervious to any known weapons, one that will crush our forces and allow him to reign free over all of Europe. With that threat hanging over our respective heads, you will understand why William feels obliged to continue his attempt to end the Moghul empire."

He made a wry face. "I think there's probably more to it than that."

"What do you mean?" I asked quickly.

"Just that there are usually two sides to every story, and I like to hear them both before making an opinion." His eyes, so oddly mismatched, and yet able to stir me right down to my soul, watched me with mild curiosity.

I was silent for a few minutes, not wanting to dwell on the direction my thoughts were headed. "I will have to smuggle you off the *Tesla* somehow. I see no other answer to this situation."

"What will happen if your buddy's men find out?"

I examined my fingertips. "The emperor has been beleaguered of late by spies sent by the Black Hand. He has decreed that anyone found guilty of a charge of espionage be executed with all due haste."

"Good God," Jack exclaimed. "You don't mean to say he'd kill you if they found out Hallie and I were on board?"

"I have no doubt I would be charged as a spy," I answered, rubbing a slight spot on one of my fingernails.

"But the emperor is a friend of yours. A ... er ... former boyfriend?"

He was fishing for that bit of information, but I let it go. Enough people knew that particular truth to keep me from spending an undue amount of energy to hide it. "The laws are quite clear. My relationship with William was long in the past, and would have no bearing on any action taken in the present. If I was found guilty of being a spy, I would be executed."

"I'm sorry," he said after a minute of silence.

I glanced up to find his expression earnest.

"I'm sorry that I've put you in such a bind. You seem like a nice woman, Octavia. I don't regret at all having the opportunity to meet you, but I regret that our being here has messed things up for you."

Several responses ran through my mind at that moment: I could tell him that it was all right (but it wasn't); I could say that he wasn't to worry or be concerned (but he should do both); I could simply say that we would cope (how?), but what came out of my mouth was something completely different. "I refuse to be attracted to you," I said, leaning forward toward him. "You can be just as charming as you like, but it will mean nothing to me. Nothing."

His eyes widened with mirth as I realized what I had said. I fought the simultaneous urge to cover my mouth in horror and run away in embarrassment.

"I find myself in the position of apologizing to you a second time," I said stiffly, wishing for a moment that I was a thousand miles away. "I assure you that I do not normally speak so unguardedly or rudely, even to strangers."

"I'm glad you did. It takes a lot of strain off of me. You have no idea how daunting it is to try to determine if a woman is interested in you without stepping into sexual harassment territory. I was wondering how I was going to do it with you all buttoned up and repressed."

"I am not repressed," I said, standing. "Not that I intend to discuss the subject with you any further. I apologize for my unwarranted comments, but let that be the end of it. If you will excuse me, I must consult with Mr. Mowen about possible ways we might hide your sister and you from the authorities when we land."

He followed me as I went to the door. I gave him a stern look that he met with an insouciant grin. "You're not going to just let me wander around alone, are you? Not a notorious airship pirate like me? I could do any number of dangerous things if I wasn't under your eye."

"You are not in the least bit subtle," I said, my hand on the doorknob.

"I always thought subtle was boring," he said, moving closer. "I may get slapped for this, but what the hell. You only live once, right?"

Before I could ask him what he was talking about, he put his hands on my hips and pulled me into a loose embrace.

"What do you think you're doing?" I asked, then damned myself for such an inane question. It was patently obvious what he was doing.

"I'm going to kiss you, Octavia Emmaline Pye."

"You may refer to me as Captain Pye, and I decline your offer," I said, a bit breathless, to be true. I wasn't normally aware of my corset, it being as much a part of me as my shoes were, but just being so close to Jack seemed to not only strip the air from my lungs but leave me with the sensation that my corset was laced several times too tight.

"Your mind says no, but your body says yes," he said, gently, persistently tugging me closer to him. I swayed into him, my fingers curling into fists as I fought the damnable attraction.

"My body is confused. Pay it no mind," I said, my gaze focused on his mouth, a few inches from mine. Somehow, my hands had moved from where they were trying to shove him away, to sliding around his ribs, outrageously pulling him closer to me.

"Your mouth says yes, too," he said, his lips brushing mine as he spoke.

I stared deep into those mismatched eyes, searching for a sign he was trying to deceive me, but there was nothing there but honest desire.

"My mouth, as you have witnessed twice, frequently does things without my explicit permission." My breath caught in my throat as my lips brushed his again, the sensation sending a kernel of heat to glow in my belly, spreading outward in a rush of warmth. "Mr. Fletcher, I am captain of this ship. I cannot indulge in untoward behav—"

His mouth closing over mine cut off the rest of my declaration. I stood passive for a second, just long enough for my desire to completely override my common sense. My fingers slid up his back as he grasped my hips, pulling me tighter against him, his lips caressing mine in a kiss that I felt down to my toenails.

It's been too long since I've had a lover, I thought to myself, but I knew that wasn't the cause of my reaction to this strange man. There was something about him, some sense that he was lost as I had once been lost, that called to me, but even that wasn't all of it. It was the way his eyes regarded me, with humor and intelligence and frank approval, that warmed me in a way I hadn't experienced in a very long time. Not since my days with Alan had any man approved of me such as I was, but our lives had just been too disparate for a relationship to be anything but fleeting.

Jack would not abandon me, no matter how great the cause. That thought flitted through my mind, startling me out of the kiss that was threatening to consume me.

"Damn," he said, his eyes crossing slightly as he tried to peer down at me. I pulled back, touching my fingers briefly to lips that felt swollen and hot. "That was one hell of a kiss, lady."

"Yes," I said, regaining my composure. "It was, but that does not change the situation, Mr. Fletcher."

"Doesn't it?" he asked with another one of his engaging grins. "I think it makes everything a lot more interesting."

I looked at him for a minute, weighing my need to get away from the temptation he posed against the growing desire to be in his presence. I knew I should lock him into the cabin set aside for him, but that thought didn't sit well with me. "Very well, you may accompany me, but what happened here will not be repeated. I am a woman, Mr. Fletcher, a normal woman who is not immune to desire, but I will not allow that to dictate my behavior or actions."

"Dignity at all costs?" he asked, one sandy eyebrow rising.

"Not entirely, no," I answered as I turned on my heel and left the mess.

Log of the HIMA *Tesla*
Monday, February 15
Forenoon Watch: Near Seven Bells

Jack followed behind me as I made my way down the gangway to the spiral stairs that led upward to the engineering deck. Air currents swirled gently past us, cold air from outside warmed only slightly by the tremendous heat generated by the boilers.

"This is amazing. I can't believe I'm in a real airship," he said, his voice filled with awe as our footsteps sounded sharply on the metal staircase. "How big is it? It seems to be several stories tall."

"The *Tesla* is seven hundred and fifty feet long, one hundred feet high, and about eighty feet wide. The gondola, which we will leave to access the engineering deck located aft, is ninety-eight feet long. The bulk of that is made up of the cargo holds, two fore and two aft of the crew's living quarters. There are seven envelopes that keep the airship aloft, run by three boilers, two aft, and one forward. Be careful here—the gangways are only wide enough for one person to pass."

We climbed a second, smaller spiral staircase to the

engineering platform that sat at the rear of the airship. I pointed out girders that ran parallel to us, but high overhead. "Those provide access to the envelopes, should they become damaged and need repair."

"Amazing," he said, his head tipped all the way back to take in the white silk envelopes that rippled above us. I entered the first room, where I had seen Mr. Mowen just a few hours before, but it was empty. "All this with steam power. Ah, the boilers, I assume?"

"Yes." I eyed the gauges as I passed by the machinery, the loud hiss and thumping of the boilers as they provided energy to the ship a familiar sound. "Mr. Mowen must be in the back. This way. Watch your step."

"You said there was a crew of eight? Wouldn't a ship this big need a lot more people to run it?"

"The *Tesla* is a simple cargo transport, Mr. Fletcher."

"Jack."

"We are not a warship that needs a significant crew to handle the weapons. Barring any disaster, my crew is able to take care of any challenge we should face on our run between Southampton and Rome."

"And pirates?" he asked.

I cast a glance over my shoulder at him.

"You were the one who got so bent out of shape over the mention of them," he said in response to my piercing look.

"The *Tesla* is small and fast, and can outrun all but the fastest of pirate airships, and none of those would be foolish enough to tackle us," I answered, moving around the second boiler to access the small room behind it. "I assure you that we are well able to avoid bringing trouble down onto ourselves. Ah, there you are, Mr. Mowen. This is Mr. Fletcher. You have no doubt heard about his presence, and that of his sister, on board the ship."

"Hi," Jack said, holding out his hand.

Mr. Mowen rose slowly from where he had been sitting at a small desk covered in technical drawings. "Welcome," he said, throwing a curious glance my way.

"I'm an engineer, as well," Jack said, looking around the tiny room. "Although steam engines are a bit out of my depths. I work on . . . er . . . if I was to say 'computer' to you both, what would you think?"

The expression on Mr. Mowen's face was interesting to behold. "Eh . . . Captain?" he said, politely gesturing for me to go first.

"It's not a word I have heard before," I said, frowning just a little. "But I would assume that a computor refers to someone who computes things. A mathematician?"

"A man who operates a steam abacus?" Mr. Mowen offered. "Although I've heard them called calculators, not computers. There was one back in the academy when I was a young lad. Great huge machine it was, and the calculator could add up the longest row of numbers just as fast as you can imagine."

"They are indeed miraculous machines," I agreed, turning my attention back to Jack. "Is that part of your profession, Mr. Fletcher? You manipulate a steam abacus?"

"Not quite," he said, his lips twitching. "Although I work on something similar. Just . . . different."

"Similar but different," Mr. Mowen repeated, pursing his lips.

"OK, a lot different. You see, I came here from another—"

"Perhaps that tale would best be left for another time," I interrupted, sending him a meaningful look. "Mr. Mowen, as you know, the emperor takes a dim view of undocumented passengers on international ships, a sentiment the Corps echoes. We have ascertained that Mr.

Fletcher and his sister were placed on the ship while they were unconscious. They are, in effect, here against their wills, and I have Mr. Fletcher's word that they mean no harm either to the ship, the cargo, the crew, or indeed any member of the empire."

It wasn't strictly true that Jack had given me his word on that, which is why I waited for him to confirm my statement.

"Absolutely." He smiled, his laugh lines crinkling in that wholly delightful manner they had. "Actually, I'm a Quaker, so I don't hold with using violence to settle anything."

"You are?" I asked, startled by his statement. "But Quakers are profoundly religious people, and you . . ."

"Swear like a sailor? Enjoy women?" His eyes practically twinkled with amusement. I ground my teeth for a few seconds. "Am highly irreverent?"

"That and much more," I said finally, well aware we had an audience. "It seems greatly at odds with such a severe religion."

"Oh, we're not severe at all. We're actually quite reasonable. Quakers believe in the goodness in all people, and don't fuss with too many ceremonies or dogma. They simply try to live good lives and treat others well. I won't say that my father hasn't lectured me about profanity a few times, but I believe it's a person's intent that matters, not the words they use."

"Yes," I said, exchanging a glance with Mr. Mowen. "We are familiar with that particular view."

Jack laughed. "Your salty Mr. Piper? I'm going to have to have a long talk with him. I bet I could pick up a few choice phrases from him."

"A frightening thought if ever I heard one." I turned back to the engineer. "Mr. Mowen, what I am going to ask you is extremely unusual, and would be frowned on by the Corps. I do not want you thinking I condone any action that would be against Corps policy, but this circumstance is of a special nature, and I am willing, this once, to go against what might be viewed as the better interests of the Corps."

"You want somewhere to hide Mr. Fletcher and his sister," Mr. Mowen said calmly.

"Yes." I searched his face. "You don't seem at all taken aback by that request."

One side of his mouth quirked up. "Your reputation is sterling, Captain. If you have a reason for breaking the Corps rules by trying to smuggle a couple of unauthorized persons across international borders, then I am willing to accept that you have due cause to do so."

"Thank you, Mr. Mowen," I said, greatly relieved that I wouldn't have to try to persuade him against his will. "I very much appreciate such support. There is the question of the crew, however—"

"They won't give you any trouble, should you explain the situation to them," he said. "They're a good crew, and will do as you ask."

"I will certainly take the first opportunity to make everything clear to them," I said, feeling a little tension go out of my shoulders.

And so I did. That night when everyone had gathered in the mess for dinner, I stood at the head of the table and looked down the length of it at the people gathered. Jack and his sister were there, on my right and left, respectively. I averted my eyes from the desirous person of Jack. I'd spent the better part of the day avoiding any further time alone with him, lest the incident in the mess be repeated, asking Mr. Mowen to keep an eye on him as the pair selected a suitable hiding spot.

That hadn't stopped Mr. Mowen from taking me aside for a few minutes while Jack was checking on his sister. "You believe his story, then?" Mowen asked as soon as Jack was out of earshot. "That he was put in the hold without his knowledge?"

"I do."

Mr. Mowen's gaze assessed me. "Seems to me there must be more to his story than what you're telling."

I allowed myself a little smile. "Of course. But the rest of the facts aren't pertinent to the situation of our landing in Rome, nor are they particularly enlightening. Suffice it to say that both Mr. Fletcher and Miss Norris were put on the ship without their agreement or approval, and since I wish to avoid any harsh repercussions to either them or this ship and its crew, I have opted for this plan of action."

"As you wish, Captain," he said, nodding before going back to his task at hand.

Mr. Ho moved around the table, bringing laden plates in from the galley, placing them before everyone— everyone but Jack.

I glanced to the end of the table where Mr. Francisco had emerged from the galley, his arms crossed. "You appear to have miscounted, Mr. Francisco."

"I did not," the Spaniard said, his eyes spitting black looks at Jack. "I will not to him give the food most extraordinary. He is the dirt beneath your feet. He is not worthy of sitting there, close enough to your divine body that he could reach out and touch your most glorious shining hair, the hair of the purest sunset, hair as bright as the fire that burns in my loins."

Jack gave him a long look. "I may have to rethink my attitude toward violence."

"That won't be necessary," I said, picking up my plate

and placing it before Jack. "Mr. Francisco, I find myself without dinner. Would you please prepare a plate for me?"

Dooley sniggered as the volatile cook swore, tossed up his hands in a dramatic gesture, then stomped off to the galley, returning shortly with a plate for me. He managed to whack Jack on the back of his head while presenting me with the dinner, but after a few harsh looks, he returned to his seat.

"Before we enjoy this delicious meal that Mr. Francisco has made for us, I would like to introduce you all to our two unexpected passengers. Mr. Fletcher and his sister, Miss Norris, will be traveling with us to Rome. Without going into lengthy details, I will simply say that they did not anticipate being with us for this journey, and in order to protect them from bureaucratic difficulties, we will not be listing them on the ship's manifest. I realize that such a procedure is highly unusual, but I assure you that it is quite necessary. I trust that no one here will have an objection to my decision?"

The seven crew members exchanged glances, but all of them shook their heads or murmured agreements with my plans.

"So they're not stowaways, then?" Dooley asked from his spot at the end of the table.

"Not in so many words, no. Please, begin," I said, gesturing toward the dinner awaiting us. I sat down and picked up my fork. "They were, for lack of a better description, placed on the ship without their consent."

Hallie Norris snorted. I slid a worried glance her way. She'd been very subdued since her brother had brought her in for the evening meal, her eyes somewhat dulled, as if she'd been beaten into submission. A quick word with Mr. Ho relieved my mind as to Hallie's mental health.

"It's all right, Captain," Mr. Ho had said shortly before the evening meal. "Miss Norris became agitated again, and I felt it appropriate to give her a tiny drop of laudanum. She'll be a bit subdued for a few more hours, but will soon be herself again."

Now Hallie stared glumly at her plate, making no move to eat.

"Eat, Hal," Jack said, shoving a piece of bread her way. "This is pretty good, even if I don't normally eat mammals. What is it?"

"Mammals!" Mr. Francisco leaped to his feet at the opposite end of the table. "You dare call my beauteous pie of the shepherd *mammals*?"

"Sit down, Mr. Francisco. A mammal is a warm-blooded animal, such as the cow that provided the beef you used to make the shepherd's pie," I said wearily.

"Hrmph." He sat down with muttered Spanish invectives.

Dooley sniggered again.

"Mr. Francisco is quite a talented cook," I said, both to smooth his ruffled feathers and to try to get Hallie talking. "Although I should warn you that we prefer simple fare on Aerocorps ships. I hope you do not mind that."

"Eh? Oh. No. I'm not one for haute cuisine," she replied, finally picking up her fork and poking it into the mound of food on her plate. She gingerly tasted a morsel. A look of surprise flickered in her eyes. "This is really good."

Mr. Francisco eyed her critically, saying, "The lady, she does not have the hair of the blazing set of the sun, but she is smart, she is much smart. She may have the flan I have so carefully made for the sweet."

"Whereas I am to go flanless?" Jack said, winking at me. "Perhaps the captain will take pity on me and share her sweet?"

I was a bit aghast at his flirtatious comment, but luckily, other than Mr. Mowen (who choked on his ale), no one seemed to understand the double entendre.

"You may have mine if there is not enough," Mr. Ho said generously. "I don't have much of a sweet tooth."

I gave Jack a stern look that was completely wasted upon such a rogue, and settled back to let the conversation move along general lines, memorable meals claiming the discussion for some time. Although I was extremely aware of Jack sitting next to me, so close I could almost feel the heat of his body, I kept my mind firmly focused elsewhere.

I did not notice the fine blond hairs that grew along his forearms, which were visible since he'd rolled back his sleeves.

I did not dwell on that little lock of hair that kept falling over his forehead, driving me almost to distraction with the need to push it back.

I refused to notice it when his knee brushed mine as he leaned forward to answer one of Mr. Mowen's questions about where in California he was from.

I didn't care one hoot about the fact that his eyes, so different in color, and yet so intriguing, had an uncanny attraction for me.

"Captain?"

"Hmm?" With a start, I realized that I was being addressed. I cleared my throat and looked attentive. "Yes, Mr. Ho?"

"I asked if there was anything in particular you wished us to do with respect to the ground crew and emperor's officials in Rome."

"No. When we are close to arrival at the aerodrome, we will land for a few minutes in a remote location to allow Mr. Fletcher and his sister to disembark." I told that lie without batting so much as an eyelash. "They won't be on the ship when we land in Rome; thus, there will be no need for you to conceal anything other than the fact that they were on board the ship for a few days."

She nodded and continued passing around cups of after-dinner coffee. Mr. Llama dropped his spoon under the table, and leaned down to pick it up.

"I know it goes against everyone's standards to conceal even that, but I think that it's for the best if—"

The sound of the door behind me gently closing had me whirling around in the chair.

"What's wrong?" Jack asked, looking up from the flan that Francisco reluctantly produced for him.

"The door . . . where's Mr. Llama?" I asked, looking suspiciously around the table. His place was empty. "Ratsbane! He's done it again. Did any of you see him leave?"

The crew all shared an unreadable look, six heads shaking in unison.

"Do you have a rule or something about people not being able to leave the table without your permission?" Jack asked as I pushed back my chair, hoisted up the edge of the tablecloth, and got on my knees to peer under the table.

"No, of course not. It's just that the blighter . . . er . . . gentleman has the habit of disappearing without anyone seeing."

"It wouldn't be a disappearance if you were watching, now, would it?" Jack said with infuriating reason.

I glared over the top of the table at him. "You don't understand—the man is positively uncanny. One moment he's here, the next he's gone. And no one ever sees him leave!"

Jack glanced over at Mr. Mowen. "Have you seen him leave a room?"

Mowen shook his head, watching me curiously as I dusted off my knees and retook my seat. "No, but then, I don't watch for folks to leave rooms."

"There you go, then," Jack said, just as if that explained everything.

"That doesn't mean anything," I argued. "The fact remains that no one has seen Mr. Llama actually in the process of leaving a room."

"I haven't seen Dooley leave the room, and yet he's gone," Mr. Christian said from farther down the table, waving his sticky spoon toward Dooley's chair.

"That's different. He probably went to use the convenience," I said, aware I was sounding grumpy. "Dooley can't sit still for more than ten minutes. And we are not discussing him—we're discussing the mystery that is Mr. Llama."

Jack pursed his lips slightly. "Does anyone else feel that this Llama person is mysterious?"

The crew, blight them all, shook their heads.

"That is misleading!" I told them before focusing my attention on Mr. Francisco. "Didn't you tell Dooley that Mr. Llama doesn't sleep in his bed at night?"

"*Sí*, but I wouldn't be in my bed if there was another for me to lie in," he said with a lecherous waggle of his eyebrows.

"Oh. You mean he spends the night—" I stopped, not wanting to put it into words.

Mr. Francisco had no such sense of propriety. "He has the mistress of love he visits."

They all looked at me.

"You can't possibly think that I would—I'm the captain!" I said, outraged.

"Aye, but ye're a right looker when ye want to be," Mr. Piper said, subjecting me to a thorough once-over. "Ye've a nice plump arse, and a pair o' ripe titties that fair make a man's cods tighten."

"That's my bustle, and you will please refrain from commenting on my chest," I said, grabbing the front edges of my jacket and jerking them closed over my blouse.

Jack grinned at me.

"You aren't helping matters," I told him.

"I'm sorry, but he's absolutely right. You do have a nice ass. And your breasts—"

"Don't say it," I said through clenched teeth.

"Aye, it could be your bustle," Mr. Piper said meditatively as he casually picked his teeth, making wet sucking noises as he did so. "But I'm of a mind that there's a fair bit o' paddin' beneath the bustle, else it wouldn't be so round."

I sent the glare down to him, then spread it amongst the other crew members as they continued to eye me speculatively. "We have left the subject of Mr. Llama and his nighttime perambulations. I assure you all that he is not visiting me. So where is he going?"

Mr. Ho calmly sipped her coffee, seemingly unaware of everyone's sudden scrutiny of her person.

I cleared my throat. Crew fraternization wasn't encouraged, but neither was it prohibited. "Oh. I . . . indeed. Well, then."

"Are there any other mysteries you'd like me to clear up for you?" Jack offered as I rose to my feet. "How the ship stays aloft? Why the sky is blue? What the meaning of life is?"

"No, thank you," I said, thinning my lips at him as he grinned at me, his eyes glittering with enjoyment.

Damnation, I would not fall for him. He was no better than any of the other rogues in my life, and if I hadn't learned by now just how bad for me such a man was, I might as well pack up my things and retire to a convent.

Sssssssteam Heat

"So really, the boiler is just a big water tank that has some tubes running through it that contain air heated from a constantly burning fire."

"That's an oversimplification of it, but yes, basically, that's correct," Matt Mowen said as we squatted next to an emergency release valve on the number three boiler.

"And the boilers produce steam that goes from here—" I stood up and visually followed the long metal pipe as it snaked up the metal girder to disappear into a gigantic pillowy shape above us that I had been informed was technically called an envelope—"and fills the envelope, which keeps the *Tesla* floating."

"Yes. Boilers one and two feed the fore and middle envelopes. Number three, here, feeds the aft envelopes, and the propellers. She's twice the size of one and two, as you can see." He gestured toward the second pipe that led down into the floor, assumably running to the back of the airship where a giant propeller gave the ship its forward thrust.

"Gotcha. And you use coal for the boilers?"

"Coal?" He scratched his head, looking puzzled. "Why would we use that?"

"I thought that's what the folks in Victorian times used."

He just stared at me.

"Sorry, that's probably not going to make any sense to you since you didn't have a Victorian age. Or did you?"

Matt gave me an odd look. "Was there something in particular you wanted with me, Mr. Fletcher?"

"Jack."

"Jack, then. You said you were an engineer yourself, so I'm confused why you would be wanting an explanation of how a simple steam engine works."

"I'm a nanoelectrical engineer. That's sort of a specialized engineer, and I didn't learn anything about steam power in college. If you don't use coal for the boilers, what do you use?"

"Aether." He frowned at a valve on the back side of the boiler.

"Er . . . that would be . . . ?"

"Aether is aether," he said, tapping the glass front of the valve. The needle inside dropped a couple of points. He nodded at it and went back to the small, rickety desk that was bolted to the floor.

"It's the same stuff used in your guns, isn't it? Some form of heated plasma or something along those lines?"

He shook his head as he picked up a small toolbox and started for the door. "I don't know what this plasma is. Aether is what's all around us."

I glanced around as I followed him, not sure what he meant. "Air? Like oxygen and carbon dioxide and those sorts of elements?"

"Aye, it's an element, but not of oxygen or those gases. The aether is what holds them up."

"OK, that's getting a little beyond me." I climbed after him as he went up a narrow metal ladder to the landing above. "It supports air? How does it do that?"

One of Matt's shoulders jerked in a shrug. "I'm no scientist. I'm just a simple engineer."

"I have a feeling that's an understatement," I said softly.

He gave a short bark of laughter. "Aye, well, my da always told me the modest man succeeds. Aether is the matter that holds the world together, lad. It binds everything. The extractors in the boilers remove it from the air, and heat it to make steam. Does that make more sense to you?"

"Actually, it does. It sounds to me like you're describing gluons."

He stopped and shot me a curious look. "A what, now?"

"Gluons. It's a way to describe the interaction of quarks." His face was blank with incomprehension. "Let's see. . . . Gluons are a way to describe how protons and neutrons are bound together."

"Binding," he said, nodding and proceeding down the narrow catwalk. "That's aether."

"Right, so your steam-powered society is using nuclear physics. I can accept that."

"Good. If there are no more questions, I'd best be getting back to work, lest the captain has my ears for talking when I should be working on the propeller slide valve. The captain thinks the valve rod isn't moving as smoothly as it should."

"Sorry, didn't mean to keep you," I said, trailing after him despite his obvious attempt to get rid of me. I had too many questions to be shooed away like that. "And I do have another question."

He stopped again and faced me with a badly concealed sigh. "You want to know how a Disruptor works? How the autonavigator functions? How aether was discovered?"

I grinned. "Actually, all of those, but for right now, I have a more burning issue uppermost in my mind. Octavia."

"The captain?" He looked me over carefully. "You fancy her?"

"Hell, yes. And I think she likes me, too," I said without a shred of modesty.

"Does she?" He pursed his lips for a moment, then continued down the catwalk.

"Well . . . yeah. I think. No, I'm sure. She's just . . ." I waved a hand to indicate the mystery that was Octavia's moods. "She seems to be avoiding me right now, but I think that's just because she didn't like the way that kiss turned out."

"Oh?" He stopped again, giving me a narrow-eyed look. "I won't have you hurting the captain. You seem likable enough, and I'm not holding with Mr. Christian's belief that you're really a thuggee, but I don't hold with men hurting those weaker than themselves. Not that the captain is weak, but you're a bright lad. You understand what I mean."

"I understand perfectly, but that's not what I meant. I didn't hurt Octavia—I think I ruffled her feathers because she liked the kiss too much."

"Ah." He almost smiled. "Women are like that sometimes." He proceeded to yet another ladder, this one leading downward.

"That's what I wanted to talk to you about." I waited until he was a safe distance below me before following him down the metal ladder. "Every time I try to talk to Octavia, she finds something she has to do, and gets away before I can do more than say hi. I want to know about her, Matt. She's infinitely interesting. I like the way she thinks—when she's around me long enough to do so, that is. I thought you could tell me something about her."

"You want to talk to her?"

It wasn't what he said—it was the way he said it, as if he was shocked I wanted to do anything that didn't involve her body pressed up against mine.

"Yes, I do." I gave him a long look. "I may not be able to keep thoughts about her being naked out of my head, Matt, but I'm not just looking for a quick lay. I want to get to know her. Maybe if I understand her better, I will be able to combat this need she feels to keep me at arm's length."

"I hardly know the captain. I met her about a week before you came on board."

"Right, but I've watched you—you notice things. You must have made some judgment about her."

He waited until I jumped down the last few rungs to land a few feet from a small wooden door. "She's lonely."

"She is?" That surprised me. "She doesn't act lonely."

"Aye, well, that's an insight into her all by itself. If your intentions towards her are honorable, and not of the sort of the other men she's filled her life with, then you might succeed. She's alone in the world now that Robert Anstruther is dead, and a smart man, one who had her best wishes at heart, might be able to fill the void he left in her heart."

"Robert Anstruther?" I tried to remember the names of the lovers that Octavia had mentioned. He hadn't been one of them.

"Her foster father, not her man friend," Matt said.

"Oh, that's right. She did mention him."

"You want to get her talking, you ask her about him. Now be off with you. There's only room for one on the propeller platform, and I don't want to be explaining to the captain why you fell overboard."

"Thanks, Matt," I said, clapping him on the shoulder. He gave me a little nod and smile, then went through the door to an outer platform, the wind whipping through it with a punch that sent me reeling backward a few steps.

"Her dad, huh?" I mused as I retraced my steps down to the main cabin area, which I'd heard Octavia refer to as the gondola. "Speak of the devil," I said as I caught sight of a red jacket and navy skirt whisk around the corner of a doorway. I followed, closing the door softly behind me. "Hello, sweetheart. All alone in here, are you?"

"Jack!" She jumped as she turned. "Er . . . that is, Mr. Fletcher, you startled me." Her gaze narrowed on me. "You wouldn't be taking lessons from Mr. Llama on how to creep up on me, would you?"

"You were right the first time—it's Jack. And I didn't mean to scare you. I just thought I'd take the opportunity of finding you alone to have a little talk with you."

She moved a bit to the side, her gaze slipping to the left. "I'm afraid that I have to set the autonavigator. Its mechanics seem to be beyond Mr. Christian's ability."

I looked at the large lump of machinery behind her. It sat on a small wooden desk, a mass of clockwork, whirring gears, and three rows of small dials. "You go right ahead. We can talk while you do that."

She didn't like that. I could tell by the way she kept glancing over my shoulder at the door. "Well . . . I suppose. What did you wish to speak about?"

I laughed. "You don't have to sound so resigned, Octavia. I'm not going to bite you. Well, I might, if you asked nicely."

She blushed. It thrilled me almost as much as the speculative light that flared in her eyes for a few seconds before reserve claimed her again. "I am not opposed to speaking with you, Mr. Fletcher. It's just that I have many tasks awaiting my attention."

"Go ahead and take care of your autonavigator. We can talk while you do that."

A little flicker of irritation was visible in those lovely velvety brown eyes. "Talk about what?"

"Whatever you like. Something of interest to us both."

Her gaze shot to my mouth, instantly making me hard. It was just that quick. One moment I was relaxed, leaning against the door, admiring her boobs when she wasn't looking at me, and the next, I was toting wood. I became even harder when the tip of her little pink tongue emerged to lick her lips, her teeth biting on her lower lip for a second making my blood boil. Damn. I wanted to kiss her again. And again after that. And probably again for several more decades.

"What's that?" she asked.

"Huh?" Maybe if I kissed her for a little bit, there would still be time to talk afterward. I wanted so badly to taste her mouth again, taste that sweetness that seemed to be a part of her, I damn near died denying myself.

"Pardon?"

I shook away the memory of her mouth so softly enticing beneath mine and made an effort to focus on the words that emerged from between those delectable, delicious lips. "Sorry, you asked me what? Oh, what would interest us both? I thought you could tell me a little bit about your father."

Her gaze left my lips, the pupils flaring. "My father? Robert Anstruther?"

"Yes. Matt said you were missing him. I take it he's dead?"

"He's gone, yes." She bowed her head. "And I do miss both him and his wife, Jane. As I mentioned, they were my foster parents, not my true parents, but I could not love them more if they had been."

"Does it upset you to talk about them?" I asked, my erection dying in the face of her grief. I wanted to comfort her, to take her in my arms and protect her from the sadness in the world, but I had a suspicion if I touched her, my dick would take control again.

She was silent a moment, then straightened her shoulders and gave me a level, if dewy-eyed, look. "No. Did you wish to know something in particular about Robert Anstruther?"

"Well, let's start with why you call him Robert Anstruther."

Twin lines formed between her brows. "That's his name."

"I understand that, but why do you refer to him by his full name?"

"It's his name," she repeated, clearly puzzled.

"OK. Let's try this—how old were you when they adopted you?"

"I was six years old."

"That's pretty young for such a big change. Matt said he was an airship captain—is that why you're one, too?"

She set down a small wrench she had been using to tighten one of the gears on what must be the autonavigator. "For the most part, yes, but I wasn't pushed into it, if that's what you're thinking. Robert and Jane told me I could choose whatever profession I desired, and they would support me." Her gaze slipped into one that looked back through time, a little smile playing with the corners of her lips.

I mentally willed down the erection that started forming the minute I thought about her mouth.

"I remember the first time I went on board an airship. It was just a domestic flight, from London to Edinburgh, where we were going for a summer holiday. I stood out on the observation deck for hours, according to Jane, and had to be forcibly brought inside. I loved the way the wind whipped around me, loved the gentle chug-chug of the propellers, even loved the whoosh of the steam as it burped out of the release valves. It was glorious, invigorating, and exciting all at once. I felt like a bird perched at the front of the gondola, and vividly remember standing with my arms stretched out, feeling as if I could take flight myself. I knew at that moment that what I wanted most of all was to fly my own ship."

"It sounds wonderful. You're a lucky woman to have achieved your dream."

Her gaze focused on me again, another faint blush pinkening her cheeks. "I am lucky. And I'm also sorry for going on at such length—I am prone to being carried away with reminiscing."

"Don't apologize. I enjoyed it. Octavia . . ."

"Yes?"

I struggled with myself for a moment, knowing I should just walk out of the room, but the sight of her there, flushed and pink and so enticing, threw all common sense out. "I want to kiss you."

Her eyes widened, her gaze once again dropping to my mouth. "I see."

"Would you be offended, appalled, or otherwise un-willing for me to do that?"

"I have work to attend to," she said, still watching my mouth with a fascination that I wholly shared.

"It won't take long," I said, and realized that I was close to babbling or pleading with her, so desperate was I to taste her again. "You can get right back to whatever it is you're doing."

"Well . . ."

That was all I needed. I slid my arms around her waist, gently pulling her toward me. "Just a quick kiss. Just the slightest brushing of mouths, all right?"

"Very well, but it must be fast. I don't have time for dalliances right now. And your hands must remain above my waist at all times," she said as I slid my hands under her bustle to feel her ass.

"If you insist," I said, cupping her breasts, instead.

"Mr. Fletcher!" she said, all breathy outrage and in-terest.

"Your boobs are above your waist."

We both looked down to where my hands were filled with cloth- and lace-covered mounds of pure ecstasy.

"No other man has ever just held them like that," she said, her breasts pressing a little more into my hands. "You are quite brazen and I should insist you stop this instant."

"Has anyone ever done this?" I asked, rubbing my thumbs across the very peak of them.

She froze, not breathing. "No. That is also quite wrong."

"How about this?" I couldn't help myself. God alone knew I tried, but I couldn't stop from dipping my head down, and licking the cleft between her boobs. She smelled like violets, and sweet, warm woman. My dick hurt so bad, it made my head spin. That or the taste and feel of her soft, heaving breasts.

She clutched my hair, writhing against me. "That would be . . . oh, mercy, could you . . . yes, right there . . . that would be beyond acceptable. You must stop immediately. Just as soon as you do that tongue thing again."

I swirled my tongue down the length of the cleft, wondering if there was any way in heaven or hell I could talk her into my bed that night. "If it's unacceptable, then I will stop."

"Good," she said, panting a little, her eyes misty with desire. I was smugly pleased that she was so receptive to the attraction that we shared.

"Yes, you are. And now, the kiss you promised me."

Her eyes widened as she took a step back, one restraining hand on my chest. "I think perhaps that will suffice. I do have things to attend to."

I frowned as she pulled up the bit of lacy top I'd dislodged when I face-dived into her cleavage. "Oh no. You promised me a kiss, and I intend to hold you to that."

Before she could say anything more, I pulled her into an embrace that allowed her to feel every inch of me, including the parts that were presently trying to burst out of my pants, and nibbled her lower lip until she parted her mouth with a sigh. "Very well, but just a quick—"

I groaned with the taste and feel of her mouth, the heat of it firing desire that already burned deep in my guts. She was like a bonfire of passion, a sweet, endlessly sweet pool of desire, and I dipped into it again and again, savoring every blessed moment. I pulled her hips closer to me, and she rewarded me with a wiggle that almost had me coming on the spot. But when she moaned into my mouth, her fingers digging into my butt, trying to pull me closer as her tongue danced around mine, I knew that something profound was happening. This wasn't just a sexual itch that badly needed scratching. This was something more, and I didn't know if there was any way I could stop it from happening.

"Captain, I—crikey! Unhand her, you murderous thuggee!"

I was rudely jerked backward out of Octavia's embrace, my body crying a lament over that fact. "You have the worst timing of anyone I've ever known, and that includes my sister," I told Al the first officer as he glowered at me. His face was almost as red as his hair.

"It's all right, Mr. Christian," Octavia said, clearing her throat a couple of times. She was almost as red as he was, and wouldn't meet my eyes. "You have nothing for which to chastise Mr. Fletcher."

"I don't?" He looked from her to me, enlightenment dawning. I didn't think it was possible, but he flushed even harder than she did. "Oh. I . . . oh. I'll just . . . yes."

He slipped out without stammering anything more. Octavia sighed. "He thinks we're lovers."

I gave her my most insouciant grin. "Nothing wrong with that idea."

"On the contrary, I can think of a number of things. And no, I will not detail them now," she added quickly, forestalling the request I was about to make. She returned to the table bearing the machinery, and picked up her wrench. "If you will excuse me, Mr. Fletcher, I have work to do."

"This isn't over, you know," I told her, opening the door.

She sighed again. "I know."

Log of the HIMA *Tesla*
Wednesday, February 17
Afternoon Watch: Five Bells

I spent the next two days avoiding the man whose very presence upset everything in my life, including my peace of mind.

Twice Jack caught me hurrying past him in the gangway, intent on some business or other. The first time he let me go with nothing but a laugh, but the second was much more disconcerting.

"You're not still avoiding me, are you?" he asked two days after he had kissed me in the navigation room.

"What an absurd question. As if I would avoid anyone," I said, adroitly sidestepping the question.

"I'm sorry if you think it's absurd, but I don't play games with people," he said, the amusement in his eyes fading. "At least not those sort. I believe in calling a spade a spade, and I've had the feeling the last day that you're deliberately keeping yourself unavailable. I had hoped we could get to know each other a little better."

"Is that a euphemism for those acts you engaged in on Monday?"

He made a little shrugging gesture, his mismatched eyes twinkling with enjoyment. "I wouldn't have any objection at all to kissing you again, if that's what you're asking. Otherwise, no, it wasn't a euphemism. I'm quite honest in my desire to get to know you better."

"It's been my experience that most men who say that simply do so in order to seduce women to their beds."

"I am not most men," he pointed out.

Oh, how I knew that. No other man had filled my mind so completely with thoughts of the most intimate nature, not to mention all the usual desires, needs, and wants that accompanied such a fascination. I glanced down the gangway toward the direction I had just come, wanting to escape, knowing if I didn't keep my distance from him, I'd end up with a bigger situation on my hands than I already had. "I am the captain, Mr. Fletcher. You might be unfamiliar with airship travel, but surely even you must realize that I have duties and obligations that do not include the entertainment of unexpected passengers. I have tasked Mr. Dooley with seeing to the comforts of your sister and you; I am sorry if he has not been able to achieve the level of service you are used to—"

"Stop," Jack said, putting his hand on my arm as I was in the process of sidling past him. I froze, feeling his hand as if it were a brand on my flesh. "I am not complaining. Neither of us are—Hallie says you have excellent taste in literature, and she's enjoying reading the books you gave her. And I'm perfectly happy following Mowen around and learning the ins and outs of steam boilers, although he's probably getting sick and tired of my questions. It's not the fact that you're busy and have a job to do that bothers me."

"I am delighted to hear that," I said, trying to edge past him again. All that did was bring me into close proximity to him, however. He took my other arm in his hand, turning me gently until I faced him.

"You're avoiding me, Octavia. And I have a bad feeling I said something to offend you."

I stared at the cross tie sitting so jauntily in the center of his two snowy collar tips. I knew his face would reflect nothing but earnestness, but I didn't want to see it. One look at those eyes, and I would be lost. It was far better that he think me a coward, a woman who didn't care how rude she was so long as she did her job. There would be no complications, no potential trouble, that way.

"Octavia?"

His voice was low and intimate, caressing me, but I hardened my heart against it. "I am wanted in the propeller room, Mr. Fletcher. If you will allow me to pass, I would be grateful."

His hands dropped away from my arms. I felt lower than a beetle as I edged around him. I made it past him, taking a deep breath as I started on my way to the rear of the airship, and congratulating myself on standing firm when my heart screamed its protest of such actions.

"I'm sorry for whatever it is I've done," Jack said from behind me. Unbidden, my feet stopped.

The pain in his voice pierced through to my soul. I turned back to face him, wanting to explain everything, wanting to tell him about Etienne, about Alan and William, about my goals and my plans and my dreams. And more than anything, I wanted to kiss him again. But I couldn't do any of those things. "You haven't done anything wrong," I said with regret for all that had been, and all that couldn't be. "If things were different—but they aren't. Tomorrow we will land in Rome. You and your sister will be free to pursue your return to wherever it is that you came from."

"Assuming we can," he said, making a wry face.

"I'm afraid I have little advice to offer you there," I said primly.

"I know. I'll find a way, I'm sure. But what about you?"

"Me?"

"What will you do?"

My gaze dropped. "I will do my duty, Mr. Fletcher. It's what I have been raised to do."

"That sounds like a very cold and unhappy future," he said, then gave me a little bow, turned on his heel, and strode off in the opposite direction.

The following day we stopped at Parcetti, a small village about an hour outside Rome. In an attempt to spare the crew of any charges of complicity, I ordered them to their quarters, assisting Mr. Mowen myself as we lowered the airship to the uneven ground of a rocky hillside. I watched the engines while he wrestled two crates out of the forward hold, depositing them without any ceremony. We regained our standard flying altitude, then continued on to Rome, having lost less than an hour from our schedule.

Buck Rogers, I Ain't

"Jack."

"Hush. You know what Matthew said—we are to stay quiet until he or Octavia knocks on the wall to let us know the coast is clear."

"I don't hear anything," Hallie whispered after a moment of silence. "And I'll go crazy if I have to just stand here being quiet. It's like being walled up alive."

I grinned despite the fact that she couldn't see it, carefully sliding my hand along the wooden wall to find her arm. I gave her fingers a little squeeze. Judging by the way she clutched my hand, I guessed she was a lot more nervous than she let on. "Afraid?"

"No. Yes. Just a little." Her voice was thin as if she was close to panic. I gave her fingers another squeeze.

"Hang in there, Hal. Octavia said the inspectors are usually pretty quick, and hardly ever glance into the engineer's rooms."

"There's only a thin sheet of wood between us and them," she whispered back. "What if they discover the bookcase has a false back? What if they trigger the mechanism that opens it like a door? What if they go around behind us and find us?"

"Octavia assured me that no one has ever given the

bookcase a second glance, and there's a big boiler on the other side of us, so there's no way anyone could shift it to find us." The throb of the boiler, which had made the wall vibrate, had slowly died down as we landed, eventually falling silent.

"One of the crew could tell someone," she persisted. "I talked to Beatrice Ho quite a bit yesterday—she said the bounty given for spies turned over would be enough for her to retire on."

"That's why Octavia set up that little scene with the two crates that were dropped off when we slipped in here—if one of the crew was going to turn us in, they'd find nothing but a couple of crates filled with barrels of salt beef."

"The engineer knows we're here. He could rat us out."

That was a valid concern. "You remember that first night when we woke up to find ourselves here?"

She shuddered. "How could I forget?"

"Octavia told me that this ship was taken from a smuggler, and although all of the other smuggling spaces had been renovated, this one had escaped detection. She suggested then that we'd have to hide here when we landed, but that Matt would have to know. That's why I spent the last few days palling around with him. He might have thought I was trying to learn about the steam engine systems, but the truth was that I wanted to have a chance to assess what sort of man he was. He doesn't strike me at all like the type of man who'd take blood money."

"You're putting a lot of faith in a few days' acquaintance," she said, stiffening at the sound of a metal clang.

"Shhh. Someone's coming. Just don't panic, and for

God's sake, don't make a noise. We'll get through this all right."

She was silent, although her fingers gripped mine with an intensity that was painful. The wooden backing to the bookcase might not have been thick—it had to swing outward in order to allow access to the narrow closetlike storage space into which we were currently packed like a pair of human sardines—but it did a great job of muffling sound. I strained my ears to pick up a clue as to what was going on out there, but all I heard was the rumble of male voices. A few minutes later and they were gone.

"See?" I whispered, letting go of her hand. "Nothing to worry abo—"

An explosion rocked the floor.

Hearing the intake of her breath, I slapped a hand over Hallie's mouth before she could scream. "Quiet!" I ordered, listening for any clue to what was going on.

"We're going to die!" she yelled, jerking down my hand. "They found us! Oh, God, I knew this would happen! We're going to die on a strange, alien world, and no one from back home will know what happened to us!"

"This isn't an alien world—," I started to say, but stopped when the wall in front of us suddenly gave way.

"Hurry," Octavia said as she yanked open the false back to the bookcase. "We must get you off the ship immediately."

"What happened?" I asked, grabbing Hallie's arm and following her. "Did they find us?"

"No. The inspectors were leaving the ship when— duck!"

I dived with her behind one of the boilers, pulling a squawking Hallie with me, my hand over her mouth as we froze.

"What is it?" I asked Octavia in an almost silent whisper. This necessitated me putting my mouth to her ear, a distracting event, since it allowed me to get another whiff of that enticing perfume she wore. Despite the danger of the situation, lust flared to life deep in my belly, spreading out a warm glow of desire that I was hard put to ignore.

"We're under attack," she said, turning her head slightly. Her mouth was suddenly close to mine, far too close for me to be able to think with any cognizance.

I stared into her lovely brown eyes, eyes that seemed to be simultaneously innocent and wise beyond their years. Her irises flared, showing she shared the attraction I felt, and I hate to admit it, but I might have just forgotten everything and kissed her right then if a shadow hadn't flickered over us.

She ducked again, and instinctively, I pulled Hallie to the ground as I flattened myself. I peered through the feet of the boiler, catching sight of several pairs of shoes. "Who?" I mouthed at Octavia.

She held her finger to her mouth and slowly, cautiously pulled herself up behind the boiler, peering out in the small space made by a pressure gauge and the body of the boiler. I did likewise.

A tall, whipcord-thin man strode past us, his coppery hair shimmering in the gaslights. He was yelling an order in French, something about securing their prize. He gestured for a moment toward the stern, then hurried out of the room. The two other people with him, both men, followed.

"Etienne," Octavia said almost inaudibly.

"Who?" I asked just as softly.

She hesitated for a moment, sliding me an unreadable glance. "Etienne Briel is the leader of the Black Hand."

"The who, now?"

"They are the revolutionary group I mentioned a few days ago."

"Oh, yeah. Them." I gave her a long look. She blushed.

"Do I take it you know this Etienne?" I couldn't help but ask.

Her blush deepened. That was all the answer I needed.

"OK, then. If you know him, why are you hiding?"

Her lips thinned. "He is stealing my cargo."

"In other words, he's using you?"

She didn't answer, but her lips tightened.

Anger boiled in my guts. Octavia's face was devoid of emotion, but she was a woman who valued her control, and I knew she had to be furious at a former lover just helping himself to her precious cargo. I also knew why she was crouched down behind a boiler rather than defending her cargo from an acquaintance—she was protecting Hallie and me.

Guilt added to the anger.

"I'm not going to hide here and let him treat you this way," I said grimly, not sure how, exactly, I was going to stop them.

"Jack?" Hallie asked as I got to my feet.

"Mr. Fletcher, get down or you'll be seen," Octavia hissed, tugging my arm.

"I don't care. It's because of us that you're in this mess, and I'm not going to stand by while someone ruins your first trip. I know how important it is to you. Hallie, stay here with Octavia. I'll come back for you when the coast is clear."

"Jack!" she moaned as I slipped around the side of the boiler.

"Mr. Fletcher, please!"

I ignored Octavia's plea and peered out into the boiler room. It was now empty, but the door had been left open to the gangway, and I could hear men's voices from the fore of the airship. I crept toward the doorway, peering around intently for any sign of a rope or cord, or something I could use to restrain the revolutionaries.

I paused at the door to pinpoint the location of the voices, and almost lost it when something bumped into me from behind.

"Octavia!" I whispered furiously as I spun around to see who had attacked me. "I thought I told you to stay with Hallie."

"You told her to stay with me, and she is."

I glared at my sister, who stood behind the captain.

"Don't give me that look. We're not weaklings," Hallie snapped back. "We're not feeble little things who have to cower in the back while the big, bad man goes out and saves the day. Stand aside, brother, and let me show you how a black belt deals with troublemakers."

She pushed past me into the gangway in a burst of short-lived bravado.

"You don't have a black belt," I pointed out, grabbing her arm to stop her.

"I could if I wanted to." She shrugged her arm out of my grasp, but I was faster and bolted ahead of her and Octavia.

"Fine. You can come with me, but I will go first. And don't give me any crap about it." I turned and marched down the gangway, realized what I was doing, and slid into a stealthy, ninjalike movement instead.

"Mr. Fletcher, this is not necessary," Octavia said, tugging at my sleeve. "The revolutionaries are very dangerous. I would feel horrible if something were to happen to you."

I tossed a grin over my shoulder at her. "Don't worry, sweetheart. I may not believe in lethal force, but I do know how to take care of myself."

"No, you don't understand." She bit her lower lip, her hands wringing themselves. "Oh, it's so complicated. . . . There are circumstances of which you are not aware, and they—"

Another blast shook the metal frame of the airship. Hallie screamed. I dashed down the spiral staircase to the level that held the entrances to the cargo holds, Octavia's boots sounding on the metal steps behind me.

"Mr. Fletcher, please stop! There is no need for you to act the hero!"

I leaped the last couple of feet down the stairs and bolted down the hallway. One of the side doors flung open, and Mowen and the lecherous cook jumped out, two oddly shaped guns in their hands.

"You go via the forward passage. I'll drop down from the rigging," Mowen ordered.

The cook stared at me in surprise for a moment. Mowen shoved him toward the front of the ship. "Move, man! There's no time to stand about gawking!"

"Mr. Mowen! Francisco! What are you both doing still on board the ship?" Octavia demanded, pushing around from behind me. "You were supposed to disembark earlier when the officials left!"

"Wanted to make sure all was well with our passengers," Mowen replied hurriedly, shoving a gun into my hands. "You take this and guard the captain."

"I do not need anyone to guard me!" she gasped, outrage visible in the fiery glare she gave him.

"I'm sorry, but I have a policy against guns," I said,

trying to give it back to him. "I make it a habit never to kill anyone."

"Shoot them in the legs, then," he snapped, and ran up the stairs we'd just come down.

Hallie, who had been descending carefully, clutched me when she reached the bottom of the stairs. "Jack, what are we going to do?"

I stared at the gun in my hand. Like the one Octavia wore strapped to her belt, it was of a rounded shape, with brass tubing and a small crystal set into the grip. The crystal glowed green now. I had a horrible feeling that indicated the safety was off it.

"We will do nothing," Octavia said firmly. "There is nothing to be done. The revolutionaries will not harm you, I promise."

"How can you promise that?" I asked, frowning.

She hesitated a moment, then grabbed my arm and pulled me into the mess. Hallie followed. "You force me into a very uncomfortable admission. I trust that it will go no further than this."

"Does it have something to do with the people attacking the ship?" Hallie asked.

She hesitated again and a dim light of understanding dawned. "You aren't at all surprised that they attacked, are you?"

She shot me an odd look.

"You expected it." The dim light grew brighter. "You knew they were going to attack and take your cargo, didn't you?"

"You're a revolutionary?" Hallie asked, looking incredulous.

Octavia closed her eyes for a moment. "I was told that the revolutionaries would be attacking when we landed, yes."

"Told by whom?" I asked.

She twisted a small garnet ring on a finger of her right hand. "Does that really matter? The fact is that we are in no danger from the revolutionaries. You, however, have shown yourself to Mr. Francisco, and although I have no reason to believe he would betray your presence, it would have been wiser had you stayed back as I asked."

I watched her closely, noted how the pupils in her lovely brown eyes constricted ever so slightly. "Just how well do you know this Etienne? *Is* he another one of your boyfriends?"

I swore she ground her teeth. She certainly gave me a look that should have dropped me dead on the spot. "Are you implying that I have carnal knowledge of every man whose name I know?"

"No, and you're changing the subject. Is he one of your lovers?"

Her fingers twitched, like she wanted to throttle someone. "Was! Since you insist on knowing, I admit it. I hope that satisfies your rampant curiosity! Now will you give me that Disruptor, and go back to the boiler room, where it's safe? I must go stop my crew from harming themselves or others!"

"That deranged cook of yours has already seen me," I said, following her as she stomped out of the mess. Hallie squeaked something and ran after us.

"I have enough to do without ensuring nothing further happens to you," Octavia answered as we hurried down the hall. She stopped to make shooing motions at Hallie and me.

"I told you I can take care of myself," I said, then realized I still had hold of the gun. I stuck it in my pocket. "And I can do it without lethal force. Let me go first and look to make sure the way is clear."

"For the love of the moon and the stars," she said, sighing loudly as I pushed past her. "Does the man not have ears? Mr. Fletcher, I told you that I will come to no harm with members of the Black Hand."

She tried to pass me as she spoke.

"Look, I may not be much of a he-man, but I *am* a man, and I consider it my duty to put myself between potential danger and people I care about, OK? So let me do my job!"

She stopped, giving me a curious look. "You . . . care about me?"

"I don't generally kiss women I dislike," I answered, pausing at the door to one of the cargo holds.

"You kissed the captain?" Hallie asked, giving her a speculative look. "Well, now. That's interesting."

"It was an aberration," Octavia said quickly.

"Like hell it was," I said, tossing a grin over my shoulder at her. "It was hot and you know it."

She opened her mouth to protest, but nothing came out.

I carefully opened the door a few inches and peered in. The far wall of the cargo hold folded back to allow access to the contents once the airship was landed. Sunlight and noise filtered in through the opened wall as a handful of men and women hurriedly removed the wooden crates filling the hold.

"You're sure those are your revolutionary buddies?" I asked as we all ducked behind the nearest crate.

"Who else would be purloining my cargo?" she countered.

"You seem to have an interesting past, and an even more interesting collection of friends," I said softly, close to her ear. I breathed in the scent of her, a light floral perfume that had overtones of honeysuckle. I've never been one for perfumes much, but this one tormented me, leaving me with an almost overwhelming urge to taste her. "I wouldn't be surprised at all if there were any number of people who wanted to get into your cargo."

She shot me a startled look, obviously not quite sure if I meant the innuendo. I let a hint of a leer curl up the edges of my smile.

"There really is no need for you both to endanger yourselves," she said. "The Black Hand will not harm me, but I cannot guarantee your safety. If you insist on staying here, remain hidden behind this crate of uniforms while I go look for Messrs. Mowen and Francisco."

"Not on your tintype," I said cheerfully, following as she skulked over to another large crate. "Whither you go, so goest me."

"You're not leaving me alone, either," Hallie said, grabbing the back of my coat as we crouched our way along the wall.

Octavia sighed heavily, but said nothing more. I beamed at her bustle as she clutched a crate and peered around it. What a smart woman she was. She knew when arguing would be futile. Smart, sexy, and fascinating—it was a heady combination, and I knew unless I watched myself, I would be a goner to her charms.

Octavia stopped, poking her head around a crate, hissing something. I peered around her. The engineer and cook had evidently been sneaking around the edges of the hold with the intention of ambushing the busy revolutionaries as they unloaded the cargo. Upon hearing Octavia, however, the pair crab-walked their way back to us, keeping their heads down.

"Captain! You shouldn't be here," Mr. Mowen said softly.

"My most luscious one, my beauty, my flame of the

brightest sun. What Mowen says is true—you should not be here. You should be in the room of bedchambers, awaiting me to pleasure you as you have never been pleasured," Francisco said, puffing out his chest even as he glared over her head at me.

"Look, I don't know why you have such a hard time understanding that Octavia isn't interested in you, but you seriously need to knock it the hell off. She's not interested—got that?"

"I hear the flying gnat buzzing," Francisco said, waving his hand in the air as if flapping away a fly. "Just a small, insignificant gnat of the most unwelcome."

I sighed. Octavia said, casting a swift glance at me, "That will be enough, Francisco. You will please both of you go back to your quarters."

"But the revolutions! They are here to take your so-precious cargo!" Francisco protested. "I cannot allow my beloved captain of the flames to be robbed!"

"I understand and applaud your reticence to allow such a thing to happen," Octavia said, her chin lifting. I loved that chin. She had a tendency to lift it when she gave commands, and the sight of it tipping up just made me want to kiss her. "But in this case, I will not have any of my crew's lives put at risk. Return to your quarters at once."

"What about you, Captain?" Matthew Mowen asked, giving first her, then me, an appraising glance.

"I'll see that she comes to no harm," I said, giving him a nod.

"I will follow shortly," she said, shooting me an annoyed look. "I just wish to make sure that the revolutionaries don't attempt to harm the ship. Then we will retreat, as well, and await the officials that are sure to come."

Mowen stood his ground for the count of twenty, but eventually he succumbed to Octavia's demands, and both men exited the cargo hold by the entrance we had just used.

"You lie very well," Hallie said, her gaze resting thoughtfully on Octavia. "I hadn't expected that of you."

A faint flush of pink rose in Octavia's cheeks. "I prefer to speak only the truth, but in this situation, I felt a lie was justified in order to save my crew members' lives."

"So no one else in the crew is a member of this group?" I asked as she crawled over to the next crate.

"No, of course not!" she whispered back. "I don't suppose it would do any good for me to request, yet again, that you and Miss Norris return to your hiding spot?"

"None whatsoever," I said cheerfully. She turned her head to glare at me and caught me ogling her ass.

"Mr. Fletcher!"

"Jack."

"Might I remind you that I am the captain of this airship?" she said, sitting abruptly on her heels.

Behind me, Hallie giggled.

"I'm a man. You're a woman, a damned attractive woman. Your ass was right there, demanding I give it the consideration due it. I couldn't help it that consideration came in the form of an ogle."

"My derriere has never demanded anything from anyone, not that you were looking at it in the first place, as the previously unwarranted discussion about bustles should have proven," she said in that huffy tone that I was beginning to love. "Now, am I going to be able to proceed without you subjecting my person to inappropriate scrutiny?"

I thought about it for a moment. "I don't think so, no. I'll try to rein it back if you're seriously offended, but as I said, I'm a man. I can't help but admire the body of a woman who I . . . well, admire. And bustle or not, if you're going to waggle your booty in front of me, I'm going to notice it."

She gestured in front of her. "Very well. Since you are unable to control your manful lusts, you may precede me."

"Manful lusts. I like that term. If Jack's manful lusts get to be too much for you, Octavia, just whisper the phrase 'sexual harassment' in his ear, and he'll stop. Probably."

I winked at Octavia as I crept past her, moving as stealthily as I could down the far wall, running at a right angle to the wall that had been folded back for unloading. I was just about to ask Octavia what we were looking for when a muffled explosion sounded. We all froze.

"That wasn't on the ship," I said, not feeling any vibration in the metal floor.

"No. It came from the aerodrome." Octavia clutched my shoulder as she peered around me, her face tight with worry.

"Are the revolutionaries blowing up the buildings?" Hallie asked, poking her head above mine to look. The workers who had been unloading Octavia's cargo ran outside, shouting to one another. In the distance, we could hear other voices, people calling out questions, and, above that, a high, droning sound.

Octavia froze for a second, her head tipped as she listened intently.

"That sounds like . . ." I stopped and dug through my memory. "It sounds like the show some Bedouins put on when I was in Saudi Arabia. What's it called? Ululation?"

"Not Bedouins," Octavia said, leaping to her feet. Hallie and I followed suit. "Moghuls!"

"What on earth are moguls doing here?" Hallie asked.

"Not the Donald Trump sort of mogul, Hal," I said. "The kind from the Moghul empire."

Gunshots sounded above the screaming, but they were hollow-sounding gunshots, not the sharp bark I was used to. We ran as a group to the edge of the opened wall, and stared out at pandemonium.

Below us, the field of the aerodrome lay, grass and dirt spread out before us like a smooth carpet, edged on one side by small one-story buildings that were probably offices or terminals of some sort. Two other airships were parked on the field—one close to us, the other visible in one of three hangars that sat on the far side of the field.

"It's Akbar," Octavia said, clutching my arm. "The imperator's son. Only he would be so bold as to attack a Black Hand raid."

"Your raid is being raided?" I asked, wondering if she saw the irony in that.

She nodded, her face pinched with worry. Evidently she didn't.

Dust rose thick and heavy in the air as madness consumed the people outside. Fifteen or so of the folks who had been loading up big wagons with the cargo had taken cover behind the wagons, and were shooting at the attackers. The Moghuls—I assumed Octavia was correct in identifying them—rode horses across the field in a wave that encircled both the hangar and the airship itself, their strange call rising high over the shouts and sounds of gunfire from the revolutionaries.

The Moghuls evidently had rifles, of a similar type to the handguns in that they made the same dull shooting sound, followed by a blast of reddish orange light.

"Akbar, huh?" I squinted through the dust, amazed she could see enough of the attackers to identify them. Their horses appeared to be wearing some sort of ornate leather and metal armor.

"Yes. That's him, there, on the black horse." She pointed as one of the galloping horses leaped over a wagon and spun around, charging the revolutionaries who had been hiding behind it. The man on the horse wore little armor, an odd choice, I thought, given the guns being fired toward him. He was dressed in some sort of a long tunic that reached to his knees, split up the sides so he could ride, with what looked like a yellow sweatshirt beneath it. His pants, also yellow, were tucked into ornately decorated leather boots, and he wore matching leather bracers on his wrists, the same type I'd seen on a friend who was heavily into archery. He had no bow, but did carry a rifle, and had a sword strapped to his belt. On his head he wore a pair of dark goggles, and a white turban, the end of which had been wrapped around the lower half of his face, no doubt to keep the dust out.

"Goggles," I told Octavia.

"Eh?" she asked, looking confused.

I pointed at the man. "See? He knows how to do steampunk. *He* has goggles."

She gave me a look that said she thought I was a few gigs short of a terabyte. While I watched, the Moghul whipped the rifle upward and began shooting at the revolutionaries, crying something at them as the dirt erupted at their feet. They scrambled backward, a few of them shooting at him, but he simply charged them with his horse. They turned tail and headed straight for us.

"Don't worry—I'll protect you!" I yelled, filled with the knowledge that I had to keep Octavia and Hallie safe from this latest threat.

"What?" Octavia said, her eyes round. "No—"

"Get back," I shouted, shoving her toward Hallie. "Both of you—go hide!"

"Mr. Fletcher, I really must object to such high-handed—"

"You can yell at me about my manners later. Hold her, Hallie!" I bellowed, grabbing up a crowbar one of the revolutionaries had left lying behind. I didn't wait to see if Hallie did as I demanded—she was a smart woman. I knew she wouldn't insist on being in the thick of a battle when she was unarmed. I just prayed that Octavia would show the same sort of good sense.

I scrambled up on a crate, leaped across it to another one that stood in the center of the opened wall, and narrowed my eyes on the Moghul prince who Octavia had said was known for his ruthlessness. The revolutionaries wouldn't hurt her, since she was obviously one of them, and I trusted her to keep Hallie safe from them. But the Moghul was another matter.

He charged toward us as the revolutionaries streamed into the hold. I felt, at that moment, in great need of a personal battle cry, something I could yell as I leaped off the box and challenged the Moghul prince, something that would summarize, in a few succinct words, both my personal attitude and beliefs, something dashing and inspiring, along the lines of the war cries that actors screamed so dramatically in period war movies. In the fraction of a second it took before the warlord reached me, I considered, and rejected, the motto of my alma mater, various Tolkien cries that were stirring, but meaningless in this context, and finally the motto of the US Army.

Akbar headed straight for me, his rifle spitting out splats of light on either side. I took a deep breath, raised my crowbar, and yelled in my best Bruce Willis impersonation, "Yippie ki-yay, motherfucker!" as I flung myself onto him.

I hit him with enough force that we both went over the back end of his horse, my arms and legs cartwheeling wildly as we fell. He was partly on the bottom as we struck the wooden ramp leading into the hold, his head making a satisfying thump on the ground as we hit.

He snarled something at me in a language I didn't understand, shoving me off him as he scrambled to retrieve the rifle I'd knocked out of his hands.

"No, you don't!" I yelled, tackling him. His head hit the ground again, leaving him dazed for a moment. I jerked him over onto his back, raising the crowbar in my hand.

From the hold, I could hear feminine voices. The gunfire had stopped, but not the screaming. I heard Octavia calling my name, and was warmed by the concern she obviously felt, but didn't want to admit.

The dazed man beneath me coughed, his eyes fluttering behind the dark green lenses of the goggles. He must have seen the heavy crowbar in my hand directly over his head, because he froze. I stared down at him for a few seconds, a war waging inside me. Part of me wanted to bash his brains in for daring to attack Octavia's ship, and possibly threatening her well-being. But I had always prided myself as having some sort of honor, so instead, I jumped to my feet, hauling him up with me. "I

could crack your head open as easily as I could an egg,"
I told him, shaking the crowbar at him. "But I'm going to
let you go so long as you leave Octavia's ship alone. Do
you understand me? You are to leave her ship alone, or
so help me, I'll make you sorry you were ever born!"

"Jack! What are you doing? Let me pass, please!" Octavia's voice was annoyed.

"It's all right," I called back, without taking my
eyes off my captive. "Tell the revolutionaries to stand
down."

"To what?" Octavia asked.

"Stop shooting at him. I've got the situation under
control."

Akbar the Moghul's eyes widened as I picked up his
rifle.

"Go on," I said, nodding toward his horse. "Take your
band of thieves and get the hell out of here."

Around and behind us, people emerged from behind
crates, looking with disbelief as I waved the crowbar at
him, more or less pushing him back toward his horse,
which had stopped at the bottom of the ramp.

"For the love of the heavens!" Octavia yelled, bursting between two revolutionaries. "Jack, stop!"

"It's all right, he's not going to steal anything from
you," I called to her. She rushed up, and I half turned my
head toward her, my eyes narrowed on Akbar. "Sorry I
can't comfort you, but this bastard looks like the type to
carry a knife in his boot."

"He does," she said, taking the rifle from me.

Both Akbar and I glanced at her in surprise.

She blushed. "That is . . . I've heard he does. The newspapers are full of tales of his atrocities."

"Well, he's not going to be performing any atrocities
here," I growled, shoving him backward another couple

of steps with the crowbar. "You heard me—get your buddies, and get the hell out of here."

I thought for a moment that he was going to fight, and I braced myself for an attack, but instead he just made me a little bow, and said in a voice heavy with accent, "I will allow you to speak to me with such insolence for the mercy you have shown me, but do not expect such again."

I slapped the crowbar against my hand in a threatening way. "Just remember that Octavia's ship isn't ripe for your picking."

He said nothing, just leaped on his horse and, calling out something, rode off, his half-dozen followers on his heels.

Octavia turned to me, her eyes wide as she watched me clutch my hand and do a little dance of pain. "You stood up to Akbar the ruthless."

"Dammit, I think I broke my hand with that damned crowbar," I said, stopping the pain dance long enough to gingerly feel my palm. "Please remind me if I ever want to slap a crowbar on my hand that it hurts like hell. And yes, I did stand up to him, but someone had to. It was clear things would have turned into a bloodbath otherwise."

She just looked at me as Hallie, making a noise of distress, took my hand and prodded at it.

"It doesn't look broken to me," Hallie said, giving it back to me.

"You challenged Akbar just because you didn't want anyone hurt?" Octavia asked me, her gaze steady on mine.

"Well, no, not just because of that. I didn't want your cargo stolen. Er . . . stolen by the wrong people," I said, gesturing with a nod toward the revolutionaries, who stood clustered around us.

"I can't believe you would endanger yourself for people you don't know," Octavia said, a frown suddenly pulling her brows together.

"I know you," I said, nudging her with my arm.

"But you could have been killed," she said slowly, little flecks of amber and black glittering in her eyes. Once again, I wanted badly to kiss her, but I figured she wouldn't appreciate it in front of everyone.

"That could happen at any time," I said, shrugging, and wishing we were alone. Clearly she wanted to express her gratitude to me for saving her cargo, and I was more than willing to have her do so, especially if that gratitude took a tangible form. I cleared my throat, ordered my groin to stop thinking about being alone with her, and arranged my expression into one of modesty. "I was happy to do it."

"Yes," she said slowly, her forehead smoothing out. She gave me a long, unreadable look. "I'm sure you were."

She turned away to the revolutionaries, speaking briefly to one before marching into the hold without another word. The revolutionaries, with a last glance toward Hallie and me, continued loading the cargo onto the wagons.

I stared after Octavia as she disappeared into the depths of the hold.

"She seems pissed all of a sudden," Hallie said, frowning after her.

"Yes, she does."

"She should be happy that you saved her cargo for her revolutionary buddies."

"You'd think so, huh?"

"Doesn't make sense," Hallie said, shaking her head, then shrugging. "Oh well. Where to now, brother mine?"

I pulled out a piece of paper that Octavia had given me. "There's a pensione not far from here, Suore della Santa Croce, that's kept by Swiss nuns. Octavia said we should be safe there."

"Safe from what?" Hallie asked as I looked back into the hold. Octavia was gone.

"That is the question, isn't it?" I said, but no one enlightened us.

Log of the HIMA *Tesla*
Thursday, February 18
Dogwatch: Five Bells

It took most of the day before we were released from the Rome offices of Southampton Aerocorps, where the entire crew had been detained by both the Corps and the emperor's officials.

"We'll provide you with an escort to the pensione," Captain MacGregor, the flight leader for this area, said as he gestured for a couple of Corps men-at-arms.

"That's not necessary," I told him, waiting for the rest of the crew to climb into the carriages that were waiting outside the main building for us. "We are prepared to take care of ourselves, and indeed would have been able to repel the Black Hand assault had the full complement of the crew been present."

"I have no doubt that you would have," Captain MacGregor said, his voice as warm as his eyes. I'd met him twice before, but was aware that there was a bit more admiration in his gaze than was purely proper, even given the situation. "You handled that attack by the barbarians quite easily. It's just too bad that the revolutionaries overpowered you and were able to get away with the rest of the cargo."

"Yes, it is quite upsetting," I said, my gaze not wavering even so much as a smidgen.

"I'm sure the emperor will have nothing but praise for you, since you tried your best to fend them off. And then there's the fact that we caught three of them. The emperor is bound to be pleased with you for that."

Drat Etienne. Why hadn't he posted guards to warn of possible reinforcements? He always was arrogant, and I had no doubt that he felt that his presence alone would guarantee the success of the raid. Now three of his men were imprisoned, and quite likely to be scheduled for execution.

"The emperor is always gracious," I murmured, thinking frantically. I'd have to contact Alan—he might be able to help with the captured revolutionaries. He wouldn't like it, since it could threaten his cover with the imperial forces, but he would just have to see the necessity in aiding me with the matter.

"I have asked the vice-provost if I might be present when he questions the revolutionaries," Captain MacGregor continued, his voice fat with satisfaction. He held open the door to a third carriage for me, his hand on my elbow as he assisted me into the vehicle. "He said that under the circumstances he thought it would be allowed."

"Really?" I paused on the top carriage step, turning around to face him. "Would it be possible for me to go with you?"

"You?" He laughed and gave me a little push into the carriage, closing the door and leaning casually against the opened window. "My dear Captain Pye, that would be the height of impropriety."

"How so? It was my ship that was attacked, my crew that was forced to undergo hours of interrogation regarding the event. I believe we are owed something for that inconvenience. I agree that it would be unreasonable for my entire crew to appear at the questioning of the revolutionaries, but surely it would be fitting for me to be present."

"On the contrary," he said, his fingers lingering on mine until I withdrew my hand. "It is out of the question. As for the so-called interrogation—surely you must realize that the present time of unrest in the empire demands that both the Corps and the emperor's officials investigate such events as what transpired today."

"Yes, of course, but—"

"You have not been in Rome in several months," he said, taking my hand again and giving it a squeeze. I was briefly thankful I had donned a pair of gloves before departing his office. "Much has changed since you were last here, my dear Captain Pye. Rome is a battleground between the barbarian Moghuls and the emperor's forces. Daily attacks are not at all uncommon, and the streets are not safe for a lady such as yourself to pass through unescorted. I would, naturally, see to your safety myself, but I promised the vice-provost that I would attend him promptly. I'm sure you will forgive me." He released my hand and gestured. Four armed men on horses moved into view, clearly there to escort our carriages to the pensione that was used by Aerocorps personnel when they were in Rome.

"You will, I hope, grant me the pleasure of your company for dinner tomorrow evening? I will call for you at eight o'clock."

"I'm afraid I will be unavailable. Another time, perhaps?" I was forced to call out as the carriage suddenly jerked forward. I sank into the cushioned back, my stomach in my boots as I considered what a horrible mess had been made of things.

I was dwelling on that, and what steps I could take to try to free Etienne's people, when we passed by the storehouses that were used to hold cargo until it could be distributed. As we passed the first one, a man emerged from the side, stepping back immediately into the blackness of the shadows between the two buildings. He wasn't fast enough, though, to escape me noting the white turban that graced his head and lower face.

I waited until the last of the carriages carrying my crew had passed the storehouses before calling to the coachman to stop at the gate.

"Is there a problem, ma'am?" he called back to me as the horses trotted smartly onward.

I glanced back toward the storehouses, slowly shrinking in the distance. "I believe the Moghuls are planning another attack on the aerodrome."

"What, again?" The man's voice was incredulous. "Well, I'll tell the guard at the gate, but I think you're mistaken. No one could get through our defenses now that the imperial troops are here."

We stopped at the guardhouse at the front gate long enough for me to insist that the man in charge send a note back to the Corps headquarters to check the storehouses. No one seemed inclined to worry.

"Now, then, Captain Pye, ye're just a bit fashed," the guard said with the same soothing tone one would use with a truculent child. "Ye've had a day, and that's no lie, but ye jest go on yer way, and leave it to us to keep the cargoes safe."

"Just do as I ask and notify Captain MacGregor," I said, returning to the carriage.

"The captain was leaving for the vice-provost, ma'am," the driver reminded me.

"Nonetheless, a message can be sent to him," I said, then told him to proceed.

The ride to the pensione was uneventful, although I saw signs on the streets of the recent attacks by the Moghuls. Several blocks had been burned, and were in disarray, while there were few people on the street who did not have an armed guard accompanying them.

I had read reports, of course, of the attacks on Rome by the Moghuls—and occasionally the revolutionaries, although they concentrated their energies on the emperor's troops—and how William, in response to a plea by the Italian king, had doubled the troops in the area. Supplying those troops was the very reason the *Tesla* had been sent out. But I had been in Rome four months before, and it had been very different then.

"Because of the incident today, we have been asked to remain available for interviews by the imperial forces," I told the crew some ten minutes later as they disembarked in front of the Hôtel d'Europe et des Îles Britanniques, a grand name for a modest pensione that was made up of a main building, a stable block that had been converted to rooms, and a small walled garden, all of which butted up against the back of a convent. It was quiet and clean, and the owners, Signore Vittorio and his wife, were most obliging and attentive to Aerocorps members. "However, I have been granted permission to give you all twenty-four hours of leave, so you may consider yourselves free from duty until tomorrow evening."

"Hurrah! I can't wait to try them Italian ices I've heard so much about," Dooley cheered, and was immediately squashed by Mr. Piper, who cuffed him on the back of the head.

"Ye'll be stayin' with me, ye will, lad. Ye're likely to end up on the end of a barbarian's sword iff'n I was to let ye run free."

"Welcome, welcome," Signore Vittorio said as he emerged from the building, wiping his hands on a large green apron as he greeted us. He was a round man, with little hair, but a broad smile. "You are most welcome. Ah, Miss Pye, is it not? I have not seen you for many months. You look well."

"It's Captain Pye now," Mr. Christian said, looking over the front of the pensione with a critical eye. Although he'd flown on the *Tesla* for over a year, this was, I knew, his first visit to Rome.

"Captain, eh?" Signore Vittorio showed blackened teeth as he beamed at me before herding us all inside the pensione. "I will tell my signora. She will be pleased, eh? She always liked you."

It took some little while to get the crew settled. Mr. Francisco took offense to having to share his room with Mr. Llama, declaring loudly, "It is the one thing that I must share on the ship. It is small and space is limited. I am a steward most accommodating there. But here? There are many rooms and I will not share!"

"I'm sorry, but Signore Vittorio says that the *Babbage* is in town, and its crew is here, as well; thus there are limited rooms available to us. We're all sharing because of that. Not even I have a room to myself," I said, hoping to end his drama scene before it worsened. "I have full confidence that everyone will be able to enjoy their leave regardless of the accommodations."

"The room, she is the bull most unbear," Mr. Francisco grumbled as he stomped into the room that had been given over to him. It took me a moment to figure out what it was he meant.

"Your room is quite delightful, and not at all unbearable—where is Mr. Llama?" I glanced around the room in growing annoyance. Not half a minute before, I'd seen the mysterious engineer's mate slink into the room, his case in hand, and now there was nothing in the room but two beds, a wardrobe, two chairs, and a stand holding a basin and ewer. The window was open, but we were on the second floor, and I doubted if he would have exited the room that way. "This is too much! I saw him come in here. I *saw* him!"

"Saw who?" Mr. Mowen asked as he strolled past the opened door, a towel over his shoulder, obviously on his way to have a bath.

"Mr. Llama. He's done it again!" I pushed past Mr. Francisco and flung open the wardrobe, expecting to see the man there, but it was empty of everything but an extremely startled mouse. "Damn!" I yelled, uncaring that I was swearing in front of the crew. I whirled around and glared at the window, rushing over to it.

"Did you see him?" I heard Mr. Mowen ask Francisco as I thrust my upper body out of the window, searching for signs that someone could have left that way. The wall was smooth, with no ledge or balcony, nothing but some climbing bougainvillea that led down to the small garden area, which was also empty of people.

"See who?"

"Llama."

"I am not the keeper of the engineers," Mr. Francisco said haughtily. "If you lose him, it is your head it is on."

"I haven't lost—oh, never mind."

"One of these days," I muttered to myself as I withdrew back into the room, my gaze darting hither and yon looking for a secret hiding spot. "One of these days I'm going to catch him in the act, and then we'll just see!"

"Captain be talkin' to herself again?" Mr. Piper asked under his breath as I stormed out of Mr. Francisco's room, and down the hallway toward mine. "Mayhap she be in need of the leave more'n we are."

I closed the door of my room on Mr. Mowen's thoughtful agreement. Mr. Ho had changed out of her uniform into a dark blue dress, and was just pinning a hat on her head. "I might not be back until late, Captain. I know you don't expect us to report in while we're on leave, but as we're sharing accommodations, I wouldn't want you worrying if you noticed I was absent."

"What you do while you're on leave is certainly your own business," I said, pulling off my wool jacket and flopping down unceremoniously onto one of the two beds in the room.

She raised an eyebrow at the priggish tone the words were spoken in.

"Oh, go on, have a good time, and enjoy yourself with whoever it is you're seeing," I said, smiling and shooing her to the door.

"It's not what you think, but thank you nonetheless."

She left and I sagged back against the wall for a moment, the events of the day swirling around me in a miasma of confusion. What was I going to do about Etienne's men?

"First things first, old girl," I told myself, reaching for my jacket. I hesitated a moment, then instead grabbed the big old leather bag that I'd had since I had been given over to Robert Anstruther's care. Quickly I stripped, had a fast wash at the basin, and pulled on a gold walking skirt, light lawn blouse, gold and Wedgwood blue rose-patterned waistcoat, and a matching moiré outing jacket. I studied myself in the mirror for a moment, tucking in a strand of hair that had come free, wondering if Jack liked the combination of blue and gold.

"Bother," I growled when I contemplated changing my clothes. I grabbed up my bag and tucked the Disruptor into it. "It doesn't matter what he likes. You have business to attend to, Octavia. Get to it."

I think it had been my third trip with Robert when he showed me the break in the tall laurel hedge that served as a boundary between the convent and the pensione.

"It will be good for you to have a way out of the pensione without detection," he had told me at the time as he pulled aside a heavy overhang of laurel and indicated a small gate that was invisible unless you knew where to look for it. "This leads to the cloister and convent gardens. If you are careful, you can escape both without being seen by the nuns in residence. The road at the front of the convent is distant enough from the entrance of the pensione to allow you to slip away unseen."

I had cause to use the hidden exit once or twice, and blessed Robert's foresight each time I did so. I added yet another blessing now as I skirted the nuns' garden, emerging at the corner of the road. I had to wait a few minutes for a patrol of the emperor's troops to pass, but they did not glance twice toward the garden, or its very climbable fence. A few minutes later I was in front of the Pensione Suore della Santa Croce, greeting the nun who answered my ring. "Good evening, Sister. I believe some friends of mine, Mr. Fletcher and his sister, Miss Norris, are staying here. Might I see them?"

The nun murmured acquiescence, moving back to allow me to enter into the pensione. The profits from it no doubt helped fund the convent, and although the pensione was small and not overly popular, it was clean, if a bit austere. I sat on an uncomfortable horsehair chair in the visitors' room, plucking a bit of laurel from where it had stuck in my collar.

"I thought you'd never come!" Jack was suddenly there in the room, and my heart lightened at the sight of his scowl. He rushed forward and took my hands, pulling me to my feet. I thought, for one giddy moment, that he was going to take me into his arms and kiss me, an act that I knew would draw censure from the nun who hovered uncomfortably in the background.

"Please, Mr. Fletcher," I said, disengaging my hands, my gaze on the nun. "We are not alone."

"To hell with that," he said, much to the nun's shock. "I tried to get hold of you, but no one would tell me where you were staying."

"Oh, for heaven's sake . . . let us go to the square," I said, apologizing to the little nun as we passed. She had one hand over her mouth, her eyes large, as I led Jack back out into the street, taking his arm and urging him forward even as I looked up and down for signs of potential trouble. "There is a small café in the square where we can have a glass of wine and—"

"Hallie's missing," he said abruptly, stopping.

A chill gripped my heart. "Missing how?"

"Missing! Don't you understand? Gone!" He ran one hand through his hair in a gesture of agitation that I found so endearing, it made my heart contract. "One minute she was there, and the next minute, she was gone."

I glanced up and down the street, but there was nothing out of the ordinary. Still, we would attract attention sooner or later if we just stood outside the convent in intense conversation. "Walk with me, Mr. Fletcher, and tell me what happened."

"Jack," he said absently, his forehead furrowed as I took his arm.

"You made it out of the aerodrome without difficulty?" I prompted.

"Yes. Your directions were spot-on, as were the ones to the hotel. We kept a casual pace, as you told me to, in order to avoid notice, and made it to the hotel without a problem. Hallie wanted to take one of those horses and carriages that run all over the place, but I didn't know how much money you had, and I felt bad enough you had to give us some to stay at the hotel, so we walked."

The muscles in his arm were tense and tight. His steps had a tendency to lag, as if he was reluctant to leave the vicinity of the pensione.

"What were the circumstances of her disappearance?" I asked.

"I'm getting to that. We made it to the hotel, took our rooms, and I told her that you'd said you would come by later to check on us. I said she should lie down for a bit, but she wanted to look around." He gave a half grimace, half smile. "I know I should have stopped her, but you have to understand—this is all a tremendous experience for us, seeing your world. It's like being transported back a hundred years, only there are things you have that we've never had. Like the hybrid bus we saw a few blocks from here—it looked like a cross between a horse-drawn bus and a steam paddler."

I frowned. "A horse-drawn bus . . . Do you mean a steam trolley?"

He shrugged. "I suppose that's as good a name as any for it. It was long like a bus, and filled with a bunch of soldiers, with a big steam engine on the back that chugged like a train."

"That sounds like a steam trolley. They are used for industrial and imperial purposes, since the engines are costly to run."

He flashed me a one-sided grin. "If I was smart, I'd invent the combustion engine, and make a fortune."

I looked at him, confused.

"I'll explain it later," he said, his grin fading as memory returned to him. "Hal and I wandered around a bit, taking in the sights, and the next thing I knew, we were in a big square."

"Rome is full of squares. Do you know which one?"

He frowned. "There was no sign, so no. There was some sort of a church on one side, a big building on the other, and a fountain with a guy blowing into a horn in the center."

"Probably the Fontana di Tritone," I said thoughtfully. "Which is in the Piazza Barberini—oh!"

My hand covered my mouth as I realized just what that meant.

"What's wrong?" Jack asked, quick to notice my distress.

"The Palazzo Barberini is the emperor's headquarters in Rome." My stomach contracted with sudden fear. "Go on. I must know what happened."

"Great, we walked right into the nest of vipers we were trying to avoid," Jack muttered to himself, his gaze on the distance, but turned inward.

"Jack," I said, squeezing his arm to bring him back to me. "What happened to Hallie?"

He gave a little shake. "We were looking at the fountain. She was fascinated by it, and was saying it was a shame we hadn't a camera to take our pictures at it. I wanted a closer look at that steam contraption, so I went to have a quick gander while she was admiring the fountain. When I was done looking, I started back across the square toward her, but I was too late. A couple of men had been passing by, and the next thing I knew, they had suddenly grabbed her, and hustled her off. It happened so fast, I didn't have time to get to her."

"Oh, no," I said, my stomach dropping to my feet.

"They sucked her into the big building," Jack continued, his hand gripping mine now. "The one with guards outside the doors. I was about to demand they release her, when another of those big steam contraptions showed up full of soldiers. A couple of them started after me, and I figured I'd better get you to help rather than end up inside with Hallie."

"Imperial soldiers chased you?" I asked, astounded, although I didn't know why I should be. Jack had shown nothing but courage ever since I had met him. Still, no one but revolutionaries had ever escaped imperial soldiers.

He shrugged. "They started to, but I lost them quick enough."

I stared at him.

"I was in the army," he said by way of an explanation. "In a . . . well, a special branch. We learned a thing or two about ditching tails."

"I don't know what a tail has to do with the situation, but that is not important now," I said, thinking furiously. "If your sister is being held by the emperor's officials . . . merciful heavens. Alan is going to be furious with me."

"Alan?"

"Alan Dubain. He is a friend whom I must call upon to help with . . . with another problem. Come." I did an about-face and took Jack with me. "I must find a messenger. Alan holds a position in the diplomatic corps. He will simply have to help us find out what happened to your sister."

By the time I located a messenger service and wrote out a plea for Alan's help, the city was in darkness. When we stepped out of the messenger office on the heels of the messenger, the sky to the east was lit with a dull orange red glow. Distant sounds of explosions drifted across the still-warm night air.

"Go straight to the palazzo," I told the messenger as he climbed onto his velocipede. The young lad cast a nervous glance over his shoulder toward the colorful skyline, but nodded, and adjusted his goggles before turning the velocipede key a few revolutions.

"A clockwork bike," Jack said softly as the boy kicked off and set on his way into the night. "And I thought I'd seen it all. If you don't mind me asking, what exactly is the purpose of the clockworks?"

"They turn the wheels, of course," I answered. "Jack, we do not have time for idle discussion. Evidently the Moghuls are making yet another assault, and we should return to the pensione to await contact by Alan."

He was resistant when I took his arm and tried to steer him toward a cab. "I was thinking that maybe we should go back to that palace and try to get in to see Hallie. She must be scared."

"Unfortunately, we wouldn't get far, not by ourselves," I told him, stopping a cab that appeared empty. "We need Alan to intervene. Can you take us to the Pensione Suore della Santa Croce, please? Via di San Basilio."

The cabdriver didn't seem any too pleased to receive us. He complained in Italian that it was dangerous for him to be out when the Moghuls were attacking, and that he was on his way home. "The sooner you take us there, the sooner you will be able to return to the safety of your home," I told him firmly, climbing into the cab.

Jack followed, his face pensive as the driver's. After the driver unburdened himself of a few opinions on my ancestry that I chose to ignore, he slapped the reins on his horse and set off at a smart trot.

"I don't like this, Octavia."

"I know you don't, but there is nothing we can do without assistance."

"What if this Alan friend of yours is gone? Or doesn't want to help us?"

"I can't imagine Alan refusing my request for assistance," I said with composure. I could feel how anxious Jack was to be doing something to free his sister. I well understood that restless need to be acting, but to act without Alan would be sheerest folly.

"Oh?" He shot me a sidelong glance, just barely visible in the dimly lit cab interior. "Is this yet *another* one of your boyfriends?"

"He's hardly a boy," I said, smoothing down the material of my skirt over my knees. "And before you pepper me with wholly inappropriate questions, yes, at one time Alan and I had an intimate relationship. That has been over for years now."

"So there's William the emperor, Etienne the leader of the revolutionaries, and now this Alan the diplomat? Aren't you ever interested in a common Joe?"

"I don't know anyone named Joe," I answered, deliberately misunderstanding.

"You know what I mean. Seems to me like you've had some pretty colorful lovers."

"And what about you?" I was irritated enough to lash out when I should have kept my tongue behind my teeth. "Why don't you detail the seven women with whom you've had relationships?"

His teeth flashed in a grin. For some reason, that irritated me even more. "Jealous, my sweet?"

"Hardly," I said, tamping down on something that felt very much like that emotion.

"Turnabout's fair play, then? OK. I've been ribbing you, so I guess it's only fair to take my medicine. I've had four girlfriends. The first two were heartless bitches who dumped me for better opportunities: one was with a stockbroker; the other ended up with a pitcher who made it into the big leagues. The third girlfriend, Samantha, was nice enough, but she was ready to settle down, and I had just gotten my job with Nordic Tech, and I wasn't up for the whole wife-and-kids scene. That was seven years ago, by the way," he said, just as if that mattered.

"Indeed," I said, curling my fingers into fists to keep from touching his leg that leaned so casually against mine.

"My last girlfriend was named Kim. She was also an engineer, worked just down the hall from me, as a matter of fact. We stuck together for a couple of years, but just kind of drifted apart." He shrugged. "I still see her occasionally, but we both know the spark is gone."

I ground my teeth at the thought of the woman continuing to cling to him. "I have always believed that one should clearly delineate the end of a relationship when it is over, so that both parties can continue on with their lives without a perpetual feeling of obligation."

"I suppose," he said after thinking about that, then proceeded to add, "I guess it's really just a matter of convenience. Sometimes . . . well, I *am* human. Sometimes if Kim isn't busy that night, we hook up, no strings attached."

I stared at him, shocked, appalled, and so angry I could spit.

"What?" he dared ask, having the nerve to look confused over my reaction to his appalling confession. "You look upset about something."

"I don't know of what you speak," I said, gathering my dignity and looking out of the window. "If you wish to bare your debauched soul with tales of your licentious, lustful habits, then it is not for me to judge."

He was silent for the count of ten, which was all I could hang on to my temper. I turned back to him, my ire a truly awesome thing to behold. "Although I will say for a man who has made repeated comments about my derriere, and kissed me freely and without my permission, and made overtures that would be clear to a blind nun, you certainly seem to have the morals of a tomcat. One who keeps several she-cats handy just in case he desires their sexual favors!"

He laughed at me, the cad. He had the unmitigated gall to laugh at me. Not only that, he wrapped an arm around me and tried to pull me onto his person. I fought him, naturally.

"Octavia, stop! That's my kidney," he pleaded, still laughing that odious laugh as I elbowed him in order to get free.

"It is not," I said, jerking my skirt out from under his leg, and straightening my waistcoat. "Your kidneys are in the back."

"Well then, it was my spleen or something," he said, chuckling. "When you get jealous, you really get jealous. I'll have to remember that."

"I am not jealous," I said somewhat huffily as I brushed out my skirt.

"You're positively pea green with jealousy, and all because I was being honest with you." Slowly, his laughter faded as he leaned over me. "Sweetheart, I figured you would prefer honesty to polite deception."

"Of course I prefer honesty," I said, lifting my chin and attempting to gaze serenely out of the window. Damn my errant heart and its telling reactions. "You are reading far too much into plain condemnation for what is a lecherous lifestyle."

"Oh? So you've never gone back and done the nasty with William or Etienne?"

"Certainly not," I said, slapping his hand when he tried to turn my face to his.

"What about this Alan you want to help Hallie? Don't you think he'll expect some sort of payment for going out of his way for us?"

There was a tight note in his voice that I found extremely interesting. "Alan is a gentleman," I said, finally looking at him. I was correct—there was a starkness about his mouth that pleased me. "He would never demand sexual favors for services rendered."

The starkness relaxed slightly. I decided that a wee morsel of revenge could be allowed.

"That's not to say that I wouldn't feel it's appropriate, but that, Mr. Fletcher, is neither here nor there to you."

"Oh, it's not, is it?" he growled, his eyes glittering with a look that made me warm down to my toes. Before I could truly enjoy his fine show of spirit, he wrapped one arm around my waist, and pulled me onto his lap.

"You really don't play fair, do you?" he said just a second before his mouth closed on mine.

I was very much aware of the open front to the cab that would allow anyone to see in to us. I was also aware that in the distance the Moghul forces were attacking the city, that my crew were probably out despite that attack, and that somewhere, buried elbow-deep in work, my former lover sat, no doubt at that moment reading my plea for his assistance.

I was cognizant of all that, and yet at that moment, I didn't care. I was honest enough with myself to admit that I wanted Jack. I wanted to taste him and touch him and lie draped across his heaving chest, fulfilled with a sense of completion that I suspected would be most gratifying with him. I kissed him back, allowing his tongue entry into my mouth, welcoming it, teasing it, tasting him even as he tasted me.

And when he growled into my mouth, "Dear God, woman, you're driving me mad," I smiled and nipped his bottom lip, soothing the sting with a long, slow rasp of my tongue. His eyes were molten with desire. "If this is the sort of reaction I'm going to get from you, I'll have to talk about Kim a lot more."

"I think once was enough," I said, sliding my hand down his chest.

"I want to sleep with you, Octavia," he murmured, his lips moving along my jawline to my ear. I shivered when he found a sensitive spot, clutching his shoulders to keep my balance on his lap. "I can't believe it's all I can think of when Hallie is in danger, but it is. Does that shock your Victorian sensibilities?"

"Not particularly. I think it's clear that I desire you, as well. I have ever since I first saw you." My back arched as his hands slid around to the front of my blouse, my breasts suddenly sensitized beneath the thin lawn of the material.

He pulled back enough to give me a jaded look. "That's not true. You wanted to toss me off your airship. You thought I was a pirate."

"Well," I allowed, kissing the tip of his nose. "Perhaps

it was after I realized that you weren't a pirate that I desired you."

He grinned. I gave in and pushed back the lock of hair that lay on his brow.

"It was my Indiana Jones–ness that got you, right? Oh, wait—you don't know who that is. How about this— it was the sense of adventure and danger that gave you the hots for me?"

"I have enough adventure and danger in my life without seeking that in a bed partner," I said, tracing the curve of his ear down to his jaw. "That's not attractive to me."

"No? Then it's my ability to make you shiver when I kiss you here?"

He bit my earlobe, then kissed the spot behind my ear, moving down in a path to the expanse of cleavage. I moaned and arched my back again as his hands swept over my breasts, the combination of that and his mouth making me burn.

"That is definitely a plus," I gasped as his tongue snaked into the valley between my breasts. I fought to hang on to my cognizance. The cab had only a few more blocks to go, and I couldn't let myself go entirely until some things were settled. "I think it's your sense of being lost that calls out to me. I was lost once, too, you see, and I know the feeling. It's as if you need me, Jack, really need me. I've never truly been needed before."

He lifted his head from my chest and looked at me with a curious expression. "Oddly enough, I feel the same thing about you—that there's a sense of kinship, just like we were strangers together. I guess it's because you were orphaned so young, and you know what it's like to have the rug yanked out from under you."

I bit my lip as I gazed down at his bright green and

brown eyes. When I was very young and just come into the care of Robert Anstruther, he had warned me against ever speaking of the time before I was found in the emperor's garden. And yet now I had an overwhelming desire to do just that. "Jack—"

The carriage stopped before I could speak more than his name.

Jack eased me off his lap, leaping out and holding his hands for me. I let him assist me down, pointed out the correct amount to give the driver, and allowed myself to be pulled across the street to the entrance of the pensione.

"I have just one question," Jack said, giving me a look that came close to melting my stays. "Your place or mine?"

"Yours," I said without hesitation. "I told Alan to send word here, rather than my pensione."

"Mine it is, my fair little squab," he said, holding open the door for me.

Now look what you've done, I told my rampant desires. *This isn't going to end well!*

Log of the HIMA *Tesla*
Thursday, February 18
First Watch: Two Bells

Luckily, Jack had enough clothing on to receive the messenger without blushing. Although judging by the activities in which we'd been engaged when the knock sounded on his bedroom door, I wasn't entirely certain the man knew how to blush. He certainly exhibited no signs of restraint or a recognition of finer feelings when it came to disrobing me in as swift a manner as possible.

"It's addressed to you," he said when I peeked out of the wardrobe into which I'd flung myself at the knock.

"Lock your door, then read the message for me," I said, grabbing his shirt from where it had been tossed unceremoniously onto the chair. I *tsk*ed at myself as I slipped into it. I wasn't normally the sort of woman who threw clothing willy-nilly.

"I assume it's from your friend—it's just signed *A* at the bottom. It says: *My very dearest Octavia*." He frowned and shot me a look. "You did say everything was over between you two?"

"Mr. Fletcher!" I said, adopting a suitably shocked expression on my face as I slid into the rumpled sheets of his bed. "I would not be here now in an advanced state of disarray if everything, as you put it, was not over."

"Sorry," he said, his frown clearing somewhat. "It's just that the *my very dearest* was a bit over-the-top."

"Alan has a very loquacious manner of speech," I admitted, settling myself against the pillows. "Go on."

"Loquacious, my ass . . . ," he murmured, then cleared his throat, and read out in a clear voice, "*My very dearest Octavia. I have received your alarming communiqué, and although I am due at the Ambassador's ball, I take pen in hand to address this matter of the gravest moment. I fear there is little I can do for your friend if she has been taken by the imperial guards, although I know you will not be content until I see the vice-provost myself and ascertain on what charges the lady is being detained. I cannot do that, however, until morning. My schedule is busy, as you are no doubt aware, but for you, my sweet Octavia, I will visit the provost's office as early as is reasonable. I must now make an appearance at the Ambassador's ball—if you have further need of me tonight, you know where to find me. Hastily, but with much regard and affection, yours, A.* I suppose I should be grateful he didn't close with hugs and kisses, eh?"

"I didn't expect there would be much he could do tonight," I said thoughtfully, hugging my knees as Jack tossed the letter onto the nightstand. "I'm sorry, Jack. I know you hoped that we would be able to see your sister tonight, but Alan is very trustworthy, and he will be at the provost's office at the first opportunity."

He frowned again, staring at nothing in particular. "You don't think . . . they wouldn't torture her, would they?"

"No! Oh, no, Jack. You must not torment yourself with such thoughts." I crawled across the bed to where he stood, wrapping my arms around his bare torso and offering him what comfort I had. He was clad only in his trousers, since I had not yet gotten to stripping them off him, but his chest, lightly bedecked with dark blond hair, was warm and inviting. "They would have no reason to do so. She did not resist them, and the provost would not have had time to see her. They likely put her in one of the nicer cells, since she is a woman, and although I'm sure she's frightened and not very comfortable, I don't think there is any reason why she should be abused."

He let me hug him for a few minutes, his tense stance finally relaxing as he accepted the fact that there was nothing more we could do. His arms went around me, and he said into my hair, "I've only known you three days, and already I'm beginning to think I can't do without you."

"That's because you're a sensible man despite your extremely unlikely circumstances."

He pulled back to eye me with those disconcerting mismatched eyes. "Circumstances which you seem to accept with more than the usual aplomb—*nnrng*."

My hand, which I had placed on the buttons of his trousers, caressed the bulge that lay therein. "If you have grown tired of seducing me, I would be happy to reciprocate."

"Dear God," he moaned, his beautiful eyes closing as I slowly undid the buttons. "Octavia, you are full of surprises."

"More than you can ever guess," I murmured, sliding his trousers down over his hips. His drawers soon followed, and I was left kneeling on the floor, cheek to jowl (so to speak) with a sight that gave me pause for measure.

Literally.

"You appear to be larger than I expected," I said,

wrapping one hand around him, and noting how much was left over.

He moaned again.

"Not grossly larger, mind you," I said, bringing my second hand into play. "Not inhumanely large. Not like an animal, for instance. Just a bit more than I expected."

Harsh breathing was the reply.

"You're not quite two hands, in case you were wondering. That is good—two hands' worth would be excessive. I could not approve of two hands' worth. But one hand and slightly more than a half of a second hand—that is reasonable. I approve of your dimensions, even if they are a bit more robust than I had anticipated."

"Flang," he said.

I frowned at the word. "Flang?"

Above me, his chest rose and fell in a rapid movement. His hands were fisted, lying not very relaxed against his bare hips. His eyes, I was interested to note, were closed. "Do that movement with your fingertips again."

I stroked the fingers in question across the underside of what was evidently a very sensitive spot.

"Flang," he repeated, his entire body trembling.

"I see." I considered that part of him that overflowed one hand, but did not fill both. "So you enjoy my fingers around you? How interesting. The other men I've been with have preferred me to use my mouth, but if you receive more enjoyment this way . . ."

"Mouth?" he said, his eyes opening quickly. Hope was in their depths, a profound hope and a pleading, desperate need. "You do that?"

"Of course I do. It is part of the act of loving, is it not?" I asked, looking back at the part in question. "Unless you have some sort of disease that would prevent me from doing so."

"No disease," he said quickly, a hint of desperation entering his voice now. "By all means, if you want to use your mouth, go right ahead. I wouldn't want to deprive you of any pleasure."

"Are you sure?" I asked, flicking my fingertips again.

His body tensed. "Yes, yes, quite sure. Full steam ahead."

"Steam?" I paused as I was about to take him into my mouth. "Mr. Fletcher—"

"Jack."

"Surely you are not going to bring up your silly conjectures about this being a society of steambumps again."

"Steampunk, sweetheart."

"Now is not the time to demand goggles, or quiz me about the use of a steam abacus, or whether or not electricity is truly as dangerous as we know it to be. I am about to pleasure you. You will please attend to that, after which you may pleasure me, and then we will proceed onward to other, equally enjoyable activities."

His eyes opened again to pin me back with a look of purest male impatience. "Do you always talk this much during sex?"

"We are not engaged in intercourse at the moment, sir," I said in my most quelling voice, emphasizing the point by shaking that part of him to which I still held on. "I am in charge of this section of the oral pleasure, and as such, it is within my right to speak when and how I choose. Now, are you done asking questions so that I might continue?"

He nodded his head rapidly, his eyes pleading with me.

"Excellent. We will proceed." I glanced at the clock sitting on the nightstand. "I shall time you, if you don't mind. I recently read of some techniques that promised to increase a man's pleasure while shortening the duration of the time needed to reach that point, and I'm curious to know if it works."

"You want to *time* me?" Jack asked, his voice filled with incredulity. "You want to time how long it takes you to bring me to an orgasm?"

"Yes. The book I purchased was very expensive, naturally, given its illicit nature, and I'd like to know that I received my money's worth from it. It promised that I would be able to speed up the act by as much as ten minutes, so if you don't mind, I shall time you."

"You are the strangest woman. . . . Whatever. Knock yourself out," he said, closing his eyes again. "But I warn you—knowing you're watching the clock is going to have the opposite effect on me than what you're shooting for."

I swirled my tongue around him. He froze solid for a second, then jerked me upward and flung me onto the bed, tearing off the shirt that I wore as he rose over me.

"That was much faster than I expected," I said, blinking as his hands and mouth possessed my now bared breasts. I arched back into him, my legs sliding up the outside of his. "Much, much faster. Oh yes, do that again."

His teeth nipped ever so gently on one nipple, causing streaks of fire to radiate outward.

"Octavia, I . . . oh, Lord, you're so soft all over. You're like satin. I'm sorry, sweetheart, I know it's my turn to do you, but I don't think I'm going to be able to last." His hips bucked as he laved his tongue along the underside of my breast, the light stubble on his jaw providing a pleasant friction. I felt proof of his impatience against my belly, hard and hot and demanding.

"That's all right, Jack," I said, kissing him as he slid upward. His lips were sweet, so sweet, and his mouth so hot, it made me burn inside for more. "There will be other times when you can reciprocate the attention. Oh!"

"Oh?" he asked, sliding his hand along my thigh to spread me farther, nestling himself at the source of my heat. "What oh? Or rather, oh what?"

"French Preventative!"

"What?"

"A French Preventative! I'm sorry, but I forgot about that. You don't happen to have one with you?" I asked, aware that my own voice was now rather hopeful.

"A French . . . you mean a condom? Oh, Lord." He quivered at my private area, his muscles tense and tight and poised to plunge inward. My muscles were trembling in anticipation of just such an event. "No, I don't have one."

"Damnation," I swore, wanting to cry with frustration. "I'm sorry, Jack. I didn't think to ask you before we arrived at the pensione. The men I've been with have always had them, so I just didn't think. . . . But all is not lost." I slid out from under him, grabbing for my petticoat. "There is a chemist a scant two blocks from here. I will simply demand that he open up his shop and sell me some French Preventatives—"

"Get back into bed," Jack said, his voice grim as he picked me up and set me back onto the mattress. "I'll get the damned things."

"But you don't know where it is—"

"I'll find it," he said in a voice that was almost a snarl. He yanked on his pants and boots with short, jerky motions.

"But—"

"Stay there, and keep your motor running," he growled, pulling on his shirt.

"My motor? Jack—"

"It's a euphemism," he said, snatching up a handful of coins. "Don't move one muscle. I'll be back in a couple of minutes."

He was gone before I could protest any further.

"What a very odd man," I said to no one as I settled back into the bed. "Keep my motor running. Ha!"

I had just enough time to worry about what might become of a man who was found on the streets of a city under siege before he eventually returned, out of breath, panting, and perspiring. He leaned against the door, his chest heaving, and just as I was about to ask him if he was all right, I heard sounds coming from the street.

"That sounds remarkably like several people running down the road," I said, eyeing him as he doubled over, his hands braced on his knees. "And that sounds like the whistles that the emperor's guards use when they are chasing someone. Say, perhaps, a man who let himself be seen by them?"

He grinned and straightened up, his breathing still rough and fast as he held up a small cardboard box. "Or one who was caught breaking into a drugstore for some emergency condoms."

"Oh, Jack, you didn't break into that nice Signore Martelli's chemist shop," I said, disapproval filling my voice even as I smiled at the sight of the box of French Preventatives. "I'll never be able to face him again."

"I left him all the money I had, so I'm sure that'll reimburse him for damage on the window. Besides, he refused to come down and open up the shop, so it was break the window and get them for myself, or return here and stare at your luscious breasts knowing I can't do anything else. And Octavia, there are many more things I want to do to them than just look."

His voice dropped significantly on that last sentence, which, coupled with the look of molten passion he was giving me as he stripped off his clothing, caused me to shiver in delight. "Yes, but, Jack, this is serious. If the emperor's men find you here—"

"They won't find me. I told you I have some skills in losing tails," he said, crawling slowly up the bed toward me.

I shivered again, and my breasts, impudent beings that they were, thrust forward to him.

"You see?" He paused as he crawled up my legs, his head dipping toward one breast. "Even your tits agree with me. They aren't worried at all about some idiot guards who are out on the streets chasing shadows. They want me to lick them. They want me to hold them, and squeeze them, and rub myself on them."

"Jack!" I squealed as he lay down on top of me. I was under the sheets, with only my breasts bared. "That word is not appropriate."

"What word?" he asked, nuzzling the underside of my left breast. "Oh, tit?"

"Yes. You should refer to a woman's upper parts as a bosom, or, if you must be specific, breasts. But never tit. That word is offensive when not referring to a small bird."

"Ah, but you are a small bird, are you not?" he asked with a decided leer before he turned his attention to my right breast. "That is the vernacular, isn't it?"

"I wouldn't know. I am not the sort of person who hangs out in bars in Marseilles, where such words and terms are bandied about," I said with dignity, moaning only a little when he nibbled on my breast. "Jack, I don't wish to complain, but you are not proceeding properly."

He looked up. "I'm not?"

"No. For one, I'm trapped beneath this sheet, and you are above. For another, we left off with you needing a French Preventative, and now you have one, so you should put it on and we should proceed from where we left off."

"Did it occur to you that a midnight run through a strange city in search of condoms might take the steam out of my engine, so to speak?"

I glanced at the part in question. "Your engine looks fully primed to me."

"That's just because I have you naked in my bed," he said with another leer. "That's enough to stiffen any man's piston."

"Thus you should proceed along the lines we were engaged upon before you left," I pointed out.

He leaned back on one elbow, looking down at me with a curious expression. "You like to be in charge, don't you?"

I blinked at him a couple of times. "I . . . I'm not sure what to say to that. In charge? I like to have things proceed in an orderly fashion, yes, but I don't think I'm domineering or selfish, if that's what you're implying."

"But you do like to call the shots," he said, sliding his hand down my breastbone, pushing the sheet down as he stroked lower, over my belly. "That's a new experience for me. The women I've been with have all been content to let me set the pace."

I felt hurt even as I squirmed under the influence of his questing fingers. "I'm sorry if I am not as passive as your other bed partners—"

"Oh, they weren't passive," he said with another of those devilish grins. This one, however, I wanted to slap off his face. "A couple of them left scratch marks. But they didn't try to give me directions. No, stop looking so offended and outraged. It's nothing bad, Octavia," he added, leaning down to kiss me. "It's just a bit different. Tell you what—we'll take turns. You let me take the lead this time, and you can have it the next time, OK?"

I was momentarily distracted by the heat of his mouth, the sensation of his chest against my breasts, the gentle tickle of his chest hair causing goose bumps to prickle along my arms. "I have no idea what you're talking about, Jack."

"I know," he said, his head dipping down to suck my lower lip. "But that's all right. I'll show you, shall I?"

"Show me what?"

He pushed the rest of the sheet off me, his hand sweeping down my hip, to my thigh. He stared down at my person for a moment before saying, "Thank God you don't wear your corset so tight it damages you. You truly are beautiful, Octavia. You're round and soft, and so silky, I just want to rub my entire body on you."

"I wouldn't be opposed to that," I said, hoping he would stop staring at me and get to the business at hand. Perhaps he needed some encouragement. I wrapped my hand around the aroused part of him.

"Oh, no. You had your turn. Now it's mine," he said, pulling my hand free.

I frowned. "I thought we discussed this earlier? You said you couldn't wait. I can see that you are quite anticipatory right now, so why don't you put on the Preventative, and we can indulge in the natural conclusion of the evening's events."

"Oh, we're going to indulge," he said, moving to sit between my legs. He slid them upward until my knees were over his arms. "Rather, I'm going to indulge you. Just relax, Octavia. You'll enjoy this."

"I always have enjoyed it," I said, watching as he nuzzled private, secret parts of me.

A slightly irritated look crossed his face. "Right, then, we'll get started. Er . . . what time is it?"

I glanced at the clock before looking back at him. "You mean to time this?"

"Why not? You were going to time me."

"Yes, but I had an expensive treatise that I was going to explore with you, not that you gave me much time to do so."

"And how do you know, my fair little pigeon, that I don't have a few tricks up my sleeve?" he asked, his eyes twinkling with lecherous delight. I raised my eyebrows at him. "So to speak," he amended.

"I have no doubt that your numerous acquaintances with women have lessoned you in many ways," I said coolly. "However, unlike you, I will not be so easily pleased. It takes me much longer to reach satisfaction. I don't wish to tell tales, but in the past, it has taxed the stamina of my lovers to get me to that point, and then only after we had known each other for some time. I do not wish to stress you unduly, however, which is why I was—and still am—happy to proceed to the main course, if you will."

"Is that a challenge?" he asked, rearing back, an outraged look on his face.

"What? No! Jack, no, I'm not challenging you, or impugning your masculinity," I said, soothing his obviously ruffled feathers. "My intention was to simply warn you that I am not quite so easily aroused as you obviously are. I didn't wish for you to be disappointed in what is lacking in me."

The angry expression faded until all that was left was heat. Pure, masculine heat. "I don't find you lacking in any way, my little squab of delight. And you haven't had me at the reins. I think you'll find I know what I'm doing."

I was about to tell him I had no doubt of that, but at that moment, he lowered his head and addressed himself to the matter at hand. Instantly, my body was suffused with warmth, a deep, burning warmth that started in my nether parts, and spread in big, rolling waves of pleasure outward to the farthest points on my body. At first, events proceeded as I expected, but then he began using his fingers, stroking me, teasing me, tormenting me until I writhed on the bed in a fever of desire. But when he curled them into me, touching me inside, finding magic parts of me that I had no idea existed, I cried out his name in wonder and amazement.

"Four minutes and twenty seconds."

Slowly, ever so slowly, I drifted down from the cloud of ecstasy and returned to the mortal coil. Jack's laughing eyes and adorable grin were there to greet me.

"Eh?" was all I managed to say. My brain seemed to have ceased functioning, and was having difficulty starting back up.

His grin became even cheekier. "Less than four and a half minutes, my delicious Octavia. I don't mean to cast any slurs on your previous boyfriends, but if they couldn't hang on that long, then they definitely have issues."

"Oh." Cognizant thought finally returned. "That was . . . four minutes, you say? I've never done that in four minutes before. Perhaps it's an anomaly. Perhaps I'm overly tired. No, that would affect me adversely, wouldn't it?" I frowned as I puzzled over this new experience. "Four minutes. I can't believe it. It's always taken me much, much longer to get to that point. Something must be wrong. I wonder if I am ill?"

"You don't feel sick to me," he said, stroking his hand down my hip. My entire body hummed and quivered in response. "You feel like a woman who's been pleasured within an inch of her life."

"You've done something to me," I accused, narrowing my eyes on him. "You've done something odd and foreign to me because you're from elsewhere. That must be it."

He laughed, and kissed my belly. The heat that had been simmering there began to spread again. My legs moved restlessly. "Sweetheart, much as I would like you to think I'm some sort of sexual superhero, I'm just a man who knows what women like. And you aren't the cold fish you seem to think you are—you were moaning and thrashing within seconds of me touching you, so I think you're going to have to let go of that claim, and move on to the one where you beg me to plant myself deep inside you, and make you scream out my name again."

I am a woman who does not take to being ordered around. I prefer to think of my sexual companion as a partner, rather than someone who feels it appropriate to treat me as a mere sexual plaything to be commanded and dictated to. For that reason, I was going to give Jack Fletcher a piece of my mind.

I opened my mouth to do so, and said simply, "Yes, please."

Log of the HIMA *Tesla*
Friday, February 19
Forenoon Watch: Two Bells

"There. What do you think?"

I looked down. "I think I'm wearing my corset on the outside of my blouse."

"Yes. Don't you think it gives you a kind of dashing look? Somewhat devil-may-care? Something that says you're not a slave to convention, that you set your own trends?"

"I think it tells more of a state of mind so confused, I would be safer locked inside an asylum than left to wander the streets with my clothing worn inside out."

"I don't know," Jack said, his head tipped to the side as he considered the bizarre sight I made. "All the steampunk ladies I met wore their corsets outside their clothes. I never once saw one hide hers."

"Whereas I and every other woman of the empire prefer to keep our undergarments hidden," I said, undoing the hooks along the front busk of the corset so I could remove it and redon it in the appropriate manner. "At this time, there are only two people whom I have approved to see me in my corset. You are one."

Rather than give me one of those endearing grins, as I expected, Jack made a face. "And this fabulous Alan who can do anything is the other?"

"Certainly not," I said, pausing for a moment. I decided Jack needed a little reward after having been true to his promise the evening prior. I had yelled out his name again—twice, both times the most amazing experiences of my life. I'd never before thought of myself as a particularly responsive woman, but with Jack, I seemed to go up in flames the minute he touched me. I pulled off my blouse, and handed Jack the corset. "I can do this by myself, but it's easier with a second person. Help me?"

"Who's the other person?" he asked, taking it.

I smiled to myself as he moved behind me, his arms coming around me as he wrapped the corset on my torso. "My corset maker. No, it goes beneath my bosom, not on it."

"Ah. Poor little boobies. Did I squash them?" His hands immediately moved to comfort my breasts, dropping the corset. I leaned back against his bare chest, a little chill of pleasure zipping up my spine at the warmth of his breath on my ear as he caressed me.

"I believe they will forgive your ignorance on the proper method of donning a corset," I murmured, amazed at the speed of my reaction to his touch. One moment I was perfectly myself; the next my mind was full of the most detailed intimate thoughts . . . thoughts of Jack splayed out in front of me, all of his delectable flesh just lying there waiting for me to touch and taste and slide upon it.

I turned my head, letting my lips nibble along his jaw. "Jack—"

He understood the warning. "We don't have time for this."

"No. Not if we are going to have time to reconnoiter before we meet Alan." I turned in his arms, intending on giving him a consolatory kiss before continuing to dress, but somehow, the second my mouth touched his, I lost all thought but one.

"Octavia?" he asked as I pushed him backward, toward the armless chair that sat next to the narrow wardrobe.

"We'll take a cab," I said, my hands on the buttons on his trousers. "It'll save fifteen minutes' walking time."

His eyes lit up. "A quickie? You want a quickie? Right now?"

"I don't know that term, but assuming it means what I think it means, then yes, I want a quickie," I said, pushing him on the shoulder. He sat down abruptly, his trousers gaping open, his hands on my waist as I hoisted up my skirt and petticoat, and settled myself on his thighs.

"Dear God, woman, you don't know what this means to me. I've always been a big fan of quickies, and ever since we got out of bed, all I could think about was making love to you againnrn."

His eyelids flickered shut as I sank down on him, my intimate self embracing and welcoming his intrusion. "Too much talking, Jack," I said, gasping as I felt him deep inside me. "Thank heavens you are so quick to arouse. I wasn't sure if you would be ready for me, but there you are, quite obviously so. A bit more ready than I expected, to be honest. Merciful saints, I can't believe you can do that. Do it again!"

He flexed his hips again, his head lolled back so I could kiss his throat and adorable face, his fingers gentle but persistent on my breasts as they teased and stroked them. "You're trying to take charge again, Octavia."

I bit his lip as I moved on him, the rhythm neither

slow nor gentle, but one driven by the intense need inside me that I knew he shared. "You said we would take turns. I am having my turn. Do it again."

He laughed, but flexed again, touching me in that magical way he had that made my eyes cross with pleasure. "You had your turn earlier this morning. Now we're back to my turn to be the boss, and I say do that swivel thing you did earlier."

I rose up until just the tip of him was gripped, then slid down him again, swiveling my hips and gripping as hard as I could with intimate muscles. He sucked in his breath, his eyes snapping open, his breath coming hard and fast. "One more like that and it'll be all over."

I tightened my thighs around his hips, the rough material of his trousers rubbing against my sensitive flesh, our bodies moving together in a way that was familiar and yet foreign to me, as if he were a stranger that I had known in a previous lifetime. He pulled my head down to capture my cry of completion in his mouth, his fingers urging me on as he found his own moment of ecstasy.

It was at that moment I realized that we had forgotten the French Preventative.

"Octavia, I can't stand this cold treatment. I said I was sorry. I didn't think you were going to fling yourself on me, so I wasn't . . . er . . . ready to go, so to speak."

I pulled myself out of the reverie that had claimed me and looked across the cab at Jack. "You're sorry about what?"

He frowned. "What do you think? You've been sitting there pouting because I forgot the damned condom earlier, and I don't know what else to say other than I won't leave you if you get pregnant because of it."

"Pregnant? Oh. I suppose that's possible, yes," I said,

considering that idea. "I don't think it's likely to happen, though."

"You're not worried about getting pregnant?" Jack asked, looking confused. He ran his hand through his hair, a gesture that always threatened to make my knees turn to jelly. I realized then that he had taken my silence as condemnation regarding the earlier comment I made about the Preventative. I moved over to his seat, tenderly pushing back the lock of hair he had dislodged down onto his forehead.

"No, although I appreciate the fact that you thought I was. I am very au courant with scientific studies, you know, including those by female doctors. I do not believe that I am currently in a fertile time of the month, although I've heard it is best to be safe, thus the Preventatives. Also, they are beneficial in guarding one's health in other ways. I thought you understood that. They are for your protection, as well, you know, although I do not have any illnesses that I'm aware of. Still—"

"You don't have to give me a birth control lecture," he interrupted, pulling me across him for a fast kiss. "And I can assure you that I'm STD free, as well, although I suppose we should probably keep using those condoms, even if it is strange seeing ones with little ribbons on the ends to tie them on. I shudder to think what they're made of, though."

"Sheep gut, I imagine. What are your Preventatives made from?"

"Latex," he said, a slow smile coming to his face. "Now, there's another fortune waiting to happen. I wonder if I could manufacture some here?"

I said nothing, my thoughts returning to the upcoming meeting with Alan.

Jack prattled on for a few more minutes, before suddenly squeezing me. "You're doing it again."

"I am not worried about becoming pregnant," I said.

"Then why are you ignoring me? You've got a distant look in your eyes like you're trying to forget I'm sitting next to you."

I was about to make a sharp retort when I saw the uncertainty in his eyes. I leaned over him, instead, licking his lips. "I assure you, Mr. Fletcher, I very much enjoy you sitting next to me."

His lips curled into a smile as I nibbled on the corners of his mouth. "I love how your eyes go all soft and shadowy when you flirt with me. If you weren't being pissed at me, what were you thinking about?"

I sat back, sighing ever so softly. "Alan."

"Oh. Him."

"Don't even think of doing that," I said, pointing my finger at his face.

He rearranged his expression from one of martyrdom to that of outrage. "Doing what?"

"Pretending that you're inferior to him. You are my lover, Jack, not him. Not anymore. If I had wanted Alan, I would still be with him, but I don't. I can't help that he's still a very dear friend, one who is in a position to help us."

Jack struggled with his pride for a moment, but eventually he slumped back against the seat of the cab. "Dammit." He suddenly stiffened up again, his eyes narrowing. "Just so he knows that you're with me, and that he's not looking to start anything with you again."

"I'm sure he won't give me a second thought beyond doing what we ask him to do," I said, turning my attention to the streets as we drove toward the square where earlier that morning we had arranged to meet Alan. I bit my lip, mentally going over the things I could say, and what would best be left unspoken.

The rest of the ride was thankfully in silence, Jack refraining from asking me exactly what I was mulling over. I was growing increasingly uncomfortable with the fact that there were secrets to be kept from him, necessary secrets, but still, my emotions concerning Jack were beginning to take on a depth and breadth that I had not anticipated.

It is the sheerest folly to have anything for him but mild affection, I lectured myself as we rolled along the now-quiet streets of Rome. *To feel anything else will only cause heartache and ultimately sorrow. Be content with a physical relationship, and don't look for anything that cannot be.*

I was still warning myself against the folly of errant emotions when we reached our meeting point. Alan's carriage was waiting, the imperial insignia on the door alerting all who saw it that the occupant was there on the emperor's business.

"Jack," I said as we paid off the cab. I eyed him, unsure of how to put into words that which I wanted to say.

Alan stepped out of his carriage and waved. I waved back.

Jack took my hand, glowered for a moment toward Alan, then, out of the blue, confused me by grinning. "This is kind of like meeting your parents, huh?"

"What is?" I asked as he tugged me forward, toward where Alan awaited us.

"Meeting the former boyfriend. Don't worry, sweetheart. I won't embarrass you. I won't growl and snap and be all he-man around your buddy. What happened before we met doesn't matter, does it?"

"I wouldn't go so far as that," I said, casting a worried glance at him, quickly rearranging my expression to be one reflecting more pleasant thoughts as Alan greeted us.

"Octavia, my dove, you look exquisite as ever," he said, bowing low over my hands.

"So that's how it's going to be, eh?" I murmured softly as he kissed my knuckles.

The look he shot me was filled with purest mischief.

"Yes, she does look exquisite, every blessed inch of her," Jack agreed, wrapping one arm around my waist and pulling me up to his side. "As I noted this morning, when I was helping her put on her corset."

"Subtlety isn't your strong point, is it, Jack?" I asked, giving him a gimlet eye.

Alan looked from me to him for a moment, before bursting into loud and very amused laughter. "I can see it's not. Jack, is it? How d'ye do. Alan Dubain."

Jack took the hand Alan offered and shook it. "Jack Fletcher. And you were worried we weren't going to be civilized about this, Octavia."

I narrowed my lips at him.

"I am frequently very uncivilized when it comes to Octavia, but I am pleased to know she has found a lover at last. I have been worried about her these last three years. She has been working so hard, she has not had time to enjoy herself in that way."

"God grant me patience," I murmured, casting my eyes upward, and indulging in a general damnation on lovers old and new.

"That's a long time for a woman to go without a man to keep her happy," Jack said, nodding his head in agreement.

"Oh, for heaven's sake—," I started to say.

"Especially a woman of Octavia's appetites," Alan said in a conspiratorial tone.

"Right. That's enough! Cease this conversation immediately. We have more important things to do than discuss my sexual well-being. This just encourages Jack in possessive behavior, and I think we can all do without that."

"Thus sayeth the woman who knows nothing of possessiveness?" Alan asked, his dark eyes lit with a teasing light I knew well.

I glared at him.

"Is she really?" Jack asked, considering me. "I had no idea. So, what would you do if I walked over to that flower seller and kissed her?"

"Bid you good riddance," I growled, ignoring the two men to climb into Alan's carriage. I gritted my teeth against their manly laughter, cursing the ill luck that not only threw Jack and his blighted sister into my lap but entangled me with the former in ways that I was beginning to fear.

Alan sat across from us as the carriage drove to the palace, his gaze alternating between Jack and myself. His appearance was as familiar to me as my own, his bronzed skin just as warm and glowing as I remembered it, his laughing eyes almost as black as the crown of shining black hair that he wore just a smidgen too long for a gentleman. His grin was not as infectious as Jack's, but it held a true warmth that I never failed to appreciate. He spoke in a drawling, languid manner common to the upper classes, but there was nothing slow about the mind behind the eyes that danced with secret mirth.

"He seems nice enough," Jack said fifteen minutes later when we stood in the lobby of the palace while Alan was speaking with a tiresome official who refused to let us pass. "I retract my earlier concern about him wanting to make a play for you. It's clear that he is what you said he is—a friend and nothing more. He doesn't seem very diplomatic, though. Not at all what I expected from someone on an ambassadorial staff. You sure he's going to be able to get Hallie free?"

"Don't allow yourself to be misled by his lighthearted appearance," I said slowly, watching Alan as he first reasoned, then joked with the official. "There is substantially more to him than what you see on the surface."

"Wise words in general," Jack acknowledged, taking my arm when Alan turned toward us and waved us forward.

"I have the utmost confidence in you, Octavia, but I think in this situation it would be best to let me handle the vice-provost," Alan told us a few minutes later as we walked down the long hallway to a suite of offices. "I am equally confident that Jack will understand the necessity to allow me to be the one to make inquiries about his sister, since I gather his presence here is not with any form of official sanction."

"What did you tell him about us?" Jack whispered in my ear as Alan strode ahead of us.

"Nothing other than you do not have official status within the empire."

"An outlaw, do you mean? Well, that's certainly close enough to the truth. Although—you don't think he's going to think I'm one of your revolutionaries?"

I hushed him, giving the guards at attention nearest us a worried glance. "It doesn't matter what he thinks you are so long as he helps us."

Jack had nothing to say to that, so we proceeded after Alan in silence, waiting patiently while an officious secretary fussed over Alan's request for a few minutes before sweeping open a set of French doors and gesturing us into a grand office where an equally officious man sat dwarfed by a huge white-and-gilt desk.

"Your Excellency, Ambassador Dubain seeks an audience with you," the secretary said, bowing and groveling as we entered.

"Yes, yes, I know all about that," the doughy man behind the desk said, his bare head shiny with perspiration despite the early hour. "I have the ambassador's letter here. It is a matter of state, I believe you said?"

"A trivial matter, I assure you," Alan said, donning his most persuasive voice. "But one, alas, that I must trouble you with."

The vice-provost barely cast a glance toward us, his shiny red face expressing dyspepsia and irritation as he gestured loftily toward Alan. "The ambassador will understand that my time is limited, what with this royal wedding almost upon us."

"The matter concerns Captain Octavia Pye," Alan said, waving a hand toward me. "Captain Pye is the commander of one of His Imperial Majesty's airships, and was the ward of a great favorite of the late emperor. She is of much value to Emperor William, as well as to the empire as a whole."

The vice-provost, whose oily glance had barely touched me, returned, this time with a glint of speculation in it. I lifted my chin and endeavored to look of great value.

"Just so," the provost said, his gaze flickering back to Alan. His fingers drummed impatiently on the table.

"Captain Pye has unfortunately lost one of her crew members, a lady, in what can only be described as a farce of miscommunication. The lady in question was mistakenly detained by imperial guards yesterday afternoon—"

"Name?" the provost interrupted, shuffling through a stack of cards.

Alan smiled. "Hallelujah Norris."

"Charged as a spy. Trial is two days hence. Deportation to England for execution on the following day," the man said in a bored voice before casually tossing the cards down onto the desk and picking up a sheet of paper.

"Execution!" Jack said, starting forward. I grasped him firmly by the arm, tightening my fingers in silent warning to let Alan handle the situation.

"That's what we do with spies," the provost said without looking up from his paper. "We don't normally send them to England, but the emperor wants a big display to be made the day of the wedding. Just more work for me, that's what it is, but does anyone think of that?" He looked up at that, narrowing his eyes on Jack. "Who're you?"

"This is another of my crew," I said quickly. "Mr. Jack Fletcher is an engineer. He came out on the *Tesla* with us, and is naturally very worried about his fellow crewmate. I can assure you that Miss Norris is not a spy."

"No more than I am," Jack growled.

Both Alan and I shot him a look of warning that thankfully he took to heart.

"You can understand how distressed Captain Pye and her crew will be to hear of this travesty," Alan said smoothly. "Since there is to be a trial, perhaps we will be able to speak on her behalf, and clear up any misunderstanding there has been regarding the identity and purpose of the lady in question."

"Trials are closed to the public," the sweaty man replied, picking his teeth for a moment before glancing up, his face tight with irritation. "As you ought to know. If there's nothing else, Ambassador, I'm a very busy man. I've nothing but work to do while you lot gad about at balls and routs, having your way with Italian princesses and such. Some of us have to work, you know! I've got all those trials to get through, and a half-dozen prisoners to ship back to England, all on the emperor's whim."

Beside me, Jack tensed.

"Sir," I said hastily, fearing what Jack might do or say. "If we could just speak with Miss Norris, it would relieve our minds—"

"Out of the question," he answered, sourly shoving away from his desk and yelling for the secretary. "Benson! Where the devil is my brandy?"

"Don't," I murmured to Jack as he strained toward the man. "You'll just end up in gaol with her, and then where will we be?"

I could feel his hesitation as I tugged him out of the room while Alan, in true diplomatic style, mouthed pleasantries and thanks that were certainly not deserved.

Jack managed to hang on to his temper until we reached the relative safety of Alan's carriage, at which point he exploded in a veritable cloud of profanity and outrageous demands.

"We have to go back in there and get her!" he repeated after the worst of the storm passed. "I'll be damned if I let my sister be executed just because she was standing in a square looking at a fountain! I'll be damned if I let her be executed for any reason! Dammit, Octavia, we have to do something."

"And we will," I said in my best soothing manner. "Alan, do you think it's worthwhile going over that repulsive man's head?"

"No. Tewksbury is a slimy slug on the underbelly of

the empire, but there's nothing I can do to force him to give us access to Jack's sister."

"What about the trial?" I asked, a sick, damp feeling clutching my belly. "Can you pull diplomatic strings to speak there? Or allow me to do so?"

"I'll look into it, but I don't hold out much hope," he said, shaking his head.

Jack's expression turned mutinous. "I am not going to sit by and let your precious emperor kill my sister as part of his wedding celebrations. We have to do something! What if we got that Etienne and his people to help us storm the palace?"

Alan's eyebrows went up.

I thought about Jack's suggestion for a moment before sighing. "No, there are simply too many guards even for the Black Hand."

"Maybe we could get in touch with that Moghul guy, the one who tried to steal your cargo. I bet he could bring down the palace."

Alan laughed. "Don't think he hasn't tried. Emperor William is well aware that the palace is a target of both the Black Hand and the Moghuls, and has seen to it that it is well protected."

"Damn."

"If we can't get her out of the palace because it's too well guarded," I said slowly, "we'll just have to free her after she's taken out of there."

"You don't want to wait until she's taken into prison in Newgate, once she's in England," Alan mused aloud. "It'll be just as impossible to get her out of there as it would be the palace here."

"We'll have to get her out en route," I agreed. "No doubt they'll use one of the troop-transport airships to take the prisoners back to England for the wedding executions."

"There is that," Jack said slowly. "Do you think you could get a job on the ship, Octavia?"

"It's doubtful. Not only will the transport ship likely have its full complement of crew already; the Southampton Aerocorps is still investigating the incident at the aerodrome yesterday, and I will not be allowed to fly in an official capacity until my status has been cleared."

"Damn."

"Alan, is there any way you could get me on the transport ship?" I asked.

He shook his head almost immediately. "Not in any way that would be useful. Besides, it would be dangerous for you."

"Dangerous? Oh . . ." I stopped, not daring to look at Jack. Unease rose again within me at the deception I was keeping from him. I sent a pleading look to Alan, but his expression was inscrutable as ever.

"That was a loaded 'oh.' What did you mean by it?" Jack asked.

I looked at him, mute, wanting to explain, but unable to risk exposing Alan if he felt the situation was not wise.

"I see," Jack said, withdrawing from me. Hurt flashed in his eyes, and I wanted to reach out and reassure him that it was nothing to do with him personally. "There are things you can say to your old friend, but not a new lover. Got it."

"Jack—" I stopped, impotent. Ire swept through me as I glared at Alan.

Alan said nothing, just watched us both.

"That's fine. Don't worry about me," Jack continued, looking out the window. "Clearly you have things to talk about that you can't say in front of me. I'll get out as soon as the carriage stops and let you have some privacy."

"Alan!" I growled, narrowing my glare on him until it could have cut iron.

He sighed and made a half shrug. "Very well, but let this be on your own head. The reason it would be dangerous for Octavia to go on the transport ship in order to rescue your sister is because she—your sister—is suspected of being a member of the Black Hand. If Octavia attempts to free her and fails, her involvement with the revolutionaries will be uncovered."

"You know Octavia is a member of the revolutionary group?" Jack asked, his pained expression thankfully fading. I took his hand, uncaring if Alan saw the gesture.

Alan said nothing. Jack turned from him to me. I raised my eyebrows.

"Holy shit. You mean he's a member, too?" Jack pointed at Alan. "But he's an ambassador!"

"There are people in all walks of life who desire to see an end to the current status of the empire," I said nonchalantly. "Naturally, Alan's involvement is known only to a very few people."

"I hope your trust is not misplaced," Alan said, giving me a warning look.

"I'd be offended by that, but I'm all too aware of the fact that you don't know me like Tavy does," Jack said, squeezing my hand. "I can keep a secret. And yes, I agree she can't go on the transport ship."

"Which means we'll have to get her off it by some other means," I said, drawing my attention away from the stroke of Jack's thumb along my fingers, and on to the issue of his sister. "We could target the confusion that happens during takeoff or landing, but there are bound to be too many guards around at either time."

"You'll have to do it en route, then," Alan said.

Jack looked up, his eyes bright. Something that I can only describe as an unholy glee lit within them, making both the green and brown eyes shine. "You know what that means, don't you, Tavy?"

I slumped back against the plush leather cushions of Alan's carriage as I realized just that very thing.

"What?" Alan asked, looking from him to me and back again.

"Octavia's just a bit disconcerted because she's about to become that epitome of steampunk adventurers."

I sighed heavily, and wished I was a good thousand miles away from this spot.

"And what's that?" Alan asked, puzzled.

Jack grinned.

"Don't say it," I snapped. "There has to be another way."

"There isn't. You said yourself that there wasn't."

I sighed again. Brought low by my own words—how mortifying.

"What are you two talking about?" Alan asked, leaning forward to pin us back with a questioning look.

"Mr. Dubain," Jack said, making a bow from where he sat next to me, donning the air of one presenting someone to an august personage. "Ambassador to the emperor William whatever-number-he-is."

"Oh, God," I moaned, and dropped my forehead to my hands. "This can't be happening."

"What is happening?" Alan demanded. "Why is Octavia groaning?"

"May I present to you Miss Octavia Pye, captain of the prestigious airship *Tesla* . . ."

"Octavia, has your lover gone mad? What is he blathering about?"

"Just kill me now and be done with it," I moaned.

". . . and now, beloved to steampunk fans the world over, that most dread of all persons . . ."

I looked up and glared at Jack as he leaned to the side and kissed the tip of my nose. "I'm not going to forget this. Just so you know."

". . . a bad-to-the-bone, genuine, one hundred percent pure airship pirate."

"Gah!" I yelled.

Alan looked thoughtful.

Log of the HIMA *Tesla*
Saturday, February 20
First Watch: Five Bells

"That's everything, I think," I said, closing the door to my cabin before sinking exhaustedly onto my bunk. "I've talked with the crew, stowed what stores we will need for the flight home, and checked the envelopes for wear. Everything is as shipshape as it can be."

Jack looked up from where he sat at the small desk that was bolted along one wall of my cabin. He raised a sandy eyebrow. I had an almost overwhelming urge to stroke the brow. "You don't sound very happy."

I considered my hands. "I don't like lying to my crew."

"Which is why I suggested you let me do it." Jack set down his pen. "I'm sorry, sweetheart. When we first talked about this plan, I didn't think about what it would mean to you. We don't have to go forward with it. We can find some way to save Hallie once she's in England."

"It will only be harder there," I said, shaking my head. "Infinitely harder. And I appreciate you offering to speak to the crew on my behalf, but I am still the captain of this ship—at least, until the Corps discovers that I have falsified flying authorization, stolen one of their airships, and turned to piracy—and I will perform my duties to the best of my abilities so long as I have them."

"You're throwing away your career because of Hallie," he said softly. "You won't be given a command of your own after this, will you?"

"The Black Hand has a couple of airships they've stolen. With luck, I will take over control of one of them," I answered. "Much as I appreciate your sympathy, I don't see any real sense in dwelling on the decision—it was necessary, and I made it."

Jack's face was filled with guilt, the knowledge that I was giving up my career showing as stark pain in his eyes. "I should never have allowed you to go ahead with this plan."

I got to my feet, dusting off my skirt, which was a bit smudged with dirt after I had scaled the scaffolding that surrounded the envelopes. "Now you are being presumptuous and arrogant. I am in control of my life, Mr. Fletcher, not you. Have you finished with your tasks? I have only the autonavigator to deal with; then I will be able to help you with anything else that needs doing."

"Almost. I was just going over the to-do list. You said you saw to the boilers?" he asked, his pen poised over an item on a lengthy list.

"Yes, both checking and filling, although Alan and I were almost seen pumping the water into them. Luckily, we saw the guard before he saw us, and we pretended to embrace in order to throw him off."

The look of pain faded slowly. One side of his mouth curled up. "Is that supposed to make me jealous? Because if it is, you're going to have to work harder than that. You'd have to say something like he had his hands down your corset and was tweaking your nipples the way that makes you squirm and beg for more in order to get a rise out of me. Or if he suddenly realized what a delectable hunk of woman he let get away from him all those years ago, and decided to fix that by pinning you against a wall, hoisting up your skirts, wrapping your legs around his hips, and plunging deep inside your heat, burying himself over and over into you, feeling every single one of your muscles tighten around him until he lost all control. Something along those lines might do it."

I stared at him, the images he was painting dancing in my mind—but with an obvious substitution. "Against the wall, Jack? One can . . . that is, I suppose there is no reason not to, but it strikes me as a wholly uncomfortable . . . with my legs around your hips? While standing? Goodness. The treatise never mentioned that."

He grinned and dropped the pen he was using to cross off an item on a long list. "I'm glad you automatically put me in there rather than Alan. Yes, it can be done that way. Both parties have to have some strength and flexibility, but it's doable. Would you like to try it?"

"Now?" I asked, glancing around the cabin, my brain a whirl of desire and need and the realization that I was fast losing all control of my baser self when around Jack. "This moment?"

"Tempting as you are, I suppose we should wait until I've finished my work with the engines. But when I'm done, my fair Octavia, then I shall show you a few things that your precious treatise didn't think of."

"The treatise was supposed to be comprehensive," I said, frowning. "If there are indeed gaps in its coverage, then I shall request my money back."

Jack laughed and gave me a look that made me feel as if he'd laced my corset too tight that morning. "There's nothing like hands-on experience, I've always said. Not that I want to change the subject, but is Alan staying on board tonight?"

"No. He has an embassy dinner to attend, and then he will meet with Etienne and confirm the plans for tomorrow. He also wishes to stay close to the vice-provost in case the prisoner-transport plans change."

"They'd better not, not after busting our respective asses for the last two days covertly getting your ship ready to fly. What time did you tell your crew to meet you here?"

"Six bells."

His forehead furrowed.

"Seven o'clock in the morning," I translated the time. "I told them to be prompt, as we would leave as soon as possible. They will not expect to be ready for immediate takeoff, but I'll simply tell them that the Aerocorps had the ship readied."

"You're sure there are no ships coming in at that time?"

I shook my head. "I asked the director of the aerodrome most specifically, pretending I was interested in a ship leaving for England, and he said there were no arrivals expected until after the wedding. There won't be but a few Corps members about at that time in the morning. The chances that one of my crew will find anyone to mention our departure are very slight."

"Excellent. All is going according to plan, Octavia. Now if I can just finish up the items on my list, I can turn my fullest attention to showing you that in matters of lovemaking nothing can beat practical experience for learning opportunities."

My body warmed at the look he gave me. "I will just go check that the rest of the stores are in place."

"That's a mighty pretty blush you have going there, sweetheart. Can it be that you're indulging in a few fantasies about me?"

"About you?" I paused at the door, straightened my shoulders, and gave him my most quelling look. "Sir, you flatter yourself. You are a scoundrel and a rogue, and I would never waste a blush on someone of your ilk."

"While you're the sexiest airship pirate who ever planned a daring midair rescue, and I can't wait to spread your thighs and—"

I shut the door rather abruptly, fanning myself for a moment before proceeding down the walkway, the muffled sound of Jack's laughter following me.

"I have never in my life met such a man as you," I murmured as I entered the mess, heading for the galley beyond. "The things you do to me . . ."

"Glorious one! You wish for your Francisco to do the things most extraordinary to you? *Madre de Dios!* I thought the day would never come, but me, I am patient, and for you I knew it must not be unneeded that your hair of the most flaming color was for me."

I whirled around at the first sound of the voice, clutching my Disruptor. "Mr. Francisco! What on earth are you doing here now? Didn't you understand that we are not leaving until tomorrow morning?"

A shadow from the galley formed into that of a man. His eyes examined me in a leisurely fashion that more or less stripped my clothing from my person. "*Sí*, but me, I am the steward most fabulous, am I not? You say that you arrange for the stores to be brought on board ship for me, but there are many little things, spicy things, things that will make you sweat and moan with pleasure when you taste them, these things only I can see to."

"I told you earlier today that I would be happy to attend to anything you needed for the trip home," I said sternly. There would be fewer guards with all airships but the *Tesla* and the transport ship gone, but I did not want to take a chance that one of those left to guard against attacks saw stores being delivered to the ship. Alan and I had worked very hard all day making sure that the copious deliveries that had been made had not drawn attention. If Francisco went and ruined everything now, I would have his hide. "I thought I made it quite clear that all of the crew were to enjoy one last night of leave before we hurry home for the emperor's wedding."

He shrugged. "But you are here, my most fiery one. And now you want me in the manner of the bull to a cow, yes?"

I blinked for a couple seconds and was about to disabuse him of such a notion when a voice behind me said, "If I am de trop, I will be happy to leave."

I whirled around, glancing at the door directly to the side of me. I pointed at it, glaring. "Mr. Llama! That door did not open!"

Both men looked at the door for a moment before returning to me.

"Don't give me that look! I *know* it didn't open. I'm all of two yards away from it, and I would have noticed if it opened. And it didn't. And there was no one in the mess when I entered it. So just where, my elusive Mr. Llama, did you come from, hmm?"

Mr. Llama had the nerve to look surprised. "Where did I come from, Captain?"

"Yes! Where? As in, how did you get into this room without me seeing you enter?"

"What's all the noise about, Tavy—oh . . . uh . . ." The

door opened and Jack stood in the doorway, looking startled. "Er . . ."

Mr. Francisco spat out a word that was not at all polite. "What is he doing here, beloved *capitán* of my hair? I thought we had left him behind, but then he is here with the revolutionaries. Why did they not take him? Why did they not cut out his heart and cook it in a tomato sauce with garlic, olive oil, and just a hint of bacon?"

"I'm back. And for the record, Octavia's hair and all the rest of her is mine, so you can just keep your lecherous eyes and whatever else is bulging out of you to yourself," Jack said, looking askance at Mr. Francisco's very tight, completely nonregulation breeches.

"I would object to such a wholesale dismissal of my personal rights, but I have more important battles to fight at the moment," I told him with a little frown before turning back to Francisco. "As it is, you must leave the . . . where is Mr. Llama?"

"Who?" Jack asked, looking around.

"Dammit!" I whirled around, grinding my teeth at the audacity of the man. "He's done it again!"

"Sweetheart, I think you're starting to get a fixation on the poor man," Jack said, giving me a long look.

By some miracle, I held my temper, but I swore to myself that I would get to the bottom of the Mr. Llama mystery by the time we landed in London. "Mr. Francisco," I said, breathing heavily through my nose. "Please leave the *Tesla*. Return here tomorrow at six bells. I will take care of any foodstuffs that you require."

"Why should I leave?" he asked, pouting even as he glared at Jack. "The one who claims your hair most fabulous is his, he will stay, but I, your most devoted servant, your slave, your worshipper, I must leave? No. It will not be. I will not allow it."

"You will leave, because I say you will," I answered, shoving him toward the door.

He resisted, his gaze narrowing on Jack. "I will not leave you with that one. He is not to be trusted. You set him down, and he returns! It is clearly that he has bad thoughts on his brains for your hair. I will not forsake you, my glorious one."

"Not only will you forsake me, you will do so right now," I said even more forcefully, putting all my weight into the act of shoving him out of the mess.

He grabbed at the doorframe. "But why should I leave when the others stay?"

I stopped shoving. "What others? Don't tell me more of the crew came on board early?"

He shrugged. "It is not for me to become the tail of tattling."

"Damnation," I swore, then slammed shut the door to the mess, and slid the bolt home before looking at Jack. "Others have come on board."

"I heard. There goes double-checking the engines."

"And setting the course for the autonavigator."

"And having wild, unbridled sex up against the wall."

My breath got caught in my chest at the look in his eyes. I cleared my throat and tried to focus on what was important. "Indeed. Well. I suppose I should go see who ignored my orders and came on board a day early. And then if there's time, I will check the autonavigator in case Mr. Christian decides to attend to his duties. He means well, but he's appalling when it comes to plotting a course and directing it to the navigator. I asked him to oil the navigator's engine shortly before you and your sister came on board, and had to spend three hours correcting the course and slipping the gears back into their proper channels. Are you sure that people do it standing up? What about balance?"

Jack grinned, and took a step toward me. "Want me to show you?"

My brain, recently having proven itself unreliable where Jack was concerned, agreed most emphatically with his suggestion, but luckily the rest of my person realized that there were more important things to do, and I unbolted the door and slipped through it before he could make good his offer.

A slight figure disappeared down the end of the corridor. "Dooley! What are you doing here?"

The lad popped his head around the corner. "Hullo, Cap'n. Mr. Piper sent me to the ship to check that all the stores were tidy-like in the hold."

"He's not here?" I asked, relieved. That would be one less person to get out from underfoot.

"No, Cap'n. He said he was going to his favorite brothel to bend one of the ladies over his capstan, and have her scrape the rusticles off his bollocks."

I absorbed that news with the silence I felt it was due.

Dooley picked his ear. "He sent me here, instead."

"Indeed. Well, at least someone had the good sense to do as I asked and not come to the *Tesla* early," I grumbled as I caught the lad by his jacket and shooed him down the passage ahead of me. "Go back to the pensione. The stores are all properly assembled in the rear hold. You may assure Mr. Piper of that when he is done having his rusticles scraped."

"But, Cap'n," the lad protested as I shoved him one step at a time down the gangway to the ground.

"Shoo. Begone. Go enjoy your last evening in Rome. I will see you at six bells."

"Cap'n, Mr. Piper'll have my dillywhacker if I don't—"

I gave him a look that probably frightened a good three years off him. "You'll lose more than your personal equipment if you don't do as I say!"

His shoulders slumped as he nodded, and shuffled off. I reentered the ship, my gaze honed to razor sharpness as I hunted down the other members of my crew. Mr. Ho I found in her cabin, putting away her clothing in a footlocker. "Mr. Ho," I said in my most disappointed tone.

She gave me a level look. "Captain Pye."

A silence grew, a rather uncomfortable silence.

"I am sorry to see you here. I had assumed you would be cherishing your last night in such a romantic city."

"I fully intend to avail myself of the city as soon as I'm through setting my things to right," she said evenly. There was a pause that was even more uncomfortable than the previous one. "I realize it is none of my business, Captain, but I could not help but notice that your bed in our shared accommodations has not been disturbed since we arrived."

"Oddly enough, I was about to remark the same about your bed," I said, lifting my chin.

She nodded an acknowledgment of that, and allowed herself a little smile. "I have greatly enjoyed our leave here."

"As have I."

"Then we are in harmony on such matters," she said rather stiffly.

"We are. You will leave the *Tesla* as soon as you have finished here?" I couldn't help but ask.

"I had wanted to make myself available to you," she said slowly, her eyes curiously examining me. "But if you have no need of me, then I shall do as you suggest."

"Everything is under control. Enjoy your last evening here," I said, closing the door and releasing a breath I hadn't known I'd been holding. There was something about Mr. Ho that simultaneously relieved me and worried me, but I couldn't for the life of me pinpoint just what.

Mr. Mowen was just coming on board when I headed for the forward cargo hold. It took some doing, but I managed to convince him that all was well with the ship, and that he needn't check anything before the morning.

I poked my head into the now empty hold after getting rid of him, just to double-check that nothing was awry, and was startled to find it occupied.

"Titties of the virgin!" Mr. Piper exclaimed as I popped into the room. He clutched his chest and staggered a couple of feet to a chair that was bolted to the floor next to the door. "Ye damn near scared the hair right off me balls jumpin' in on me like that!"

"Mr. Piper," I said, hands on my hips. "I thought you were off having your rusticles scraped! What are you doing here?"

His startled expression melted into one of smug masculine pleasure. "Aye, Captain, that I was. I went t'see Two-Guinea Tandy, finest whore in all of Italy. She's got muscles in her Suez Canal that can grip a man like a pair of hands. Fair stripped the foreskin right off me rod, they did, the first time I had her. Scared me 'alf to death until she told me that she's known far and wide for her ability to milk a man without layin' so much as a finger on him."

"Mr. Piper," I said firmly, straightening my shoulders and giving him a look that I hoped he read with great accuracy. "I am not interested in your leisure-time activities except so far as they concern you being on the *Tesla* when you are supposed to be elsewhere. You have the rest of the evening free, so I suggest you go back to your friend and allow her to ... er ... grip you again."

"But, Captain," he said, lifting a wan hand. "Once ye've been milked by Two-Guinea Tandy, yer cods is drained dry. There be'nt any use in me goin' to see her again. Not until twenty-four hours has passed to allow me sacs to refill."

"Surely a man of your lusty appetite can find something to do with Tandy," I said, pulling him to his feet.

"Nay, Captain. 'Tis the truth I'm tellin' ye. Look, I'll show ye—here're me tallywags. See how they just hang there, swayin' ever so forlornly in the wind, like a pair of empty plums?"

Before I could stop him, Mr. Piper dropped his trousers and pulled up the front of his shirt, gesturing toward his groin. I averted my gaze immediately, but not before getting sight of that which I hoped never to see again.

"Have ye ever in yer life seen a pair of cods as drained?" he demanded, prodding at himself. "I couldn't mount a flight of stairs, let alone a whore as demanding as Tandy be, not without givin' me clappers time to recover."

"How goes the—what the hell is going on here?"

I whirled around at the sound of Jack's outraged voice. "Oh. Jack. Um ... I found Mr. Piper."

"So I see," Jack said, glaring at the bosun. "What's he doing exposing himself to you? That's what I'd like to know."

"The captain didn't believe me when I told her that Two-Guinea Tandy had drained me oysters dry," Mr. Piper said, gesturing once again toward his crotch. "But ye be a man of the world, and ye'll be able to tell her the truth in what I say. Er ..." Mr. Piper thankfully hiked up his trousers, squinting at Jack as he did up the buttons. "If ye don't mind me askin', didn't we leave ye off outside of Rome a few days ago?"

"Yes. I'm back." Jack gave me a look that had me clearing my throat. "I assume you are finished showing the captain your nuts? Good. If you don't mind, I need her to look at something."

"Oh, aye?" Mr. Piper looked speculatively at me before leaning toward Jack and saying in what was supposed to be a confidential tone, "I wouldn't be showin' her yer middle leg and baubles just yet, lad. She looks to be in a right mood, and the ladies, they need a bit of sweet-talking before they welcome ye to fix their plumbin'."

I rubbed my forehead as Mr. Piper, with a wink at Jack, and a leer at me, staggered off to parts unknown. "In a way, I shall miss the crew. But on the other hand, the thought of having a normal crew, one that does not possess individuals who can disappear and reappear at will, and a bosun obsessed with all things sexual, is strangely attractive. What is it you wanted to see me about? I assume it wasn't to show me your—" I waved toward his fly.

"Not until later, no. Your chief officer is here. He . . . uh . . . took exception to finding me in the navigation room, and seemed convinced that I was holding you captive, and that it was his duty to alert the authorities."

"Oh, no." I bolted from the room, heading down the corridor to the spiral stairs leading up to the small navigation room housing the machinery that piloted the airship, Jack right on my heels. "You didn't let him leave, did you?"

"You should know me better than that," Jack said,

grabbing my arm as I charged up the stairs and reached for the door to the navigation room. "Tavy, I should warn you—it looks a lot worse than it really is."

I opened the door, looked in, then closed it quietly again.

"Jack."

He winced at the expression in my eyes. "I can explain."

"I should hope so." I took a deep breath, then asked, "Why is my chief officer hanging upside down, naked, with my best corset strapped to his chest?"

Jack opened the door. "I couldn't find any rope. You'd think that an airship would have great big coils of rope lying around, but no, I couldn't find so much as a ball of string, and I had to have something to immobilize his arms, Tavy. Your corset was the only thing I had, so I used it to strap him down so he won't be able to escape."

"Today seems to be my day for seeing members of my crew sans clothing. He appears to be unconscious."

Jack rubbed his chin. "Ye-es, I thought you'd notice that, too. He put up a bit of a fight, so I used the Vulcan Neck Pinch on him. Or the real-world equivalent."

The naked chief officer swayed ever so slightly as the ship moved with the wind. "I believe I'll forgo inquiring about this Vulcan Neck Pinch, and instead ask you why you felt it necessary to strip Mr. Christian."

The look he gave me was pitying. "I forget you haven't seen *MacGyver*, but you can take it from me that it greatly increases your chances of escape if you're fully clothed. But string someone up naked and hang them by their feet, and you're just about guaranteed to keep them where you want them."

I sighed, and gestured toward the man, entering the small room. "Get him down."

"He was pretty violent, Octavia. Punched me in the jaw, as a matter of fact, but I didn't hold that against him, since he thought I was abducting you. Maybe we should keep him up there for a bit until he wakes up. You wouldn't want him to escape to warn the authorities if we were distracted, would you?"

"For a man who professes to follow the doctrine of doing unto others as you would have them do unto you, you're rather imaginative with your methods of restraint," I said, gesturing toward the chief officer again.

Jack hauled a chair over and stood on it, pulling out a small penknife to slash what appeared to be a pair of my best wool stockings that bound Mr. Christian's feet to the framework that ran over our heads. "Just because I'm a Quaker doesn't mean I'm a wimp, sweetheart. I don't kill people, but I don't have a problem restraining someone who will cause us grief. And it wasn't easy getting him up here on my own, you know. Took some doing. Watch out below."

I managed to grab Mr. Christian's head so it would not strike the floor with the rest of him. "I have every confidence that I will be able to reason with him when he wakes up. Until then, we will leave him bound on the floor. Will that suffice for security measures?"

"MacGyver would escape in about ten seconds," Jack said, shaking his head.

"Then let Mr. MacGyver's captain worry about him. I will just see to the autonavigator while we're here."

"And I'll go off to finish checking the engines in the boiler room. That sheet of start-up procedures you found in Mowen's room was very detailed. I'll have the engines primed and ready to go. Oh, and Octavia?"

I consulted the navigation charts, making note of the course I would need to enter into the navigator. "Hmm?"

His eyes positively danced with pleasure. "My engine will be primed and ready to go, as well. If you're up to seeing a third set of genitalia for the evening."

I smiled. There really was nothing to be said.

Women Are Complicated Creatures

"Here you are. Now, why did I have a feeling I'd find you here, Jack?"

I stopped imagining Octavia flat on her back, writhing beneath me, urging me on in that husky, breathy voice she had, and smiled. "Because you're a very intelligent woman, that's why. Have I mentioned that I think smart is sexy?"

She blushed, just as I knew she would, closing the door to her cabin in a pretty confusion that never failed to delight me. "I can't imagine anyone would find ignorance attractive, so it makes sense that the opposite must be true."

"You don't like being complimented, do you? It's something I've noticed about you, Tavy. Usually feelings of inferiority accompany that sort of mentality, but I don't think you feel that way."

"Then you would be wrong," she said with a primness that, again, delighted me. "I feel less than secure on a number of issues. This engaging in sexual acts while standing is one example. I wish I had a pamphlet on it, Jack. I wish I could see some diagrams about where one's hands go, and how one's legs are to be dealt with."

She was a mystery, my Octavia was, a woman who

was both strong and yielding, sophisticated and yet na-
ive. She had the manner of a prude, but once her passion was stirred, she was a wildcat, demanding more and
more until I thought my eyes were going to roll back in
my head and I'd just flat-out die of sexual gratification.
She was a conundrum, a puzzle, and I loved every interesting facet to her intriguing personality.

And that was what worried me. "I'm no Alan Alda,
you know," I said as she moved over to a large brass-
bound trunk and began taking off her clothes. "I don't
like quiche. I get bored at Jane Austen movies, and I'd
rather have my ball hair plucked out than sit around discussing what I feel at any given moment."

She paused in the act of pulling off her shirt, surprise
and confusion written on her adorable face. "I beg your
pardon?"

I sat up, swinging my legs over the side of her bed.
I was, naturally, naked, and even though I felt it was
important to make a few points, I couldn't help but be
pleased by the way in which her gaze lingered on me.
"I try to be sensitive to a woman's wants and needs, of
course. I'm not a selfish pig, after all. I want to give you
as much pleasure as you give me. But that's just sex, and
what we're talking about here isn't sex."

Her expression was confused. "It isn't?"

"No. You need help?" I got to my feet and moved
behind her, peeling off her shirt and tossing it onto the
chest, quickly loosening the corset strings as she'd shown
me a few days ago, bringing my hands around to caress
her tits before undoing the hooked part of the corset
front. I moaned into her hair as she filled my hands, so
warm and soft and mouthwateringly wonderful. "Oh,
God, I'm never going to get enough of this, am I?"

"No," she said on a long breath, leaning back against

me, her hands covering mine as I kneaded the soft globes. "No, you never will."

I breathed in the scent of her, something that held a faint hint of honeysuckle, but was mostly a pure, womanly smell that had my balls tightening with pleasure. "I've been in love before, Tavy. I don't want you to think I haven't, because I have."

"Have you?" She shivered as I sucked on the spot behind her ear that always made her knees buckle. I loved her knees.

"Yes. I always hoped it would last, but it never did. I think it's something to do with me, the way I work or the way I process emotions. I don't blame the women—they gave it their best shot. I think it's me."

"Yes, yes, it's definitely you," she said, her voice becoming increasingly ragged as I slid my hands down, peeling off first the thin gauzy chemise she wore beneath the corset, then working the buttons on her skirt until I could slide it over her hips. It settled on the floor around her feet with a sigh that I echoed. "About this standing up—"

"This is important, Tavy," I said, unbuttoning her petticoat to the long underwear she wore beneath the skirts, pushing them, too, down over her hips until she stood naked except for a pair of knee-high silk stockings, held up by a pair of garters. I turned her around, curling my fingers down around the plump lines of her ass, parting her legs until I could feel the heat of her, heat that glowed only for me.

"What is?" She was having problems speaking, her breath coming in short spurts as I dipped my fingers inside, teasing her soft flesh. "Merciful heavens, Jack! Do that again!"

A sense of possession shook me for a moment, the

knowledge that this woman was mine, and mine alone. I rubbed my thumb in the circular manner she found so pleasing, feeling her passion clear down to my bones as she writhed and panted soft little breaths that made me as hard as a rock.

"It's important that you realize that what we have probably won't last. It never has before, and although you're different, Tavy, completely and utterly different from any woman I've been in love with before, it never lasts. There'll come a time when we both will be ready to move on. I don't want you hurt when that happens."

She quivered in my arms, her fingernails digging into the flesh on my shoulders, as I pleasured her. But a few seconds after I delivered my warning, her eyes snapped open. She stopped quivering. In fact, she downright glared at me, as if I'd done something to piss her off.

Before I could explain again that I was just trying to keep her from being hurt when the inevitable happened, she let go of my left shoulder, made a fist, and punched me as hard as she could in my gut.

"Hey!" I said, releasing her to rub my abused belly. "What the hell was that for?"

Her glare was truly monumental now. "I think I agree with you, Jack."

Surprise felt somewhat hollow in my stomach. I rubbed it again, wondering if it was just because she'd hit me there that acknowledgment of the rightness of what I said felt so cold and clammy. "About us having no permanent future?"

"About it being more enjoyable to have your testicular hair plucked out than indulge in a discussion of your feelings." Her fingers twitched, as if she wanted to start the plucking immediately.

I took a prudent step back. "I'm just trying to think of you. I'm trying to be sensitive and caring."

"By telling me that the time will come when you will tire of me and look for another woman?"

I was lucky there wasn't a large, heavy object within her reach at that moment, because I think she would have brained me with it if there had been. Clearly, she misunderstood how thoughtful I was being. "No, by telling you that I love you. It's not easy for a man to say that, Tavy, or at least it's not easy for me. But I do love you, and I know you want to hear that. I just don't want you to think that it's going to be a forever sort of thing, because based on my past history, it doesn't last."

She stopped looking like she wanted to kill me, a thoughtful expression settling across her face. Her lips softened as she considered me. "You love me?"

"Yes. I just said that." I waited, but she didn't reciprocate. "Er . . . did I mention how hard it is for me to say that?"

"Yes," she said, continuing to look thoughtful. She moved over to the bed and sat, removing first her shoes, then her stockings.

"I don't want to hurry you or anything, but now would be a good time for you to tell me you feel the same way, and then we can get on to the sex part of the evening," I said, a little surprised that she hadn't taken the hint. Normally she was so quick.

Her eyebrows rose. "You wish for me to tell you what?"

"That you . . . er . . . love me, too." I suddenly felt vulnerable and winded, as if I'd been playing a game of dodgeball and someone knocked me backward with a ball to the gut. I didn't like the feeling at all, but I couldn't very well tell her that after I'd just explained that I didn't want to talk about my emotions. "You do, don't you?" I couldn't help but ask, clearing my throat when the words came out unsure.

She was back to looking thoughtful. She rose and strolled over to me, her hips swaying in a way that sent a warm glow through the cold pit that was my stomach. There was something about the curve of her hips that drove me wild, something about that long, sinuous line that started at her rib cage, swept inward to her waist, then flared out in a curve that begged my hands to trace it. I wanted to simultaneously touch, taste, and bite her, marking her as mine, claiming everything that she had for me and me alone.

"I'm very fond of you, naturally, Jack. I should not have gone to bed with you if I had not been fond of you. *Very* fond. But if you are so determined that our relationship not be anything but the most fleeting of moments, then it seems to me that it would be the purest folly for me to indulge my emotions in anything but such a fondness, and an appreciation for the time we have together. Don't you agree?"

The dodgeball hit me dead in the gut again. "No, I don't agree. I think if one person loves someone, then that person should love the other person back."

Her eyebrows rose again, damn them. "But there is no sense in that at all. Your way, both of us will suffer heartache when the time comes that we part. If I remain just fond of you, then only you will be heartbroken, and surely that has to be better than both of us suffering?"

Suddenly, I hated her cool, calm intellect. "The least you could do is love me back, Octavia. I just bared my soul to you! Do you have any idea how hard that is for a man?"

"Quite difficult, I'm sure," she said, placing a hand on my chest. I was distracted for a moment by the feeling of her stroking the line of my pectoral muscle. "And I can understand your ire. I tell you what—every time you tell me that you love me, I will reciprocate. Does that sound fair?"

Relief filled my still-clammy-feeling belly. "Very fair." I slid my arms around her, pulling her soft, warm, lush body against mine, bending my head until my lips steamed against hers. "I love you, Octavia."

"And I fond you, Jack," she murmured back.

It took a few seconds for the word to sink through the lust-induced haze that always seemed to grip me when I was around her. I reared back, scowling down at her.

Her brown eyes regarded me with frank amusement.

"You *fond* me?"

"I realize it's not a verb, but I felt that under the circumstances we can be a bit free with the rules of linguistic syntax."

At that moment, I knew fury as no man had ever known it. "By God, I am going to make you pay for that, woman."

"Oh really?" Her head tipped to the side. "How?"

I grabbed her shoulders and hauled her up to me, kissing her fast and hard and not even letting her respond. I whipped my tongue into her mouth, sucked hers, and then released her just as she began to moan. "I'm going to make you love me! You're going to love me so much that you're going to want to die from it!"

She giggled at the words rather than looking horrified, as she ought. I had a nagging suspicion I was making a fool of myself, but at that moment, I didn't care. I was filled with a righteous purpose, a holy grail that I would pursue to the end of time—she would love me as much as I loved her, or I would die trying.

"I see. And just how do you expect to make me love you?"

"Sex," I snarled, grabbing her breast, immediately gentling the touch so I wouldn't hurt her. "Lots and lots of sex. So much sex, you won't be able to walk straight for a month of Sundays."

"There is more to love than just sexual compatibility," she pointed out with that annoying rationality that normally I adored, but just at the moment was as irritating as sandpaper on diaper rash.

"Do not mock my holy vow," I said, spinning her around so she was against the wall of the cabin. I pressed myself against her, my body reveling in the feeling of her curves so soft and warm against me.

"Oh, it's a holy vow," she said, and I swear there was a giggle in her voice, although her face was almost without expression. "I see."

"You don't yet, but you will," I promised, and had another go at her mouth. This time she managed to get her tongue back in time to twine it around mine, her hands moving down my back to my hips.

"Jack, there is something I read in the pamphlet, something that was mentioned as being particularly enjoyable to some gentlemen. I don't see it, myself, but I am prepared to try if it would bring you pleasure." Her voice was deep with arousal now, just the way I liked it.

I rubbed my hips against her, catching my dick between her thighs. I almost lost it all right then and there. "What is involved in it?" I managed to gasp out as her hands slid lower, to my butt.

"Evidently there is a very sensitive spot that I can reach by inserting my—"

I covered her mouth with my hand, shaking my head as her eyes widened. "Any suggestion that involves the word 'inserting' with reference to me is not going to float my boat."

She relaxed, and flexed her fingers on my ass. "I didn't think it sounded very enjoyable, but I am not a man, and thought that perhaps it was different for you."

"Some men, yes. Not for me. I'm a traditionalist where that is concerned. And now, my fair little captain, are you ready to be plundered? Because I don't think I'm going to be able to take much more of you wiggling like that."

She wiggled again, the impudent hussy. "I am quite ready. I have been since the moment I came into the cabin and found you stretched out on the bed naked. Jack, do you really love me?"

"With all my heart," I murmured into her neck, wrapping my hands around the backs of her thighs, and hoisting her upward. She locked her legs around my hips, her arms around my neck as I nibbled a path along her collarbone. I paused and gave her a look. "At least so long as it lasts."

She bit me on the shoulder. Hard.

I dipped my fingers inside her, found her more than ready, and, without any sort of warning, thrust deep into her.

Her back arched against the wall, her eyes wide, as her legs flexed on me. "Mercy! You're so deep within me! I . . . I . . ."

I couldn't talk, couldn't tell her how she felt to me, couldn't even think. I just kissed her long and hard, our bodies moving against each other in a rhythm that had no beginning or end. It just was, and I gloried in every single moment of it. By the time she was yelling her pleasure into my mouth, I was ready to promise her the sun and moon if only she would swear to stay with me forever.

"I love you, you insanely wonderful woman," I gasped as my brain started working again. We clung together, her legs still around my hips, the heat of her still holding me tight, my legs shaking with the intensity of the moment. "I love you more than anything else in the world."

"Oh, Jack." Her eyes were misty with the strength of her orgasm, her breath hot on my mouth. "I shouldn't say this after you were so beastly, but I—"

"Captain Pye? My arms seem to be tied down. Do you know what's happened to me?"

The door next to us opened and the naked figure of a man staggered in, still bound by Octavia's corset.

Joy filled me at the words she'd almost spoken. "You shouldn't say what, my love?"

"I . . ." She looked from me to the chief officer, who stared at us in horror. I let her slide down me until her feet were on the floor, while I shielded her with my body.

"Gark!" the chief officer said, swaying and toppling over onto the floor.

"Mr. Christian?"

"What was it you were going to say?" I demanded, shaking her gently so she would stop staring at the unconscious man and get back to admitting she loved me.

"I think he fainted," she said, peering around me. "How very peculiar."

"Octavia."

"Hmm?" She was all innocence when I grabbed her chin and turned her head toward me.

"What was it you shouldn't say, but were about to when that idiot burst in on us?"

She blinked for a couple of seconds, then kissed the tip of my nose. "I was going to say that I'm not just fond of you, Jack. I'm also *very* fond of that new position."

I growled. Women!

Log of the HIMA *Tesla*
Tuesday, February 23
Afternoon Watch: Three Bells

"Do you have a minute to spare me?"

Jack looked up from where he was examining a recalcitrant valve on one of the boilers. His eyes regarded me warily. "That depends. Are you going to tell me you fond me again, or is there some other form of fresh hell you wish to inflict upon me?"

I bit back the smile that seemed to be arising more and more often when I was around Jack. It wasn't easy keeping a placid countenance around him when he was in full possession of what he thought of as his wholly righteous ire, but the man had brought this upon himself. The nerve of him telling me in one breath that he loved me, and the next that he fully expected it wouldn't last.

"I hadn't planned on saying that at this exact moment, but if you feel the need to hear it—"

He made a sharp movement with his hand. "Thanks, I think I'll pass. What did you need?"

Determined though I was to make him see the error of his ways, I couldn't resist pushing back that lock of hair that insisted on falling over his brow. For a moment, I considered weakening and admitting that my feelings for him had grown, as well, giving him the reassurance that my heart was wholly his, but for such an intelligent man, he could exhibit some profound stupidity. If he hadn't guessed that I was madly in love with him by the time we rescued his sister and were all safe in London, then I would admit the same. But until then, he could simmer in the stew of his own making. "I seek advice regarding Mr. Mowen."

"Matthew giving you trouble? I thought of all your crew, he was the one you were worried least about." He sat back on his heels and wiped his hands on a repulsive rag splotched black with grease.

"He is. Or rather, he's not. Everyone has been fine since we left Rome—they believed that I was called back to England suddenly, and no one questioned our hasty departure thanks to the royal wedding in two days' time."

"Is he giving you grief about me? I thought your crew bought the story about us meeting up in Rome by chance."

"No, it has nothing to do with you."

"Good, because one raving lunatic on board determined to kill me and take my place in your bed is enough." He grinned.

"I have spoken most firmly to Mr. Francisco," I informed him, momentarily diverted from my purpose. "He knows now that I will confine him to his quarters if he tries sneaking into my cabin again in order to stab you. I expressed myself in no gentle terms about that matter, you may rest assured!"

He took my chin in his hand and kissed me, very swiftly, but it was enough to send heat flashing through me. "And you, my adorable one, may rest assured that I also had words with him, and warned him that if he wanted to ever have children, he'd best leave us alone."

I couldn't help but smile. "You are such a terribly bloodthirsty man for a Quaker."

"I told you before—being a Friend doesn't mean I'm a pushover. I am quite capable of defending what's mine." He knelt and made a small adjustment to the bearing before returning to his feet.

"Would you prefer that I object to being considered as a possession now, or later?" I inquired politely.

He laughed. "I thought you'd like that. It wouldn't be good for your spleen to hold it in, so go ahead, tell me you're not mine."

"Damn you," I grumbled, wrapping my arms around his waist and reveling in the warmth and hard strength of him against me. "You know full well I'm yours body and soul."

"And heart?" he asked, something serious behind the laughter in his eyes.

"You know that I'm very fon—"

He stopped me with his mouth, growling even as he kissed me. "Dammit, Tavy, it's only fair that we should suffer together."

"Perhaps I prefer that we should enjoy life together, instead," I said lightly.

He set me away from himself, gathering up the handful of tools on the floor and returning them to a small wooden box that Mr. Mowen was seldom without. "Be that way. What was it you wanted my help with if it's not someone pestering you?"

"It's the plan for today," I said, watching as he tidied up. I frowned as I mentally ran over the note Alan had sent me the morning we left Rome. "I'm not easy in my mind what we'll tell Mr. Mowen. He knows something is up."

"Yes, he does." Jack rubbed his nose, leaving a black smear of grease on it. "Matt's no fool. You think he'll hinder us when we see the *Aurora*?"

"I don't know. He's been with the Corps for a very long time. The others will be no problem—we will simply lock them into the mess as we planned, thus keeping them from any charges of complacency when we attack the *Aurora*. But we will need Mr. Mowen's assistance in order to be successful, and I fear he might not feel the excuse of your sister is enough motivation to assist. I will naturally reassure him that we will swear that he had no part in the attack, but he is the sort of man who would not be easy in his mind about lying."

Jack rubbed his chin. I *tsk*ed, and pulled out a handkerchief, unable to stand him spreading any more grease marks. I cleaned off the side of his nose and his chin, pressing a kiss to the latter.

"I don't think you have anything to worry about. He seems a reasonable enough man. Once he understands that Hallie will be executed if we don't save her, he will help us. I'm sure of that."

"I wish I was so confident," I said, sighing as I consulted my pocket watch. "Two hours to go."

"You're sure the *Aurora* is following?"

"Alan said it was scheduled to leave after us, and we are unladen, and thus faster. It could not have passed us, and according to my calculations, we should find her before we pass over Angers."

"I still say we should have attacked right out of Rome." Jack shook his head. "Rather than waiting until we're right at the English Channel."

"It just wouldn't be prudent. The king of Italy has

ships leaving Rome to travel to London, as well. They take a slightly different flight path to England than imperial ships, and now that we are two days out, our paths have separated. Should the *Aurora* call for assistance, there will be no one to aid them. I know you hate the delay, but it is far better to catch the transport ship by surprise when she least expects it. That element of surprise is going to have to carry us far."

"It still seems like waiting until the last minute. And speaking of your friend, where is your precious Alan? I thought the plan was for him to come with us and help," Jack grumbled as he took my hand, leading me from the boiler room, his fingers warm on mine.

I was silent, uncomfortable when it came to that subject. I wanted badly to tell Jack what Alan had said in his letter to me, but there were secrets that were not mine to divulge. Still, it left me feeling dishonest, and I struggled with my need to speak frankly to Jack, and the knowledge that I held Alan's life in my hands.

"He was so gung ho about the whole idea of attacking the *Aurora*, you'd think he'd want to be here for it," Jack continued.

I felt lower than a slug's belly. "He sent me a note saying he was asked by the king to travel with his entourage. His hands are tied, although he did promise to do whatever he could to help," I said with a lameness that made me wince.

Jack shrugged. "Fat lot of good he can do us if his ship isn't even nearby. Aw, sweetheart, that's such a long face. I'm sorry. I won't pick on him anymore if it's going to make you uncomfortable. As penance, I'll help you talk to Mowen, OK?"

I bit my lip, not wanting to say anything that would condemn either myself or Alan. Luckily, Jack was distracted by the sight of Mr. Francisco looming in the passageway, and didn't bother to press me for reassurances that I badly wanted to avoid.

Our conversation with Mr. Mowen a short while later was eye-opening. Jack quickly explained the circumstances of Hallie's incarceration, and the travesty of a trial that had been held in Rome. To my surprise, Mr. Mowen simply nodded.

"You'll be wanting to take the lass off the ship in flight, then?"

"Yes," I said. "I realize this is asking you to go against everything you believe in, every moral value held dear by the Aerocorps, but it is literally a matter of life or death. We cannot do this without you. Naturally, we will arrange it to appear that you were an unwilling participant in the event, so that your career will not suffer for your kindness."

Mr. Mowen gave me a lopsided smile. "I've been thinking of retiring soon anyway. Perhaps this will be the event that pushes me down that path."

"Thanks, Matt," Jack said, clapping him on the shoulder while tossing me a triumphant "told you so" grin. "I knew we could count on you. Octavia is going to handle positioning the ship for the attack. If you can deal with making sure she has the power she needs, that'll let us handle subduing the crew of the *Aurora* once we're in place."

Mr. Mowen gave Jack a curious look. "What will happen to the other prisoners on the ship if you kill the crew?"

I made a face while Jack laughed.

"If you only knew how bloodthirsty your captain is," he said, grinning at me.

"I am not bloodthirsty. It was a natural assumption on

my part to assume that when you decreed we would become airship pirates, we would use force to overpower the crew of the *Aurora*. I hardly see how that makes me some sort of a monster crying out for innocent people's blood!"

Mr. Mowen gave me a very long look.

"Tavy and I had a bit of an argument over what to do with the crew," Jack explained.

"It was not an argument. I never once said, 'Let's go in with our Disruptors blazing and take out everyone we possibly can!' I simply assumed that you would wish to use Disruptors on one or two crew members or guards in order to show the rest that we were serious."

"That does seem reasonable," Mr. Mowen said.

"Thank you. I'm glad someone understands," I said with much dignity.

"It's a bit sadistic to make examples of the poor innocents, but more reasonable than slaughtering the entire crew and leaving the other prisoners to die on an unmanned ship," he added.

I sighed.

"So after I took a firm stand with Tavy and told her no, she couldn't turn into a steampunk version of Blackbeard, she demanded to know just how we were going to get Hallie free if she couldn't bathe the decks in blood."

"Bathe the decks in blood!" I gasped, outraged.

"To which I had four words for her. And those words are what, sweetheart?"

I ground my teeth for a moment at Jack's teasing, finally managing to get out, "Better living through chemistry."

"That's right." He nodded and beamed at Mr. Mowen, who just looked confused.

"Chemistry? You're going to bomb the ship?"

"Nope. In Tavy's cabin, hidden away in a nice little box, we have several syringes prefilled with the best, strongest, most potent form of liquid knockout drops money could buy in Rome."

Mr. Mowen looked even more confused.

"It's a sedative," I explained. "Jack wanted to make some sort of tapir, but wasn't sure how to do so."

"Taser."

"So instead, he suggested that we simply drug people on the ship, remove his sister and the other five prisoners, and fly away without anyone coming to harm. By the time the crew of the *Aurora* comes to, we will be far away and they will not be able to catch us."

"Neat trick, huh?" Jack asked, looking inordinately proud of himself.

I gave him a little smile. I was rather proud of his ingenuity, too.

"Very neat. But won't that take a bit of time, drugging all those people?"

"Not really." I looked at Jack. He nodded for me to continue. "The *Aurora* is running with just a skeleton crew. The only people they are transporting are half a dozen prisoners. There are no other troops on board, and only enough crew as is needed to fly the ship. We'll be able to take them out quite quickly, I believe."

"Aye, that would help things along. You'd be well met to take along a Disruptor or two just in case your sedative doesn't work."

Jack protested that his plan couldn't fail, but Mr. Mowen waited until he had left to gather up the syringes to press his Disruptor on me.

"Give it to your man. Just in case."

I took it with a murmur of thanks. "You're not at all

surprised by any of this, are you?" I couldn't help but ask. "Not by Jack being here, or the need to rescue his sister, or my decision to do so."

"Not really, no," he said with a slow smile.

"I fear you must be disappointed in how things turned out, that I will never be the captain of whom you had such high hopes."

He shook his head. "On the contrary—it would have been my pleasure to serve under a captain who thought more of others than herself. I knew your guardian, you know."

"You knew Robert?" I was frankly surprised. Robert Anstruther was such a man that those who knew him were usually quick to identify themselves.

"Aye. I sailed with him briefly during the war with the Americas. I was a gunner's mate then, but I knew him to be a fair man, a just man who thought the world of his crew, and we him. I remember one day, when we were in port and about to set off for the east coast of America, he came on board with a little girl who had the reddest hair I'd ever seen. She was a solemn little mite, but curious, and when I twisted a bit of packing cotton used to cushion the aether tubes into a doll, she smiled at me. It was like a ray of sunshine piercing my heart. Captain Anstruther was very pleased, for he told me later the little girl hadn't smiled up to that time."

"I don't remember that at all," I said sadly, searching my memory for anything about that time. "It must have been when I was very young."

"Aye, you were, just a sprite of about ten. I knew that you'd be fine with him, and so you have been. He'd be proud of you now, Captain."

I blinked back a few tears that stung my eyes. "Thank you. I'd like to think he would."

" 'Tis a shame he is no longer around. I think he'd like your choice of men, as well."

His tone was even, but there was a note in it that made me look sharply at him. I couldn't tell if he was simply making a slight dig at the men of my past, of whom Robert had most definitely not approved, or if he was implying something else, something far more sinister. "Indeed. Do you have any questions about the plans?"

"None. I'll be on duty in the rear boiler room at the appointed time. You just give me the word, and I'll open the boilers wide up."

"Thank you. I believe what Jack calls a speedy getaway will be most propitious."

Slightly less than three hours later, I entered the mess and smiled at everyone present. "Good afternoon. Thank you all for answering the summons of this impromptu crew meeting. Mr. Llama alone is missing, I see."

"And Mr. Mowen," Dooley said, jumping up from his chair at the long table. "I'll fetch him."

"Stay where you are, Dooley. Mr. Mowen is excused from this meeting." I felt rather than heard a presence behind me. Without turning around to look, I added, "Ah, Mr. Llama, how nice of you to join us. Won't you sit down?"

He gave me an odd look as he sidled past me, gliding his way over to stand in a far corner.

"No doubt you are all very curious as to what this meeting is about," I said, looking from one face to another. "Jack?"

"Right here." The far door, the one leading to the galley, opened, and Jack stood there.

Mr. Francisco forcibly shoved back his chair and leaped to his feet, scattering Spanish curses as he did so.

"I'm afraid we're taking a little detour. It shouldn't take long," I said over the cursing. "But you all are going to have to stay here while we do so. I have placed a case of ale under the table—you're free to enjoy that until we are back on course."

I nodded to Jack, and before any of the crew could protest, ask a question, or charge the door, I slipped out it, locking it from the outside. Jack, I knew, would do the same to the galley door.

"Do you have everything?" I asked him as he met me on the upper level.

"Think so. Syringes, set of skeleton keys, goggles . . . yup. Got everything."

"Goggles? What are those for?" I asked as I ran up the spiral stairs to the navigation room.

"You can't be a proper airship pirate without goggles, Tavy. Everyone knows that. Here, I got a pair for you."

"You are the strangest man I've ever met," I said, taking the goggles. "I shan't wear them, you know."

"We'll see," he said, donning his pair and grinning at me.

"For mercy's sake . . . Jack." I bit my lower lip, holding his arm as he was about to leave. "I know how you feel about weapons, but please take this. Just in case you need it."

He looked down at the Disruptor that Mr. Mowen had given me, his eyes hidden behind the dark green glass of the hideous brass-and-leather goggles. "I don't need a gun, Tavy."

"I know you don't, but if something untoward happens, it would make me feel better to know you had it."

He pushed the goggles back onto his forehead, his eyes considering me with something that looked very much like sorrow. "Do you expect me to use it?"

I looked down at my hands for a moment. What he was really asking me was whether I wanted him to use it, whether I wished for him to violate his moral beliefs. "I believe that the sight of it will dissuade people without you having to use it."

"That's not what I asked, sweetheart."

"I know." I took his hand and rubbed his knuckles against my cheek. "But it is the best answer I can give you, Jack. Take it. Keep it prominently visible so the crew of the *Aurora* sees you have it. That's all I ask."

The pain in his eyes was deep, but it was nothing compared with the pain I felt at the thought of losing him. He nodded and tucked the Disruptor into the pocket of his Corps jacket. "I won't need it, Tavy. Our plan is foolproof."

"I pray that's so." I released his hand, and would have turned to the autonavigator, to begin our swing around to intercept the *Aurora*, but Jack's hand on my arm stopped me.

"There's only one woman in the world—in any world—I would carry a firearm for," he said, pulling me into a hard embrace. "Now give me a kiss for luck, pirate Octavia."

His lips were demanding, but I was of no mind to take issue with that. I put every ounce of love I had into the answering kiss, smiling when he pulled the goggles into place, made a dashing salute, and hurried out of the room to take up his position on the forward deck.

I had qualms about calling any plan foolproof, having had ample example during my lifetime to see how even the best of plans could go astray, but luck was with us. The *Aurora* was an hour behind where I had calculated she would be, but she did eventually show up, and upon seeing the signal lights that Jack was waving from the forward deck, she slowed as I knew she would.

By the time Jack was using semaphore to indicate we were in distress, the *Aurora* had stopped her engines, and two crewmen were on their promenade deck with grappling hooks. I waited until we were within hailing distance, then appeared on our forward deck, assisting Jack as the *Aurora*'s hooks were thrown across to us and we were reeled in.

"Our boilers are down," I called across in answer to a question about the nature of our emergency. "I believe it is sabotage by the Black Hand."

A man appeared, pulling on the scarlet jacket bearing the insignia of a ship's captain. "What's going on here?"

"If you would allow us to board, I will be happy to explain," I called across to him. The ships were not able to pull close together because of the size of the envelopes, but one of the grappling hooks carried with it a heavy line, which Jack secured to a ring bolted into the *Tesla*'s frame.

"Come across, then," the captain said, holding a finger up to the air. "You'll have a bit of a rocky ride, but you should be safe enough."

"You're sure this is not going to come loose?" Jack murmured as one of the *Aurora* crewmen attached a pulley to the line that tethered us, and hooked a basket underneath it. "It doesn't look very sturdy."

"It's the only way to get across. I've done it before, and had no problems. Just don't look down," I advised as I reached out to receive the basket. "I'll go first. Use the pulley to move across to the *Aurora*. The wind will buffet you a little, but if you brace your legs in the bottom of the basket, you'll be fine."

Jack didn't look like he believed me, but he had no

other choice. By the time I knelt in the basket, hauling myself across the gap between the two airships, he had evidently steeled his nerve, for he did not hesitate at all when the basket was sent back to him.

"Captain Octavia Pye," I said, greeting the *Aurora*'s captain. "That is Mr. Fletcher, my chief officer. If you have a moment, we'd like to consult with your engineer."

Jack arrived on the deck of the *Aurora*, his color high, but in one piece.

"Captain Armand. We don't have time for dillydallying, Captain Pye. We're on a very tight schedule to reach England, and although I would normally take the time to help you, I'm afraid the best we can do is to spare you a half hour."

I smiled, and put my hand in my coat pocket, sliding off the hard lump of wax from the tip of a syringe. "I believe that will be ample time."

The captain and the first of the two crewmen stared at us in surprise when we leaped at them and jabbed them with syringes.

"What the devil—," the captain started to say before his eyes rolled back and he slumped to the floor.

The second crewman on the deck shouted and reached for his Disruptor, but Jack knocked it out of his hand, quickly disabling him with another syringe of sedative.

"This is quite a bit more potent than I imagined," I said as we hurried into the interior of the airship. "I had no idea it would work so fast."

"I told you—better living through chemistry. Which way?"

"Down," I said, pointing to a spiral staircase. "The containment cells are bound to be at the bot—"

An explosion rocked the ship. I grabbed at the metal handrail, slipping down a couple of steps, Jack falling heavily into me.

"What the hell was that?" he demanded to know, righting me. "Are you OK?"

"I'm fine, but I think we'd better hurry up and get Hallie."

Another blast shook the ship. "Damnation," I swore under my breath as I tumbled down a couple more steps, the hard iron railing burning my hands as I clutched it frantically to keep from falling farther.

"You get Hallie," Jack ordered, hauling me to my feet before turning and starting up the stairs. "I'll go see what's going on."

"No, Jack, it's too dangerous," I yelled, aware of a wetness on my hip. Jack ignored me, bolting to the top of the stairs and disappearing down a catwalk that stretched behind the nearest envelope. "Ratsbane! Jack! My syringes are broken!"

A third blast hit, this time accompanied by the hissing sound that indicated one of the envelopes had been breached. The ship listed to the fore, forcing me to cling to the railing in order to keep from falling. A distant, more muffled explosion sounded, and I knew with a horrible prescience that someone had fired on the *Tesla*.

I swore under my breath as I half ran, half slid down the stairs. Two more crewmen raced past me, none of them giving me a second look. "I'm from the *Tesla*," I yelled after one of them. "What's happening?"

"Who're you?" he asked as he bolted for the stairs, pausing long enough for me to answer.

"Captain Pye, from the *Tesla*."

"Well, Captain Pye, we're in the middle of a Moghul attack. Bronson! Get the prisoners out and bring them aloft! They can man the cannons with us. Your ship's being fired on, as well, Captain Pye. I'd advise you to see to her and leave us to defend ourselves."

Two more muffled explosions had my stomach clenching in fear. I stood indecisive for a moment, torn between trying to rescue Hallie and saving my crew. If the prisoners were being forced to man the cannons with the crew, I would never get her free. Not without more sedatives.

I hauled myself up the stairs, calling for Jack.

"Here! Tavy, they're shooting the *Tesla*. Did you get Hallie?"

He pulled me up the last few stairs, looking expectantly beyond me.

"No, I couldn't. They're using the prisoners to man their aether cannons. Jack, we have to get across now, while we can, or we'll be stuck on the *Aurora*. And the *Tesla* will go down."

"I'm not leaving without Hallie," he said grimly, trying to push past me to the stairs.

"We can't get to her! The first blast broke my syringes, and you don't have enough left to disable the remaining crew."

Another explosion sounded. I grabbed Jack's arm and dragged him toward the door. "Jack, we have to go now!"

"But Hallie!"

"This ship is well armed, and the Moghuls appear to be targeting the *Tesla* now. Hallie will be fine. We'll just have to rescue her at a later time."

Jack hesitated, pain lacing his face, but in the end he saw reason and jerked open the door, taking me with him as we slid down the tilted deck to where the basket waited.

The *Tesla* was listing heavily to the port side, toward us, causing the rope that tethered the two ships to hang slack. I pulled it tight while Jack held out the basket for me.

"Get in," he ordered.

"There's no time for two trips," I said, stepping into the basket. "We'll have to go together."

"Will it hold us?"

"It should." A flame appeared briefly in the forward-most envelope. I grabbed Jack by his coat and hauled him into the basket, kneeling beside him as he fed out the line that pulled us across.

I fervently hope I never again have to make such a journey as the one from the *Aurora* to the *Tesla*. Both ships continued to tilt, the *Tesla* starting to roll over on her side. Blasts of aether from the *Aurora*'s cannons split the air, sending the basket rolling. Jack yelled something as I clutched the side of the basket with one hand, and him with the other, praying fervently all the while that the line hold just long enough to deposit us on the deck of the *Tesla*.

It did, of course. It even held a good two minutes after we got there, but once Jack and I had managed to get inside the ship, release the crew, and order a very shaken Mr. Mowen to open up the boilers, the *Tesla* was beginning to show the effect of taking several broadside blasts of Moghul aether cannons.

"Mr. Christian, set a new course twenty-five degrees to the north. Jack, can you help Mr. Mowen with the boilers? We'll need maximum speed immediately. Dooley, go with Mr. Ho and see to the envelopes. I must know how badly damaged they are. Mr. Llama, would you likewise assess structural damage in the frame?"

"Captain, what's happenin'?" Mr. Piper asked, limping after me as I dashed down the hall. The rest of the crew scattered, their faces pale and strained. "Who's attackin' us? Why did ye lock us in the mess?"

"Moghuls, and no time to explain now. I smell smoke! Mr. Francisco, you come with me to the forward holds while Mr. Piper deals with the aft."

Another explosion ripped into the ship, this one causing the floor to shake horribly under my feet. A rush of air and a long, inhuman scream warned me that yet another envelope had suffered damage. I shoved the pressurized water cylinder we kept for fires into Mr. Francisco's arms. "Put out any fires you see in the forward holds. I must go aloft and see how many envelopes are intact."

"I will not leave you alone, my glorious *capitán* of the hair!" he said stoutly.

I shoved him none-too-gently down the corridor, and took off, deaf to his shouts and demands that he be allowed to save my hair. I scrambled up three flights of stairs to the repair balcony that ran the length of the airship, gasping in horror at the sight. Of the seven envelopes, four were damaged, two collapsed upon themselves, with the other two sagging inward at a fast rate. "Dear God in heaven. Why are they doing this to us?" I asked, clutching the railing as one of the three remaining envelopes suddenly shuddered and began to lose its form.

The ship was going down. I was staring straight into the face of disaster, and there wasn't anything I could do to save the *Tesla*.

"Abandon ship!" I bellowed, throwing myself back down the stairs to the floor below. The *Tesla* had rocked over about thirty degrees onto her side, making it impossible to walk on the exposed upper gangways. I made it down to the main floor, falling down the last half of the flight, just in time to see Jack race past yelling my name.

"Octavia! The ship is—"

"I know. Help me get to the mess. No, it's all right, I'm not hurt seriously. We must sound the alarm and get everyone off the ship before she lists any more."

"Matt says the boilers will explode," he said, half-carrying me down the corridor. "How are we going to get off the ship? Have parachutes been invented yet?"

"Of course they have. Do you think we would conquer the skies without having a method of getting down in the case of an emergency?" We reached the mess just as Dooley and Mr. Ho came barreling down the corridor, yelling at the top of their respective lungs.

"We're abandoning ship," I called to them, then jerked down on the emergency cord just inside the doorway. A loud Klaxon horn sounded, adding to the confusion. "Help me pull up the floor," I commanded, and kicked back the small rug that covered a panel in the floor.

Jack and I hauled up the panel, bracing ourselves when the ship groaned and leaned even farther over. "Go to the gangway off the forward hold," I yelled over the sound of the Klaxon and the noise the ship was making as she died. "Jump from there."

Jack yanked up an armful of canvas bags, shoving one each into the arms of Dooley and Mr. Ho.

"I can stay and help—," Mr. Ho started to say.

"Go! Get out while you can!" I yelled back, lying on my belly to grab the remainder of the parachutes from their storage locker under the floor.

By the time the rest of the crew appeared, the ship was listing at a forty-degree angle.

"The boilers won't hold much past forty-five," I told

Jack, helping him buckle on the harness of the parachute. "I don't suppose you would jump without me?"

He gave me a chastising look. I summoned up a grim smile. "I didn't think so. I wouldn't leave you, either. Where's Mr. Mow—thank God, there you are. You're injured!"

A blood-drenched Mr. Mowen staggered into the room, Mr. Christian holding grimly on to his arm. "I found him on the gangway above," Mr. Christian said. "He'd been knocked out."

"Get into your parachute and jump," I told him, shoving a parachute bag at him before grabbing up another one. "Mr. Mowen, can you hear me? Do you understand what's happened? Here, Jack, help me get this on him."

My fingers were slick with Mr. Mowen's blood as we frantically buckled the harness straps around him. He said nothing as we did so, his eyes glazed and unfocused.

"Should I wait—?" Mr. Christian said, hesitating at the door.

"Go," I ordered, shoving him. "We'll see to Mr. Mowen."

"Godspeed," was all he said before sliding his way down the gangway.

"You take one side, and I'll take the other," Jack said, shoving his shoulder under Mr. Mowen's arm. I did likewise, and we started our perilous journey down the gangway. "We'll never get him down the stairs at this angle without killing ourselves."

"No. We won't need to. There's an exit hatch ahead. It's small, but we should fit through it."

"Will he be able to open his chute in this state?" Jack asked as he kicked open the door to one of the storerooms.

"Open the chute?"

"Pull the cord to open it. I don't know that he's aware enough of what's happening to do it in time."

"There's no cord, Jack. You simply open the bottom of the sack and the parachute comes out while you fall."

"Oh, God. That sounds horribly unsafe."

I shoved aside a crate and grasped the metal crank that would open up the emergency hatch. "I've never had cause to use one before, but I understand that they have saved many lives. We'll put him through first. If you can lift his legs, I'll ready the parachute, and we can slide him through."

"You don't think it would be better for me to hold him?" Jack asked, his face pinched and white.

"That would be disastrous. Your parachute would tangle with his, and you would spiral down to your death. Ready?"

We got Mr. Mowen's lower body through the opening. He moaned, and feebly moved his arms, but didn't seem to understand what was happening. "You'll be all right, I know you will," I told him before Jack released him. Mr. Mowen slid out of view.

I leaned out, relieved when I caught sight of the black silk twisting, fluttering, and then opening into an umbrella shape.

"You next," I told Jack.

"Right," he said, grabbing me about the waist and stuffing me headfirst through the hatch. "Octavia—"

"I know," I said, kicking my feet as I looked over my shoulder at him. "I'll see you below."

My emotions as I was cradled by nothing but the air were tangled together in a mess that was hard to sort. I felt relief when my parachute opened, jerking me upward for a few feet as the canopy caught the air. Even more relief followed when I looked upward and saw Jack, silhouetted against his parachute. From my vantage point below her, I could see just how badly damaged the *Tesla* was, and wondered that she'd stayed aloft as long as she had. Almost her entire starboard side was in flames now, the envelopes tattered and charred, and as I watched, she gave a hiccuping lurch; then a roar exploded down the length of her.

"The boilers," I said softly, feeling wetness on my cheeks. Whether it was from tears or moisture in the air I didn't know, but I felt a profound sadness as my ship, my first and probably only command, died before my eyes.

Beyond her and above, the *Aurora* sat, her guns now silent, bearing scars of the attacks against her, but I noted that she had suffered little in comparison. Hallie and the others would be safe.

Jack yelled something, his arm jutting out to point behind me. I craned my head to look. The Moghul ship was moving away, but my breath caught in my throat when I counted the aether cannons that bristled out of her. She was small and fast, a ship clearly built for one thing—to destroy. Even as my dazed eyes counted the cannons, she maneuvered a tight turn, gained altitude, and left the scene of the carnage, evidently not wishing to tangle any further with the bigger, and better armed, *Aurora*.

"Why?" I asked the ship, the wind snatching away my voice. "Why would you do that to us?"

Personal Log of Octavia E. Pye
Wednesday, February 24
Midwatch: Three Bells

"If I was to kiss you right here, what would you do?"
I opened my eyes and looked at Jack as he hovered over my left knee. "Probably moan."

"Would that be a good moan, a 'he's kissing his way up my legs and will soon sup at the gates of my own personal paradise, making me squirm and writhe and become a true believer in the power of oral sex' sort of moan, or a bad moan, a moan that indicates you're in pain and just want to be left alone to sleep?"

"Unfortunately, it's a bad moan, although I don't want you to leave me. And indeed, I don't have time to sleep." I made an effort to sit upright in the rather uncomfortable inn bed, and swung my good leg over the edge. My wounded knee protested at the very thought of moving, but I steeled my nerve, gritted my teeth, and pulled it over the edge, as well.

"Oh, no, you don't," Jack said, gathering my legs and putting them back on the bed. "If you're not well enough for me to make you writhe, you're not well enough to get up."

"I'm not injured seriously, just a little bruised," I said, struggling against him for a few seconds before giving up and slumping back against the headboard. "Jack, I have many things to see to. I know you mean well, but you must let me up."

"I'll take care of anything you need to do," he said firmly. "You just rest that knee. You're lucky you didn't break your leg the way you landed."

"I was trying to see in which direction the Moghul ship was going," I said, allowing him to tuck me in. "I wasn't watching the ground."

"I know. Scared at least ten years off my life," he said, and I noticed for the first time since we'd staggered our way to the small inn outside of Angers that there were deep lines of stress on either side of his mouth. I touched them gently.

"You were wonderful, Jack. I doubt if I could have managed Mr. Mowen on my own. Are you sure he's—"

"The doctor said he's concussed, has a couple of broken ribs and a bruised ankle, but he'll recover."

"I just wish we knew what happened to Mr. Llama," I said, fretting the embroidered bedcover. "Has no one seen any sign of him?"

"Not yet, no."

"I hope he wasn't seriously injured."

"I doubt if he was. The others came through all right. Speaking of which, your chief officer is being a big pain in the ass about seeing you. He insists it's his right or some such bull. I told him you needed rest, but he says he wants to make sure I haven't done away with you and am trying to hide the fact."

"He is . . . imaginative," I said, smiling. "You may let him in."

"Nope. You're too tired."

"Please, Jack. It would make me feel better to see that everyone is safe."

He hesitated for a moment, then bent and gave me a swift kiss. "You're going to wrap me around your little finger any time you like, aren't you?"

"I'm a woman," I said with a nonchalant shrug. "That's my job, isn't it?"

It took over an hour to see all of the crew, since Jack would allow them to enter my room only singly. They all looked hale and hearty—a few cuts, bruises, and, in Dooley's case, burns aside. They were all animated and excited, and wanted to know just what had happened. Noting that I was fast losing strength, Jack told them we would have a group meeting the following morning, and explanations and plans would be made then.

"We can't stay here overnight," I told him when he saw out the last of the crew.

"Why not? You said yourself that the *Aurora* would take two more days to get to England, and that we could make it there by one on a train."

"I said if I was captain, I would make repairs first, and those would take a day. But we have no guarantee that the *Aurora*'s captain will do any such thing. He might feel that he's vulnerable to another attack, and make all haste to get safely to England. We must leave tonight, Jack, if we are to arrive in England in time to intercept the transfer of prisoners from the *Aurora* to the prison."

His shoulders slumped as he sat next to me on the bed. "Poor Hallie. She must be scared to death, and God knows what she thinks of me just letting her be carried off like that."

"I have no doubt she's frightened—I would be in her situation—but she's a strong woman. You've told me that many times. And although I regret that she is no doubt very worried and scared, we have to focus our energies on rescuing her, not ruing what has happened."

"And that means letting you walk around on a leg that should be resting," he said, his shoulders slumping even more.

I leaned into him and rubbed my cheek on his shoulder. "If I told you that it's feeling better, will you kiss me?"

"I'd kiss you anyway," he said in a voice that sounded very close to exhaustion.

"Ah, but I didn't specify where the kiss would land."

He straightened up at that, a familiar light of interest glowing in his mismatched eyes. "Captain Pye, are you by any chance flirting with me?"

"Yes, Mr. Fletcher, I am. Is it working?"

"As a distraction, you mean? Yes. Although I'm not going to make love to you as you deserve. No," he said, holding up a hand to interrupt the protest I was about to make. "Don't beg, it's not becoming in a captain. You need time to physically recover from the incidents today, and if we are to get to England before morning, I will have to go out and figure a way there."

I bristled at him. "I never beg!"

He grinned.

"Well, almost never," I amended, recalling an event just two nights past when I pleaded with him to repeat a particularly effective tongue swirl. I cleared my throat and adopted a placid expression. "The ice you brought for my knee has worked wonders, so I should have no trouble booking our passage."

He hesitated. "I suppose it will be all right, but only because I have no idea how to go about doing that. Although I would if you wanted me to."

"I know you would." I kissed him softly, my lips lingering on his. "I can't tell you how much I appreciate all your help and support, Jack. I really would have been lost without you."

"You are a horrible liar," he said, pulling me onto his lap. When I stiffened with outrage, he just tickled my ribs. "Don't get all prissy on me, Tavy. It was actually a compliment."

"You have a very strange idea about what consists of a compliment," I grumbled, my breath suddenly hitching in my throat as he began unbuttoning my blouse.

"Mmmhmm," he murmured, burying his face in my chest.

I clutched his shoulders and gave myself over to the pleasure he provided, but only for a few minutes, sighing when I caught a glimpse of my pocket watch lying on the nightstand. "I'd better get going. Jack, please, you're to make me embarrass myself when I go out."

He pulled his head back from where he'd been sucking on my nipple right through my chemise. The flesh pebbled, the skin tightening into hard little knots of desire and pleasure that wanted nothing more than for Jack to pay them a good deal more attention.

"Sorry," he said, not at all contrite as I buttoned up my blouse. He grinned wickedly at my breasts before I buttoned my jacket.

"What are we going to do with the crew?" he asked as we slipped out of the inn.

"I hate to say it, but we'd probably have more luck of getting to England quickly if there are just two of us. I will try to book them passage with us, but if I can't, they must simply go later."

As I suspected, there were limited openings on a train that left Angers an hour after we spoke to a booking agent. "Only three spots left, madame," the agent told me when I inquired as to the fastest route to England. "The train, she leaves from Angers and arrives at Paris at two of the clock in the morning. The boat train leaves on the half of the hour, and arrives in Calais at the hour of five. If the channel crossing is not delayed due to weather, you will arrive in London by nine of the clock in the morning. Will that suit Madame?"

"Very much so, yes. Two, please."

"What time is the *Aurora* due to land?" Jack asked in a quiet voice.

"Four bells," I said, glancing at the clock. It was just twenty minutes to that time now. "But I'm hoping that the attack slowed her down somewhat. We might just make it there before her, especially if she was forced to make repairs."

"*Mon Dieu!* You are from the *Aurora*?" the ticket man asked, obviously overhearing a word or two from our muted conversation. "That was most terrible, the attack of the Moghuls. It is said that they swept out of the sky like a giant black bird of prey, and tore apart the *Aurora* and a smaller ship, which crashed near here."

"We were on the *Tesla*, the other ship," I said, glancing at Jack.

"And you are not killed? I hear that no one was saved, and yet here you stand! You are sure you are from that ship and not the *Aurora*?" he asked somewhat suspiciously.

"I am the captain of the *Tesla*. I assure you we know which ship we were on," I said stiffly.

"How did you happen to hear about the attack on the *Aurora*?" Jack asked as I tucked the tickets away in my bag. "I imagine someone noticed the *Tesla* falling to the ground, but the *Aurora* didn't crash, did it?"

"*Mon Dieu*, no! But she is here, in Angers, getting the repairs most necessary."

Jack and I exchanged glances. If the *Aurora* was on the ground, perhaps now was our chance to extricate Hallie from it. Just as my hopes rose that we could manage that, they were dashed again. "The emperor, he has sent ground troops from Paris to guard her. It is said that the Moghul airship haunts the skies around us, waiting for another chance to destroy her."

Jack and I both slumped a little at the news. "Do you happen to know when the *Aurora* is expected to get under way?"

The man gave a Gallic shrug. "*Non.* But it cannot be long because it is said that the ship holds a present most *magnifique* for the emperor William to give to his bride, and the wedding, it is tomorrow, yes?"

I managed to keep from grimacing. Jack didn't even bother to try to hide his disgust. "Some present," he muttered under his breath.

I squeezed his arm and was about to leave, but the agent suddenly peppered us with a thousand questions about the attack. It took some time to curb his interest, but as we left the train station, we had much to chew over.

"The captain of the *Aurora* didn't say anything about us attacking them," I said to Jack as we settled back in a cab.

"Evidently not. I wonder if the sedatives had some sort of amnesia effect?"

"More likely things were just so confused and desperate after the attack by the Moghuls, they didn't remember the prick of the needles."

"I hope not. The question is, what are you going to do about the *Tesla*? If your Aerocorps doesn't know you had turned to piracy, you might still have a job there."

"Possibly, although there's the crew to think of. Surely they must have an inkling that we were up to something nefarious when we locked them into the mess."

"I don't know," Jack said slowly, his fingers stroking over mine in a way that had me thinking wholly inappropriate thoughts. "They were full of questions for you tonight, but if you think about it, none of them asked you why we locked them in—they all wanted to know about the Moghul attack."

"That is true."

"And why the Moghul seemed to target the *Tesla* over the *Aurora*."

My lips tightened. I wanted very much to know that, as well. "The *Aurora* did have cannons, and we did not."

"I suppose that would explain it. You know I'm opposed to violence, but if I could get my hands on that Moghul prince guy, that Abdullah—"

"Akbar."

"—Akbar, then I'd wring his neck. He could have killed you!"

I said nothing because really, what was there to say?

We returned to the inn and slipped inside without being seen by any of the crew, most of whom I suspected had retired to recover from the day's ordeal. By the time Jack paid the innkeeper for all our rooms, I had written a brief note to Mr. Mowen, and enclosed the crew's tickets to London on a train that would leave early the next morning.

"I told Mr. Mowen that we had to be in London to meet the *Aurora* when she landed," I informed Jack as I sealed the envelope. "And that no one seems to be aware of our attack on the *Aurora*. I trust he will keep his silence about that."

"I'm sure he will," Jack said, draping a shawl he'd acquired somehow around my shoulders. "He's a good guy, Matt is. We can trust him."

We escaped the inn a second time without being seen. I was about to ask Jack where he found the shawl when suddenly we were surrounded.

MacGyver Makes It Look Way Too Easy

"What the hell—" Before I could do more than swing around to face the men that loomed up out of a dark doorway Octavia and I were passing, one of them grabbed me in a choke hold, and pressed a cloth across my face. Two others held my arms as the sickly-sweet scent of something I knew must be an anesthetic seeped into my lungs. I fought as best I could, but the men were expert in close combat and avoided most of my attempts at stopping them.

"No!" Octavia cried, throwing herself on one of the men. They were all swarthy in color, clad in brown-and-gold outfits with white turbans, the ends of which covered their lower faces, just like those worn by the Moghul attackers in Rome. . . .

"Moghuls!" I yelled through the cloth as a synapse sparked. "Run, Octavia!"

"Leave him be!" she cried, pulling at the man's arm that held the anesthetic to my face. Her voice seemed to be rather distant, her beloved face growing fuzzy. I was being drugged, knocked out, but there wasn't a damned thing I could do about it.

"If you hurt her, you'll spend the rest of your life

regretting . . ." I fell face-first into a thick black pool of nothingness.

I swam around there for a bit; then a nagging worry started to make me feel uneasy. Just as I pinpointed the source of the emotion as being concern for Octavia, a tidal wave hit me dead in the face.

"Blah!" I sputtered, jerking upright, wiping water from my eyes.

"You didn't have to drown him! Jack, are you all right? I couldn't wake you, and I was beginning to worry."

My eyes were a bit blurry, but at last I got them to focus on the most beautiful of sights. "Hello, Tavy. Why am I wet?"

"Azahgi Bahajir felt the best way to wake you was to dump a bucket of water on you. How do you feel?"

"Damp, headachy, and confused. How long have I been out?"

"About an hour."

"Hell. Who's Azerbaijan?"

"Azahgi Bahajir," Octavia said, handing me a rough bit of blanket from the bunk.

"Azenburger . . . oh, screw it. Who is he?" I asked as I used the blanket to wipe my face.

"I am. Come," a deep voice answered. I turned to frown at the man standing in the doorway. It was one of the thugs who'd attacked us. "Prince Akbar has commanded you be brought to him."

"Why do I have a bad feeling that we're not in Kansas anymore?" I asked Octavia as she helped me get to my feet. The room spun for a few seconds but quickly settled back the way it should be.

"I'm not sure where Kansas is, but we *were* in France," Octavia answered with a delightful little frown between her equally delightful eyebrows. "Perhaps you're muddled. Did you hit your head? Are you seeing double?"

I put my arm around her and glared at the behemoth in the doorway. He had to be at least a foot taller than me, and I'm no slouch at six foot three. "It was a joke, love. All right, Az. Take us to your leader."

The Moghul rolled his eyes as he gestured for us to precede him.

I kept Octavia close to my side as we walked down a narrow corridor, and said softly to her, "The floor is vibrating."

"Yes."

"We're on an airship, aren't we?"

She glanced behind us to where the giant Moghul walked. "Not just any airship, but Akbar's."

"Damn."

"My thoughts exactly. Jack, perhaps you ought to let me handle the situation with the prince."

We reached the end of the corridor.

"Up," Azahgi said, prodding me in the back with a scimitar and nodding toward a set of metal spiral stairs. "Prince Akbar awaits you on the observation deck."

I let Octavia go first, tearing my mind from the contemplation of her legs as she climbed above me. "Why? Wait a minute. Don't tell me he's yet another of your boyfriends. I know you're not on some sort of a guys-in-power kick because I'm just an average Joe, but damn, Tavy. Do you think we could go a couple of days without running into yet another former lover?"

"I told you before—I've only had three lovers, and you know about them," she answered in what sounded like a growl. I reached the top of the stairs to find her glaring at me. I grinned.

"My apologies. You can talk to this Akbar guy all you

want, but I'm not going to let him hurt you. And before you get all prickly again and tell me that you can take care of yourself, let me remind you that I'm the man in this relationship, and we like to do the protecting when it's called for. Makes us feel like we're doing our job."

She continued to glare at me as Azahgi gave me a shove down the passageway. "Forward."

"I'm very well aware that you're a man," Octavia said with only a fleeting glance at my crotch. "And I understand that, as such, you feel the need to be protective and aggressive toward those you consider a threat, but I am fully capable of taking care of myself, and moreover, I am more experienced in dealing with Moghuls. Thus it is logical that I should be the one to deal with Akbar."

"It may be logical, but I've been kidnapped, drugged, and soaked with water. I'm going to have a few things to say about his idea of hospitality," I grumbled as Octavia opened the door ahead of us.

"You have no idea what sort of person he is," she answered.

"Oh, I think I took his measure pretty well the other day when I scared him off from raiding your ship," I said. "Yes, he's a warlord, but from what I saw, he's not a maniac, and thus, he can be reasoned with. I fully intend to do the latter."

"Jack—"

Wind hit us as the door swung wide, causing Octavia's skirts to flutter behind her. She said nothing more, just gave me a warning glance before entering the observation platform. Unlike the forward version on the *Tesla*, this one was mounted on the side of the gondola, a long rectangular stretch open to sky above and earth below, with substantial black metal railing that presumably kept folk from plummeting off the airship.

A man stood at the railing, his arms braced as he leaned out, obviously watching the world slip by beneath him. He turned at the sound of the door closing behind us. I was a bit surprised that Azahgi had left us alone with the prince, but one look at the two aether guns strapped to either hip explained a lot.

"You are awake," Akbar said in the same heavily accented voice I remembered from Rome. He was dressed much the same, in a long gold coat, white turban wrapped partially around his face, and dark goggles, no doubt to protect him from the wind on the platform. He pulled down the tail of the turban, revealing a fierce black mustache the approximate size of a dachshund.

"I tend to do that when people dump a pail of water on me," I said, pulling Octavia close.

She made an annoyed sound and jammed her elbow into my ribs. "Jack, stop it."

"I'm the man, dammit," I told her. "I get to do this."

"Not in front of others," she hissed.

I gave her a look that spoke volumes, which she pretty much ignored, just as I knew she would. "Look, I have a job to do here—that's to keep you safe. I'm not saying you can't do that on your own. I'm simply pointing out that thousands of years of evolution have primed me for this very moment. I am biologically and emotionally engineered to protect you in times of threat. He"—I pointed at Akbar—"is a threat."

"Actually, I don't believe I've threatened either one of you." Akbar thought a moment. "Yet."

"Therefore," I continued, ignoring the prince, "I will pull you to my side in an attempt to show him that you're mine, just in case he has any funny ideas about you, as well as warn him that he's going to have to go through me to get to you. I'm sorry if that offends your delicate sensibilities, but a guy's got to do what a guy has to do. So just let me do my job, and you can do yours, and everyone will be happy."

Akbar, his goggles glinting in the sun, nodded.

"And just what is my job?" Octavia asked, elbowing me again. "To stand around and look frail? To allow you to have your way without any regard to what is right or proper? To subjugate myself to you?"

I grinned at her, and leaned forward to give her a quick kiss. "Ah, Tavy, you're so damned adorable when you're pissed. I like it when your eyes shoot sooty sparks at me. In fact, I think I'll kiss you again just to rile you up a little more."

"Jack!" she said, giving a startled glance at the prince.

"Eh? Oh. Sorry," I told him.

"That's all right," he said with a shrug. "I understand."

"You do?" I asked, surprised.

"No, he doesn't."

"You are the man, as you say," he said with another shrug. "It's what we do. Women, they do not understand that. They say they do, but they really don't."

"I understand just fine!"

"I hear you," I told him. "They tell us to be sensitive and understanding, to spill our guts about every little thought that goes through our heads, and the next minute, they're screaming about a spider in the bathtub, and demanding we be macho spider-squashing he-men."

"I like spiders! I would never squash one!"

"Frequently they do not make any sense," Akbar agreed. "And the discussions they expect us to have regarding emotions—bah! It makes my blood curdle. It is one thing to admit to a woman that she is yours, that you regard her well, but that is not enough for them. They must have daily announcements of the state of your affections toward them."

"That's it. I'm leaving. You two can stand out here and be masculine together. I wash my hands of the pair of you."

I tightened my arm around Octavia as she tried to leave the deck. "I have to admit that I don't mind that so much. Usually if you tell a woman you love her, one thing leads to another and . . . well. You know."

Beneath that giant black mustache his lips pursed for a moment. "Ah. There is that."

We both looked at Octavia.

She glared first at Akbar, then at me. "You are sorely mistaken if you think I'm going to do anything but scorn you the next time you declare your love for me."

"She's crazy about me," I told Akbar, giving her a squeeze.

"Argh!"

"I can see that," he answered, putting his hands behind his back. "It makes the situation that much more regrettable that you have once again interfered with my plans."

"What plans?" I asked, my amusement with Octavia fading as I realized that Akbar might not be quite the pushover I assumed he was.

"My plans to end the empire, naturally." He turned to Octavia. "I understand that your ship was shot down by mistake. I would apologize for the inexperience on the captain's part, but I find it difficult to mourn the loss of an enemy ship."

"We could have been killed," I said, anger firing inside of me. "Any of the crew could have."

One shoulder lifted. "Perhaps. But you were not

killed, and thus you were in Angers, and I knew you would make an attempt to stop us from reaching England. You will therefore be my guests until after we destroy your emperor. And as time is short, you will do me the goodness of telling me just what you intended to do to stop my attack."

Octavia and I exchanged glances. "We had no plan to attack anyone," she said, looking somewhat confused.

"You didn't?" Akbar frowned. "Then what were you doing in the vicinity of my ship?"

"Trying to get tickets," I answered sharply. "Because one of your men shot down Tavy's ship. We didn't even know you were in the area."

Through the smoky lenses of the goggles I could see him eyeing me. "Did you not? Unfortunately, that matters little. We are, as you see, well across the Channel. Whether or not you intended on interfering with my plans, you will remain with us until we reach London in a few hours' time. At that point, I will decide what is to be done with you. Until then, you may return to your quarters."

"You're taking us to London?" Octavia asked, an odd expression on her face. It was almost as if she wanted to laugh, but was struggling to keep her face straight.

"Yes." He turned to look out over the English Channel. "I always prefer to keep my enemies within my sight."

"That just means you have to watch your back," I warned him as he waved a dismissive hand toward us. As if by magic, the door behind us opened, and Azahgi gestured for us to leave.

Akbar swiveled around to look at us. "From attack? By whom? You?"

"If you try this crap again, yes," I said, trying like the

devil to keep from whooping with joy. I scowled for good measure, and thought about shaking a fist at him, but decided it was too over-the-top.

Octavia waited until we were returned to the small cabin that was our cell before she collapsed with a weary sigh. "He's taking us to London."

I picked her up and twirled her around, kissing her soundly as I set her down. "Hours ahead of the train, right?"

She nodded, nibbling my lower lip. "At least four hours."

"Then we'll have that much more time to get to Hallie. Right." I set her down and rubbed my hands as I looked around the room. "Let's start planning our escape. We have a bed, a broken chair, something that I assume is a chamber pot, but don't really want to know, and two thumbtacks in the wall. I bet MacGyver could manufacturer a flamethrower or small thermonuclear device from that, but we'll have to make do with a simple smash and dash."

"The simpler the better," she said, then smiled, her eyes lighting with a glow that made my dick come to life. "Until then . . ."

She patted the narrow bunk.

Personal Log of Octavia E. Pye
Thursday, February 25
Forenoon Watch: One Bell

"Which way now?" Jack asked a few hours later as we caught our breaths.

I leaned against the rough wall of a warehouse, peering around him to make sure we hadn't been followed from the Moghul ship. Jack was barely breathing hard, the uncorseted rotter.

"We're at the river, so northwards. If we can get to a main street, we can get a cab," I said. "I think we lost them when you insisted we double back."

He beamed with pride. "Told you I knew how to handle a tail, even when it's made up of seven murderous Moghuls."

"Yes, well, they wouldn't have been quite so murderous if you hadn't been brandishing that chamber pot so effectively. I do hope you didn't hit Azahgi too hard."

"You of all people should know that I'm not going to whack someone's brains out. I just tapped him lightly on the head."

"Mmm. Let's try this way, shall we?" I pushed myself

away from the wall, and took Jack's hand as we hurried down the street.

"Are you sure this Etienne guy is going to be willing to attack a full contingent of your emperor's soldiers?" Jack asked after I briefly explained my plan to enlist the aid of the Black Hand. "Based on that raid on your ship in Rome, I have to say I don't have a whole lot of confidence in their black ops skills."

I frowned in confusion.

"Black ops means covert activities, such as freeing a prisoner from almost overwhelming odds."

"Oh. Well, the odds aren't overwhelming with regards to your sister—just very daunting. With the power of the Black Hand, I'm hoping we can overcome the troops that will be present to guard the prisoners. But even beyond that, Etienne will want to rescue the three members of the Hand who were captured in Rome. No doubt he has a plan of his own in place, and if it comes down to it, we can simply go along with him and rescue her at the same time."

"I hope you're right," he said, shaking his head, exhaustion and worry etched into the lines around his mouth. "Because we aren't going to have too many chances to save Hallie."

His words echoed in my head as we made our way through London, haunting me when we arrived travel-stained and crumpled at the headquarters of the Black Hand. I knew that Etienne had a plan in mind for disturbing the royal wedding, so I was confident he would be present in that city, hidden away as he marshaled his forces and honed his plans.

"Jack, my dear," I said as we were shown into the inner sanctum of what appeared to be a commonplace block of insurer's offices, but was in fact the headquarters of the Black Hand, "you know I have every respect for you—"

"But let you do the talking?" Jack grinned as he interrupted me. "This is getting to be a habit."

"Jack—"

"Don't worry, sweetheart, I'm not such a pushy bastard that I have to be the one to make all the arrangements. I'm well aware that you have more experience with this guy than I do."

"I would never refer to you as a pushy bastard, let alone think it," I told him gently.

"OK, then, I'm not so jealous that I have to put on a show in front of all your ex-lovers." He eyed me for a second. "Although I hope you don't mind if I make it clear that we are a couple. I may not be overly jealous, but I wouldn't like him getting the wrong idea and thinking he could have you all to himself again."

I kissed his earlobe. "I assure you that Etienne wouldn't dream of thinking that."

"Oh really? What's wrong with him?" Jack's eyes narrowed in suspicion. "Just how long were you two together?"

"About the length of time it took me to discover that he had no intention of having a monogamous relationship—three days."

Jack looked uncertain for a moment, then relaxed. "His loss, my gain, so I'm not going to complain."

The wrought iron lift door opened, and we stepped out onto the fourth floor, swept immediately into pandemonium. Black Hand folk choked the hallway as they bustled hither and yon, many of them talking as they did so, although whom they were conversing with was difficult to detect.

"—said we wouldn't have enough time to rally all the

steam carriages, but would they listen to me? No! And now what am I to do? Those carriages go two miles an hour. They can't possibly make it here in time to do any good—"

"—blasted William suddenly decided to forgo the Carmelite nuns at the wedding, which means a good six months' work wasted, utterly wasted, not to mention all that cloth it took to make up the habits—"

"—Please, Mr. Hanson, you must sign the chit or else the quartermaster will not release the bombs, and I ask you, what good are bombardiers without bombs?"

"So this is what a revolutionary headquarters looks like," Jack said, holding my arm tightly as people swarmed against and around us as they attended to the last-minute business connected with the royal wedding. Or rather, the attack that was planned against it. "Not quite what I expected."

I eased my way between two women who were arguing about the merits of beards and wigs as disguises, and headed for the double doors at the end of the hallway. "What was it you expected?"

"A lot less chaos and more order," Jack replied as I ducked when two men emerged from a room bearing a portable aether cannon on their shoulders. "Just how effective are these people?"

"Enough so that the emperor has made it his top priority to eliminate them," I answered, tugging on his hand. I stopped before the double doors and raised my hand to knock. "It may look chaotic, but I assure you there is a method to Etienne's plans."

"There is more than method. There is brilliance," a voice answered me as the door swung open. "Which you of all people should know, Octavia. I thought you were in Italy."

"We were. We came back," I said simply, noting the fevered glint to Etienne's dark green eyes. He always reminded me of a cat, sly and purposeful, as if he had a thousand secrets that consumed him. He stood looking at me now, his expression mildly annoyed.

"We need to see you for a few minutes," I said, pushing past him into his office.

"I am busy. The emperor is getting married today, if you hadn't noticed," he said with acid sarcasm.

"There are still three hours before the first of the festivities begins," I said, glancing at the clock. "And it is about that we have come to seek help."

Etienne looked for a moment like he was just going to walk out of the room, but his gaze slid over to Jack, assessing him quickly before returning to me. He closed the door and leaned against it. "I can give you five minutes, no more."

"Thank you. This is Jack Fletcher. He is American."

Etienne's coppery brown eyebrows rose, but he said nothing. I'm sure he noticed the possessive manner with which Jack slid his arm around my waist as he said, "Octavia has spoken highly of you, Etienne. Pleased to meet you."

"Jack's sister was taken by the emperor's forces in Rome. Unjustly, naturally."

"Naturally," Etienne said, his voice waspish.

Jack stiffened.

I elbowed him and continued. "She was brought to England to be part of the wedding executions along with the three who were captured during your raid on the *Tesla*. The executions are to be held at noon today. I thought we could piggyback on whatever plan you have to rescue your men."

"What plan?" he asked.

"You don't have a plan?" I asked, horrified.

"On the contrary, I have lots of plans. None of them concern the execution, however."

Jack and I exchanged glances fraught with frustration and despair. "All right, then you can assist us in rescuing your men. We'll simply release them when we get Jack's sister."

"No."

I continued, ignoring his refusal. "Since the emperor and his bride are to attend the executions, I thought you would relish the chance to disrupt it, and we could join forces and work together to achieve both ends."

"No," Etienne said again, this time turning to open the door.

"Etienne!" I jumped forward and grabbed his arm. "You can't mean that. Your own people are there! You wouldn't let them die unnecessarily, would you?"

"I never say things I don't mean," he answered, frowning at my hand on his arm.

"Listen here, this isn't a game," Jack said, his hands fisted as he moved up beside me. "This is my sister's life we're talking about, and the lives of the people who look to you for leadership, people who were following *your* orders when they were captured. Aren't you supposed to be protecting people from this emperor you want out of the way so badly?"

Etienne's cool green gaze passed over Jack for a few seconds. "Not in the least. Our goal is to overthrow the government, not protect the common man."

"For God's sake—"

"Etienne, please." I tightened my hold on his arm. "I have never asked you for a favor. I have worked untiringly for you since I was sixteen. I ask now that you honor my work, honor that done by Robert Anstruther, and give me the aid we need."

He shook his head before I had more than a few words out. "It would serve no purpose, Octavia."

"But the emperor will be there!"

"It doesn't matter."

I stared at him for a moment or two. "I can't believe you can be so callous."

He shrugged. "You say callous—I say discriminating. I have no wish to waste time and resources on another attack on a prison. I would have thought after the last one you organized, you'd feel the same way."

"Well, I don't!"

"It matters not. We have more important plans in place."

"You're so willing to throw away the lives of innocent people?" Jack asked, his voice thick.

Etienne shrugged again. "It is the way things are. Every member of the Black Hand is willing to give his life if needed." His eyes slid over to me. "And that is how it will remain. Now, since you are in town, Octavia, I can put you to a much better use. The reception is to be held on the grounds of the palace. We have several airships ready and waiting outside of town, and we could use your ability to pilot in order to bomb the reception."

"I'm sorry, I will be too busy rescuing the prisoners," I said coolly, taking Jack's hand.

Etienne frowned. "I have mentioned before, Octavia, that one of your shortcomings is that you do not see the overall picture. Do you not realize that the death of the innocent prisoners will do more for our cause than rescuing them ever could? The public will be incited. They will protest the death of an innocent woman. It will engender hard feelings amongst them. I regret that the innocent must suffer for our cause, but they will die a glorious death, for a just and right cause."

"I'm sorry, Octavia," Jack said softly as he shook off my hand.

"Oh, Jack, no—"

The words had barely left my lips when Jack punched Etienne in the face, the sickening sound of a bone cracking and flesh meeting flesh making me grimace as Etienne dropped to the ground.

Jack shook his hand as Etienne curled up into a ball, moaning loudly. "The sign of a good leader is one who values *all* life, a concept you clearly fail at. You may think that sacrificing my sister is a glorious thing, but we aren't going to let that happen."

Etienne uncovered his face, his nose slanted to the side, blood streaming out of it to wash over his mouth and chin. "You'll die for this."

"Not before I see my sister safe," Jack vowed, and, grabbing me, hauled me over Etienne's prone self, making sure, I noticed with a stab of amusement, of stepping on Etienne's hand as he did so.

"I would suggest haste in getting out of here," I said, spinning off to the left and pushing past a number of people who were toiling up a small set of back stairs. "Etienne will not hesitate to have us confined."

"Right with you," Jack said as we sprinted down the stairs. Above us, I could hear Etienne shouting orders to stop us.

Luckily, there was so much noise and confusion as everyone went about their business, we managed to slip out of the building without being restrained. It wasn't until we were blocks away, however, out of breath from running, that I felt secure enough to stop and hail a cab.

"What the hell?" Jack asked as a steam carriage stopped at my direction. "You have cars?"

I gave the cabbie my address and climbed into the front seat, Jack following. "This is a steam carriage. They are commonplace in London."

"I'll be damned." Jack peered around behind us. The cabbie watched him with a wary expression. "Where's the steam? I can hear it hiss, but I can't see anything."

"The boiler and engine are beneath us. Jack, please, now is not the time to examine it." I yanked on his coattails as he hung his upper body over the edge of the carriage to get a glimpse at the mechanisms underneath. "We have more important things to discuss," I added in a lower tone of voice.

He rubbed the knuckles of his right hand, red and somewhat swollen. "I'm not going to apologize for punching him."

"I wouldn't ask you to. Etienne is far too narrow-minded for his own good. If you hadn't struck him, I might have been inclined to do it. But that's neither here nor there—we have slightly less than three hours to come up with plan of rescue." I consulted my pocket watch. "The *Aurora* is probably landing at this moment. The prisoners will be sent up to London via train."

"Then we won't have time to get to her there?"

"No." I slumped in defeat. "It's going to have to be here, in London."

Jack took my hand and, after a moment, kissed my fingers. "If it's too much for you, Octavia—"

"Don't be ridiculous. We'll find a way to save her," I interrupted, forcing a smile to my lips. "I have a few cards up my sleeves yet."

"Really?" He made a show of looking up my sleeve. "I don't see anything there. What do you have in mind?"

"Well, Alan should be in London by now, too," I said, shying away from a thought that had been hanging in the back of my mind ever since Etienne had refused us. "He will help us."

"How?"

"I don't know," I admitted. "But he is a resourceful man, and he will give us whatever aid is within his ability."

"Will it be enough?" Jack asked morosely.

I was unable to answer that question. We rode in silence to the house Robert Anstruther had left me, my stomach sick with the knowledge that we were fast running out of time.

Personal Log of Octavia E. Pye
Thursday, February 25
Forenoon Watch: Four Bells

"So there's nothing you can do to help us?"

"I wish I could, Jack, but my hands are tied." Alan cast me a forlorn gaze. "As it is, I'm juggling the emperor's demand that all diplomats be present at the wedding, and Etienne's plan to have me single-handedly knock out a troop of guards and open up one of the sealed entrances so the Black Hand can infiltrate the reception. I really only came to warn Octavia about the Moghul attack that is evidently imminent."

I searched his face, but didn't find any answers there. "You're sure that it's the same ship that attacked us?"

"The report Etienne slipped me was that a black Moghul warship was seen crossing the channel this morning. It had a complement of twenty-four cannons, and was heading for London," he said, his voice neutral.

"That sounds like the one that destroyed Tavy's ship," Jack said, momentarily distracted.

"I'd give a lot to know why they did that," I said, picking a piece of lint off my sleeve. "The *Tesla* posed no direct threat to them."

"Perhaps it was just an inexperienced captain," Alan said, shrugging. "Or someone who didn't know what he was doing. I am surprised they attacked the *Tesla*, too, when just two hours behind you was the ambassador's ship with several officials from the Italian court, along with myself, naturally."

"You wouldn't think the Moghuls would allow their warships to run amok in the hands of inexperienced crews."

"They seem a rather brutal lot," Jack said. "Perhaps they just attack anything that isn't part of their empire."

"Perhaps," I said, reaching for the teapot to refresh both men's cups.

Jack accepted his tea with a little frown. "What I find amazing is that both the Moghuls and the revolutionaries are going to attack at the same time. It's going to be a madhouse out there. Although, you know, we might be able to use that to our benefit."

"That's a thought," Alan said, trying to look cheerful and failing miserably. He glanced at the clock and sighed heavily. "I must go. The emperor asked specifically to see me before the ceremony, and if I am to have time to deal with Etienne's request, I must see William first. My dear, you will both be in my thoughts."

I rose with him, allowing him to take my hand and press a kiss to the back of it. "Thank you for warning us about the Moghul attack, Alan. I know you're pressed for time, too."

"I wanted to make sure that you would be well out of it," he said simply, his dark eyes warm with affection and regret. "I only wish I could help you free Jack's sister."

My gaze dropped, my fingers growing cold, a polite

murmur all I could utter. There were things I had not told anyone, not even Alan. Now was not the time to unburden myself.

"I'm going to reconnoiter the prison where they're taking Hallie," Jack said, pulling on his jacket. "If we can find a weakness there, we can exploit it. You coming with me?"

I shot him an outraged look. "Jack, you know full well that I am wholly devoted to the idea of freeing your sister. I would not now change my intention of doing so."

He pulled me into a gentle embrace. "I didn't mean to ruffle your feathers, sweetheart. I just didn't know if there was someone you could see about getting her released."

My gaze fell to his neck. I said nothing.

Jack's hands tightened on my arms. "Octavia? Is there someone?"

I bit my bottom lip, my stomach in turmoil. "Yes."

"Really?" Relief and hope filled his voice. "Then for God's sake, woman, let's go see him. We have only a little over two hours left."

"It's not that easy, Jack," I said slowly, wanting nothing more than to fold myself in his arms and hide from the world. I looked at his face, infinitely dear to me now, and didn't want to acknowledge the truth.

"Why not?"

"I love your eyes," I said. "Have I mentioned that? I love that they don't match. I love how they sparkle when you tease me, and how they seem to radiate heat when you make love to me."

He searched my face for a moment, his thumb brushing along my cheekbone. "What is it you don't want to tell me?"

Pain and regret and despair roiled within me. I closed

my eyes for a moment so he wouldn't see it. "I can save your sister's life."

Silence filled the small front sitting room of the red-brick house that had been my home for most of my life.

"But?" Jack asked.

I opened my eyes again. "But it will cost me mine."

He turned to stone in my arms, his muscles tightening, as did his expression, his eyes going flinty. "No."

"It's the only way," I said, wanting to cry. "We cannot breach the prison on our own. There will be nothing to exploit."

"You don't know that until we go and check it out," Jack said, pulling me to the door. "Let's go and look."

"I do know," I said, my voice thick with tears. I pulled to a stop, not wanting to bare my secrets, but knowing I had no other option.

"How?" he asked.

"Do you remember what Etienne said about it being foolish to attack the prison?"

"Yes, damn him."

"My guardian, Robert Anstruther, was arrested for treason. He and his wife were taken to the prison. I convinced Etienne to help me free them." Pain at the memory lashed me with freshly honed barbs. "Seven people died in the attempt, Jack. Seven people died because of my insistence that we try to free my guardians. We were not successful. I thought perhaps this time it would be different, but I fear Etienne is right. It would end in disaster just as the last attempt did."

"We have to try," Jack said, and the agony in his voice almost brought me to my knees.

I swallowed back my misery, and nodded. "There is no other decision to be made. I will go and see to your sister's freedom."

"No." Jack grabbed me as I marched resolutely past him. "I'm not going to let you sacrifice yourself."

"There is no other way," I said, warmed despite the chilly knowledge of what would transpire.

"I love you, Tavy," he said, his forehead against mine as his arms wrapped around me in a steely embrace. "I love you with all my heart."

"You love your sister, too."

"I love you both. I want you both in my life."

Tears pricked at my eyes. "You don't know me, Jack. There are things about me that would change your mind. I'm not who I seem to be. You must believe me that it's best this way."

His arms loosened, his voice oddly without emotion. "You'd rather die than spend your life with me?"

"No, oh no," I wailed, flinging myself onto his chest, kissing his neck. "But there are things I've kept from you—secrets, things you don't know about me—"

"Stop it," he said, shaking me. "Do you think I've told you every little thing there is to know about me? Learning about each other is going to be one of the delights to come, Tavy. And I fully intend for us to have that."

His jaw set, he pulled me down the stairs to the front door.

"There's no time," I protested.

"Yes, there is." He searched the street for a cab, didn't see one, and, with my hand firmly in his, proceeded down the street to a busy intersection. Five minutes later we were in yet another of the steam carriages that jetted about London at the legal limit of two miles per hour. "Now, tell me about this person who we're going to see, and why you think the only way you can save Hallie is to sacrifice yourself."

I fought my inner demons for a second, then turned

around in my seat and yelled a new direction to the driver. I had to yell it twice, since the sibilant hiss of the steam coming from beneath the carriage was enough to mask our conversation.

"Did I hear you right?" Jack asked as I sat back in my seat. "You want to go to a palace?"

"There is only one person who can save your sister now—the emperor. It is to him we must plead our case."

"But . . ." Jack's brow furrowed. "Didn't you say that you and he used to be together? Why would you think he'd want to kill you?"

"We were together." I smoothed my gray leather gloves over my fingers. "We were until he discovered something about me, something that changed our relationship."

"What was that?" Jack asked.

I shook my head. "I will tell you that later. For now, you must simply know that our parting was not . . ."

"Amicable?" he suggested.

"That would be an understatement. William allowed me to leave and, for the sake of what we once had, appeared to forget about my existence. But it was made very clear to me that should I push myself upon his notice again, I would pay for what he viewed as the gravest of crimes."

Jack fought with his curiosity for a few seconds before nodding. "All right. You may think I don't know you, Octavia, but I have faith in your character enough to let you tell me whatever it is you have to tell me in your own time."

I was touched, very touched, warmth swelling over me at the gesture of belief. "Thank you," I managed to say.

"So you think that if you go to the emperor and ask for Hallie's life, he'll release her, but what—put you in prison in her place?"

"Quite likely." Or worse.

Jack made a face and held my hand. "I won't let that happen."

"You can't go against William, Jack—he's the emperor," I said, unable to keep from laughing at the obstinate expression on his face.

"Says who? There's more than one way to skin an emperor, Octavia, and I mean to show you just that."

I eyed him. He spoke with determination, his jaw set, his gaze resolute. All warning signs that he had some plan in mind, a plan that would quite likely spell his own doom unless I did something to avert that. "I hope you don't intend on doing anything foolish, Jack. As I said, I am not in favor, and I would have absolutely no influence on anyone should you run afoul of William."

"You just get us in to see him, and leave the rest to me."

"Yes, well, getting in to see him isn't the problem." I glanced out of the window. The crowds had been building on the sidewalks, several people deep by now—citizens of the empire who clutched little flags bearing pictures of the emperor and the duchess, and who were willing to endure a long wait just to glimpse the emperor and his bride as they passed on the way to the cathedral.

"I take it you have a way for us to get in?"

"More or less. There is a well-hidden secret gate to the gardens. Only the imperial family and one or two trusted retainers know of it. I gather it was put in place in order to provide an exit should an emergency occur. William showed it to me when I was a very small child. We will hope the way to it is clear."

"You know, in my world, the queen lives in Buckingham Palace," Jack said as we drove slowly toward Kew Gardens. We passed a bystreet that I recognized, and prayed Jack wouldn't.

"Really? How very odd. I don't believe William has ever even been in Buckingham House," I said, patting his knee so he'd stop looking out the window. He obliged me by waggling his eyebrows. I smiled at him, catching the sight of the freshly erected gallows in my peripheral vision. "Emperors have always lived in Kew Palace. It's actually a very nice palace as a grand house goes. Not too large, but warm."

"If I ask you how you met the emperor, will you be able to tell me?" he asked, the smile still in his eyes.

I let my gaze drop. "I was lost. I ended up in the garden. William heard me crying, and came to investigate. He was only a few years older than me, and had escaped his tutor for a little illicit tree climbing in the back garden."

"And your parents never came forward to claim you?" Jack asked, his face now full of sympathy.

"No. The emperor, William's father, tried to locate them, but was not successful. We'll get out here, I think. We have to go to the very far end of Kew Gardens. I'll tell the driver to stop."

The gardens were thankfully not very occupied since most people were on the streets, so it didn't take us long at all to get to the distant corner that touched on the high brick wall marking the boundary between the palace gardens and the public garden. I stopped at a distinctive yew bush, once cut in the shape of a topiary, but now sadly grown out so its former shape was almost unrecognizable, and counted out seven paces. After a quick check to make sure we were unobserved, I pressed the twelfth brick from the bottom, and was rewarded with a dull grinding noise.

"Push," I told Jack, putting both hands on the wall and heaving.

Jack did likewise, and the wall sagged inward a few inches.

"I'll be damned. There is a secret gate."

"It's more of an opening than a gate, and it feels like no one has used it since I was a child. We'll have to widen it more."

Five minutes' work gave us a gap that was big enough to allow us to slip through. We put the wall back into place before hurrying along the tall yew hedge.

"Jack, I should warn you—"

"I know, I know. Let you do the talking." He sighed. "Some day we're going to go back to my world, and then I'll get to boss you around."

"I'm not bossing you. I'm simply requesting that you let me handle the situation with the palace, since I am more familiar with it. And as for returning to your world—"

Jack's hand clamped over my mouth as he pulled me more or less into the yew hedge. Just as he did so, I heard feminine voices. On the other side of a short brick wall that designated what was referred to as the children's garden, a small gaggle of women strolled. We could just see their heads and shoulders as they perambulated the pathways. The woman in front was familiar to anyone who had read recent newspapers, or attempted to purchase a tea towel.

I turned my head and put my mouth next to Jack's ear. "That's the duchess."

"I gathered as much. What are they doing out here?"

I listened to their chatter for a few minutes. Before

I could comment, a footman approached and informed the duchess that she was wanted. She and her ladies-in-waiting followed him back to the palace.

"That was close. But it does bring up a point," Jack said as we emerged from the hedge, brushing twigs and leaves and small insects from our persons. "Just how are we going to get in to see the emperor if there are all sorts of people running around inside?"

I took the hand he offered, plucked a beetle from his hair, and pulled him a few yards down the hedge before stopping and scrabbling in the dirt at the corner of the hedge.

Jack whistled as I peeled back a bit of lawn and revealed a brass ring set into a flat stone.

"You don't think a palace as old as this isn't riddled with secret passages," I said, moving back to allow him to pull up the trapdoor.

"I'm so glad I've never been one to scoff at a cliché," he grinned, grunting as he strained at the stone.

I pulled a small narrow cylinder from my bag, shaking it several times. A dull glow emanated from it, not as bright as an oil lantern, but providing enough light to see by.

"I don't believe it. You have glow sticks?" Jack asked as I crawled backward down the unevenly cut stones that led into the earth.

"I have no idea what that is. This is called a ghost lantern. It's made by exciting particles of aether. As they rub against each other, they release a bit of energy which manifests itself in light. They don't last very long, but I remember my way into the emperor's suite well enough."

Jack lowered the trapdoor over our heads as he followed. The passageway was exactly as I remembered

it—close, smelling of earth and damp and things long
dead, the air musty and thick. It made me nervous to
feel so buried beneath the earth, but I held the ghost
lantern aloft and took comfort from both its gentle glow
and the feel of Jack's hand on my waist.

"I've never been in a secret passageway before. I
think the only thing this adventure is missing is a trip to
the dungeon."

"I fervently hope we shall not be forced to endure
that," I said, my voice sounding as muffled and flat as his.
"Now, let me see. . . . There should be some stairs to our
left soon, and then . . . ah yes, there they are."

After sloping slightly downhill, the passage changed
from earth walls and floors to ones of stone and wood.

"I take it we're in the palace now," Jack whispered
as I held the light up on the narrow stone staircase that
melted into the darkness on our left.

"Yes, although you don't really need to whisper until
we're outside of the emperor's chamber. The walls are
stone on the lower levels, and quite thick."

The glow from the ghost lantern was enough to warn
the things that lived in the passage of our coming, so
luckily, we did not see any of the occupants, although
we noted signs of their demises. I do not have an undue
aversion to rodents, but neither do I seek their company,
and for that reason, I made a bit more noise than I normally would have as we made our way up two flights of
narrow, ill-cut stone stairways, and down a passage so
narrow that we had to walk in single file.

"The opening to the emperor's bedchamber should
be somewhere along here," I whispered, pressing the
dark wood panels. "There is a panel that is hidden beneath a tapestry that slides . . . Ah, here it is."

I pressed the wood inward and up. It gave way a few

inches, sliding along an invisible track in the paneling with only a whisper of sound.

The tapestry smelled as musty as the passageway when I pushed it aside and peeked out into the room. Sounds that had been muffled by it were only too clearly audible as I stared in horror at the sight of a man standing at the end of a bed, a pair of legs clad in stockings wrapped around his hips.

Jack was close behind me, obviously about to follow me into the room. As I hurriedly dropped the tapestry and stepped back into the passage, he grunted in pain. I put my hand over his mouth to warn him before sliding the panel back into place.

"I'm sorry I stepped on you," I whispered once it was closed again.

"Those boots have damned deadly heels," he said, hopping on one foot as he pulled the other out of his shoe and rubbed the toes. "What's wrong? Isn't he there?"

"Erm . . ." I shook the ghost lantern again and set it on the ground so I could examine Jack's foot. "Yes, he's there."

"Ow. Stop moving my toes. I think they're broken."

"They're not broken, just bruised. And I do apologize about stepping on them. I had no idea you were that close behind me. Here, let me wrap them together. That may ease the pain somewhat."

Jack sat on the ground, his foot propped up on his knee, as I pulled a handkerchief from my bag, using it to bind his abused toes together.

"OK, if he's there, then why didn't we go in to talk to him?"

"He was busy." I pulled his sock on, and assisted him to slide the foot into his shoe.

"Busy with what? Octavia, we have"—he pulled out his pocket watch and tipped it so the face caught the glow of the lantern—"slightly less than two hours before my sister is hanged. I don't care if he's busy. We have to save her *now*."

"I can guarantee you that if we were to talk to William now, we would not receive any favor from him. In fact, quite the opposite."

"Why? What's he doing?"

I coughed and brushed off my skirt. "He's just . . . busy."

"I don't have time for this," Jack muttered, pressing against the panel.

"Jack, no—" I clamped my lips closed as he slid it open again, my hand on his arm as he shoved aside the tapestry and looked into the room. I averted my gaze.

Jack pulled back, slid the panel home, and gave me a sour look. "What sort of a man bonks his bride hours before the wedding?"

"Evidently one who couldn't wait. Unfortunately, that is exactly what we will have to do."

"I agree that interrupting him while he's getting a jump on his honeymoon isn't a good idea, but we don't have time to sit around and wait for him to finish. And I'll be damned if I let my sister hang because the emperor is too busy getting it off to save her."

I leaned against the wall and crossed my arms. "I don't see that we have any other choice. We're just going to have to wait for him to finish."

"Well, how long will that take?"

"How on earth do you expect me to know that?" I asked.

"You've slept with him. You must know how long he takes."

"As long as is needed," I answered somewhat waspishly, I admit.

"Great." Jack slumped against the wall. "So we just sit here and wait for him to finish."

I took his hand. "We can check on the ... er ... progress periodically. Until then, we can talk."

"About what?"

"Whatever you wish to talk about. What interests you?"

"You." He sounded cross and irritable.

I smiled in the almost darkness. "What else?"

"Making love to you."

"I agree that's a subject I am most interested in, as well, but hardly suitable for our location."

Jack turned to look at me, the petulant expression fading into something that made my belly suddenly feel warm. "You think not? Then let's can the talk and just do the deed itself."

I blinked at him in surprise. "You want to make love here?"

"Sure."

He started unbuttoning his trousers.

I gestured toward the walls. "But this is a filthy passage. There are rats here."

"Not around us. Tell you what, I'll volunteer to be on the bottom. You can climb on top."

I was about to refuse, as any sane woman would, when he pulled me down onto his legs, and nuzzled my cleavage. "Jack, no, we shouldn't. Really, we shouldn't. This is a secret passage, not a bed."

"Sweetheart, there's nothing I want more than to get into your secret passage," he mumbled into my breasts, pulling aside my blouse, corset cover, and chemise to reveal a breast. I shivered at the combination of the cool air of the passageway and the heat of his mouth as it descended upon my flesh.

"Your double entendres . . . oh, yes, please, right there . . . leave much to be desired. . . . Could you . . . ? Thank you. My breasts get jealous if you pay attention to only one of them." I clutched Jack's shoulders and gave in to my inner wanton, arching my back as he moved over to the other breast, laving it with the same sweet heat that threatened to set all of me alight. "No, no, Jack, we must stop. This isn't right."

Jack looked up, grinning, the ribbon from my corset cover clenched between his teeth. "I know. It's very dirty of us, isn't it?"

"Dirty isn't so much the word as unwise," I said with dignity, or as much dignity as one could have when one's bosom was bared and slick with moisture.

"Come on, Octavia. Let go of that reserve. I guarantee you'll enjoy yourself if you do."

"We are in a filthy secret passageway, just a few feet away from the emperor. I don't know why this makes you quite so determined to make love, but I assure you, it's not a setting that arouses me in the least," I said, aware that I sounded prim and prudish, but clearly, someone had to keep her head in this situation.

"Oh really?" Jack's mismatched gaze positively glittered with wickedness as he flicked his thumb over my bare nipple. "So that doesn't do anything for you at all?"

"No, of course not." I cleared my throat as I pulled up my chemise, inwardly cringing at the patent lie.

He raised both eyebrows at my nipple. It was beaded and tight and rosy, and looked very much like a nipple that had been pleasured within an inch of its life.

I cleared my throat again. "I'm a little chilly, that's all."

"Uh-huh. So, despite the fact that we're alone here together, just you and me and no one else, just the two of us, you sitting on my thighs and a mere couple of inches away from my dick, despite all that, you're wholly unmoved and don't want me to make love to you until your eyes cross, your legs shake, and your body does that delicious convulsive thing that damn near wrings my balls dry?"

Something resembling the sound of a whimper emerged from my lips as I pulled up my corset cover. "Um . . . I'm sorry, I wasn't paying attention. What was the question?"

"Octavia?" Jack's voice was even, but there was an undertone that told me he was about at the end of his tether.

"Yes?"

"You're the worst liar I've ever met in my life. I hope to God you're ready."

Before I could open my mouth to dispute such base abuse, he lifted my hips, and impaled me. I was, naturally, more than ready for him, but still, the invasion of him so hard and hot inside me took my breath away. For as long as he held still, that is, but the second he started moving, urging my hips into a motion that consumed me, all thoughts of things as mundane as breathing left my mind.

"Lovemaking should never be done under such unhygienic circumstances," I panted as I rose on him, flexing my muscles as I did so, trying to make him groan nonstop. "We could catch who knows what here."

Jack's fingers dug deep into my hips. Luckily my corset kept him from hurting me, but I knew by both the strength of his thrusts upward, and the extremely ragged nature of his breathing—not to mention the fact that it was his eyes that were, at that moment, crossed—that he was enjoying himself as much as I was. "You're doing that deliberately, aren't you?"

I sank down on him slowly, savoring the feeling at once so alien and yet so familiar, as my body welcomed him into its depths. "What? Lecturing you?"

His entire body jerked as I tightened my newfound muscles around him. "No, that. That squeezing thing."

"I did that before, Jack. You seemed to enjoy it, so—" I rose until only the very tip of him was inside me. I clenched my inner muscles as tight as I could, and swiveled my hips as I sank downward again. "—so I thought I would do it again."

"You may have done something before, but it wasn't like this. You've been working out!"

I froze for a moment, staring down into his outraged eyes. "I beg your pardon?"

"Admit it! You weren't this strong the other day when you did that swivel move. You almost ripped my dick off then with it—now you're about to emasculate me entirely. The only way you could get that strong is if you've been working out."

"Working out?"

"Your muscles." He pulled one hand from my hip to gesture at the juncture of our bodies. "Down there. Don't deny it."

I stared at him for a moment, trying to sort out what he was saying with the emotion that was so stark in his face.

"Jack."

"Look! You're doing it again. Holy Jesus and all his saints! You're going to kill me! Don't stop!"

I released the muscles that were gripping him so tightly and leaned forward to kiss him. "You really are the strangest man I've ever met. I have no idea why I love you so much, I really don't. Now be quiet so I can continue emasculating you, not that I will because your parts seem to be just fine after we're done. More than fine, quite hale and hearty and usually ready to go again in a surprisingly short amount of time—"

Jack stopped me from continuing by the simple act of wrapping his hand into my hair and pulling me down to kiss all thoughts from my brain. Our movements became frantic, the lovely rhythm changing to that of a primal nature, a glorious end in sight that we strained against each other to achieve.

Jack pushed me over the edge by sliding his hands under my skirt and petticoat, cupping my behind in his hands as he leaned backward, altering the angle of his attack. My moans of pleasure mingled with his as rapture broke over me, the waves of climax rippling outward in a seemingly never-ending moment that seemed to stop time itself.

I opened my eyes to the sound of an echoed roar, words that were as sweet to me as the purest honey.

"I love you, too," I said, leaning down to kiss him as he lay collapsed against the wall, his body limp, his head lolling.

He opened one eye and glared at me. "What happened to you fonding me?"

I nipped the tip of his nose. "You grew on me."

He shifted me, a devilish glint in his eyes. "I'll grow inside—"

A noise from behind us had me leaping to my feet, jerking up my chemise and blouse, as Jack hurriedly buttoned his trousers. He pulled me behind him as light suddenly flooded the passage.

I peered over his shoulder as I finished buttoning

the last buttons, my eyes growing wide with dismay as I noted who had opened the panel.

Three men wearing the imperial livery were accompanied by two more who bore the police uniform.

"There they are," one of the men said. I recognized him from years past as being William's valet. "Just as I thought—dirty revolutionaries trying to kill the king. Well, you failed, you filth. The king is gone, but he'll enjoy seeing you strung up with the rest of the scum. Take them away!"

Personal Log of Octavia E. Pye
Thursday, February 25
Forenoon Watch: Eight Bells

"Let me see if I have all this straight."

A rough hand shoved me forward, accompanied by the smell of stale garlic and old ale, and a rougher voice. "Forward, you lot! You've got a date with the emperor, you have!"

I ignored the snickers of the men lining the dank, dimly lit passage, and thought furiously.

"You and Jack, in an attempt to rescue me from the gallows, were having sex in a hallway."

"It was a secret passageway, not a hallway," I corrected Jack's sister before continuing to try to come up with some sort of plan.

"You and Jack were having sex in a secret passageway in the mistaken belief that this would somehow save me from being killed?"

"It was part of our plan," I said, stumbling when the gaoler shoved me again. With manacles on my feet and my hands tied to a long rope that snaked down the line of condemned prisoners, I had little hope of saving myself from a fall should he continue to do that.

"Prisoners will be silent!" the gaoler roared, and pushed me aside to move up to the front of the line, where the men were tied together. "Else you'll wish you had been!"

"Well, it must have been a hell of a plan," Hallie said, managing to give me a half smile. "Too bad it didn't work."

"You seem remarkably at peace," I said, keeping my voice low, and one eye on the gaoler as we shuffled our way along the passage. "I didn't think you would be ill-treated, but if you will not mind my saying so, I expected you to be a good deal more distraught."

"Oh, I was, right up until I realized the truth." She made an airy gesture.

"What truth?"

"Shhh!"

The woman behind me gave me a none-too-gentle push to remind me of the gaoler's threats.

I spun around and glared at her. "Do you mind? I am attempting to have a conversation with my friend."

"Ooh, ain't you the hoity-toity one," the woman said, sneering at me from beneath unkempt hair and a filthy face. I mentally compared her with Hallie, who, although somewhat rumpled, was clean and appeared civilized. "Well, you can just stick your pride up your arse, 'cause you ain't no better'n anyone else here."

"I don't believe a debate about the class structure in modern-day England is at all appropriate at the moment; however, I will point out that I am here wholly through a set of unfortunate circumstances. I have done nothing wrong."

"They all say that," the woman's companion said, jerking her line and sniffing. "None of us here done anything wrong, but you try getting the judge to believe that."

"I have not seen a judge, nor have I been charged with anything, let alone had a trial," I pointed out, righteous indignation swelling within me. "My ... er ... companion and myself were simply hauled away from the emperor's palace and told we were to be executed for unnamed and unproven crimes which we did not commit."

"Go on," the first woman said, and curled her upper lip at me.

"It's really best if you don't rile them," Hallie said, tugging at my sleeve. I heeded her advice and returned my attention to the line of prisoners, staring at the back of Jack's head.

"What truth?" I asked her.

"Huh?"

"What truth is it you discovered that has relieved your mind so greatly?"

"Oh." Her face took on a serene expression. "Once I realized that my way out of this world was right in front of me, I stopped fighting everything."

"Your way out?" I shook my head. "Hallie, I know this has been a most difficult experience for you, but death is not the answer. I admit things look a little bleak right now, but I have an idea, and if I can just see it through to fruition, then we will all of us be safe."

"No, no, you don't understand—I'm not suicidal. Far from it! I have a lot to live for. Don't you see? If I die here, then I get returned to my own world."

I stared at her, my heart filled with sadness. "No, Hallie, you don't."

"Pfft." She dismissed me with a complacent smile. "You don't know anything about it. You're part of this world, so you probably can't imagine anything outside it. But I know I'm right."

"Hallie, I assure you that—"

"Prisoners, halt!"

We had shuffled our way through the dismal prison to a sort of antechamber. Beyond it, through an open doorway, sunlight poured in. Although the air was almost balmy for February, a chill rippled down my arms and back at the sight of a new wooden structure standing stark and raw on the far side of the courtyard. A dull hum sounded, as if a beehive were somewhere close by, but I knew it for what it was—the noise of a crowd, gathered to watch people hang.

A sudden spurt of fear gripped my gut, and I clutched Hallie's hand as I stared again at the back of Jack's head. Would William listen to me? Would he stop the proceedings in time? Or would he simply laugh in my face and send us all to our deaths?

A handful of officials darkened the doorway. There was a brief altercation when the sadistic guard refused to yield control of us poor wretches, but he was more or less shoved aside by men wearing the imperial crest.

"Lovely," I grumbled under my breath as my spirits fell with leaden weight to my feet. "William sent his own personal guards to hang us."

"I think the first thing I'll do when I get back to my world is have a fish taco from a really fabulous beach-Mex place just down the street from my apartment. Or perhaps I'll go shopping. No, a bath first, then the chili lime salmon taco, then shopping."

"Prisoners, march!"

My mind whirled around like the gear spinning on a giant steam clock that Robert Anstruther had once taken me to see.

"Don't look so glum, Octavia," Hallie said, patting

my hand awkwardly before releasing it. "You don't have to worry about rescuing Jack and me anymore. And I'm sure whatever plan you have percolating in your head will work out just fine. So all's well that ends well."

The hum rose to a roar of excitement as we stumbled our way out into the pale February sunlight. On our left were two gallows, the smell of the fresh wood a stark note in the dusty courtyard. Steps led up to where the nooses dangled, swaying ever so gently in the wind. An executioner stood silent beside the gallows, his head covered in the traditional black hood, two slighter figures, also hooded, behind him.

"How lucky, we get the day when the apprentice hangmen are here," I muttered.

Hallie giggled under her breath.

I turned to face the crowd, which was simultaneously cheering and jeering us.

Jack turned to look at me, his expression unreadable. I gave him the best smile I could manage, and turned to scan the crowd, looking for a face that I so desperately wanted to see.

The crowd filled part of the courtyard, spilling out through the large gates to the street beyond. In addition, several of the more athletic and daring boys had managed to clamber up the sides of the brick and wrought iron fence, and were perched along the top, their legs dangling as they laughed and called.

"Rotten little blighters," I said.

"Ghoulish, definitely. So, this plan of yours—is it going to take place soon?" Hallie asked as the emperor's men consulted one another in a tight clutch before suddenly moving down the line of prisoners, a blade flashing as they severed the ropes binding our wrists to the leading line.

A slight figure with the imperial busby pulled down low over his head knelt as he worked his way along the prisoners, unlocking their shackles.

I looked out at the crowd again. "It's supposed to, but William isn't here."

"William?"

"The emperor."

She raised her eyebrows. "You know the emperor?"

"Yes. Why the devil isn't he here? I cannot begin to tell you how peeved I will be if he doesn't even bother to show up," I complained.

A scuffle broke out up front. I craned my neck to see around the other prisoners, watching with dismay as Jack rolled on the ground with one of the guards. Suddenly he froze, and the other guards seized that moment to haul him to his feet.

"Before we begin with the scheduled executions, we have two assassins to deal with," the man I recognized as the prison warden declared.

The crowd yelled their approval of this idea. I glared at them all.

The warden stood to one side of the dual scaffolds, his chest puffed up importantly. He rubbed a hand along his hair, smoothing it back, leaving him with a pronounced resemblance to a seal. "Two assassins were discovered just a short while ago in Emperor William's bedchamber."

The crowd gasped.

"Oh, rubbish," I told them.

"Atta girl, Octavia," Hallie said, picking at a fingernail. "You tell them."

Desperately, I hunted through the crowd for the tall, blond figure who was the only one who could save our lives.

"Today, in honor of the emperor's nuptials, we will hang the assassins!"

The crowd cheered madly.

"Dammit, William, why can't you be on time just once in your life?" I mumbled as one of the imperial guards grabbed my arm and hauled me along to the steps leading up to the noose.

"I give you the notorious assassin Octavia Pye, and her lover, Jack Fletcher."

The crowd booed and threw several items of produce that were long past their prime.

"Jack," I said when he was pulled toward the steps. "I'm so sorry. I'm so very, very sorry."

He looked surprised, to my complete and utter stupefaction. "Sorry about what?"

"About all this. All right! You do not need to shove me! I will walk up the stairs on my own."

"Octavia—"

Jack's voice was cut off in a spontaneous roar of pleasure. I turned to see the crowd ripple; then a familiar figure strode forward, the sun glinting off the rows of gold trim and gold buttons that graced his navy blue military uniform. The trim was almost as burnished as his hair and neatly trimmed mustache.

"William!" I bellowed the second the noise had dropped. "William!"

A hand on my shoulder stopped me from flinging myself forward.

The emperor looked startled for a moment, glancing around, finally realizing who was calling him. He frowned and squinted at me, taking a few steps forward.

"Octavia?"

I shrugged my way free of the restraining hand and ran down the few stairs I had mounted, intending on forcing my way over to William, but several of his guards rushed before him to protect him.

He shouldered them aside, marching over to me in a glorious display of arrogance and masculinity. "Octavia, what the devil are you doing here? A hanging is no place for a lady."

"*I* am being hanged," I said, gritting my teeth at his obtuseness. "Evidently at your direct command."

"My command? My command?" He turned to the nearest member of his entourage. "Billings, do you recall me asking that Miss Pye be executed?"

"No, Your Majesty," the man promptly replied.

Jack had joined me at that point. He thoroughly examined William, who, noticing the bold examination, returned the compliment. "Who is this man, Octavia?"

"Jack Fletcher. He is a friend of mine."

Jack put his arm around my waist and pulled me up close. "We're a hell of a lot more than friends, Tavy."

"Tavy!" William looked shocked. "Did he just call you Tavy?"

"Yes." I sighed. "He was intent on finding a nickname, and settled on that."

"But you wouldn't let me use a nickname, not even when we were . . ." William coughed and stopped that particular train of thought. "Tavy. I would have never imagined such a thing."

"William, we really do not have the time to stand here discussing my nickname."

"No, indeed we don't. I've only got an hour before I have to head over to the cathedral, but I didn't want to miss the hangings. Always did like them. I'm a bit surprised to see you here, though. You always refused to come to the other ones." He turned to the executioner. "Shall we proceed?"

"No!" I shrieked, then took a step closer to William. That's all I could manage, what with Jack holding tight to my waist. "William, you seem to be missing the point."

The crowd, which had been watching us with bated breath, gasped again in surprise.

I hurried to correct my faux pas. One did not ever tell an emperor that he was missing a point. "I am not here to see the executions. I am here to be hung because Jack and I were trying to see you earlier today, but you were . . . and we were . . . er . . . and then some very rude men came barging into our secret passageway and arrested us, saying we were there to assassinate you."

"People try to assassinate me all the time," William said, waving away the very idea. "I never counted you amongst my enemies, though, Octavia. I must say that I'm very disappointed. My father would be disappointed, too. He thought the world of you."

"I am *not* your enemy," I said firmly. "In fact, I will prove our friendship to you by telling you something of the gravest import."

Jack glanced curiously at me, understanding slowly dawning as he saw what had just at that moment struck me—a bargaining chip.

"Octavia," Jack said softly, rubbing his hand on my back. "You don't have to."

"There's no other way, Jack. Not if we all want to survive."

"It'll cost you everything," he warned.

"We'll be alive," I answered with a grim smile. "At this point, I'm willing to consider that a victory in itself."

"This is all very intriguing and mysterious, but I'm afraid I have a rather tight schedule today," William said, consulting his pocket watch. "Delightful as it is to see you again, Octavia, I'm afraid I must ask that the executions proceed so that I might dash off and be married."

"Would you like me to do this?" Jack asked me.

I thought for a moment before shaking my head. "No, it'll be better coming from me."

"Executioner!" William waved over the three hooded figures. "You may as well get started."

"William, we would have a few words with you." His personal guards moved forward as I took hold of William's sleeve to stop him from returning to the crowd. "I assure you that what we have to say will be worth a little delay."

William's cool blue eyes assessed me for the span of three seconds. "My dear Octavia, surely we have said all that can be said?"

"Not if you wish to live out this day," I answered, taking Jack's hand.

William might be many things—his strong suit was not mental agility, and he tended to be distracted by shiny things, much like a magpie—but he was no fool.

"Very well," he said, sighing and gesturing toward the antechamber from which we had just emerged. "We'll use this room. I don't suppose you mind if we carry on with the other executions?"

"Actually, I mind very much. In fact, your survival depends on you not hanging anyone."

"No hangings?" He looked incredulous. "This is a royal wedding, dammit! I can't have a royal wedding without hangings!"

I took him by the arm and, with Jack on my other side, marched both men into the antechamber. William's guards followed, but I knew them to be trustworthy, so I ignored them as best I could. "Jack and I have information that will be vital to you. We are willing to impart this information to you if you will grant everyone here pardons."

"No," William said, and, to my utter surprise, turned around and walked out the door.

"No? Did he just say no?"

"He said no," Jack answered. "Here, you! Emperor! You can't say no!"

I followed Jack when he charged out after William, who turned at the admittedly undignified address.

"I just did," William said.

"Well, stop it," I snapped, pushed beyond the limits of my patience. "What we have to tell you is important, William. Very important."

"Not important enough to ruin my executions," he answered.

"Not when it has to do with a Moghul warship that is unlike anything ever seen?" I asked.

William, in the act of returning to the audience, stopped, and slowly turned to face us. "What Moghul warship?"

"If you want to know that, and just what it has to do with the safety of you and your duchess, then I would suggest you call over the warden and tell him that all of us standing here awaiting the hangman have been pardoned." I folded my hands and waited for his response.

He looked over the line of prisoners, clearly weighing the enjoyment to be had in watching us all hang (William always did have a morbid sense of fun), against the need to stay au courant with news of his enemy.

He considered for an entire minute, then shook his head and said, "No. It's just not worth it, Octavia. I'm sorry that you tried to assassinate me and now must hang, but really, it is your own fault, and perhaps next time you won't be so hasty to attack an old friend such as me."

"William!" I shrieked, and would have jumped on the man to throttle some sense into him, but the guards and one of the hangmen grabbed me, pulling Jack back when he tried to assist. "Are you completely out of your mind?"

He struck a pose and thought about the question for a few seconds. "Not entirely, no."

"Argh!" I screamed, so frustrated I could spit, if I did that sort of thing, which I don't. Instead, I did the next best thing—I gave William a piece of my mind. "I really wish I had been an airship pirate, because I would have made it my life's ambition to plunder every damned one of your ships!"

He looked shocked. He actually looked shocked at my statement. "Octavia! I am aghast!"

"Atta girl, sweetheart," Jack said, giving me a thumbs-up. "Tell him what you really think."

"And when we were done plundering your airships, we'd blow them up!" I yelled, waving my hands around in wild abandon.

William staggered back a step as if he'd been struck.

"While we were wearing our goggles!" Jack added.

"Yes! With our goggles on!" I paused to throw Jack a quick glance. "One day we really must have a discussion about your unhealthy obsession with goggles."

He grinned and winked.

"Octavia, I have never been so shocked—what?" One of William's private guards whispered into his ear. He looked furious and directed the bulk of his fury at me. "Bloody hell! Now do you see what you've done? You've wasted all my execution time! I have to go to the cathedral without seeing a single prisoner die! Of all the selfish acts I've known you to perform, Octavia, this is the most selfish. I hope you're happy that you've completely ruined my wedding day!"

With a flourish that would do a Shakespearean actor proud, he spun around on his heel and plowed through the avid crowd to the grand gold-and-silver steam carriage that waited for him outside the prison gates.

"You actually dated this guy?" Jack asked in a voice rife with disbelief.

"I was young at the time," I said, wanting to cry and scream and shoot someone, all at the same time. "And very stupid."

"I'll say."

I glanced at Jack.

He coughed. "I meant, we all make mistakes."

"I doubt if yours are going to cost you your life."

"Yours aren't, either." He gave me an odd look as the guards bundled us toward the platform. "Haven't you noticed—"

"Prisoners to the scaffold!" the warden cried, waving an imperious arm.

"Jack, I really want to say—"

"Don't," he interrupted as we were shoved up the stairs. My guard stopped me behind a rough-looking rope noose. I glared at it for a moment before transferring my glare to the man whom I had more or less murdered with my own folly and inability to carry through a plan.

"I'm trying to apologize," I snapped, then realized that my final moments would be spent in anger and irritation. I took a deep breath as a musty-smelling black bag was shoved over my head. Someone pulled my arms behind me and bound them. "I just want to say that I'm sorry, Jack. Sorry that I couldn't rescue your sister—"

"Oh, I'm fine. Don't worry about me!" a voice called out from behind me. "I'm going home! Maybe I'll have *two* chili lime salmon tacos...."

"—sorry that we were captured, sorry that William is such an ignoramus and that he wouldn't know a good thing if it came up and bit him on the bottom—"

A gasp of shock was heard from the crowd, who no doubt were enjoying the scene greatly. They were hushed and expectant, as if they were holding their collective breath in anticipation of our deaths.

"—and most of all, I'm sorry that I haven't told you the truth about me. Jack, I—"

"I love you, Octavia Pye," he interrupted me.

The rope was drawn over my head, and tightened behind my neck.

"I love you now, but not nearly so much as I'm going to love you five minutes from now."

"Poor man, his mind has snapped under the strain," I murmured to myself as I felt the attendants stepping away. I sent up a little prayer that death would be instantaneous and painless for us both. "Poor Jack. Poor, adorable—"

The floor dropped out from under my feet.

Personal Log of Octavia E. Pye
Thursday, February 25
Afternoon Watch: One Bell

"I don't know why you're mad at me, Tavy. I *tried* to tell you."

"You did no such thing!"

"Duck!"

I ducked, then spun around and fired the Disruptor at the prison guard who was heading for us.

"I was going to knock him out," Jack snarled, his fists covered in blood as he gestured toward the man I shot. "You didn't have to kill him!"

"I didn't kill him. I shot him in the leg, which you can see for yourself if you would take the opportunity to—" Jack shoved me to the side, landing a hard right to the jaw of a guard who just emerged from the prison antechamber.

"Well, thank you for that!" he snapped.

"Why are you angry with me?" I yelled, jumping up onto the top of the platform and shooting at the next two guards who streamed out of the prison.

"I'm not! You're the one who's mad! And why? Just because you didn't notice what I did."

"Captain! Over here!"

I glared at Jack as he knocked out the last guard. "I was a little busy at the time, if you didn't notice! I was trying to save our lives!"

"And yet if you'd just opened up your eyes, you would have seen that the so-called executioners were not what they seemed."

Jack grabbed my arm and hustled me toward the gate. I thought up several scathing replies to his comment, but the truth was, I *had* been so distraught and determined to get William to see reason that I hadn't paid attention to our surroundings as I should have.

A guard bearing a bayonet charged at us. Before I could fire, a figure hobbled across my line of sight and cracked the guard over the head with a stout staff. "Ye try that again, me laddie, and ye'll be wearin' me lance up yer peewaddin!"

"What's a peewaddin?" I asked Jack as Mr. Piper shooed us forward, toward the gate.

"I don't know, but I don't think a lance would be very comfortable shoved up it. This way."

I shook my head to clear the confusion. My crew, my very own crew that I had left sleeping in France, had somehow managed to get to the prison, disable the regular hanging attendants, and take their places with the intention of rescuing us. It fair boggled the brain.

"Over here!" Hallie yelled, waving at us from the street. Mr. Christian, still clad in the executioner's outfit, held his Disruptor at arm's length as he swept the area for any lingering guards. "There's a carriage here for us!"

Mr. Ho and Mr. Mowen slammed shut the door to the prison antechamber, racing toward us with their black hoods stuffed unceremoniously in their trouser pockets. Mr. Mowen limped heavily, and was somewhat hunched over and battered about the face, but appeared hale enough otherwise.

"Quick," Mr. Ho said, panting a little. She looked excited and thrilled. I boggled a bit more at the fact that they were helping us. "Hurry, Captain. We don't know how long the barricade will hold them."

"You came to save us?" I asked Mr. Mowen as we ran, telling myself I could boggle later, when speed wasn't such an issue.

"Of course," he answered, wheezing. "You're the captain."

"I don't understand any of this," I mumbled as we dashed out of the now-empty prison courtyard. There were a couple of inert forms (Jack knew several nonfatal ways of disabling people), more that were moaning and crawling toward the guardroom door (barricaded handily by Mr. Piper and Dooley), but no corpses. The crowd had bolted the second the first shot of aether had been fired, their fascination with the rescue having been overthrown by an urgent need to get away from aetherfire, the other prisoners following immediately on their respective heels. As we ran, I was aware of a sting around my neck, and touched it gingerly. "I can still feel the rope."

"Yeah, it was a nice touch, huh?" Jack said as he followed me. "You've got to hand it to Matt—when he comes up with a rescue plan, he really does it whole hog."

"Whereas my plans just fail miserably," I said, panting slightly as we raced down the street toward two black carriages. Ahead, Mr. Christian was assisting Hallie into one of them. Mr. Mowen awkwardly jumped into the driver's seat, taking the reins.

"*Mi capitán!*" A man standing at the second carriage waved. "My glorious captain of the sunset hair! Hurry, oh, splendid one. I shall take you to the place of much safety, where you can lay down on your back on the grass, and spread out your so tingly hair, and I will roll around on it, pressing it to my naked flesh, and you will at last know the true depths of the desire that is mine."

"Can we go in the first carriage?" I asked Jack.

"That sounds good to me—damn!"

The carriage took off as we ran past it, Mr. Ho being pulled inside by Dooley and Mr. Christian. Hallie waved as the horses sprang forward.

"Get out of me way, ye puss-filled boil on the underside of a gangrenous rod!" Mr. Piper bellowed as he heaved himself up into the driver's seat of the second carriage, the one we were fated to take.

"I am driving the most glorious *capitán*," Mr. Francisco argued, scrambling up to sit beside him and attempting to wrestle the reins from him. "It is to me the *capitán* will be most thankful and allow me to have my way with her hair."

"Yer daft, do ye know that?"

"I may be daft, but I do not always talk of the peepees and walk like a so bent crab!" Mr. Francisco countered.

A man wearing a long black cape and tricorne hat stood at the side of the carriage, holding the door open. He gestured for us to hurry.

"This is too much," I said, stopping, suddenly overwhelmed by a sense of failure. "I can't, Jack. I just can't."

"Sure you can. Aw, sweetheart, don't cry."

"I'm not crying. I'm just upset because I failed," I said, ashamed to feel the heat of tears in my eyes. I rubbed at them with the back of my hand. "I tried everything I knew how, and I still failed."

"You did your best. That's all anyone can ask for," Jack said.

"Not if my best isn't enough. Really, Jack, I've failed horribly in everything I've tried to do since I met you. My ship has been destroyed, I've lost my position as captain, William was ready to see me hang for something I didn't do, and I couldn't save your sister, let alone us. I don't wish to doom you to that, too. You must go without me."

"You always were a perfectionist," the coachman next to the carriage told me before looking at Jack. "She never was happy unless everything went exactly the way she intended it to go. It looks like she hasn't changed."

I gawked at the man in the tricorne, outright gawked at him. *"William?"*

He winked at me as he shoved me into the carriage. "A little bird told me you might need some help. And for the record, I do know a good thing when it bites my arse. Now stop complaining and get in before those blasted guards get free."

"But—you left us—you said—"

"I promised my father a long time ago that I'd watch after you. He really was very fond of you," he said with a little smile. "I've never been one to go back on a promise."

"But at the prison, you said . . ."

Jack climbed into the carriage after me, slamming the door closed. William leaned in through the window, grabbed my hair, and pulled me forward into a quick, hard kiss. "Just kissing the bride," he told Jack with a grin as he released me.

Jack narrowed his eyes. "*You're* the one getting married today."

"That's right. But if you don't make an honest woman out of Octavia, I really will have you hanged. Off you go!"

William slapped the carriage door as he stepped back.

I stared at Jack in bemusement when Mr. Piper, having pushed Mr. Francisco off the perch so he had to cling to the railing in order to avoid being dumped into the street, cracked his whip and urged the horses forward into a gallop. "That was William."

"Yeah."

"He helped us."

"He also kissed you. I don't think that was at all called for," Jack replied, looking very disgruntled. "You don't see me going around kissing his girl."

"He helped us escape." I couldn't seem to get my brain to accept that fact.

"Who the hell does he think he is just grabbing you right in front of me and laying his lips all over you?"

"William helped us."

"I always ask permission before kissing someone who is taken. That's the way things are done. But no, Mr. Emperor evidently feels he can do whatever the hell he wants to do without any consideration how others might feel about their girlfriends being tongued in front of them."

Jack's words finally penetrated the thick fog of bemusement that had wrapped me up so firmly. My lips twitched with the need to smile, but one look at his glower had me trying my best to keep my expression neutral. "Just so you don't demand we turn around so you can challenge William to a duel over the kiss, I'll point out that there was no tongue involved. It was a farewell kiss, Jack. Nothing more."

"A duel," Jack said thoughtfully, his fingers twitching. "Now, there's a thought...."

"No, it isn't a thought. Jack, are you always going to be this jealous?"

"Jealous? Me?" He looked honestly surprised at such an accusation. "I haven't a jealous bone in my body. I'm a very reasonable man."

"Yes, of course you are. My mistake," I murmured, struggling to keep from laughing. "Well, I still don't quite know how it happened, but we're alive, Jack."

"You thought all along that the emperor would help us. You were right. It just took a different form from what you expected."

I flopped back in the carriage and lifted a feeble hand. "Yes, but after what he said . . . well, it took me completely by surprise."

"Me, too." His lips twisted in a wry smile as he finally stopped frowning. "I figured he was an idiot, like you said."

"I said he was an ignoramus, not an idiot. Good heavens, and I told him I wanted to blow up his airships. Jack, what's going on? Why is everyone helping us?"

He pulled me onto his lap. "Because you're their captain, and you're adorable, and the look in your eyes when you want me to make love to you would bring anyone, man or woman, to their respective knees." His lips were as sweet as marmalade as he gently kissed my mouth, and the sting along my neck. "Mowen's trick with the noose was clever, but I can see a mark it left on you. I'll have to tell him he'll need to be more careful next time."

"There will be no next time," I said firmly, tilting my head to allow Jack better access.

"No? We'll discuss that later," he murmured, his fingers busy on the buttons of my blouse before they slid inside the material to stroke my straining flesh.

"I'm just overwhelmed by it all." I bit his ear and licked away the sting. "The crew saved us. They really saved us."

"Mmhmm." His mouth moved lower, to my breastbone.

A thought struck me, one that had nothing to do with the warm waves of desire that were slowly rippling out from my belly. "Except Mr. Llama! I just bet he—"

A loud slapping noise from behind me had me jumping in surprise. I stared in stark disbelief at the shade that had been pulled down to cover the rear window. Of its own accord, it had rolled itself up, revealing the smiling face of Mr. Llama. He must have been clinging to the rear of the carriage. Even as I watched, he waved and disappeared from the window.

"Did you see that?" I asked, wondering for a moment if I had just imagined seeing the man.

"See what?"

"Mr. . . . never mind." I looked down at the head that nuzzled my bosom, and smiled. "It doesn't matter."

I rose from the bench as Jack and Mr. Mowen emerged from the darkness of the inn into the shaded garden where the crew and I had been reposing for the last hour or so, enjoying unusually balmy weather for February. Both men's faces wore identical grim expressions. My stomach lurched and tightened into a leaden ball. "You weren't successful?"

Jack took my hands in his, his thumbs sweeping over my fingers in a gentle caress meant to reassure and comfort. "We tried everything we could to get a message to him, but the security at the cathedral was impossible to get through. We looked for Alan, but couldn't find him, either."

"The ambassadors are sure to be almost as protected as the emperor," I said, the feeling of dread in my gut growing. "Jack, we can't let him die. Not after everything he's done for us."

"We gave your message to the guard and told him to give it to the emperor as soon as possible, that it was most urgent and it had to do with his safety and security."

"But will he get it in time?" I asked, leaning against Jack, my spirits mourning the potential disaster. "Etienne and the Moghuls could attack at any time."

"Which is why we need to get moving," Jack said.

I hesitated. It didn't feel right to run away from the attack when I wasn't sure that William would get the information about it in time to save himself and as many people as he could.

"Captain, you did all that was possible," Mr. Mowen said.

The other crew members, who had been lounging around the small garden in various attitudes of celebration as they enjoyed the innkeeper's prized ale, slowly gathered around us—all but Mr. Llama, who was seated in the shade of a small lime tree.

"The emperor isn't stupid," Jack said, sensing my continued reluctance to leave. "You said that yourself. He will have standing orders that any information that might have an impact on him would be given top priority and passed along immediately."

"That's right," Mr. Mowen agreed. "And his guards recognized your name."

"They will give William the message as soon as possible," Jack finished.

"Listen to my brother. He knows about intelligence stuff," Hallie said from where she lounged on a chaise, availing herself of the rarely seen February sun, and sipping an exotic beverage.

"It's true that William always did value his network of information," I said, hope beginning to flare to life in the wasteland of despair. I looked up, into Jack's lovely eyes, and was overwhelmed with a feeling of gratitude. How lucky I had been to find him. How lucky I was to have a crew . . . no, *friends* who risked everything to save us. "All right. We'll trust to fate that William will be told about the attack in time to do something about it."

"There's . . . er . . . something else." Mr. Mowen looked at Jack.

Jack avoided my eye.

"What?" I asked.

Jack sighed and reached into his coat to pull out a white sheet of paper. He held it out to me. I read it with growing indignation.

"That . . . that . . . he put a bounty on our heads?"

"So it would appear." Jack considered the paper. "I assume five thousand pounds is a lot of money. You should be flattered."

"Flattered that the man who informed me he had sworn to watch over me now has plastered the city with notices that we are—what did he say?" I snatched the paper from his hand and read through it again. "Ah, here it is. 'Crimes of a most heinous and appalling nature against His Imperial Majesty, his guards, and the respected warden of the Newgate Prison . . .' That he would dare do that after he had me convinced he really meant what he said! Oh! The nerve of him!"

"You attacked an entire prison in front of witnesses," Jack pointed out. "What did you expect?"

I wadded up the paper and wished I could set William's head alight. "I don't know. I assumed he'd come up with some sort of a story."

"I think even he has limits to the sort of whitewash he can pull off," Jack said mildly. "Even if an attack by the Moghuls wasn't imminent, I think it would be best for us to get out of town."

"I agree, but the question is, where are we to go? The *Tesla* is destroyed, and the Corps isn't going to give me another ship, not after the *Aurora*'s captain finally overcame his drug-induced haze to realize that it was I who attacked them. And then there's the question of the crew. Once we get you all to safety, there's still the issue of dealing with the Aerocorps. We can't let the recent events adversely affect your careers."

"We've been thinkin' about that," Mr. Piper said, blatantly scratching himself.

"Aye, we had a long discussion on our way to England," Mr. Mowen agreed, taking a pint of ale from Dooley. He took a long pull on it before sighing in relief, wiping his mouth, then continuing. "We agreed that since we were your crew, we'd let you decide what direction our careers would take."

My jaw wanted to drop, but I had myself well in hand now, and I would not allow it to do anything so feeble-minded. "I am beyond flattered, beyond honored by your faith and trust, not to mention the fact that you all risked your lives for those of Jack and Miss Norris and myself, but I cannot let you throw away your careers like that. My actions can be interpreted in no other way by the Aerocorps, but you all have not been so damned."

"Damned, me scaly-lipped foreskin," Mr. Piper snorted, belching loudly as he slammed down his empty glass. "A crew sticks together. Where the captain goes, we go. Ain't that right?"

The crew, to a man, nodded. "We don't mind a bit of adventure," Mr. Christian said after clearing his throat. "So long as it's not too rough, and doesn't involve disgusting things, like bodies and entrails and severed limbs." He shuddered.

Mr. Piper eyed him. "Ye've not lived till ye've slipped on a deck wet with guts and blood and brains and bowels, lad."

Mr. Christian weaved and turned green. Mr. Ho, sitting beside him, hastily moved out of the way and took up a position on the other side of the table.

"I am very flattered," I said, feeling a change of subject was in order lest Mr. Christian embarrass himself. "And if you are all sure you wish to toss away your sterling careers at the Aerocorps—"

"Aye," Mr. Mowen said, and the others all nodded their agreement. "It's time for a change."

"Well, then. I guess we'll have to consider what we wish to do, since we will all remain together." I thought for a moment. "We could open up a boardinghouse somewhere. Or perhaps go into some sort of a trade, perhaps a shop of some form . . ."

"Pfft," Hallie said, waving a hand. "Boardinghouse! Shop! Why don't you just say what everyone wants you to say?"

I cocked an eyebrow at her. "And what would that be?"

"Everyone knows you're a whatchamacallit. Airship guy. Right? I mean, that's why your airship corps won't have you back? So do that! Boy, this gin is really good. I had no idea it could be so very yummy. Never drank the stuff back home."

"There you go," Jack said, smiling down at me. "You told the emperor you wished you really were an airship pirate. Well, sweetheart, here's the perfect opportunity to be that."

"You're jesting," I said, searching his face for signs he was pulling my leg.

He looked in all earnestness.

"Aye, that's a right good idea," Mr. Piper said, burping again. "Fetch me another pint, would ye, lad? Aye, Captain, there's good money to be made in piratin', they do say."

"And easy pickings, what with the war and all," Mr. Christian added, his Adam's apple bobbing up and down excitedly. His face paled suddenly. "I wouldn't have to shoot anyone, would I?"

Mr. Piper patted him on the arm. "Nay, lad."

Mr. Christian's face cleared.

"We'll put ye on the entrail-cleanup duty," Mr. Piper added with a wicked glint to his eyes.

Mr. Christian keeled over.

"Piracy is illegal," I pointed out to everyone as Mr. Mowen and Jack propped the unconscious chief officer against the brick wall. "I couldn't do that. It would be wrong, morally wrong."

"Sweetheart . . ." Jack took my hand and kissed my knuckles. "Your Aerocorps already considers you a pirate for attacking the *Aurora*. The emperor has put a price on your head. The Black Hand is after your blood for refusing to help them. I don't think you have a lot of choices."

"Even if I agreed to that—and I'm in no way saying that I do—where would we get a ship? The Corps aerodromes will all be too well guarded to get in and take one, even if I thought our situation merited something so immoral as stealing, which I don't, but even if I did, it would be impossible."

"There's the revolutionaries," Mr. Ho suddenly said.

We all turned to look at her. She gazed back at us with steady eyes.

"Well, I assume by what Jack said that you have some sort of a . . . relationship . . . with them, and if that's so, then you must have access to their aerodrome."

I thought for a moment, glancing at Jack. "She's right."

He grinned. "Your precious Etienne would be furious with you."

"Extremely so." My lips curled in a small, satisfied smile. "It would serve him right for using me all those years."

"Excellent plan," Mr. Mowen said, wiping his mouth again, burping discreetly, and rising from the table. "If you'll excuse me, Captain, I'll head out to the Black Hand's aerodrome and see what ships are likely prospects."

I stared at him in surprise. "You know where their aerodrome is?"

"Aye, have for years." He leaned down and said softly, "You're not the only one with a few secrets."

"Rouse yerself, lad," Mr. Piper said, hauling the limp form of Mr. Christian to his feet. "We'll be helpin' Mr. Mowen find us a worthy ship. Dooley, ye take his feet. Francisco! Ye comin'?"

Mr. Francisco, who had been strangely silent since arriving at the inn, rose to his feet and glared at Jack. His eye was swollen shut, the area around it currently a deep maroon color, and darkening quickly.

Jack grinned and flexed his hands.

"I am the *capitán*'s most devoted one. Of course I will

come," he said with great dignity, bowing toward me. His gaze wandered along the top of my head for a few seconds before dropping once again to Jack. "Bah!" was all he added before storming out of the garden after the others.

"Was it really necessary to give him a black eye?" I asked Jack.

"Sometimes, the fist is mightier than the sword."

"Oh, very Quaker, brother," Hallie said, sliding her feet off the chaise so she could sit up. She weaved a little bit.

"I didn't kill him. I just reminded him that Octavia is taken, and he needs to keep his hands off her."

"Where's Mr. Llama?" I asked, looking around the small garden. "He was right over there a few minutes ago. Dammit, he's done it again! I can't believe it! He was right there!"

"Who's Mr. Llama when he's at home?" Hallie asked, yawning.

"He was one of the crew on Octavia's ship. The dark-haired guy."

"Oh. Him. Nice looking in a mysterious sort of way."

"Mysterious doesn't begin to cover it," I muttered. "So help me God, one day I will have him!"

"Uh-huh. Well, this has all been fascinating, but I'm afraid this is where I leave you." Hallie stood up and stretched, then looked expectantly at her brother.

"Leave us?" he asked.

"Yes. I want to go home, please."

"Hallie—" He raised his hands and let them drop again. "I don't know what to tell you. I haven't had time to do any sort of research on what brought us here in the first place, let alone how we're going to get home. Not that I want to go home. There's so much here for us, I don't know why you can't just be happy here."

"Happy? Here?" She shook her head. "You may be happy in this technologically ass-backward society, but I'm not. I want malls. I want the Internet. I want my laptop and my cell phone and my life back! Just send me back, and you can stay here and play steampunk adventurer to your heart's desire, although why you'd want to is beyond me."

"I wouldn't leave Octavia even if I could go back," Jack said, sliding an arm around me.

I smiled up at him. "I wouldn't stand in the way of your happiness, you know. If you really wanted to go back, I would not stop you."

He stared down at me, those lovely eyes of his filled with curiosity. "Do you really mean that?"

"Not in the least," I said, kissing his chin. "I just thought I should say it."

"Is it any wonder I love you?" he said, pulling me up to his chest.

"None whatsoever."

"Wait just a second!" Hallie pulled me back before I could kiss Jack as he so obviously deserved. "You guys can get all lovey-dovey after you send me back. I'm not going to stand around waiting for you to get out of the land of lust to do your duty."

"Hallie, I've told you—I can't send you back."

I felt Jack's exasperation, and knew what I had to do. The garden was empty of everyone but us and a small wren that was warbling to itself. I turned to Jack and asked, "Do you remember me telling you that I had a secret, something I knew I should tell you, but couldn't at that moment?"

"Yes," he said slowly.

"Look, I don't want to interrupt your *Oprah* moment of baring your soul to Jack, but this really is important to me," Hallie said, her face tight with anger.

"And this is important, too, Hallie. I promise you it has some bearing on you." I turned so I was facing them both. "You think I'm English because I sound like everyone here, but the truth is that I was born in Oregon."

Jack looked mildly surprised.

"So?" Hallie asked, tapping her foot impatiently, her arms crossed.

"I was born in 1977. My mother was . . . well, not worth discussing right now. I don't have any memories of my father but one—I remember a day when he took me with him to work. I was so excited and thrilled at being with him as he made his rounds."

"Fascinating, but not quite pertinent, I think," Hallie said.

I looked at Jack. He was watching me silently, his eyes speculative. "My father worked at an electrical power plant."

"So? Mine worked at . . . hey . . ." Hallie frowned in puzzlement. "Did you say *electrical* power plant?"

"Yes."

I saw the exact second when Jack understood. "You're the same as us?"

"I am. Something happened that day. What, I have no idea—I was only six at the time. One moment I was with my father, sitting in a room while he showed me a panel of dials and lights, and the next moment, there were loud sirens and an explosion. Then there was nothing until I woke up and found myself wandering around the emperor's garden."

"You got zapped here, too?" Hallie asked, her expression frozen for a few seconds in incredulity. It swiftly changed to that of sheer, unadulterated horror. "Oh God! There's no way back, is there?"

I shook my head. "I don't think so. If there is, I haven't found it."

She fell over in a dead faint.

To Boldly Go

"Penny for your thoughts."

Octavia turned from where she was gazing out at the clouds and endless blue-gray sky. Her eyes warmed as they always did when she looked at me, and I was filled with a sense of well-being. I would forever rank the fact that we found each other as a miracle of the most profound nature.

"I was feeling thankful that William paid attention to our warning in time. All those people might have been killed . . . but it ended well, although Etienne must be positively livid that his grandiose attack plans were for nothing."

"I'm sure the bastard will recover. His sort always do," I said, wishing I could punch him in the face again.

"Unfortunately, that's true. That Moghul ship worries me, though. No one knows where it has gone to."

"You said this ship could outrun it," I said, not liking the faint line of worry between her brows.

"And so we can. I would simply feel better if I knew where it was."

"Ah."

She leaned into me, warm and soft, and so wonderful, it made my heart swell. It made other parts swell, as

well, but I was getting used to wanting to pounce on her
every time I saw her. I contented myself with just holding her close to me, breathing in her heady scent, and
wondering how soon I could reasonably introduce the
idea of going back to her cabin. Since we'd just left her
bed an hour ago, I figured I'd give her another half hour
to recover before I broached the subject.

"And lastly, I was thinking about what's in store for
us."

"I love how you think the same way I do," I said, cupping her breasts. "Why don't we go back to your cabin,
and I can tie you down and have my wicked way with
your fair, soft, deliciously responsive body."

She turned a dusky pink, delighting me once again.
"But we just got done. . . . Jack, you really do say the
most inappropriate things. Someone could overhear
us. Sounds echo quite well down these passages, not
to mention the fact that it's wholly inappropriate for a
chief officer to mention having his way, wicked or not,
with his captain."

"I'm your first and only mate, my love," I said, taking her
in my arms in my very best impression of a pirate. "Chief
officers are for the Aerocorps. What we are, my adorable
little squab, are pirates. Nonlethal, but still very manly and
tough pirates. And you are our pirate captain."

"I still don't feel right about that," she said, squirming
slightly when I spread my hands across her chest and
stroked her breasts beneath the soft linen of her blouse.
"I would have been fine with you being captain, you
know."

"I don't know anything about flying an airship, and
you do. Besides, I'm secure enough to let my girlfriend
have a superior position, especially when it involves riding me like a sweaty mule."

"Sweaty mule?" Her eyes brightened. "Is that something new you haven't told me about? I wonder if it's in the pamphlet."

"It is—they just don't call it sweaty mule. But I have a few ideas on things we can do to go above and beyond your precious pamphlet. Yeah? What is it?"

I released Octavia and turned when the gangly Aldous Christian approached. "I thought you would like to know that we've crossed over into France, sir, and to ask for coordinates for the navigation machine. The rest of the crew is interested to know where you and the captain think we should go."

I turned back to Octavia. She was biting her delectable pink lip, looking slightly frustrated. I leaned down and whispered, "You told him he could be navigator when I took over his job. Let him prove himself."

She sighed. "I know. It's just that he'll make such a muck out of the autonavigator. He always has."

"He wants to learn. Just give him a chance."

She nodded and raised her voice, giving the young man a list of numbers. "I thought we would go to North Africa."

"Aye, aye, Captain," he answered, saluting awkwardly before grinning at me, and rushing off to deal with the odd machine used to pilot the airship.

"What's in North Africa?" I asked her.

She gave me a long look out of those sloe eyes. "Someone I'd like you to meet."

"Not another lover?" I asked, pretending to be shocked.

She hit me on the arm. "No. The man who raised me."

I frowned and poked around in my memory. "Robert

Anstruther? The famed captain? I thought you said he died?"

"I did." Her gaze was steady on mine.

I smiled. "It's like that, is it?"

"I'm afraid so. There are some secrets that are not mine to tell, Jack. I hope you can understand that."

"I can." I took her in my arms and captured her sweet breath. "So long as I have you."

"You have me," she answered, gently pushing back a bit of my hair off my forehead. "You had me from the first moment you started talking the most incomprehensible gibberish."

"If you left our world as a small child, I guess it would have been incomprehensible to you," I allowed. "When I think of the stuff you've missed . . . it's a shame."

"I've learned to celebrate rather than regret," she said, leaning in and nibbling on my lower lip. "I had wonderful foster parents who loved me and taught me as best they could. I have good friends who would risk their lives for me. And most of all, I have you."

"Now you're getting all sappy on me," I teased. "It's a good thing Hallie is off embracing her inner pirate and learning how to shoot those damned guns, or she'd be all over you for that."

Her brown eyes sparkled as she pushed back, reaching into the pocket on her skirt. "That reminds me, I have something for you. Something to celebrate your new position as first mate."

"An eye patch? A hook? Please tell me it's not a huge wig of dreadlocks? I don't know how Johnny Depp stood wearing one."

She frowned for a moment.

"Never mind, it's not important," I said.

"Why would I want you to wear a wig? . . ." She shook her head. "Hold out your hands."

I did so, gazing in delight at the object she deposited there.

"I had it engraved with your name, and since you named the ship we took from the Black Hand, I had the engraver put that on, as well. I'm sorry that the last few letters are a bit squashed. I think he ran out of room."

On my hands lay a beautiful specimen, black leather, oiled and rich, brass highly polished, the light from the gas jet glittering brightly off the round glass lenses. Over one lens my name was inscribed; the other bore the word *Enterprise*.

"I hope you like them. I don't in the least understand your fascination with goggles, but I decided that you should have a pair worthy of a . . ." She narrowed her eyes in concentration. "Steampunk pirate."

"Airship pirate," I corrected her, setting the goggles down so I could thank her properly.

"First and *only* mate," she added, melting in my arms.

Glossary

aether: The material that binds everything together on a molecular level. Can be extracted and converted to energy.

Akbar: Crown prince of the Moghul empire, Akbar is the only surviving son of Aurangzeb III. Akbar leads the Moghul army in its attempt to capture new territories, and is acknowledged to be one of the best fighters of the time.

Anstruther, Robert, Captain: Held the post of captain in the Southampton Aerocorps. He was the husband of Jane, and foster father to Octavia Pye, having accepted her as his charge when she was six years old. He and his wife died in a tragic airship explosion, although their bodies were never identified.

Aurangzeb III: Imperator (emperor) of the Moghuls, and father to Prince Akbar. Aurangzeb had four wives, three of whom are deceased. He has one son and seven daughters.

Black Hand, the: The name of the revolutionary group bent on breaking William's empire, most particularly Prussia's inclusion in it. The Black Hand is led by Etienne Briel, who operates primarily in England, Italy, and Prussia.

bosun: Abbreviated version of the word "boatswain." A bosun's typical duties include inspecting the vessel, dealing with cargo, and maintaining structures not covered by engineering.

Briel, Etienne: Leader of the Black Hand revolutionary group. He is of French and Prussian ancestry, and holds a degree in architecture.

chief officer: A second-in-command, the chief officer on the *Tesla* is responsible for navigation, assisting other officers as needed, and attending to such duties as the captain commands.

Constanza, Duchess of Prussia: The hereditary ruler of Prussia, Constanza is eight years the junior of her fiancé, William VI. She is considered a witch because she bears six fingers on her left hand.

Disruptor: The name of the weapons carried by Southampton Aerocorps members; they fire blasts of molten aether rather than bullets.

emperor: Male sovereign who rules over more than one nation. William VI rules over the United Kingdom (consisting of England, Scotland, and Ireland) as well as Prussia.

engineer: Maintains and monitors the machinery on the vessel. On the *Tesla*, this includes the propellers, engines, weapons, and boilers.

HIMA: His Imperial Majesty's Airship, a prefix for all ships flown on imperial business, including those leased to the Southampton Aerocorps.

Iago, king of Italy: Constanza's first cousin, and childhood friend. Iago rules the kingdom of Italy, which is sorely beset upon by the Moghuls. He went to Oxford with William VI, and considers the English emperor one of his closest friends.

imperator: Another name for an emperor or supreme ruler. The Moghuls refer to their leaders using this term.

Marseilles: Port on the southern French coast, known for its particularly tough inhabitants, and the wide popularity of its bordellos.

Moghuls: Persianates who originally dominated the Indian subcontinent; now the Moghul empire stretches across parts of Russia and Eastern Europe, encompassing India, Kazakhstan, Ukraine, Romania, Bulgaria, Serbia, and Croatia. Battles for Turkey, Bulgaria, Greece, and Italy are ongoing.

Prussia: Originally part of the German empire, the historic state of Prussia was formed when in 1626 Prince Otto, the Margrave of Brandenburg, married Jocaste, the only child of Frederick, Duke of Prussia. Their son, William (Wilhelm) inherited both the duchy and the margravate, combining them into the state of Prussia. William's grandson, another Otto, married the eldest daughter of King James V. Their son, William III, brought Prussia into the British empire, where it has remained to the present date.

Rome: City in the southern part of Italy, capital of the Italian kingdom, and home to Iago. William VI maintains troops in the city as part of the defense against Moghul attacks.

Southampton Aerocorps: Private company that provides both passenger services and contracted military work for the emperor. Ships owned outright by the Aerocorps do not bear the designation HIMA.

steward: Responsible for the maintenance of the habitation areas of the vessel, such as the galley, mess, and crew quarters.

thuggee: The name commonly given to a cult of murderers and thieves known in parts of India.

watches: In naval tradition, the twenty-four-hour day was divided into seven watches, two of which, first and second dogwatches, are frequently combined into just one, since each dogwatch is only two hours long.

Bells were rung every half hour, allowing seamen to know what time it was. The table below translates watches and bells to a twenty-four-hour clock:

Midwatch	Morning	Forenoon	Afternoon	Dogs	First
0030—1 bell	0430—1 bell	0830—1 bell	1230—1 bell	1630—1 bell	2030—1 bell
0100—2 bells	0500—2 bells	0900—2 bells	1300—2 bells	1700—2 bells	2100—2 bells
0130—3 bells	0530—3 bells	0930—3 bells	1330—3 bells	1730—3 bells	2130—3 bells
0200—4 bells	0600—4 bells	1000—4 bells	1400—4 bells	1800—4 bells	2200—4 bells
0230—5 bells	0630—5 bells	1030—5 bells	1430—5 bells	1830—5 bells	2230—5 bells
0300—6 bells	0700—6 bells	1100—6 bells	1500—6 bells	1900—6 bells	2300—6 bells
0330—7 bells	0730—7 bells	1130—7 bells	1530—7 bells	1930—7 bells	2330—7 bells
0400—8 bells	0800—8 bells	1200—8 bells	1600—8 bells	2000—8 bells	2400—8 bells

Read on for a look at
Katie MacAlister's next novel

LOVE IN THE TIME OF DRAGONS

A Novel of the Light Dragons

Available in May 2010 from Signet

"You're going to be on your knees saying prayers for hours if Lady Alice finds you here."

I jumped at the low, gravelly voice, but my heart stopped beating quite so rapidly when I saw who had discovered me. "By the rood, Ulric! You almost scared the humors right out of my belly!"

"Aye, I've no doubt I did," the old man replied, leaning on a battered hoe. "Due to your guilty conscience, I'm thinking. Aren't you supposed to be in the solar with the other women?"

I patted the earth around the early-blooming rose that I had cleared of weeds, and snorted in a delicate, ladylike way. "I was excused."

"Oh, you were, were you? And for what? Not to leave off your sewing and leeching and all those other things Lady Alice tries to teach you."

I got to my feet, dusting the dirt off my knees and hands, looking down my nose at the smaller man, doing my best to intimidate him even though I knew it wouldn't do any good. Ulric had known me since I was a wee babe puling in her swaddling clothes. "And what business is it of yours, good sir?"

He grinned, his teeth black and broken. "You can

come over the lady right enough, when you like. Now, what I'm wanting to know is whether you have your mother's leave to be here in the garden, or if you're supposed to be up learning the proper way to be a lady."

I kicked at a molehill. "I *was* excused . . . to use the privy. You know how bad they are—I needed fresh air to recover from the experience."

"You had enough, judging by the weeding you've done. Get yourself back to the solar with the other women before your mother has my hide for letting you stay out here."

"I . . . er . . . can't."

"And why can't you?" he asked, clearly suspicious.

I cleared my throat and tried to adopt an expression that did not contain one morsel of guilt. "There was an . . . incident."

"Oh, aye?" The expression of suspicion deepened. "What sort of an incident?"

"Nothing serious. Nothing of importance." I plucked a dead leaf from a rosebush. "Nothing of my doing, which you quite obviously believe, a fact that I find most insulting."

"What sort of an incident?" he repeated, ignoring my protests of innocence and outrage.

I threw away the dried leaf and sighed. "It's Lady Susan."

"What have you done to your mother's cousin now?"

"Nothing! I just happened to make up some spiderwort tea, and mayhap I did leave it in the solar next to her chair, along with a mug and a small pot of honey, but how was I to know she'd drink all of it? Besides, I thought everyone knew that spiderwort root tea unplugs your bowels something fierce."

Ulric stared at me as if it was my bowels that had run free and wild before him.

"Her screams from the privy were so loud, Mother said I might be excused for a bit while she sought one of Papa's guards to break down the privy door, because her ladies were worried that Lady Susan had fallen in and was stuck in the chute."

Ulric's look turned to one of unadulterated horror.

"I just hope she looks on the positive side of the whole experience," I added, tamping down the molehill with the toe of my shoe.

"God's blood, you're an unnatural child. What positive side is there to spewing out your guts while stuck in the privy?"

I gave him a lofty look. "Lady Susan always had horrible wind. It was worse than the smell from the jakes! The spiderwort tea should clear her out. By rights, she should thank me."

Ulric cast his gaze skyward and muttered something under his breath.

"Besides, I can't go inside now. Mother said for me to stay out of her way because she is too busy getting ready for whoever it is who's visiting Father."

That wasn't entirely true—my mother had actually snapped at me to get out from underfoot and do something helpful other than offer suggestions on how to break down the privy door, and what could be more helpful than tending the garden? The whole keep was gearing up for a visit from some important guest, and I would not want the garden to shame her.

"Get ye gone," Ulric said, shooing me out of the garden. "Else I'll tell your mother how you've spent the last few hours rather than tending to your proper chores. If you're a good lass, perhaps I'll help you with those roses later."

I smiled, feeling as artless as a girl of seventeen could feel, and dashed out of the haven that was the garden and along the dark overhang that led into the upper bailey. It was a glorious almost-summer morning, and my father's serfs were going about their daily tasks with less complaint than was normal. I stopped by the stable to check on the latest batch of kittens, picking out a pretty black-and-white one that I would beg my mother to let me keep, and was just on the way to the kitchen to see if I couldn't wheedle some bread and cheese from the cooks when the dull thud of several horses' hooves caught my attention.

I stood in the kitchen door and watched as a group of four men rode into the bailey, all armed for battle.

"Ysolde! What are you doing here? Why aren't you up in the solar tending to Lady Susan? Mother was looking for you." Margaret, my older sister, emerged from the depths of the kitchen to scold me.

"Did they get her out of the privy, then?" I asked in all innocence. Or what I hoped passed for it.

"Aye." Her eyes narrowed on me. "It was odd, the door being stuck shut that way. Almost as if someone had done something to it."

I made my eyes as round as they would go, and threw in a few blinks for good measure. "Poor, poor Lady Susan. Trapped in the privy with her bowels running amok. Think you she's been cursed?"

"Aye, and I know by what. Or rather, whom." She was clearly about to shift into a lecture when movement in the bailey caught her eye. She glanced outside the doorway, and quickly pulled me backward, into the dimness of the kitchen. "You know better than to stand about when Father has visitors."

"Who is it?" I asked, looking around her as she peered out at the visitors.

"An important mage." She held a plucked goose to her chest as she watched the men. "That must be him, in the black."

All of the men were armed, their swords and mail glinting brightly in the sun, but only one did not wear a helm. He dismounted, lifting his hand in greeting as my father hurried down the steps of the keep.

"He doesn't look like any mage I've ever seen," I told her, taking in the man's easy movements under what must be at least fifty pounds of armor. "He looks more like a warlord. Look, he's got braids in his hair, just like that Scot who came to see Father a few years ago. What do you think he wants?"

"Who knows? Father is renowned for his powers; no doubt this mage wants to consult him on arcane matters."

"Hrmph. Arcane matters," I said, aware I sounded grumpy.

Her mouth quirked on one side. "I thought you weren't going to let it bother you anymore?"

"I'm not. It doesn't," I said defensively, watching as my father and the warlord greeted each other. "I don't care in the least that I didn't inherit any of Father's abilities. You can have them all."

"Whereas you, little changeling, would rather muck about in the garden than learn how to summon a ball of blue fire," Margaret laughed, pulling a bit of grass from where it had been caught in the laces on my sleeve.

"I'm not a changeling. Mother says I was a gift from God, and that's why my hair is blond when you and she and Papa are redheads. Why would a mage ride with three guards?"

Margaret pulled back from the door, nudging me aside. "Why shouldn't he have guards?"

"If he's as powerful a mage as Father, he shouldn't need anyone to protect him." I watched as my mother curtsied to the stranger. "He just looks . . . wrong. For a mage."

"It doesn't matter what he looks like—you are to stay out of the way. If you're not going to tend your duties, you can help me. I've got a million things to do, what with two of the cooks down with some sort of a pox, and Mother busy with the guest. Ysolde? Ysolde!"

I slipped out of the kitchen, wanting a better look at the warlord as he strode after my parents into the tower that held our living quarters. There was something about the way the man moved, a sense of coiled power, like a boar before it charges. He walked with grace despite the heavy mail, and although I couldn't see his face, long ebony hair shone glossy and bright as a raven's wing.

The other men followed after him, and although they, too, moved with the ease that bespoke power, they didn't have the same air of leadership.

I trailed behind them, careful to stay well back lest my father see me, curious to know what this strange warrior-mage wanted. I had just reached the bottom step as all but the last of the mage's party entered into the tower, when that guard suddenly spun around.

His nostrils flared, as if he'd smelled something, but it wasn't that which sent a ripple of goose bumps down my arms. His eyes were dark, and as I watched them, the colored part narrowed, like a cat's when brought from the dark stable out into the sun. I gasped and spun around, running in the other direction, the sound of the strange man's laughter following me, mocking me, echoing in my head until I thought I would scream.

New York Times bestselling author
KATIE MACALISTER

Playing with Fire
A Novel of the Silver Dragons

Gabriel Tauhou, the leader of the silver dragons, can't take his eyes off of May Northcott—not even when May, who has the unique talent of being able to hide in the shadows, has slipped from everyone else's sight. May, however, has little time for Gabriel—not when she's hiding from the Otherworld law, hunting down a blackmailer, and trying to avoid a demon lord's demands. But her ability to withstand Gabriel's fire marks her as his mate, and he has no intention of letting her disappear into the darkness she seems to prefer. When May is ordered to steal one of Gabriel's treasures—an immensely important relic of all dragonkin—he must decide which to protect: his love or his dragons.

ALSO AVAILABLE IN THE SERIES
Up in Smoke
Me and My Shadow

Available wherever books are sold or at
penguin.com